FROM THE PAGES OF *DAISY MILLER*
AND *WASHINGTON SQUARE*

Some people had told him that, after all, American girls were exceedingly innocent; and others had told him that, after all, they were not. He was inclined to think Miss Daisy Miller was a flirt—a pretty American flirt. (from *Daisy Miller*, page 14)

"I like a lady to be exclusive; I'm dying to be exclusive myself." (from *Daisy Miller*, page 21)

"Whether or no being hopelessly vulgar is being 'bad' is a question for the metaphysicians. They are bad enough to dislike, at any rate; and for this short life that is quite enough." (from *Daisy Miller*, page 33)

They desired to express to observant Europeans the great truth that, though Daisy Miller was a young American lady, her behaviour was not representative—was regarded by her compatriots as abnormal. (from *Daisy Miller*, page 54)

"She sent me a message before her death which I didn't understand at the time. But I have understood it since. She would have appreciated one's esteem." (from *Daisy Miller*, page 62)

The ideal of quiet and of genteel retirement, in 1835, was found in Washington Square, where the doctor built himself a handsome, modern, wide-fronted house, with a big balcony before the drawing-room windows, and a flight of white marble steps ascending to a portal which was also faced with white marble. (from *Washington Square*, page 76)

There were portions left over, light remnants and snippets of irony, which she never knew what to do with, which seemed too delicate for her own use; and yet Catherine, lamenting the limitations of her understanding, felt that they were too valuable to waste, and had a belief that if they passed over her head they yet contributed to the general sum of human wisdom.

(from *Washington Square*, page 83)

"She would be enchanted to be able to prove to herself that she is persecuted." (from *Washington Square*, page 101)

"There is something I should greatly like—as a moral satisfaction. I should like to hear you say—'He is abominably selfish!'"

(from *Washington Square*, page 133)

"If you see him, you will be an ungrateful, cruel child; you will have given your old father the greatest pain of his life."

(from *Washington Square*, page 153)

"If he marries her, and she comes into Austin's money, they may get on. He will be an idle, amiable, selfish, and doubtless tolerably good-natured fellow. But if she doesn't get the money and he finds himself tied to her, Heaven have mercy on her! He will have none. He will hate her for his disappointment, and take his revenge; he will be pitiless and cruel." (from *Washington Square*, page 177)

"When persons are going to be married, they oughtn't to think so much about business." (from *Washington Square*, page 204)

Catherine, meanwhile, in the parlour, picking up her morsel of fancy-work, had seated herself with it again—for life, as it were.

(from *Washington Square*, page 240)

DAISY MILLER

and

WASHINGTON SQUARE

Henry James

With an Introduction
by Jennie A. Kassanoff

George Stade
Consulting Editorial Director

BARNES & NOBLE CLASSICS
NEW YORK

𝒜𝓑

BARNES & NOBLE CLASSICS
NEW YORK

Published by Barnes & Noble Books
122 Fifth Avenue
New York, NY 10011

www.barnesandnoble.com/classics

Originally published in trade paperback format in 2004 by Barnes & Noble Classics with
new Introduction, Notes, Biography, Chronology, Appendix, Comments & Questions, and
For Further Reading. This hardcover edition published in 2009.

Introduction, Notes, and For Further Reading
Copyright © 2004 by Jennie A. Kassanoff.

Note on Henry James, The World of Henry James, *Daisy
Miller* and *Washington Square*, and Comments & Questions
Copyright © 2004 by Barnes & Noble, Inc.

Daisy Miller and Washington Square
ISBN-13: 978-1-59308-389-2
ISBN-10: 1-59308-389-0
2008941956

Produced and published in conjunction with:
Fine Creative Media, Inc.
322 Eighth Avenue
New York, NY 10001

Michael J. Fine, President and Publisher

Printed in the United States of America

MV

1   3   5   7   9   10   8   6   4   2

HENRY JAMES

The writer Henry James was born into a wealthy family in New York City in 1843. His father, Henry, Sr., was a religious freethinker and follower of the philosopher Swedenborg, and associated with many of the literary men of his day, including Nathaniel Hawthorne and Ralph Waldo Emerson. Young Henry was educated privately in New York, Geneva, Paris, and London; the family lived alternately in Europe and the United States for much of his childhood.

He began his literary career writing for magazines. Having dropped out of Harvard Law School to pursue writing, he associated with the literary set in Cambridge, Massachusetts, and was a good friend of budding novelist and critic William Dean Howells. In 1864 James's first published piece of fiction, the story "A Tragedy of Error," appeared in the *Continental Monthly*. He also wrote reviews and articles for the *Atlantic Monthly* and the *Nation*. He frequently traveled to Europe and in 1876 settled permanently in London.

James is often cited as one of literature's great stylists; it has been said that his writing surrounds a subject and illuminates it with a flickering light, rather than pinning it down; according to Virginia Woolf in her diaries, he spoke in the same way. His style became more and more indirect as he moved from his early period, when he produced novels that considered the differences between American and European culture and character—*Roderick Hudson* (1876), *The American* (1877), *The Europeans* (1878), *Daisy Miller* (1879), *Washington Square* (1881), and *The Portrait of a Lady* (1881)—to his middle period, when he wrote two novels about social reformers and revolutionaries, *The Bostonians* and *The Princess Casamassima*, both in 1886, as well as the novellas *The Aspern Papers* (1888) and *The Turn of the Screw* (1898) .

In 1898 James retreated to Lamb House, a mansion he had purchased in Rye, England. There he produced the great works of his final period, in which in complex prose he subtly portrayed his characters' inner lives: *The Wings of the Dove* (1902), *The Ambassadors* (1903), and *The Golden Bowl* (1904). He returned to the United States for the last time to supervise production of a twenty-six-volume edition of his most important fictional works that was published between 1907 and 1917. *The American Scene* (1907), an account of his last journey to America, is highly critical of his native land. He became a British citizen in 1915. Shortly after receiving the Order of Merit, Henry James died, on February 28, 1916, leaving behind a prodigious body of work: twenty novels, 112 stories, and twelve plays, as well as voluminous travel writing and literary journalism and criticism.

TABLE OF CONTENTS

THE WORLD OF HENRY JAMES AND

DAISY MILLER AND *WASHINGTON SQUARE*

1789   William James, Henry's grandfather, emigrates to the United States from Ireland.

1811   Henry James, Sr., the author's father, is born.

1826   Washington Square is dedicated as a public place and military parade ground. Originally a marsh, then a graveyard, it served as a spot for duels and executions prior to this transformation.

1828   Construction begins on the first house on the north side of Washington Square; over the next thirty years Washington Square North will become the most expensive and fashionable street bordering Washington Square.

1832   William James dies, leaving a $3 million estate to his twelve children.

1835   Henry James's maternal grandmother, Elizabeth Walsh, moves into a townhouse at 18 Washington Square North (now part of 2 Fifth Avenue), occupying it until 1847. James visits her often as an infant and toddler.

1836   Ralph Waldo Emerson publishes his essay "Nature," setting forth the main principles of Transcendentalism.

1837   William Dean Howells is born; he will be James's colleague, an important editor, and a founder of American "realism."

1842   Henry's brother William is born.

1843   On April 15, Henry James, Jr., is born at 21 Washington Place, in New York City, around the corner from his grandmother. In October the James family relocates to Europe.

1844   The family returns to New York City.

1849   Henry, Sr.'s social circle comprises philosophers and writers, including Nathaniel Hawthorne and Ralph Waldo Emerson. Henry, Jr., is educated privately in the United States and Europe. His exposure to the Old World during his formative years establishes in him a lifelong preference for Europe over America.

1853   The New York City Commission pays $5,000,000 for land
       that will become Central Park, a vast public recreation space
       in the European style. The first portion of the park will open
       in 1858; it will be complete some sixteen years hence.

1857   The *Atlantic Monthly* is founded by Moses Dresser Phillips
       and Francis H. Underwood. Early contributors include Ralph
       Waldo Emerson, Henry Wadsworth Longfellow, James Rus-
       sell Lowell (the magazine's first editor), and Oliver Wendell
       Holmes. In coming years James will be a frequent contri-
       butor.

1859   In October Henry, Sr., takes his family to Geneva.

1860   The family returns to America in September and settles in
       Newport, Rhode Island.

1861   The American Civil War begins.

1862   James enrolls at Harvard Law School but drops out after a
       year to pursue a writing career. He becomes friendly with
       William Dean Howells.

1864   In February James publishes his first piece of fiction, the story
       "A Tragedy of Error," in the *Continental Monthly*. Nathaniel
       Hawthorne dies.

1865   James begins to write reviews for the *Nation*, a new liberal
       weekly. The American Civil War ends.

1866   The first permanent transatlantic telegraph cable links
       Europe and America, vastly increasing the speed of informa-
       tion transmittal.

1869   In England James meets George Eliot and writes reviews of
       her works, including *Romola*, *Middlemarch*, and *Daniel
       Deronda*, which are published in the *Atlantic Monthly* and
       the *Galaxy*, a literary journal. Mark Twain publishes the
       best-selling travel book *The Innocents Abroad*, based on let-
       ters he had written while journeying by steamship to Europe
       and the Holy Land; it treats hallowed Old World landmarks
       with irreverence and parodies the manners and mores of
       Europeans and Americans.

1870   James's cousin Mary ("Minny") Temple dies in March, and
       the author, devastated, moves back to New York. His social
       opportunities are abundant; he spends time at Emerson's
       house in Concord, Massachusetts, and meets Henry Adams,
       who has just been appointed editor of the *North American*

Review. The Metropolitan Museum opens in New York City.

1871 James publishes his first novel, *Watch and Ward*, in installments in the *Atlantic*; it introduces what will be a prominent Jamesian theme: the development of a young girl into womanhood.

1872 Assigned to write a travel series for the *Nation*, James sails to Liverpool and spends time in Europe. Susan B. Anthony casts a vote in the presidential election in Rochester, New York, and is arrested.

1873 Financial panic grips New York with the failure of Jay Cooke and Company, the nation's preeminent investment bank. After a ten-year economic boom, the United States enters its worst depression to date, although New York continues its prodigious growth.

1875 James publishes in the *Atlantic Monthly* the novel *Roderick Hudson*, about an American sculptor in Rome and his struggle to reconcile art and passion. During his early period (also called his international period), he compares the people and cultures of the United States and Europe, focusing especially on the differences. While living in Paris, James associates with the writers Gustave Flaubert and Émile Zola, as well as Russian expatriate authors, including the novelist Ivan Turgenev. He works on his novel *The American*, about a self-made American millionaire who tries to marry the daughter of French aristocrats.

1876 *Roderick Hudson* is published in book form. Impatient with America's foreign policy and disaffected with the United States in general, James joins other expatriates in London and settles permanently there. Throughout the rest of the 1870s, he associates with many leading English writers and thinkers and becomes an important presence on the Anglo-American literary scene.

1877 *The American* is published in book form. James is friendly with Alfred Tennyson, William Gladstone, and Robert Browning. While in Rome, James hears about an American "child of nature and of freedom" who consorted with a "good-looking Roman, of vague identity." James is immediately inspired to turn this story into a novel, *Daisy Miller*.

1878   James publishes the short novel *The Europeans*. The Macmillan Publishing Company of London asks him to write a biography of either Washington Irving or Nathaniel Hawthorne.

1879   James publishes *Daisy Miller*, about a young American woman in Rome, in book form. He signs a contract for the British copyright on *Hawthorne*, which is published in the English Men of Letters series in London.

1880–   The focus of James's writing shifts to social and psy-
1881   chological drama. *Washington Square* is serialized in *Cornhill Magazine* and *Harper's* (1880) and released in book form (1881); the novel concerns a young American woman whose father rejects the man she wants to marry. *The Portrait of a Lady* is serialized in *Macmillan's Magazine* and the *Atlantic Monthly* (1880–1881), and in book form (1881); this brilliant novel depicts a young American woman who out of a kind of generosity marries the wrong man. James vows "never again to return" to New York, in a fit of disdain over the way the city's "oppressive" economic growth has lowered the quality of life.

1882   James travels to Washington, D.C., where he briefly meets Oscar Wilde.

1886   James publishes the first novels of his middle period: *The Bostonians*, the story of a struggle between a southern conservative and an embittered suffragist, and *The Princess Casamassima*, an exploration of the personal dangers involved in taking up anarchism and revolution.

1888   James publishes the short novel *The Aspern Papers*, about a man who woos the custodian of letters by a poet he idolizes.

1889   Psychologically and financially depressed by the failure of *The Bostonians*, James shifts his focus to playwriting for the next six years.

1890   He publishes *The Tragic Muse*, about art and theater in London and Paris. His brother William publishes his groundbreaking and influential *Principles of Psychology*, in which pragmatism and "radical empiricism" are key elements.

1891   James's dramatization of *The American* fares moderately well.

1892   After a life beset by illness, Alice James dies in England, with Henry at her side.

1895 James's first dramatic work written as such, *Guy Domville*, is booed by the opening-night audience and receives mostly negative reviews, though George Bernard Shaw praises it. After little success with playwriting, James returns to writing fiction. The United States increases its involvement in a conflict between Spain and Cuba, which wants independence from Spanish rule. James opposes this involvement, calling it "none of our business."

1897 He publishes *What Maisie Knew*, the story of a preadolescent girl who must choose between her parents and a governess.

1898 James publishes the ghost story *The Turn of the Screw*. He purchases Lamb House, in Rye, England, where he will write his last novels and letters. The Spanish-American War takes place.

1900 During the final stage of his writing career, James's style becomes increasingly complex and convoluted. Over the next few years, he produces what are often considered his greatest works.

1902 He publishes *The Wings of the Dove*, about a group of people who scheme to inherit a dying woman's fortune.

1903 *The Ambassadors*, about an American suspicious of European ways who is won over by life in Paris, is published, as is "The Beast in the Jungle," a story of a man who believes he is intended for something remarkable. In London, James meets Edith Wharton.

1904 His novel of adultery *The Golden Bowl* is published. He travels to the United States to oversee the production of a revised collection of his most important works of fiction.

1907 James publishes *The American Scene*, his observations on what America has become. Publication of the twenty-six volumes of the revised fiction collection, *The Novels and Tales of Henry James*, begins; it will continue until 1917.

1908 James publishes the story "The Jolly Corner," an oblique commentary on the America he has left behind.

1910 In January James becomes very ill. He is nursed by his brother William and William's wife, Alice, and the three return to North America. William, also ill, dies shortly thereafter. James visits New York, where he receives psychiatric care.

1911   In August he returns to England.
1914   James begins work on two novels, *The Ivory Tower* and *The Sense of the Past*, which he will not complete before his death.
1915   James's health deteriorates. He becomes a British subject.
1916   On New Year's Day he receives the Order of Merit. On February 28 Henry James dies. His ashes are taken to Cambridge, Massachusetts, to be buried in American soil.
1917   *The Ivory Tower* and *The Sense of the Past* are published in their unfinished state.

INTRODUCTION

"It is, I think, an indisputable fact," Henry James remarked in 1879, "that Americans are, as Americans, the most self-conscious people in the world." This striking claim was delivered the year his first success, *Daisy Miller: A Study*, was published in book form, and a year prior to the serial publication of his quintessentially New York novel, *Washington Square* (published in book form in 1881); it highlights James's fascination with his native land and equally reveals his own share in its self-consciousness. As James remarked in *Hawthorne* (1879), his extended study of the writer, the "experimental element" had not "as yet entirely dropped out of the great political undertaking" of the United States, and as a result, Americans were singularly "conscious of being the youngest of the great nations, of not being of the European family." Like adolescents exiled to the children's table at some big family celebration, Americans felt themselves the victims of an international "conspiracy to undervalue them." As James noted, they had been "placed on the circumference of the circle of civilization rather than at the centre," a geometric and constellational vantage point that offered few consolations. In orbit around the cultures of Britain and France, America was troubled by a lurking "sense of relativity." While Europe's ancient monarchies luxuriated in a "quiet and comfortable sense of the absolute, as regards [their] own position[s] in the world," the United States was forced to renegotiate its national contract with every election, submitting to vote decisions that, in Europe, were the divine right of kings.

Like many of his contemporaries, James saw democracy as an ongoing challenge not only to traditional politics and aesthetics, but equally to America's national identity. In the decade following the Civil War, as the country's centennial loomed on the horizon, Americans found themselves deliberating anew on the core possibilities of democracy. As James himself admitted in *Hawthorne*, the postwar world was "a more complicated place than it had hitherto seemed, the future more treacherous, success more difficult." Within this increasingly pluralist context, democracy seemed less an abstract aspiration than a hardscrabble process. As Dana D. Nelson has observed, citizens had to "develop their social and political subjectivities in relation to multiple, local, and nonidealized relationships with others," rather than in accordance with a single, stylized, aristocratic model ("Representative/Democracy," p. 220; see "For Further Reading"). In coming to terms with the postwar period's unwieldy new "sense of proportion and relation," James found himself faced with two competing models of democratic practice: an "abstract universality" associated with antebellum democracy, and the "embodied particularity" of direct, postwar political engagement (Berlant, "Uncle Sam Needs a Wife," p. 144). Drawing on the curiously relevant debates circulating around late-nineteenth-century mathematics, James offered a critique of America's "great political undertaking" in both *Daisy Miller: A Study* and *Washington Square*.

James described *Daisy Miller* as the "little tragedy . . . of a light, thin, natural, unsuspecting creature being sacrificed as it were to a social rumpus that went on quite over her head and to which she stood *in no measurable relation*" (quoted in Edel, *The Life of Henry James*, p. 520; emphasis added). The story is indeed a meditation on measurability. When the American expatriate Frederick Winterbourne first encounters the "strikingly, admirably pretty" Daisy Miller, he straightaway sets out to quantify and categorize her. From the outset, she is not singular, but plural—an aggregated type rather than a distinctive individual: "How pretty they are!" he thinks (p. 8). In his quest for "the formula that applied to Miss Daisy Miller" (p. 14), Winterbourne is not alone. The majority of his American colony similarly seeks to account for Daisy's particularity in mathematically generic terms. Like Mrs. Walker, the American hostess who collects "specimens of her diversely-born fellow-mortals to serve, as it were, as text-books" (p. 46), and Mrs. Costello, who can barely distinguish Miss Miller from her nearly identical cohorts ("that young lady's—Miss Baker's, Miss Chandler's—what's her name?" [p. 51]), so Winterbourne himself struggles to identify "how far [Daisy's] eccentricities were generic, national, and how far they were personal" (p. 55). "Were they all like that, the pretty girls who had a good deal of gentlemen's society?" (p. 14). When the members of his expatriate circle in Rome accuse "poor little" Miss Miller of "going really 'too far,'" Winterbourne's regret takes a predictably fixed form: "It was painful to hear so much that was pretty and undefended and natural assigned to a vulgar place among the categories of disorder" (p. 53). Like his itemizing compatriots, Winterbourne cannot imagine disorder beyond its paradoxical categorization.

Winterbourne judges Daisy according to a set of conventional norms rather than a cluster of metaphysical truths. For all his inner debates, he ultimately agrees with the verdict of those who "intimated that they desired to express to observant Europeans the great truth that, though Miss Daisy Miller was a young American lady, her behaviour was not representative—was regarded by her compatriots as abnormal" (p. 54). In the normative world of *Daisy Miller*, there can be no decree more damning. Daisy's behavior is not so much wicked as it is atypical. As Winterbourne's aunt Mrs. Costello blandly observes, "Whether or no being hopelessly vulgar is being 'bad' is a question for the metaphysicians. They are bad enough to dislike, at any rate; and for this short life that is quite enough" (p. 33).

Like Winterbourne and his cohort of reproving Americans, early critics of *Daisy Miller* took pains to classify and typologize James's heroine. The *Nation*, marveling that "no American book of its size has been so much read and so much discussed," saw the story as a cautionary tale. "It is a perfect study of a type not, alas! uncommon." Daisy was the garish American tourist par excellence. The journal could only hope that *Daisy Miller* would find its way aboard "all the ocean steamers" that set sail across the Atlantic, and thereby "be so presented to the 'moral consciousness' of the American people that they, being quickwitted, may see themselves here truthfully portrayed, and may say, 'Not so, but otherwise will we be'" (*James's "Daisy Miller,"* p. 106). The critic for the *North American Review*, Richard Grant White, agreed that "in Daisy Miller Mr. James has undertaken to give a characteristic portrait of a certain sort of American young woman, who is unfortunately too common." The text, he hoped, would have a "corrective effect" on American travelers: "It is perhaps well that [James] has made this study, . . . which should show European critics of American manners and customs the light in which the Daisy Millers are regarded by Americans themselves" (*James's "Daisy Miller,"* p. 107).

Other readers, however, were not so sanguine. Daisy Miller was "an outrage on American girlhood," they declared (James, *Daisy*

Miller; Pandora; The Patagonia; and Other Tales, p. v). Indeed, her story was so scandalous as to cast doubt on James's patriotism. The *New York Times*, for one, took this charge seriously enough to mount a spirited rebuttal. Mr. James, the *Times* insisted, was obviously "possessed by a sincere patriotism": Only someone truly committed to his country could "[consecrate] his talents to the enlightening of his countrywomen in the view which cynical Europe takes of the performance of the American girl abroad" (*James's "Daisy Miller,"* p. 103).

For his own part, James grew weary of the debate and eventually tried to put the matter to rest. In the twenty-four-volume New York Edition (1909), he summarily dropped the story's subtitle, "A Study," and insisted that the tale had neither prescriptive nor descriptive designs on American womanhood. "My little exhibition is made to no degree whatever in critical but, quite inordinately and extravagantly, in poetical terms," James explained (*Daisy Miller*, p. vi). His readers were not to confuse art with life: "My supposedly typical little figure was of course pure poetry, and had never been anything else" (p. viii). This effort to contain Daisy's multiple meanings, however, seems nothing if not a self-conscious parody of Winterbourne's own effete aestheticism. As Winterbourne strolls into the malarial Roman arena, blithely quoting Byron, he belatedly recalls that "if nocturnal meditations in the Colosseum are recommended by the poets, they are deprecated by the doctors" (p. 57). As a fictional character himself, Winterbourne's insistence on the difference between art (the poets) and life (the doctors) is an awkward one. An aesthetic taxonomist of the worst kind, his empirical observations are too little and too late.

In probing such distinctions between art and life, and the generic and the specific, *Daisy Miller* exposes the tension between what Russ Castronovo has called the conservative "true democrat" and the more revolutionary "radical democrat." According to Castronovo, the true democrat is the citizen who imagines freedom as a freedom *from* society. His activist counterpart, the radical democrat, however, sees freedom as the "freedom *to* participate in the daily forms and activities that constitute community" (*Necro Citizenship*, p. 142). Winterbourne is, in this respect, the cautious "true democrat." Because he worships conformity, stasis, and polite restraint, he relies on the bland certitude of standard categories. Faced with Daisy's "extraordinary mixture of innocence and crudity," Winterbourne can only accuse her of "a want of finish" (p. 10). Displaying the true democrat's antipathy toward inconclusiveness and disorder, he rejects her unfinished appearance—an appearance that threatens democratic consensus and closure (see Nelson, p. 240).

Unlike Winterbourne, who begins and concludes *Daisy Miller* in the same place—"'studying' hard" in Geneva and rumored to be "much interested in a very clever foreign lady" (p. 62)—Daisy herself charts a dynamic path through the text. Resisting the docent culture of museums where "dreadful old men . . . explain about the pictures and things" (p. 38), she insists instead upon unscripted, unmediated encounters with the real. She rejects tour guides of all sorts, balking at the repeated interference of the "vigilant matrons" who would police her behavior. Like her literary successor, Isabel Archer in *The Portrait of a Lady* (1881), Daisy wants to "see for [her]self" (James, *The Portrait of a Lady*, p. 203). She longs to generate "a little fuss"—to experience the messy turmoil of direct, democratic engagement (p. 26). Thus, when the American ingénue bids goodnight to Winterbourne after their second meeting, she playfully remarks, "I hope you are disappointed, or disgusted, or something!" (p. 27). Craving dissent, Daisy seeks a public sphere in which one can speak one's mind without the stifling intervention of self-styled representatives or chaperones. Hers is a world of direct democracy. Unlike Winterbourne, who cloaks his desire to see her beneath the conventional pretense that he has come to Rome to visit his aunt, Daisy is alarmingly direct: "I don't want you to come for your aunt, . . . I want you to come for me" (p. 30). Like her frank gaze ("she avoided neither his eyes nor those of any one else; she blushed neither when she looked at him nor when she saw that people were looking at her" [p. 28]), Daisy covets the electric possibilities of direct connection. When Winterbourne questions the wisdom of her intention to speak to her Italian suitor, Giovanelli, in a public park, she immediately replies, "Do I mean to speak to him? Why, you don't suppose I mean to communicate by signs?" (p. 39). For Daisy, communicating by signs would be the equivalent of trailing a curator around a museum: Both would frustrate her desire for immediate participation in the unpredictable possibilities of the real. She thus rejects Winterbourne's abstract devotion to honor and gallantry, insisting instead on the candor and volatility of original, local experience. To Winterbourne's lurid insinuation that she has been "walk[ing] about the streets" with her Roman beau, Daisy responds with vibrant literalism: "About the streets? . . . Where then would he have proposed to her to walk? The Pincio is not the streets, either" (p. 48).

In insisting on "a little fuss," Daisy rejects Winterbourne's empty iconoclasm. Whereas Mrs. Costello's nephew plans his most spontaneous gestures and daydreams in set pieces, Daisy relies on the capricious dynamics of flirtation. In this respect, James's heroine exposes what Chris Castiglia has called "a skeptical space within conventional commitments" (Castiglia, "The Genealogy of a Democratic Crush," p. 210). By challenging those customs that demand the sacrifice of local loyalties to the seemingly greater good of "abstract national allegiance," flirtation "opens . . . a realm of practical democracy" (Castiglia, p. 209). It contests the conservative true democrat's allegiance to contractual institutions like religion, law, social etiquette, and representational politics, and instead requires "the operation of trust on a local and contingent basis" (Castiglia, p. 211).

Winterbourne himself acknowledges that flirtation is a loaded and potentially subversive activity. "Little American flirts," he silently observes, are "the queerest creatures in the world" (p. 49). "He had known, here in Europe, two or three women—persons older than Miss Daisy Miller, and provided, for respectability's sake, with husbands—who were great coquettes—dangerous, terrible women, with whom one's relations were liable to take a serious turn" (p. 14). Yet despite this amusing hyperbole, Winterbourne's observations only partly account for the "fearful, frightful" potential of the flirt (p. 48). Daisy's playful, narrative-defying "prattle" and her circular, coquettish habit of "going round" undermine the linear link between cause and effect. Refusing to speculate on the future, she focuses instead on the inchoate pleasures of the here and now.

Daisy's insistence on seeing the Colosseum by moonlight draws its dramatic force precisely from such participative urges. The Roman ruin, the scene of an ancient culture's violent sport, grounds the narrative in the rough-and-ready world of visceral engagement. Despite his exhilarated discovery of Daisy's compromised state—she is, after all, alone with a man near midnight—Winterbourne cannot renounce his habit of "cautious criticism" (p. 58). Turning to Giovanelli, he remonstrates, "I wonder . . . that you, a native Roman, should countenance such a terrible indiscretion." The Italian's reply, "Ah, . . . for myself, I am not afraid," highlights the difference between the two men. Whereas Giovanelli has imbibed Daisy's radical ethic of personal agency ("when was the Signorina ever prudent?" he asks), Winterbourne relies on the true democrat's system of political substitutions: "I am speaking for this young lady." Daisy, however, insists on her own embodied self-determination: "I never was sick, and I don't mean to be! . . . I don't look like much, but I'm healthy!" (p. 59). Unlike Mrs. Walker and her taxonomic collection of "diversely-born fellow-mortals," Daisy treats herself and her friends as living, breathing human beings. Rejecting her countrywoman's bookish sensibilities, she focuses instead on the Roman's physical charm: He is the "handsomest man in the world" (p. 36), the "beautiful Giovanelli" (p. 37).

Daisy's insistence on Giovanelli's tangible embodiment stands at odds with Winterbourne's canned depictions of Daisy herself: She is either "a delicate young girl lounging away the evening in this nest of malaria" (p. 58) or "a young lady whom a gentleman need no longer be at pains to respect" (p. 58). From this perspective, Winterbourne's desire to know whether Daisy and Giovanelli are "engaged" takes on a great deal of significance. In glibly dismissing the matter—"it makes very little difference whether you are engaged or not!" (p. 59)—he implies that Daisy's intimacy with the Italian has little to do with conventional professions of marital intent. For all of Winterbourne's flippancy, however, the very fact that Daisy, on her deathbed, insists that "she never was engaged to that handsome Italian" (p. 60), underscores the importance of the question to the story's outcome. Had she been formally engaged, Daisy would have put an end to the indeterminate and fundamentally playful dynamics that animated her status as a radical democrat. Instead of ceding her political options to a man—the ultimate chaperone for the nineteenth-century middle-class woman—Daisy embraces the flirtatious limbo that postpones the static certainty of marriage. "I have never allowed a gentleman to dictate to me, or to interfere with anything I do," she insists (p. 39). Indeed, inasmuch as Daisy uses her parasol to transform public spaces into furtively private enclaves, so she equally converts abstract issues into material matters. After knowing Winterbourne for only a few days in Vevey, she "[made] it a personal matter that [he] should have left the place"—much to Mrs. Walker's astonishment (p. 44). To borrow Castiglia's formulation, Daisy "shift[s] the balance of power, making public spaces private, abstract functionaries familiar, powerful men needy, and abject citizens possessed of the power to satisfy a national hunger" (p. 211). While she is not engaged in a marital sense, she is deeply engaged in a political one.

Daisy's death by malaria exposes the perils of this visceral type of democratic participation. In a story peppered with petty somatic complaints (Mrs. Miller's dyspepsia, Randolph's tooth loss, Mrs. Costello's headaches), Daisy alone falls victim to a genuine contagion so fierce that it withstands the palliations of Eugenio's "splendid pills" (p. 59). Although she is "dying to be exclusive," it is Daisy's flesh-and-blood genericism that ultimately seals her fate. Transformed from a cause célèbre into "a terrible case" (p. 61), she experiences the inevitable mortality of the embodied subject. Despite her nine-year-old brother's childish insistence on American exceptionalism ("in America there's always a moon!" [p. 60]), Daisy's death transforms national identity into a matter of clinical epidemiology. The "dusky circle of the Colosseum" (p. 57) mocks "that self-enclosed exceptionalist circle" wherein Americans consider themselves of paramount importance (Giles, "Transnationalism and Classic American Literature," p. 72). As mosquitoes trump manifest destiny, so the body seals Daisy's radically democratic fate: "The poor girl died" (p. 61).

Ever the conventional true democrat, Winterbourne balks at the material historicity crudely evinced by the "raw protuberance" of Daisy's grave (p. 62). Seizing upon Giovanelli's assertion that Daisy "was the most innocent" (p. 61), he tries instead to embalm his fair young compatriot in the sublime rhetoric of transcendence and purity, abstracting her virginal body "beyond the touch of history" (Castronovo, *Necro Citizenship*, p. 122). For Winterbourne, Daisy's metaphysical innocence annuls malaria's ghastly effects. Her death becomes less a bodily phenomenon than a singular act of Christian martyrdom, a beatific sacrifice in a realm of latter-day Roman tyrants. Unlike the notoriously misnamed Pope Innocent X, a pontiff whose duplicity was presciently captured in the "superb portrait . . . by Velasquez" (p. 53), Daisy is, in Winterbourne's eyes, genuinely, epiphenomenally pure. Armed with this conviction, he all but exonerates himself from his own political inaction. Noting that "it was on his conscience that he had done her injustice," he mildly confides to his aunt that Daisy "would have appreciated one's esteem" (p. 62). Yet Winterbourne's passive retreat from first-person accountability and his withdrawal into the anonymity of the pronoun "one" speak more loudly than words. Content with the idealized identifications of symbolic citizenship, and repelled by the messy responsibilities of actual intervention, Winterbourne can only acknowledge that he was "booked to make a mistake" (p. 62). As with everything else in his life, his errors are literally and figuratively made with reservations.

Two years after *Daisy Miller* appeared in book form, James brought out a novel entitled *Washington Square*. Like its predecessor, the 1881 publication would stage a conflict between two kinds of democracy—the calculating abstraction of a man and the spontaneous empiricism of a woman. The geometric precision of the novel's title is significant, for *Washington Square* charts the subtle machinations of a mathematically minded doctor, Austin Sloper, as he systematically prevents his lovelorn daughter, Catherine, from marrying a handsome fortune hunter, Morris Townsend. A physician, Sloper has made a career of calculation: "He had passed his life in estimating people (it was part of the medical trade), and in nineteen cases out of twenty he was right" (p. 124). From his quantifying perspective, the lavish "red satin gown trimmed with gold fringe" (p. 75) that Catherine wears to her cousin's engagement party makes her look as though she "had eighty thousand a year" (p. 83). When his embarrassed daughter "illogically" denies the charge, Sloper's rejoinder gives brutal testimony to his own relentless logic of equivalency: "So long as you haven't you shouldn't look as if you had" (p. 83). Like other such ironic barbs, Sloper's comments are "perfectly calculated" to dumbfound the deferential child. As a student boggled by the complexities of life's long division, Catherine must make sense of the world's messy remainders. To extract the least scrap of happiness from her father's mordant remarks, she must perform a kind of linguistic surgery, cutting "her pleasure out of the piece, as it were" and ignoring the "portions left over, light remnants and snippets of irony, which she never knew what to do with, which seemed too delicate for her own use" (p. 83).

For his part, Sloper is fascinated by a different mathematical concept: that of a limit. According to the *Oxford English Dictionary*, "limit" is a "finite quantity to which the sum of a converging series progressively approximates, but to which it cannot become equal." Although Catherine acknowledges that "her deepest desire was to please" her father, she has in fact "never succeeded beyond a certain point," and "to go beyond the point in question seemed to her really something to live for" (p. 72). When Catherine's Aunt Almond accuses the doctor of toying with his daughter's filial devotion, Sloper coolly responds that he is merely interested in locating the limit of Catherine's affection: "It is the point where the adoration stops that I find it interesting to fix" (p. 164).

Sloper meets his mathematical match in Morris Townsend — a good-looking scoundrel whose name itself postulates a limit — a town's end. Like his would-be father-in-law, Morris reckons his relationship with Catherine in mathematical terms. "Dr. Sloper's opposition," he observes, "was the unknown quantity in the problem he had to work out. The natural way to work it out was by marrying Catherine; but in mathematics there are many short cuts, and Morris was not without a hope that he should yet discover one" (p. 169). Nonetheless, when Catherine returns from Europe, the young man's confidence begins to flag. "He will never give us a penny; I regard that as mathematically proved," he impatiently tells Catherine's Aunt Penniman (p. 197). Like Sloper, Townsend subscribes to a rigid logic of quid pro quo. When Catherine pleads with him to stay — "Think of what I have done! . . . Morris, I have given up everything!" — Townsend replies with "a sort of calculated brutality," "You shall have everything back!" (p. 206). Despite the mathematical tidiness of this response, and the geometric precision of Townsend's farewell note — a letter of some "five large square pages" — Catherine again confronts the shabby remainders of a broken heart.

As its title would suggest, geometry is *Washington Square*'s mathematical discipline of choice. The story itself takes place on a square, itself the geographic border between Manhattan's irregular network of roads snaking across the island's southern tip, and its neat grid of avenues and streets that was then beginning to extend northward (see Bell, " 'This Exchange of Epigrams,' " p. 53). Like the square in which he dwells, Sloper adheres to the systematic principles of Euclidean geometry. When Mrs. Almond, testing his resolve, asks whether he plans to yield to Catherine's importunities, Sloper icily replies, "Shall a geometrical proposition relent? I am not so superficial." Hearing his sister's clever rejoinder, "Doesn't geometry treat of surfaces?" Sloper only reaffirms the tenets of his mathematical faith: "Yes; but it treats of them profoundly. Catherine and her young man are my surfaces; I have taken their measure" (p. 164).

Sloper's confidence in the incontrovertibility of Euclid's time-honored axioms reveals and fortifies his low opinion of women. Like the majority of nineteenth-century educators, Sloper believes that "geometry [is] impossible for women to understand" due to the latter's "insufficient abstract reasoning power" (Cohen, *A Calculating People*, p. 8). Indeed, the doctor finds his "idea of the beauty of *reason* . . . on the whole meagrely gratified by what he observed in his female patients" (p. 70). To this axiom, Catherine is no exception. From her father's pitiless perspective, "she is about as intelligent as the bundle of shawls" (p. 178). In Sloper's binary world, boys are "sent to college or placed in counting-rooms," and girls are "married very punctually" (p. 78). In such a world, the gendered discourse of geometry admits no exceptions.

Yet when Sloper asks, "Shall a geometrical proposition relent?" (p. 164), James invites us to take a critical, rather than merely rhetorical, view of the matter. Indeed, by the late nineteenth century, geometrical propositions *were* relenting. In the mid-1870s, mathematicians in England, where James lived while writing *Washington Square*, were learning of the first fundamental challenge to the gold standard of mathematical thought in nearly two thousand years. Based on the work of Carl Friedrich Gauss and Georg Riemann, both German geometers, the Russian mathematician Nikolai Ivanovich Lobachevsky, a Hungarian named János Bolyai, and their English-language spokesmen—Hermann von Helmholtz, William Clifford and, ultimately, Albert Einstein himself—Euclidean geometry underwent a major revolution. At the base of this transformation was a startling mathematical premise: that Euclid had not exhausted the possibilities of spatial knowledge, and that other spaces were equally possible—including curved spaces. These so-called "hyperbolic spaces," though difficult to imagine, yielded a radically new insight: that, in the words of Leonard Mlodinow, "Euclidean form is approachable but not attainable, like the speed of light, or your ideal weight" (*Euclid's Window*, p. 121). In these new, non-Euclidean spaces, brave new worlds were possible. The sum of a triangle's angles, for example, was always less or more than 180 degrees; similar triangles did not exist, and parallel lines intersected (Mlodinow, p. 121). The "curved space revolution" challenged the most fundamental tenets of nineteenth-century thought, among them, the concepts of absolute space, absolute time, and Immanuel Kant's moral imperative (Mlodinow, p. 95). As the British geometer William Clifford declared in 1875, "the idea of the Universe, the Macrocosm, the All, as subject of human knowledge, and therefore of human interest, has fallen to pieces" (quoted in Richards, *Mathematical Visions*, p. 112). A new spirit of empiricism had raised doubts about Euclid's formerly absolute truths. In Clifford's words, "Immensity and Eternity [are] replaced by knowledge of Here and Now."

In christening his doctor "Sloper," James puts the physician's cherished Euclidean certainties in doubt. The trigonometric concept of a slope — "the rate at which a curve rises or falls per horizontal unit" — connects Sloper to the new, curved notions of space that, by the 1870s, were rendering the doctor's axiomatic metaphors out of date (Kline, "Geometry"). Inasmuch as the new, non-Euclidean universe was governed by dynamic, empirical forces like gravity, so notions of space and time changed accordingly. When Einstein later observed that space-time assumed the form of a "curvature" when confronted with a massive body, he was working from a set of assumptions in which "the propositions of Euclidean geometry cannot hold exactly," and the very "idea of a straight line also loses its meaning" (Einstein, quoted in Dimock, "Rethinking Space, Rethinking Rights," p. 256). In *Washington Square*, such curvature necessarily undermines not only Dr. Sloper's sanguine view of surface geometry, but also the "moral satisfaction" that such mathematical assumptions produce (p. 133).

Indeed, the rejection of Euclidean absolutism had a seismic impact on Western political philosophy. To challenge Euclid was to challenge the presumption of pure reason that his axioms had inspired. Within the Kantian world of categorical imperatives, moreover, democracy existed as a vaunted if speculative set of civic promises. In the hyperbolic world of empirical events and sensate bodies, however, democracy became a matter of concrete, practical choices (see Dimock, p. 249). In such a new, relativistic space, as Wai Chee Dimock observes, "compromises and concessions, rather than absolute victories, mark the endpoint . . . of democracy" (p. 263).

James's vision of non-Euclidean democracy is evident in his representation of Catherine Sloper, the character he modestly regarded as "the only good thing in the story" (*Henry James: Letters*,

p. 316). Catherine's robustly corporeal embodiment—her "clear, fresh complexion," her physical resilience, and her status as someone "strong and solid and dense," indeed someone who "would live to a great age—longer than might be generally convenient"—all highlight her physical immediacy. Hers is a somatic sturdiness that belies the abstract postulates deployed by those around her. Unlike her fellow characters, for example, Catherine can distinguish form from content. She can appreciate the aesthetics of a given representational strategy, that is, without losing track of the underlying import. Thus, despite the fact that her father speaks ill of Morris, she nonetheless admires the "neatness and nobleness" of the Doctor's expression—"even while she felt that what he said went so terribly against her" (p. 117). Later, after reading Townsend's devastating farewell letter and letting "her sense of the bitterness of its meaning and the hollowness of its tone . . . [grow] less acute," Catherine "admire[s] its grace of expression" (p. 217). This skill arms her with the ability to distinguish radical democracy from its more conventional counterpart, true democracy, and real participation from mere political show. Although she fails to recognize Townsend's duplicity, Catherine's myopia is less a testament to her foolhardiness than it is a mark of her fundamental trustfulness. Whereas her father dismisses Townsend as a generic rogue, Catherine appreciates the embodied presence of the "beautiful young man." Indeed, we are mistaken if we see the rightness of Sloper's verdict as vindication of his jaded approach. While Catherine's naive devotion to Morris is misguided, it is also genuine. By refusing to marry anyone else (even, as it turns out, an older but none the wiser Townsend), Catherine demonstrates the authenticity of her trust. Refusing to marry, she rejects formal commitments, and instead remains faithful to the contingent and radically local secrets of her own heart. Like *The Scarlet Letter*'s Hester Prynne, who stays steadfastly loyal to her erotically insurgent act and refuses to leave the town of her punishment, so Catherine clings to her dynamic (if wrongheaded) trust—a commitment forged in intimacy and perpetually outside of formal consecration. Democracy, as it turns out, is less concerned with mistakes than it is with the participative process by which one makes them. Catherine may have chosen the wrong man, but at least she chose. Like a voter who has mistakenly cast her ballot for a corrupt candidate, Catherine's willingness to participate and

DAISY MILLER

and

WASHINGTON SQUARE

DAISY MILLER:
A STUDY

I

AT THE LITTLE TOWN of Vevey, in Switzerland, there is a particularly comfortable hotel. There are, indeed, many hotels; for the entertainment of tourists is the business of the place, which, as many travellers will remember, is seated upon the edge of a remarkably blue lake—a lake that it behoves every tourist to visit.* The shore of the lake presents an unbroken array of establishments of this order, of every category, from the "grand hotel" of the newest fashion, with a chalk-white front, a hundred balconies, and a dozen flags flying from its roof, to the little Swiss *pension* of an elder day, with its name inscribed in German-looking lettering upon a pink or yellow wall, and an awkward summerhouse in the angle of the garden. One of the hotels at Vevey, however, is famous, even classical, being distinguished from many of its upstart neighbours by an air both of luxury and of maturity.† In this region, in the month of June, American travellers are extremely numerous; it may be said, indeed, that Vevey assumes at this period some of the characteristics of an American watering-place. There are sights and sounds which evoke a vision, an echo, of Newport and Saratoga.[1] There is a flitting hither and thither of "stylish" young girls, a rustling of muslin flounces, a rattle of dance-music in the morning hours, a sound of high-pitched voices at all times. You receive an impression of these things at the excellent inn of the "Trois Couronnes,"‡ and are transported in fancy to the Ocean House or to Congress Hall.[2] But at the "Trois Couronnes," it must be added, there are other features that are much at variance with these suggestions: neat German waiters, who look like secretaries of legation; Russian princesses sitting in the garden; little Polish boys walking about, held

---

*Lake Geneva, the largest alpine lake in Europe, has an area of 224 square miles; located in southwestern Switzerland and southeastern France, it is a popular tourist destination.

†The Grand-Hôtel de Vevey and Palace Hotel, a fashionable watering-place on Lake Geneva.

‡The Hôtel des Trois Couronnes was a hotel on the Quai Perdonnet in Vevey.

by the hand, with their governors; a view of the snowy crest of the Dent du Midi* and the picturesque towers of the Castle of Chillon.†

I hardly know whether it was the analogies or the differences that were uppermost in the mind of a young American, who, two or three years ago, sat in the garden of the "Trois Couronnes," looking about him, rather idly, at some of the graceful objects I have mentioned. It was a beautiful summer morning, and in whatever fashion the young American looked at things, they must have seemed to him charming. He had come from Geneva the day before, by the little steamer, to see his aunt, who was staying at the hotel—Geneva having been for a long time his place of residence. But his aunt had a headache—his aunt had almost always a headache—and now she was shut up in her room, smelling camphor, so that he was at liberty to wander about. He was some seven-and-twenty years of age; when his friends spoke of him, they usually said that he was at Geneva, "studying." When his enemies spoke of him they said—but, after all, he had no enemies; he was an extremely amiable fellow, and universally liked. What I should say is, simply, that when certain persons spoke of him they affirmed that the reason of his spending so much time at Geneva was that he was extremely devoted to a lady who lived there—a foreign lady—a person older than himself. Very few Americans—indeed I think none—had ever seen this lady, about whom there were some singular stories. But Winterbourne had an old attachment for the little metropolis of Calvinism;[3] he had been put to school there as a boy, and he had afterwards gone to college there[4]—circumstances which had led to his forming a great many youthful friendships. Many of these he had kept, and they were a source of great satisfaction to him.

After knocking at his aunt's door and learning that she was indisposed, he had taken a walk about the town, and then he had come in to his breakfast. He had now finished his breakfast; but he was drinking a small cup of coffee, which had been served to him on a little table in the garden by one of the waiters who looked like an *attaché*.‡ At last he finished his coffee and lit a cigarette. Presently

---

*Mountain of 10,686 feet in the Swiss Alps, near the French border.
†Medieval fortress built in the thirteenth century on the eastern shore of Lake Geneva and made famous by George Gordon, Lord Byron (1788–1824), in his poem "The Prisoner of Chillon" (1816).
‡Functionary who has been assigned to serve on the staff of a diplomatic mission.

a small boy came walking along the path — an urchin of nine or ten. The child, who was diminutive for his years, had an aged expression of countenance, a pale complexion, and sharp little features. He was dressed in knickerbockers,* with red stockings, which displayed his poor little spindleshanks;† he also wore a brilliant red cravat. He carried in his hand a long alpenstock,‡ the sharp point of which he thrust into everything that he approached — the flower-beds, the garden-benches, the trains of the ladies' dresses. In front of Winterbourne he paused, looking at him with a pair of bright, penetrating little eyes.

"Will you give me a lump of sugar?" he asked, in a sharp, hard little voice — a voice immature, and yet, somehow, not young.

Winterbourne glanced at the small table near him, on which his coffee-service rested, and saw that several morsels of sugar remained. "Yes, you may take one," he answered; "but I don't think sugar is good for little boys."

This little boy stepped forward and carefully selected three of the coveted fragments, two of which he buried in the pocket of his knickerbockers, depositing the other as promptly in another place. He poked his alpenstock, lance-fashion, into Winterbourne's bench, and tried to crack the lump of sugar with his teeth.

"Oh, blazes; it's har-r-d!" he exclaimed, pronouncing the adjective in a peculiar manner.

Winterbourne had immediately perceived that he might have the honour of claiming him as a fellow-countryman. "Take care you don't hurt your teeth," he said, paternally.

"I haven't got any teeth to hurt. They have all come out. I have only got seven teeth. My mother counted them last night, and one came out right afterwards. She said she'd slap me if any more came out. I can't help it. It's this old Europe. It's the climate that makes them come out. In America they didn't come out. It's these hotels."

Winterbourne was much amused. "If you eat three lumps of sugar, your mother will certainly slap you," he said.

---

*Loose-fitting breeches, gathered in at the knee, worn by boys, sportsmen, and others who required free use of their legs.
†Long, thin legs.
‡Long staff, with an iron point, used by mountain climbers.

"She's got to give me some candy, then," rejoined his young interlocutor. "I can't get any candy here—any American candy. American candy's the best candy."

"And are American little boys the best little boys?" asked Winterbourne.

"I don't know. I'm an American boy," said the child.

"I see you are one of the best!" laughed Winterbourne.

"Are you an American man?" pursued this vivacious infant. And then, on Winterbourne's affirmative reply—"American men are the best," he declared.

His companion thanked him for the compliment; and the child, who had now got astride of his alpenstock, stood looking about him, while he attacked a second lump of sugar. Winterbourne wondered if he himself had been like this in his infancy, for he had been brought to Europe at about this age.

"Here comes my sister!" cried the child, in a moment. "She's an American girl."

Winterbourne looked along the path and saw a beautiful young lady advancing. "American girls are the best girls," he said, cheerfully, to his young companion.

"My sister ain't the best!" the child declared. "She's always blowing at me."*

"I imagine that is your fault, not hers," said Winterbourne. The young lady meanwhile had drawn near. She was dressed in white muslin, with a hundred frills and flounces, and knots of pale-coloured ribbon. She was bare-headed; but she balanced in her hand a large parasol, with a deep border of embroidery; and she was strikingly, admirably pretty. "How pretty they are!" thought Winterbourne, straightening himself in his seat, as if he were prepared to rise.

The young lady paused in front of his bench, near the parapet of the garden, which overlooked the lake. The little boy had now converted his alpenstock into a vaulting-pole, by the aid of which he was springing about in the gravel, and kicking it up not a little.

"Randolph," said the young lady, "what *are* you doing?"

---

*Verbally attacking or reprimanding.

"I'm going up the Alps," replied Randolph. "This is the way!" And he gave another little jump, scattering the pebbles about Winterbourne's ears.

"That's the way they come down," said Winterbourne.

"He's an American man!" cried Randolph, in his little hard voice. The young lady gave no heed to this announcement, but looked straight at her brother. "Well, I guess you had better be quiet," she simply observed.

It seemed to Winterbourne that he had been in a manner presented. He got up and stepped slowly towards the young girl, throwing away his cigarette. "This little boy and I have made acquaintance," he said, with great civility. In Geneva, as he had been perfectly aware, a young man was not at liberty to speak to a young unmarried lady except under certain rarely-occurring conditions; but here at Vevey, what conditions could be better than these?— a pretty American girl coming and standing in front of you in a garden. This pretty American girl, however, on hearing Winterbourne's observation, simply glanced at him; she then turned her head and looked over the parapet, at the lake and the opposite mountains. He wondered whether he had gone too far; but he decided that he must advance farther, rather than retreat. While he was thinking of something else to say, the young lady turned to the little boy again.

"I should like to know where you got that pole," she said.

"I bought it!" responded Randolph.

"You don't mean to say you're going to take it to Italy."

"Yes, I am going to take it to Italy!" the child declared.

The young girl glanced over the front of her dress, and smoothed out a knot or two of ribbon. Then she rested her eyes upon the prospect again. "Well, I guess you had better leave it somewhere," she said, after a moment.

"Are you going to Italy?" Winterbourne inquired, in a tone of great respect.

The young lady glanced at him again. "Yes, sir," she replied. And she said nothing more.

"Are you—a—going over the Simplon?"* Winterbourne pursued, a little embarrassed.

_____

*Mountain pass in southern Switzerland between the Pennine and Lepontine Alps.

"I don't know," she said. "I suppose it's some mountain. Randolph, what mountain are we going over?"

"Going where?" the child demanded.

"To Italy," Winterbourne explained.

"I don't know," said Randolph. "I don't want to go to Italy. I want to go to America."

"Oh, Italy is a beautiful place!" rejoined the young man.

"Can you get candy there?" Randolph loudly inquired.

"I hope not," said his sister. "I guess you have had enough candy, and mother thinks so too."

"I haven't had any for ever so long—for a hundred weeks!" cried the boy, still jumping about.

The young lady inspected her flounces and smoothed her ribbons again; and Winterbourne presently risked an observation upon the beauty of the view. He was ceasing to be embarrassed, for he had begun to perceive that she was not in the least embarrassed herself. There had not been the slightest alteration in her charming complexion; she was evidently neither offended nor fluttered. If she looked another way when he spoke to her, and seemed not particularly to hear him, this was simply her habit, her manner. Yet, as he talked a little more, and pointed out some of the objects of interest in the view, with which she appeared quite unacquainted, she gradually gave him more of the benefit of her glance; and then he saw that this glance was perfectly direct and unshrinking. It was not, however, what would have been called an immodest glance, for the young girl's eyes were singularly honest and fresh. They were wonderfully pretty eyes; and, indeed, Winterbourne had not seen for a long time anything prettier than his fair countrywoman's various features—her complexion, her nose, her ears, her teeth. He had a great relish for feminine beauty; he was addicted to observing and analysing it; and as regards this young lady's face he made several observations. It was not at all insipid, but it was not exactly expressive; and though it was eminently delicate Winterbourne mentally accused it—very forgivingly—of a want of finish. He thought it very possible that Master Randolph's sister was a coquette; he was sure she had a spirit of her own; but in her bright, sweet, superficial little visage there was no mockery, no irony. Before long it became obvious that she was much disposed towards conversation. She told him that they were going to Rome for the winter—she and her mother and Randolph. She asked him if he was a "real

American"; she wouldn't have taken him for one; he seemed more like a German—this was said after a little hesitation, especially when he spoke. Winterbourne, laughing, answered that he had met Germans who spoke like Americans; but that he had not, so far as he remembered, met an American who spoke like a German. Then he asked her if she would not be more comfortable in sitting upon the bench which he had just quitted. She answered that she liked standing up and walking about; but she presently sat down. She told him she was from New York State—"if you know where that is." Winterbourne learned more about her by catching hold of her small, slippery brother and making him stand a few minutes by his side.

"Tell me your name, my boy," he said.

"Randolph C. Miller," said the boy, sharply. "And I'll tell you her name"; and he levelled his alpenstock at his sister.

"You had better wait till you are asked!" said this young lady, calmly.

"I should like very much to know your name," said Winterbourne.

"Her name is Daisy Miller!" cried the child. "But that isn't her real name; that isn't her name on her cards."*

"It's a pity you haven't got one of my cards!" said Miss Miller.

"Her real name is Annie P. Miller," the boy went on.

"Ask him *his* name," said his sister, indicating Winterbourne.

But on this point Randolph seemed perfectly indifferent; he continued to supply information with regard to his own family. "My father's name is Ezra B. Miller," he announced. "My father ain't in Europe; my father's in a better place than Europe."

Winterbourne imagined for a moment that this was the manner in which the child had been taught to intimate that Mr. Miller had been removed to the sphere of celestial rewards. But Randolph immediately added, "My father's in Schenectady.† He's got a big business. My father's rich, you bet."

"Well!" ejaculated Miss Miller, lowering her parasol and looking at the embroidered border. Winterbourne presently released the

---

*Visiting cards bearing a person's written or printed name, or name and address, were used chiefly in making social calls.

†City in east-central New York State; site of an economic boom catalyzed by the opening of the Erie Canal in the 1820s and the railroad manufacturing boom that began in the 1830s.

child, who departed, dragging his alpenstock along the path. "He doesn't like Europe," said the young girl. "He wants to go back."

"To Schenectady, you mean?"

"Yes; he wants to go right home. He hasn't got any boys here. There is one boy here, but he always goes round with a teacher; they won't let him play."

"And your brother hasn't any teacher?" Winterbourne inquired.

"Mother thought of getting him one, to travel round with us. There was a lady told her of a very good teacher; an American lady—perhaps you know her—Mrs. Sanders. I think she came from Boston. She told her of this teacher, and we thought of getting him to travel round with us. But Randolph said he didn't want a teacher travelling round with us. He said he wouldn't have lessons when he was in the cars.* And we *are* in the cars about half the time. There was an English lady we met in the cars—I think her name was Miss Featherstone; perhaps you know her. She wanted to know why I didn't give Randolph lessons—give him 'instruction,' she called it. I guess he could give me more instruction than I could give him. He's very smart."

"Yes," said Winterbourne; "he seems very smart."

"Mother's going to get a teacher for him as soon as we get to Italy. Can you get good teachers in Italy?"

"Very good, I should think," said Winterbourne.

"Or else she's going to find some school. He ought to learn some more. He's only nine. He's going to college." And in this way Miss Miller continued to converse upon the affairs of her family, and upon other topics. She sat there with her extremely pretty hands, ornamented with very brilliant rings, folded in her lap, and with her pretty eyes now resting upon those of Winterbourne, now wandering over the garden, the people who passed by, and the beautiful view. She talked to Winterbourne as if she had known him a long time. He found it very pleasant. It was many years since he had heard a young girl talk so much. It might have been said of this unknown young lady, who had come and sat down beside him upon a bench, that she chattered. She was very quiet, she sat in a charming tranquil attitude; but her lips and her eyes were constantly moving. She had a soft, slender, agreeable voice, and her tone was decidedly

---

*Railway passenger cars.

sociable. She gave Winterbourne a history of her movements and intentions, and those of her mother and brother, in Europe, and enumerated, in particular, the various hotels at which they had stopped. "That English lady in the cars," she said—"Miss Featherstone—asked me if we didn't all live in hotels in America. I told her I had never been in so many hotels in my life as since I came to Europe. I have never seen so many—it's nothing but hotels." But Miss Miller did not make this remark with a querulous accent; she appeared to be in the best humour with everything. She declared that the hotels were very good, when once you got used to their ways, and that Europe was perfectly sweet. She was not disappointed—not a bit. Perhaps it was because she had heard so much about it before. She had ever so many intimate friends that had been there ever so many times. And then she had had ever so many dresses and things from Paris. Whenever she put on a Paris dress she felt as if she were in Europe.

"It was a kind of a wishing-cap," said Winterbourne.

"Yes," said Miss Miller, without examining this analogy; "it always made me wish I was here. But I needn't have done that for dresses. I am sure they send all the pretty ones to America; you see the most frightful things here. The only thing I don't like," she proceeded, "is the society. There isn't any society; or, if there is, I don't know where it keeps itself. Do you? I suppose there is some society somewhere, but I haven't seen anything of it. I'm very fond of society, and I have always had a great deal of it. I don't mean only in Schenectady, but in New York. I used to go to New York every winter. In New York I had lots of society. Last winter I had seventeen dinners given me; and three of them were by gentlemen," added Daisy Miller. "I have more friends in New York than in Schenectady—more gentlemen friends; and more young lady friends too," she resumed in a moment. She paused again for an instant; she was looking at Winterbourne with all her prettiness in her lively eyes and in her light, slightly monotonous smile. "I have always had," she said, "a great deal of gentlemen's society."

Poor Winterbourne was amused, perplexed, and decidedly charmed. He had never yet heard a young girl express herself in just this fashion; never, at least, save in cases where to say such things seemed a kind of demonstrative evidence of a certain laxity of deportment. And yet was he to accuse Miss Daisy Miller of actual or potential *inconduite*,* as they said at Geneva? He felt that he had lived at Geneva so long that he had lost a good deal; he had become dishabituated to the American tone. Never, indeed, since he had grown old enough to appreciate things, had he encountered a young American girl of so pronounced a type as this. Certainly she was very charming; but how deucedly sociable! Was she simply a pretty girl from New York State—were they all like that, the pretty girls who had a good deal of gentlemen's society? Or was she also a designing, an audacious, an unscrupulous young person? Winterbourne had lost his instinct in this matter, and his reason could not help him. Miss Daisy Miller looked extremely innocent. Some people had told him that, after all, American girls were exceedingly innocent; and others had told him that, after all, they were not. He was inclined to think Miss Daisy Miller was a flirt—a pretty American flirt. He had never, as yet, had any relations with young ladies of this category. He had known, here in Europe, two or three women—persons older than Miss Daisy Miller, and provided, for respectability's sake, with hus-bands—who were great coquettes—dangerous, terrible women, with whom one's relations were liable to take a serious turn. But this young girl was not a coquette in that sense; she was very unsophisticated; she was only a pretty American flirt. Winterbourne was almost grateful for having found the formula that applied to Miss Daisy Miller. He leaned back in his seat; he remarked to himself that she had the most charming nose he had ever seen; he wondered what were the regular conditions and limitations of one's intercourse with a pretty American flirt. It presently became apparent that he was on the way to learn.

"Have you been to that old castle?" asked the young girl, pointing with her parasol to the far-gleaming walls of the Château de Chillon.

"Yes, formerly, more than once," said Winterbourne. "You too, I suppose, have seen it?"

"No; we haven't been there. I want to go there dreadfully. Of course I mean to go there. I wouldn't go away from here without having seen that old castle."

"It's a very pretty excursion," said Winterbourne, "and very easy to make. You can drive, you know, or you can go by the little steamer."

"You can go in the cars," said Miss Miller.

---

*Unsuitable behavior (French).

"Yes; you can go in the cars," Winterbourne assented.

"Our courier* says they take you right up to the castle," the young girl continued. "We were going last week; but my mother gave out. She suffers dreadfully from dyspepsia.† She said she couldn't go. Randolph wouldn't go either; he says he doesn't think much of old castles. But I guess we'll go this week, if we can get Randolph."

"Your brother is not interested in ancient monuments?" Winterbourne inquired, smiling.

"He says he don't care much about old castles. He's only nine. He wants to stay at the hotel. Mother's afraid to leave him alone, and the courier won't stay with him; so we haven't been to many places. But it will be too bad if we don't go up there." And Miss Miller pointed again at the Château de Chillon.

"I should think it might be arranged," said Winterbourne. "Couldn't you get some one to stay—for the afternoon—with Randolph?"

Miss Miller looked at him a moment; and then, very placidly—

"I wish *you* would stay with him!" she said.

Winterbourne hesitated a moment. "I would much rather go to Chillon with you."

"With me?" asked the young girl, with the same placidity.

She didn't rise, blushing, as a young girl at Geneva would have done; and yet Winterbourne, conscious that he had been very bold, thought it possible she was offended. "With your mother," he answered very respectfully.

But it seemed that both his audacity and his respect were lost upon Miss Daisy Miller. "I guess my mother won't go, after all," she said. "She don't like to ride round in the afternoon. But did you really mean what you said just now; that you would like to go up there?"

"Most earnestly," Winterbourne declared.

"Then we may arrange it. If mother will stay with Randolph, I guess Eugenio will."

"Eugenio?" the young man inquired.

"Eugenio's our courier. He doesn't like to stay with Randolph; he's the most fastidious man I ever saw. But he's a splendid courier.

---

*Servant, employed by a traveler or traveling party, responsible for making arrangements connected with the journey.

†Term that described various digestive maladies involving weakness, loss of appetite, depression, and indigestion.

I guess he'll stay at home with Randolph if mother does, and then we can go to the castle."

Winterbourne reflected for an instant as lucidly as possible— "we" could only mean Miss Daisy Miller and himself. This programme seemed almost too agreeable for credence; he felt as if he ought to kiss the young lady's hand. Possibly he would have done so—and quite spoiled the project; but at this moment another person—presumably Eugenio—appeared. A tall, handsome man, with superb whiskers, wearing a velvet morning-coat and a brilliant watch-chain, approached Miss Miller, looking sharply at her companion. "Oh, Eugenio!" said Miss Miller, with the friendliest accent.

Eugenio had looked at Winterbourne from head to foot; he now bowed gravely to the young lady. "I have the honour to inform mademoiselle that luncheon is upon the table."

Miss Miller slowly rose. "See here, Eugenio," she said. "I'm going to that old castle, any way."

"To the Château de Chillon, mademoiselle?" the courier inquired. "Mademoiselle has made arrangements?" he added, in a tone which struck Winterbourne as very impertinent.

Eugenio's tone apparently threw, even to Miss Miller's own apprehension, a slightly ironical light upon the young girl's situation. She turned to Winterbourne, blushing a little—a very little. "You won't back out?" she said.

"I shall not be happy till we go!" he protested.

"And you are staying in this hotel?" she went on. "And you are really an American?"

The courier stood looking at Winterbourne, offensively. The young man, at least, thought his manner of looking an offence to Miss Miller; it conveyed an imputation that she "picked up" acquaintances. "I shall have the honour of presenting to you a person who will tell you all about me," he said smiling, and referring to his aunt.

"Oh, well, we'll go some day," said Miss Miller. And she gave him a smile and turned away. She put up her parasol and walked back to the inn beside Eugenio. Winterbourne stood looking after her; and as she moved away, drawing her muslin furbelows over the gravel, said to himself that she had the *tournure** of a princess.

---

*Bearing (French).

II

H<small>E HAD, HOWEVER, ENGAGED</small> to do more than proved feasible, in promising to present his aunt, Mrs. Costello, to Miss Daisy Miller. As soon as the former lady had got better of her headache he waited upon her in her apartment; and, after the proper inquiries in regard to her health, he asked her if she had observed, in the hotel, an American family—a mamma, a daughter, and a little boy.

"And a courier?" said Mrs. Costello. "Oh, yes, I have observed them. Seen them—heard them—and kept out of their way." Mrs. Costello was a widow with a fortune; a person of much distinction, who frequently intimated that, if she were not so dreadfully liable to sick-headaches, she would probably have left a deeper impress upon her time. She had a long pale face, a high nose, and a great deal of very striking white hair, which she wore in large puffs and *rouleaux** over the top of her head. She had two sons married in New York, and another who was now in Europe. This young man was amusing himself at Homburg, and, though he was on his travels, was rarely perceived to visit any particular city at the moment selected by his mother for her own appearance there. Her nephew, who had come up to Vevey expressly to see her, was therefore more attentive than those who, as she said, were nearer to her. He had imbibed at Geneva the idea that one must always be attentive to one's aunt. Mrs. Costello had not seen him for many years, and she was greatly pleased with him, manifesting her approbation by initiating him into many of the secrets of that social sway which, as she gave him to understand, she exerted in the American capital. She admitted that she was very exclusive; but, if he were acquainted with New York, he would see that one had to be. And her picture of the minutely hierarchical constitution of the society of that city, which she presented to him in many different lights, was, to Winterbourne's imagination, almost oppressively striking.

---

*Rolls, ringlets (French).

17

He immediately perceived, from her tone, that Miss Daisy Miller's place in the social scale was low. "I am afraid you don't approve of them," he said.

"They are very common," Mrs. Costello declared. "They are the sort of Americans that one does one's duty by not—not accepting."

"Ah, you don't accept them?" said the young man.

"I can't, my dear Frederick. I would if I could, but I can't."

"The young girl is very pretty," said Winterbourne, in a moment.

"Of course she's pretty. But she is very common."

"I see what you mean, of course," said Winterbourne, after another pause.

"She has that charming look that they all have," his aunt resumed. "I can't think where they pick it up; and she dresses in perfection—no, you don't know how well she dresses. I can't think where they get their taste."

"But, my dear aunt, she is not, after all, a Comanche savage."

"She is a young lady," said Mrs. Costello, "who has an intimacy with her mamma's courier."

"An intimacy with the courier?" the young man demanded.

"Oh, the mother is just as bad! They treat the courier like a familiar friend—like a gentleman. I shouldn't wonder if he dines with them. Very likely they have never seen a man with such good manners, such fine clothes, so like a gentleman. He probably corresponds to the young lady's idea of a Count. He sits with them in the garden, in the evening. I think he smokes."

Winterbourne listened with interest to these disclosures; they helped him to make up his mind about Miss Daisy. Evidently she was rather wild. "Well," he said, "I am not a courier, and yet she was very charming to me."

"You had better have said at first," said Mrs. Costello, with dignity, "that you had made her acquaintance."

"We simply met in the garden, and we talked a bit."

"*Tout bonnement!** And pray what did you say?"

"I said I should take the liberty of introducing her to my admirable aunt."

"I am much obliged to you."

---

*Just so! (French).

"It was to guarantee my respectability," said Winterbourne.

"And pray who is to guarantee hers?"

"Ah, you are cruel!" said the young man. "She's a very nice girl."

"You don't say that as if you believed it," Mrs. Costello observed.

"She is completely uncultivated," Winterbourne went on. "But she is wonderfully pretty, and, in short, she is very nice. To prove that I believe it, I am going to take her to the Château de Chillon."

"You two are going off there together? I should say it proved just the contrary. How long had you known her, may I ask, when this interesting project was formed? You haven't been twenty-four hours in the house."

"I had known her half-an-hour!" said Winterbourne, smiling.

"Dear me!" cried Mrs. Costello. "What a dreadful girl!"

Her nephew was silent for some moments. "You really think, then," he began, earnestly, and with a desire for trustworthy information— "you really think that——" But he paused again.

"Think what, sir?" said his aunt.

"That she is the sort of young lady who expects a man—sooner or later—to carry her off?"

"I haven't the least idea what such young ladies expect a man to do. But I really think that you had better not meddle with little American girls that are uncultivated, as you call them. You have lived too long out of the country. You will be sure to make some great mistake. You are too innocent."

"My dear aunt, I am not so innocent," said Winterbourne, smiling and curling his moustache.

"You are too guilty, then!"

Winterbourne continued to curl his moustache, meditatively. "You won't let the poor girl know you then?" he asked at last.

"Is it literally true that she is going to the Château de Chillon with you?"

"I think that she fully intends it."

"Then, my dear Frederick," said Mrs. Costello, "I must decline the honour of her acquaintance. I am an old woman, but I am not too old—thank Heaven—to be shocked!"

"But don't they all do these things—the young girls in America?" Winterbourne inquired.

Mrs. Costello stared a moment. "I should like to see my granddaughters do them!" she declared, grimly.

This seemed to throw some light upon the matter, for Winterbourne remembered to have heard that his pretty cousins in New York were "tremendous flirts." If, therefore, Miss Daisy Miller exceeded the liberal license allowed to these young ladies, it was probable that anything might be expected of her. Winterbourne was impatient to see her again, and he was vexed with himself that, by instinct, he should not appreciate her justly.

Though he was impatient to see her, he hardly knew what he should say to her about his aunt's refusal to become acquainted with her; but he discovered, promptly enough, that with Miss Daisy Miller there was no great need of walking on tiptoe. He found her that evening in the garden wandering about in the warm starlight, like an indolent sylph,[5] and swinging to and fro the largest fan he had ever beheld. It was ten o'clock. He had dined with his aunt, had been sitting with her since dinner, and had just taken leave of her till the morrow. Miss Daisy Miller seemed very glad to see him; she declared it was the longest evening she had ever passed.

"Have you been all alone?" he asked.

"I have been walking round with mother. But mother gets tired walking round," she answered.

"Has she gone to bed?"

"No; she doesn't like to go to bed," said the young girl. "She doesn't sleep—not three hours. She says she doesn't know how she lives. She's dreadfully nervous. I guess she sleeps more than she thinks. She's gone somewhere after Randolph; she wants to try to get him to go to bed. He doesn't like to go to bed."

"Let us hope she will persuade him," observed Winterbourne.

"She will talk to him all she can; but he doesn't like her to talk to him," said Miss Daisy, opening her fan. "She's going to try to get Eugenio to talk to him. But he isn't afraid of Eugenio. Eugenio's a splendid courier, but he can't make much impression on Randolph! I don't believe he'll go to bed before eleven." It appeared that Randolph's vigil was in fact triumphantly prolonged, for Winterbourne strolled about with the young girl for some time without meeting her mother. "I have been looking round for that lady you want to introduce me to," his companion resumed. "She's your aunt." Then, on Winterbourne's admitting the fact, and expressing some curiosity as to how she had learned it, she said she had heard all about Mrs. Costello from the chambermaid. She was very quiet and very *comme il faut;** she wore white puffs; she spoke to no one, and she never dined at the *table d' hôte.*† Every two days she had a headache. "I think that's a lovely description, headache and all!" said Miss Daisy, chattering along in her thin, gay voice. "I want to know her ever so much. I know just what *your* aunt would be; I know I should like her. She would be very exclusive. I like a lady to be exclusive; I'm dying to be exclusive myself. Well, we *are* exclusive, mother and I. We don't speak to every one — or they don't speak to us. I suppose it's about the same thing. Any way, I shall be ever so glad to know your aunt."

Winterbourne was embarrassed. "She would be most happy," he said; "but I am afraid those headaches will interfere."

The young girl looked at him through the dusk. "But I suppose she doesn't have a headache every day," she said, sympathetically.

Winterbourne was silent a moment. "She tells me she does," he answered at last — not knowing what to say.

Miss Daisy Miller stopped and stood looking at him. Her prettiness was still visible in the darkness; she was opening and closing her enormous fan. "She doesn't want to know me!" she said, suddenly. "Why don't you say so? You needn't be afraid. I'm not afraid!" And she gave a little laugh.

Winterbourne fancied there was a tremor in her voice; he was touched, shocked, mortified by it. "My dear young lady," he protested, "she knows no one. It's her wretched health."

The young girl walked on a few steps, laughing still. "You needn't be afraid," she repeated. "Why should she want to know me?" Then she paused again; she was close to the parapet of the garden, and in front of her was the starlit lake. There was a vague sheen upon its surface, and in the distance were dimly-seen mountain forms. Daisy Miller looked out upon the mysterious prospect, and then she gave another little laugh. "Gracious! she *is* exclusive!" she said. Winterbourne wondered whether she was seriously wounded, and for a moment almost wished that her sense of injury might be such as to make it becoming in him to attempt to reassure and comfort her. He had a pleasant sense that she would be very approachable for

---

*Proper in behavior or etiquette (French).
†At a hotel or inn, communal dining offered to guests as part of the cost of the stay (French).

consolatory purposes. He felt then, for the instant, quite ready to sacrifice his aunt, conversationally; to admit that she was a proud, rude woman, and to declare that they needn't mind her. But before he had time to commit himself to this perilous mixture of gallantry and impiety, the young lady, resuming her walk, gave an exclamation in quite another tone. "Well; here's mother! I guess she hasn't got Randolph to go to bed." The figure of a lady appeared, at a distance, very indistinct in the darkness, and advancing with a slow and wavering movement. Suddenly it seemed to pause.

"Are you sure it is your mother? Can you distinguish her in this thick dusk?" Winterbourne asked.

"Well!" cried Miss Daisy Miller, with a laugh, "I guess I know my own mother. And when she has got on my shawl, too! She is always wearing my things."

The lady in question, ceasing to advance, hovered vaguely about the spot at which she had checked her steps.

"I am afraid your mother doesn't see you," said Winterbourne. "Or perhaps," he added—thinking, with Miss Miller, the joke permissible—"perhaps she feels guilty about your shawl."

"Oh, it's a fearful old thing!" the young girl replied, serenely. "I told her she could wear it. She won't come here, because she sees you."

"Ah, then," said Winterbourne, "I had better leave you."

"Oh no; come on!" urged Miss Daisy Miller.

"I'm afraid your mother doesn't approve of my walking with you."

Miss Miller gave him a serious glance. "It isn't for me; it's for you—that is, it's for *her*. Well; I don't know who it's for! But mother doesn't like any of my gentlemen friends. She's right down timid. She always makes a fuss if I introduce a gentleman. But I *do* introduce them—almost always. If I didn't introduce my gentlemen friends to mother," the young girl added, in her little soft, flat monotone, "I shouldn't think I was natural."

"To introduce me," said Winterbourne, "you must know my name." And he proceeded to pronounce it.

"Oh, dear; I can't say all that!" said his companion, with a laugh. But by this time they had come up to Mrs. Miller, who, as they drew near, walked to the parapet of the garden and leaned upon it, looking intently at the lake and turning her back upon them. "Mother!" said the young girl, in a tone of decision. Upon this the elder lady turned round. "Mr. Winterbourne," said Miss Daisy Miller, introducing the young man very frankly and prettily. "Common," she was, as Mrs. Costello had pronounced her; yet it was a wonder to Winterbourne that, with her commonness, she had a singularly delicate grace.

Her mother was a small, spare, light person, with a wandering eye, a very exiguous nose, and a large forehead, decorated with a certain amount of thin, much-frizzled hair. Like her daughter, Mrs. Miller was dressed with extreme elegance; she had enormous diamonds in her ears. So far as Winterbourne could observe, she gave him no greeting—she certainly was not looking at him. Daisy was near her, pulling her shawl straight. "What are you doing, poking round here?" this young lady inquired; but by no means with that harshness of accent which her choice of words may imply.

"I don't know," said her mother, turning towards the lake again.

"I shouldn't think you'd want that shawl!" Daisy exclaimed.

"Well—I do!" her mother answered, with a little laugh.

"Did you get Randolph to go to bed?" asked the young girl.

"No; I couldn't induce him," said Mrs. Miller, very gently. "He wants to talk to the waiter. He likes to talk to that waiter."

"I was telling Mr. Winterbourne," the young girl went on; and to the young man's ear her tone might have indicated that she had been uttering his name all her life.

"Oh, yes!" said Winterbourne; "I have the pleasure of knowing your son."

Randolph's mamma was silent; she turned her attention to the lake. But at last she spoke. "Well, I don't see how he lives!"

"Anyhow, it isn't so bad as it was at Dover," said Daisy Miller.

"And what occurred at Dover?" Winterbourne asked.

"He wouldn't go to bed at all. I guess he sat up all night—in the public parlour. He wasn't in bed at twelve o'clock: I know that."

"It was half-past twelve," declared Mrs. Miller, with mild emphasis.

"Does he sleep much during the day?" Winterbourne demanded.

"I guess he doesn't sleep much," Daisy rejoined.

"I wish he would!" said her mother. "It seems as if he couldn't."

"I think he's real tiresome," Daisy pursued.

Then, for some moments, there was silence. "Well, Daisy Miller," said the elder lady, presently, "I shouldn't think you'd want to talk against your own brother!"

"Well, he *is* tiresome, mother," said Daisy, quite without the asperity of a retort.

"He's only nine," urged Mrs. Miller.

"Well, he wouldn't go to that castle," said the young girl. "I'm going there with Mr. Winterbourne."

To this announcement, very placidly made, Daisy's mamma offered no response. Winterbourne took for granted that she deeply disapproved of the projected excursion; but he said to himself that she was a simple, easily-managed person, and that a few deferential protestations would take the edge from her displeasure. "Yes," he began; "your daughter has kindly allowed me the honour of being her guide."

Mrs. Miller's wandering eyes attached themselves, with a sort of appealing air, to Daisy, who, however, strolled a few steps farther, gently humming to herself. "I presume you will go in the cars," said her mother.

"Yes; or in the boat," said Winterbourne.

"Well, of course, I don't know," Mrs. Miller rejoined. "I have never been to that castle."

"It is a pity you shouldn't go," said Winterbourne, beginning to feel reassured as to her opposition. And yet he was quite prepared to find that, as a matter of course, she meant to accompany her daughter.

"We've been thinking ever so much about going," she pursued; "but it seems as if we couldn't. Of course Daisy—she wants to go round. But there's a lady here—I don't know her name—she says she shouldn't think we'd want to go to see castles *here*; she should think we'd want to wait till we got to Italy. It seems as if there would be so many there," continued Mrs. Miller, with an air of increasing confidence. "Of course, we only want to see the principal ones. We visited several in England," she presently added.

"Ah, yes! in England there are beautiful castles," said Winterbourne. "But Chillon, here, is very well worth seeing."

"Well, if Daisy feels up to it——," said Mrs. Miller, in a tone impregnated with a sense of the magnitude of the enterprise. "It seems as if there was nothing she wouldn't undertake."

"Oh, I think she'll enjoy it!" Winterbourne declared. And he desired more and more to make it a certainty that he was to have the privilege of a *tête-à-tête* with the young lady, who was still strolling along in front of them, softly vocalising. "You are not disposed, madam," he inquired, "to undertake it yourself?"

Daisy's mother looked at him, an instant, askance, and then walked forward in silence. Then — "I guess she had better go alone," she said, simply.

Winterbourne observed to himself that this was a very different type of maternity from that of the vigilant matrons who massed themselves in the forefront of social intercourse in the dark old city at the other end of the lake. But his meditations were interrupted by hearing his name very distinctly pronounced by Mrs. Miller's unprotected daughter.

"Mr. Winterbourne!" murmured Daisy.

"Mademoiselle!" said the young man.

"Don't you want to take me out in a boat?"

"At present?" he asked.

"Of course!" said Daisy.

"Well, Annie Miller!" exclaimed her mother.

"I beg you, madam, to let her go," said Winterbourne, ardently; for he had never yet enjoyed the sensation of guiding through the summer starlight a skiff freighted with a fresh and beautiful young girl.

"I shouldn't think she'd want to," said her mother. "I should think she'd rather go indoors."

"I'm sure Mr. Winterbourne wants to take me," Daisy declared. "He's so awfully devoted!"

"I will row you over to Chillon, in the starlight."

"I don't believe it!" said Daisy.

"Well!" ejaculated the elder lady again.

"You haven't spoken to me for half-an-hour," her daughter went on.

"I have been having some very pleasant conversation with your mother," said Winterbourne.

"Well; I want you to take me out in a boat!" Daisy repeated. They had all stopped, and she had turned round and was looking at Winterbourne. Her face wore a charming smile, her pretty eyes were gleaming, she was swinging her great fan about. No; it's impossible to be prettier than that, thought Winterbourne.

"There are half-a-dozen boats moored at that landing-place," he said, pointing to certain steps which descended from the garden to the lake. "If you will do me the honour to accept my arm, we will go and select one of them."

Daisy stood there smiling; she threw back her head and gave a little light laugh. "I like a gentleman to be formal!" she declared.

"I assure you it's a formal offer."

"I was bound I would make you say something," Daisy went on.

"You see it's not very difficult," said Winterbourne. "But I am afraid you are chaffing me."

"I think not, sir," remarked Mrs. Miller, very gently.

"Do, then, let me give you a row," he said to the young girl.

"It's quite lovely, the way you say that!" cried Daisy.

"It will be still more lovely to do it."

"Yes, it would be lovely!" said Daisy. But she made no movement to accompany him; she only stood there laughing.

"I should think you had better find out what time it is," interposed her mother.

"It is eleven o'clock, madam," said a voice, with a foreign accent, out of the neighbouring darkness; and Winterbourne, turning, perceived the florid personage who was in attendance upon the two ladies. He had apparently just approached.

"Oh, Eugenio," said Daisy, "I am going out in a boat!"

Eugenio bowed. "At eleven o'clock, mademoiselle?"

"I am going with Mr. Winterbourne. This very minute."

"Do tell her she can't," said Mrs. Miller to the courier.

"I think you had better not go out in a boat, mademoiselle," Eugenio declared.

Winterbourne wished to Heaven this pretty girl were not so familiar with her courier; but he said nothing.

"I suppose you don't think it's proper!" Daisy exclaimed. "Eugenio doesn't think anything's proper."

" I am at your service," said Winterbourne.

"Does mademoiselle propose to go alone?" asked Eugenio of Mrs. Miller.

"Oh, no; with this gentleman!" answered Daisy's mamma.

The courier looked for a moment at Winterbourne—the latter thought he was smiling—and then, solemnly, with a bow. "As mademoiselle pleases!" he said.

"Oh, I hoped you would make a fuss!" said Daisy. "I don't care to go now."

"I myself shall make a fuss if you don't go," said Winterbourne.

"That's all I want—a little fuss!" And the young girl began to laugh again.

"Mr. Randolph has gone to bed!" the courier announced, frigidly.

"Oh, Daisy; now we can go!" said Mrs. Miller.

Daisy turned away from Winterbourne, looking at him, smiling and fanning herself. "Good night," she said; "I hope you are disappointed, or disgusted, or something!"

He looked at her, taking the hand she offered him. "I am puzzled," he answered.

"Well; I hope it won't keep you awake!" she said, very smartly; and, under the escort of the privileged Eugenio, the two ladies passed towards the house.

Winterbourne stood looking after them; he was indeed puzzled. He lingered beside the lake for a quarter of an hour, turning over the mystery of the young girl's sudden familiarities and caprices. But the only very definite conclusion he came to was that he should enjoy deucedly "going off" with her somewhere.

Two days afterwards he went off with her to the Castle of Chillon. He waited for her in the large hall of the hotel, where the couriers, the servants, the foreign tourists were lounging about and staring. It was not the place he would have chosen, but she had appointed it. She came tripping downstairs, buttoning her long gloves, squeezing her folded parasol against her pretty figure, dressed in the perfection of a soberly elegant travelling-costume. Winterbourne was a man of imagination and, as our ancestors used to say, of sensibility; as he looked at her dress and, on the great staircase, her little rapid, confiding step, he felt as if there were something romantic going forward. He could have believed he was going to elope with her. He passed out with her among all the idle people that were assembled there; they were all looking at her very hard; she had begun to chatter as soon as she joined him. Winterbourne's preference had been that they should be conveyed to Chillon in a carriage; but she expressed a lively wish to go in the little steamer; she declared that she had a passion for steamboats. There was always such a lovely breeze upon the water, and you saw such lots of people. The sail was not long, but Winterbourne's companion found time to say a great many things. To the young man himself their little excursion was so much of an escapade—an adventure—that, even allowing for her habitual sense of freedom, he had some expectation of seeing her regard it in the same way. But it must be confessed that, in this particular, he was disappointed. Daisy Miller was extremely animated, she was in charming spirits; but she was apparently not at all excited; she was not fluttered; she avoided neither his eyes nor those of any one else; she blushed neither when she looked at him nor when she saw that people were looking at her. People continued to look at her a great deal, and Winterbourne took much satisfaction in his pretty companion's distinguished air. He had been a little afraid that she would talk loud, laugh overmuch, and even, perhaps, desire to move about the boat a good deal. But he quite forgot his fears; he sat smiling, with his eyes upon her face, while, without moving from her place, she delivered herself of a great number of original reflections. It was the most charming garrulity he had ever heard. He had assented to the idea that she was "common"; but was she so, after all, or was he simply getting used to her commonness? Her conversation was chiefly of what metaphysicians term the objective cast; but every now and then it took a subjective turn.

"What on *earth* are you so grave about?" she suddenly demanded, fixing her agreeable eyes upon Winterbourne's.

"Am I grave?" he asked. "I had an idea I was grinning from ear to ear."

"You look as if you were taking me to a funeral. If that's a grin, your ears are very near together."

"Should you like me to dance a hornpipe on the deck?"

"Pray do, and I'll carry round your hat. It will pay the expenses of our journey."

"I never was better pleased in my life," murmured Winterbourne.

She looked at him a moment, and then burst into a little laugh. "I like to make you say those things! You're a queer mixture!"

In the castle, after they had landed, the subjective element decidedly prevailed. Daisy tripped about the vaulted chambers, rustled her skirts in the corkscrew staircases, flirted back with a pretty little cry and a shudder from the edge of the *oubliettes,** and turned a singularly well-shaped ear to everything that Winterbourne told her about the place. But he saw that she cared very little for feudal antiquities, and that the dusky traditions of Chillon made but a slight impression upon her. They had the good fortune to have been

---

*Dungeons with a trapdoor in the ceiling that serves as the only means of entrance or exit.

able to walk about without other companionship than that of the custodian; and Winterbourne arranged with this functionary that they should not be hurried—that they should linger and pause wherever they chose. The custodian interpreted the bargain generously—Winterbourne, on his side, had been generous—and ended by leaving them quite to themselves. Miss Miller's observations were not remarkable for logical consistency; for anything she wanted to say she was sure to find a pretext. She found a great many pretexts in the rugged embrasures of Chillon for asking Winterbourne sudden questions about himself—his family, his previous history, his tastes, his habits, his intentions—and for supplying information upon corresponding points in her own personality. Of her own tastes, habits and intentions Miss Miller was prepared to give the most definite, and indeed the most favourable, account.

"Well; I hope you know enough!" she said to her companion, after he had told her the history of the unhappy Bonivard.[6] "I never saw a man that knew so much!" The history of Bonivard had evidently, as they say, gone into one ear and out of the other. But Daisy went on to say that she wished Winterbourne would travel with them and "go round" with them; they might know something, in that case. "Don't you want to come and teach Randolph?" she asked. Winterbourne said that nothing could possibly please him so much; but that he had unfortunately other occupations. "Other occupations? I don't believe it!" said Miss Daisy. "What do you mean? You are not in business." The young man admitted that he was not in business; but he had engagements which, even within a day or two, would force him to go back to Geneva. "Oh, bother!" she said, "I don't believe it!" and she began to talk about something else. But a few moments later, when he was pointing out to her the pretty design of an antique fireplace, she broke out irrelevantly, "You don't mean to say you are going back to Geneva?"

"It is a melancholy fact that I shall have to return to Geneva tomorrow."

"Well, Mr. Winterbourne," said Daisy; "I think you're horrid!"

"Oh, don't say such dreadful things!" said Winterbourne—"just at the last."

"The last!" cried the young girl; "I call it the first. I have half a mind to leave you here and go straight back to the hotel alone." And for the next ten minutes she did nothing but call him horrid. Poor

Winterbourne was fairly bewildered; no young lady had as yet done him the honour to be so agitated by the announcement of his movements. His companion, after this, ceased to pay any attention to the curiosities of Chillon or the beauties of the lake; she opened fire upon the mysterious charmer in Geneva, whom she appeared to have instantly taken it for granted that he was hurrying back to see. How did Miss Daisy Miller know that there was a charmer in Geneva? Winterbourne, who denied the existence of such a person, was quite unable to discover; and he was divided between amazement at the rapidity of her induction and amusement at the frankness of her *persiflage.** She seemed to him, in all this, an extraordinary mixture of innocence and crudity. "Does she never allow you more than three days at a time?" asked Daisy, ironically. "Doesn't she give you a vacation in summer? There's no one so hard worked but they can get leave to go off somewhere at this season. I suppose, if you stay another day, she'll come after you in the boat. Do wait over till Friday, and I will go down to the landing to see her arrive!" Winterbourne began to think he had been wrong to feel disappointed in the temper in which the young lady had embarked. If he had missed the personal accent, the personal accent was now making its appearance. It sounded very distinctly, at last, in her telling him she would stop "teasing" him if he would promise her solemnly to come down to Rome in the winter.

"That's not a difficult promise to make," said Winterbourne. "My aunt has taken an apartment in Rome for the winter, and has already asked me to come and see her."

"I don't want you to come for your aunt," said Daisy; "I want you to come for me." And this was the only allusion that the young man was ever to hear her make to his invidious kinswoman. He declared that, at any rate, he would certainly come. After this Daisy stopped teasing. Winterbourne took a carriage, and they drove back to Vevey in the dusk; the young girl was very quiet.

In the evening Winterbourne mentioned to Mrs. Costello that he had spent the afternoon at Chillon, with Miss Daisy Miller.

"The Americans—of the courier?" asked this lady.

"Ah, happily," said Winterbourne, "the courier stayed at home."

---

*Mockery (French).

"She went with you all alone?"

"All alone."

Mrs. Costello sniffed a little at her smelling-bottle.* "And that," she exclaimed, "is the young person you wanted me to know!"

---

*Vial containing smelling-salts, used as a restorative in cases of faintness or headache.

III

WINTERBOURNE, WHO HAD RETURNED to Geneva the day after his excursion to Chillon, went to Rome towards the end of January. His aunt had been established there for several weeks, and he had received a couple of letters from her. "Those people you were so devoted to last summer at Vevey have turned up here, courier and all," she wrote. "They seem to have made several acquaintances, but the courier continues to be the most *intime*.* The young lady, however, is also very intimate with some third-rate Italians, with whom she rackets about in a way that makes much talk. Bring me that pretty novel of Cherbuliez's—'Paule Méré'[7]—and don't come later than the 23rd."

In the natural course of events, Winterbourne, on arriving in Rome, would presently have ascertained Mrs. Miller's address at the American banker's and have gone to pay his compliments to Miss Daisy. "After what happened at Vevey I certainly think I may call upon them," he said to Mrs. Costello.

"If, after what happens—at Vevey and everywhere—you desire to keep up the acquaintance, you are very welcome. Of course a man may know every one. Men are welcome to the privilege!"

"Pray what is it that happens—here, for instance?" Winterbourne demanded.

"The girl goes about alone with her foreigners. As to what happens farther, you must apply elsewhere for information. She has picked up half-a-dozen of the regular Roman fortune-hunters, and she takes them about to people's houses. When she comes to a party she brings with her a gentleman with a good deal of manner and a wonderful moustache."

"And where is the mother?"

"I haven't the least idea. They are very dreadful people."

Winterbourne meditated a moment. "They are very ignorant—very innocent only. Depend upon it they are not bad."

---

*Intimate (French).

"They are hopelessly vulgar," said Mrs. Costello. "Whether or no being hopelessly vulgar is being 'bad' is a question for the metaphysicians. They are bad enough to dislike, at any rate; and for this short life that is quite enough."

The news that Daisy Miller was surrounded by half-a-dozen wonderful moustaches checked Winterbourne's impulse to go straightway to see her. He had perhaps not definitely flattered himself that he had made an ineffaceable impression upon her heart, but he was annoyed at hearing of a state of affairs so little in harmony with an image that had lately flitted in and out of his own meditations; the image of a very pretty girl looking out of an old Roman window and asking herself urgently when Mr. Winterbourne would arrive. If, however, he determined to wait a little before reminding Miss Miller of his claims to her consideration, he went very soon to call upon two or three other friends. One of these friends was an American lady who had spent several winters at Geneva, where she had placed her children at school. She was a very accomplished woman and she lived in the Via Gregoriana.* Winterbourne found her in a little crimson drawing-room, on a third floor; the room was filled with southern sunshine. He had not been there ten minutes when the servant came in, announcing "Madame Mila!" This announcement was presently followed by the entrance of little Randolph Miller, who stopped in the middle of the room and stood staring at Winterbourne. An instant later his pretty sister crossed the threshold; and then, after a considerable interval, Mrs. Miller slowly advanced.

"I know you!" said Randolph.

"I'm sure you know a great many things," exclaimed Winterbourne, taking him by the hand. "How is your education coming on?"

Daisy was exchanging greetings very prettily with her hostess; but when she heard Winterbourne's voice she quickly turned her head. "Well, I declare!" she said.

"I told you I should come, you know," Winterbourne rejoined, smiling.

"Well—I didn't believe it," said Miss Daisy.

---

*Street near the Spanish Steps in central Rome.

"I am much obliged to you," laughed the young man.

"You might have come to see me!" said Daisy.

"I arrived only yesterday."

"I don't believe that!" the young girl declared.

Winterbourne turned with a protesting smile to her mother; but this lady evaded his glance, and seating herself, fixed her eyes upon her son. "We've got a bigger place than this," said Randolph. "It's all gold on the walls."

Mrs. Miller turned uneasily in her chair. "I told you if I were to bring you, you would say something!" she murmured.

"I told *you!*" Randolph exclaimed. "I tell *you*, sir!" he added jocosely, giving Winterbourne a thump on the knee. "It *is* bigger, too!"

Daisy had entered upon a lively conversation with her hostess; Winterbourne judged it becoming to address a few words to her mother. "I hope you have been well since we parted at Vevey," he said.

Mrs. Miller now certainly looked at him—at his chin. "Not very well, sir," she answered.

"She's got the dyspepsia," said Randolph. "I've got it too. Father's got it. I've got it worst!"

This announcement, instead of embarrassing Mrs. Miller, seemed to relieve her. "I suffer from the liver," she said. "I think it's this climate; it's less bracing than Schenectady, especially in the winter season. I don't know whether you know we reside at Schenectady. I was saying to Daisy that I certainly hadn't found any one like Dr. Davis, and I didn't believe I should. Oh, at Schenectady, he stands first; they think everything of him. He has so much to do, and yet there was nothing he wouldn't do for me. He said he never saw anything like my dyspepsia, but he was bound to cure it. I'm sure there was nothing he wouldn't try. He was just going to try something new when we came off. Mr. Miller wanted Daisy to see Europe for herself. But I wrote to Mr. Miller that it seems as if I couldn't get on without Dr. Davis. At Schenectady he stands at the very top; and there's a great deal of sickness there, too. It affects my sleep."

Winterbourne had a good deal of pathological gossip with Dr. Davis's patient, during which Daisy chattered unremittingly to her own companion. The young man asked Mrs. Miller how she was pleased with Rome. "Well, I must say I am disappointed," she answered. "We had heard so much about it; I suppose we had heard too much. But we couldn't help that. We had been led to expect something different."

"Ah, wait a little, and you will become very fond of it," said Winterbourne.

"I hate it worse and worse every day!" cried Randolph.

"You are like the infant Hannibal,"* said Winterbourne.

"No, I ain't!" Randolph declared, at a venture.

"You are not much like an infant," said his mother. "But we have seen places," she resumed, "that I should put a long way before Rome." And in reply to Winterbourne's interrogation, "There's Zurich," she observed; "I think Zurich is lovely; and we hadn't heard half so much about it."

"The best place we've seen is the City of Richmond!" said Randolph.

"He means the ship," his mother explained. "We crossed in that ship. Randolph had a good time on the City of Richmond."

"It's the best place I've seen," the child repeated. "Only it was turned the wrong way."

"Well, we've got to turn the right way some time," said Mrs. Miller, with a little laugh. Winterbourne expressed the hope that her daughter at least found some gratification in Rome, and she declared that Daisy was quite carried away. "It's on account of the society—the society's splendid. She goes round everywhere; she has made a great number of acquaintances. Of course she goes round more than I do. I must say they have been very sociable; they have taken her right in. And then she knows a great many gentlemen. Oh, she thinks there's nothing like Rome. Of course, it's a great deal pleasanter for a young lady if she knows plenty of gentlemen."

By this time Daisy had turned her attention again to Winterbourne. "I've been telling Mrs. Walker how mean you were!" the young girl announced.

"And what is the evidence you have offered?" asked Winterbourne, rather annoyed at Miss Miller's want of appreciation of the zeal of an admirer who on his way down to Rome had stopped neither at Bologna nor at Florence, simply because of a certain sentimental impatience. He remembered that a cynical compatriot had

---

*Carthaginian general who fought against Rome in the third century B.C.

once told him that American women—the pretty ones, and this gave a largeness to the axiom—were at once the most exacting in the world and the least endowed with a sense of indebtedness.

"Why, you were awfully mean at Vevey," said Daisy. "You wouldn't do anything. You wouldn't stay there when I asked you."

"My dearest young lady," cried Winterbourne, with eloquence, "have I come all the way to Rome to encounter your reproaches?"

"Just hear him say that!" said Daisy to her hostess, giving a twist to a bow on this lady's dress. "Did you ever hear anything so quaint?"

"So quaint, my dear?" murmured Mrs. Walker, in the tone of a partisan of Winterbourne.

"Well, I don't know," said Daisy, fingering Mrs. Walker's ribbons. "Mrs. Walker, I want to tell you something."

"Motherr," interposed Randolph, with his rough ends to his words, "I tell you you've got to go. Eugenio'll raise something!"

"I'm not afraid of Eugenio," said Daisy, with a toss of her head. "Look here, Mrs. Walker," she went on, "you know I'm coming to your party."

"I am delighted to hear it."

"I've got a lovely dress."

"I am very sure of that."

"But I want to ask a favour—permission to bring a friend."

"I shall be happy to see any of your friends," said Mrs. Walker, turning with a smile to Mrs. Miller.

"Oh, they are not my friends," answered Daisy's mamma, smiling shyly, in her own fashion. "I never spoke to them!"

"It's an intimate friend of mine—Mr. Giovanelli," said Daisy, without a tremor in her clear little voice or a shadow on her brilliant little face.

Mrs. Walker was silent a moment, she gave a rapid glance at Winterbourne. "I shall be glad to see Mr. Giovanelli," she then said.

"He's an Italian," Daisy pursued, with the prettiest serenity. "He's a great friend of mine—he's the handsomest man in the world—except Mr. Winterbourne! He knows plenty of Italians, but he wants to know some Americans. He thinks ever so much of Americans. He's tremendously clever. He's perfectly lovely!"

It was settled that this brilliant personage should be brought to Mrs. Walker's party, and then Mrs. Miller prepared to take her leave. "I guess we'll go back to the hotel," she said.

"You may go back to the hotel, mother, but I'm going to take a walk," said Daisy.

"She's going to walk with Mr. Giovanelli," Randolph proclaimed.

"I am going to the Pincio,"* said Daisy, smiling.

"Alone, my dear—at this hour?" Mrs. Walker asked. The afternoon was drawing to a close—it was the hour for the throng of carriages and of contemplative pedestrians. "I don't think it's safe, my dear," said Mrs. Walker.

"Neither do I," subjoined Mrs. Miller. "You'll get the fever† as sure as you live. Remember what Dr. Davis told you!"

"Give her some medicine before she goes," said Randolph.

The company had risen to its feet; Daisy, still showing her pretty teeth, bent over and kissed her hostess. "Mrs. Walker, you are too perfect," she said. "I'm not going alone; I am going to meet a friend."

"Your friend won't keep you from getting the fever," Mrs. Miller observed.

"Is it Mr. Giovanelli?" asked the hostess.

Winterbourne was watching the young girl; at this question his attention quickened. She stood there smiling and smoothing her bonnet-ribbons; she glanced at Winterbourne. Then, while she glanced and smiled, she answered without a shade of hesitation, "Mr. Giovanelli—the beautiful Giovanelli."

"My dear young friend, " said Mrs. Walker, taking her hand pleadingly, "don't walk off to the Pincio at this hour to meet a beautiful Italian."

"Well, he speaks English," said Mrs. Miller.

"Gracious me!" Daisy exclaimed, "I don't want to do anything improper. There's an easy way to settle it." She continued to glance at Winterbourne. "The Pincio is only a hundred yards distant, and if Mr. Winterbourne were as polite as he pretends he would offer to walk with me!"

Winterbourne's politeness hastened to affirm itself, and the young girl gave him gracious leave to accompany her. They passed down-stairs before her mother, and at the door Winterbourne perceived Mrs. Miller's carriage drawn up, with the ornamental courier

---

*Public park where nineteenth-century Romans traditionally promenaded toward sunset.
†Malaria.

whose acquaintance he had made at Vevey seated within. "Good-bye, Eugenio!" cried Daisy, "I'm going to take a walk." The distance from the Via Gregoriana to the beautiful garden at the other end of the Pincian Hill is, in fact, rapidly traversed. As the day was splendid, however, and the concourse of vehicles, walkers, and loungers numerous, the young Americans found their progress much delayed. This fact was highly agreeable to Winterbourne, in spite of his consciousness of his singular situation. The slow-moving, idly-gazing Roman crowd bestowed much attention upon the extremely pretty young foreign lady who was passing through it upon his arm; and he wondered what on earth had been in Daisy's mind when she proposed to expose herself, unattended, to its appreciation. His own mission, to her sense, apparently, was to consign her to the hands of Mr. Giovanelli; but Winterbourne, at once annoyed and gratified, resolved that he would do no such thing.

"Why haven't you been to see me?" asked Daisy. "You can't get out of that."

"I have had the honour of telling you that I have only just stepped out of the train."

"You must have stayed in the train a good while after it stopped!" cried the young girl, with her little laugh. "I suppose you were asleep. You have had time to go to see Mrs. Walker."

"I knew Mrs. Walker——" Winterbourne began to explain.

"I knew where you knew her. You knew her at Geneva. She told me so. Well, you knew me at Vevey. That's just as good. So you ought to have come." She asked him no other question than this; she began to prattle about her own affairs. "We've got splendid rooms at the hotel; Eugenio says they're the best rooms in Rome. We are going to stay all winter—if we don't die of the fever; and I guess we'll stay then. It's a great deal nicer than I thought; I thought it would be fearfully quiet; I was sure it would be awfully poky. I was sure we should be going round all the time with one of those dreadful old men that explain about the pictures and things. But we only had about a week of that, and now I'm enjoying myself. I know ever so many people, and they are all so charming. The society's extremely select. There are all kinds—English, and Germans, and Italians. I think I like the English best. I like their style of conversation. But there are some lovely Americans. I never saw anything so hospitable. There's something or other every day. There's not much dancing;

but I must say I never thought dancing was everything. I was always fond of conversation. I guess I shall have plenty at Mrs. Walker's — her rooms are so small." When they had passed the gate of the Pincian Gardens, Miss Miller began to wonder where Mr. Giovanelli might be. "We had better go straight to that place in front," she said, "where you look at the view."

"I certainly shall not help you to find him," Winterbourne declared.

"Then I shall find him without you," said Miss Daisy.

"You certainly won't leave me!" cried Winterbourne.

She burst into her little laugh. "Are you afraid you'll get lost — or run over? But there's Giovanelli, leaning against that tree. He's staring at the women in the carriages: did you ever see anything so cool?"

Winterbourne perceived at some distance a little man standing with folded arms, nursing his cane. He had a handsome face, an artfully poised hat, a glass in one eye and a nosegay in his buttonhole. Winterbourne looked at him a moment and then said, "Do you mean to speak to that man?"

"Do I mean to speak to him? Why, you don't suppose I mean to communicate by signs?"

"Pray understand, then," said Winterbourne, "that I intend to remain with you."

Daisy stopped and looked at him, without a sign of troubled consciousness in her face; with nothing but the presence of her charming eyes and her happy dimples. "Well, she's a cool one!" thought the young man.

"I don't like the way you say that," said Daisy. "It's too imperious."

"I beg your pardon if I say it wrong. The main point is to give you an idea of my meaning."

The young girl looked at him more gravely, but with eyes that were prettier than ever. "I have never allowed a gentleman to dictate to me, or to interfere with anything I do."

"I think you have made a mistake," said Winterbourne. "You should sometimes listen to a gentleman — the right one?"

Daisy began to laugh again. "I do nothing but listen to gentlemen!" she exclaimed. "Tell me if Mr. Giovanelli is the right one."

The gentleman with the nosegay in his bosom had now perceived our two friends, and was approaching the young girl with obsequious rapidity. He bowed to Winterbourne as well as to the latter's companion; he had a brilliant smile, an intelligent eye; Winterbourne thought him not a bad-looking fellow. But he nevertheless said to Daisy—"No, he's not the right one."

Daisy evidently had a natural talent for performing introductions; she mentioned the name of each of her companions to the other. She strolled along with one of them on each side of her; Mr. Giovanelli, who spoke English very cleverly—Winterbourne afterwards learned that he had practised the idiom upon a great many American heiresses—addressed her a great deal of very polite nonsense; he was extremely urbane, and the young American, who said nothing, reflected upon that profundity of Italian cleverness which enables people to appear more gracious in proportion as they are more acutely disappointed. Giovanelli, of course, had counted upon something more intimate; he had not bargained for a party of three. But he kept his temper in a manner which suggested far-stretching intentions. Winterbourne flattered himself that he had taken his measure. "He is not a gentleman," said the young American; "he is only a clever imitation of one. He is a music-master, or a penny-a-liner,* or a third-rate artist. Damn his good looks!" Mr. Giovanelli had certainly a very pretty face; but Winterbourne felt a superior indignation at his own lovely fellow-countrywoman's not knowing the difference between a spurious gentleman and a real one. Giovanelli chattered and jested and made himself wonderfully agreeable. It was true that if he was an imitation the imitation was very skilful. "Nevertheless," Winterbourne said to himself, "a nice girl ought to know!" And then he came back to the question whether this was in fact a nice girl. Would a nice girl—even allowing for her being a little American flirt—make a rendezvous with a presumably low-lived foreigner? The rendezvous in this case, indeed, had been in broad daylight, and in the most crowded corner of Rome; but was it not impossible to regard the choice of these circumstances as a proof of extreme cynicism? Singular though it may seem, Winterbourne was vexed that the young girl, in joining her *amoroso*,† should not appear more impatient of his own company, and he was vexed because of his inclination. It was impossible to regard her as

---

*Hack writer for a newspaper or journal who was paid a penny a line or a similarly low rate; the term is contemptuously used to refer to writers with an overblown style.
†Lover (Italian).

a perfectly well-conducted young lady; she was wanting in a certain indispensable delicacy. It would therefore simplify matters greatly to be able to treat her as the object of one of those sentiments which are called by romancers "lawless passions." That she should seem to wish to get rid of him would help him to think more lightly of her, and to be able to think more lightly of her would make her much less perplexing. But Daisy, on this occasion, continued to present herself as an inscrutable combination of audacity and innocence.

She had been walking some quarter of an hour, attended by her two cavaliers, and responding in a tone of very childish gaiety, as it seemed to Winterbourne, to the pretty speeches of Mr. Giovanelli, when a carriage that had detached itself from the revolving train drew up beside the path. At the same moment Winterbourne perceived that his friend Mrs. Walker—the lady whose house he had lately left—was seated in the vehicle and was beckoning to him. Leaving Miss Miller's side, he hastened to obey her summons. Mrs. Walker was flushed; she wore an excited air. "It is really too dreadful," she said. "That girl must not do this sort of thing. She must not walk here with you two men. Fifty people have noticed her."

Winterbourne raised his eyebrows. "I think it's a pity to make too much fuss about it."

"It's a pity to let the girl ruin herself!"

"She is very innocent," said Winterbourne.

"She's very crazy!" cried Mrs. Walker. "Did you ever see anything so imbecile as her mother? After you had all left me, just now, I could not sit still for thinking of it. It seemed too pitiful, not even to attempt to save her. I ordered the carriage and put on my bonnet, and came here as quickly as possible. Thank heaven I have found you!"

"What do you propose to do with us?" asked Winterbourne, smiling.

"To ask her to get in, to drive her about here for half-an-hour, so that the world may see she is not running absolutely wild, and then to take her safely home."

"I don't think it's a very happy thought," said Winterbourne; "but you can try."

Mrs. Walker tried. The young man went in pursuit of Miss Miller, who had simply nodded and smiled at his interlocutrix in the carriage and had gone her way with her own companion. Daisy, on learning that Mrs. Walker wished to speak to her, retraced her steps with a perfect good grace and with Mr. Giovanelli at her side. She declared that she was delighted to have a chance to present this gentleman to Mrs. Walker. She immediately achieved the introduction, and declared that she had never in her life seen anything so lovely as Mrs. Walker's carriage-rug.

"I am glad you admire it," said this lady, smiling sweetly. "Will you get in and let me put it over you?"

"Oh, no, thank you," said Daisy. "I shall admire it much more as I see you driving round with it."

"Do get in and drive with me," said Mrs. Walker.

"That would be charming, but it's so enchanting just as I am!" and Daisy gave a brilliant glance at the gentlemen on either side of her.

"It may be enchanting, dear child, but it is not the custom here," urged Mrs. Walker, leaning forward in her victoria with her hands devoutly clasped.

"Well, it ought to be, then!" said Daisy. "If I didn't walk I should expire."

"You should walk with your mother, dear," cried the lady from Geneva, losing patience.

"With my mother dear!" exclaimed the young girl. Winterbourne saw that she scented interference. "My mother never walked ten steps in her life. And then, you know," she added with a laugh, "I am more than five years old."

"You are old enough to be more reasonable. You are old enough, dear Miss Miller, to be talked about."

Daisy looked at Mrs. Walker, smiling intensely. "Talked about? What do you mean?"

"Come into my carriage and I will tell you."

Daisy turned her quickened glance again from one of the gentlemen beside her to the other. Mr. Giovanelli was bowing to and fro, rubbing down his gloves and laughing very agreeably; Winterbourne thought it a most unpleasant scene. "I don't think I want to know what you mean," said Daisy presently. "I don't think I should like it."

Winterbourne wished that Mrs. Walker would tuck in her carriage-rug and drive away; but this lady did not enjoy being defied, as she afterwards told him. "Should you prefer being thought a very reckless girl?" she demanded.

"Gracious me!" exclaimed Daisy. She looked again at Mr. Giovanelli, then she turned to Winterbourne. There was a little pink flush in her cheek; she was tremendously pretty. "Does Mr. Winterbourne think," she asked slowly, smiling, throwing back her head and glancing at him from head to foot, "that—to save my reputation—I ought to get into the carriage?"

Winterbourne coloured; for an instant he hesitated greatly. It seemed so strange to hear her speak that way of her "reputation." But he himself, in fact, must speak in accordance with gallantry. The finest gallantry, here, was simply to tell her the truth; and the truth, for Winterbourne, as the few indications I have been able to give have made him known to the reader, was that Daisy Miller should take Mrs. Walker's advice. He looked at her exquisite prettiness; and then he said very gently, "I think you should get into the carriage."

Daisy gave a violent laugh. "I never heard anything so stiff! If this is improper, Mrs. Walker," she pursued, "then I am all improper, and you must give me up. Good-bye; I hope you'll have a lovely ride!" and, with Mr. Giovanelli, who made a triumphantly obsequious salute, she turned away.

Mrs. Walker sat looking after her, and there were tears in Mrs. Walker's eyes. "Get in here, sir," she said to Winterbourne, indicating the place beside her. The young man answered that he felt bound to accompany Miss Miller; whereupon Mrs. Walker declared that if he refused her this favour she would never speak to him again. She was evidently in earnest. Winterbourne overtook Daisy and her companion, and, offering the young girl his hand, told her that Mrs. Walker had made an imperious claim upon his society. He expected that in answer she would say something rather free, something to commit herself still farther to that "recklessness" from which Mrs. Walker had so charitably endeavoured to dissuade her. But she only shook his hand, hardly looking at him, while Mr. Giovanelli bade him farewell with a too emphatic flourish of the hat.

Winterbourne was not in the best possible humour as he took his seat in Mrs. Walker's victoria. "That was not clever of you," he said candidly, while the vehicle mingled again with the throng of carriages.

"In such a case," his companion answered, "I don't wish to be clever, I wish to be *earnest!*"

"Well, your earnestness has only offended her and put her off."

"It has happened very well," said Mrs. Walker. "If she is so per-fectly determined to compromise herself, the sooner one knows it the better; one can act accordingly."

"I suspect she meant no harm," Winterbourne rejoined.

"So I thought a month ago. But she has been going too far."

"What has she been doing?"

"Everything that is not done here. Flirting with any man she could pick up; sitting in corners with mysterious Italians; dancing all the evening with the same partners; receiving visits at eleven o'clock at night. Her mother goes away when visitors come."

"But her brother," said Winterbourne, laughing, "sits up till mid-night."

"He must be edified by what he sees. I'm told that at their hotel every one is talking about her, and that a smile goes round among the servants when a gentleman comes and asks for Miss Miller."

"The servants be hanged!" said Winterbourne angrily. "The poor girl's only fault," he presently added, "is that she is very uncultivated."

"She is naturally indelicate," Mrs. Walker declared. "Take that example this morning. How long had you known her at Vevey?"

"A couple of days."

"Fancy, then, her making it a personal matter that you should have left the place!"

Winterbourne was silent for some moments; then he said, "I sus-pect, Mrs. Walker, that you and I have lived too long at Geneva!" And he added a request that she should inform him with what par-ticular design she had made him enter her carriage.

"I wished to beg you to cease your relations with Miss Miller—not to flirt with her—to give her no further opportunity to expose herself—to let her alone, in short."

"I'm afraid I can't do that," said Winterbourne. "I like her ex-tremely."

"All the more reason that you shouldn't help her to make a scandal."

"There shall be nothing scandalous in my attentions to her."

"There certainly will be in the way she takes them. But I have said what I had on my conscience," Mrs. Walker pursued. "If you wish to rejoin the young lady I will put you down. Here, by-the-way, you have a chance."

The carriage was traversing that part of the Pincian Garden which overhangs the wall of Rome and overlooks the beautiful Villa Borghese.[8] It is bordered by a large parapet, near which there are several seats. One of the seats, at a distance, was occupied by a gentleman and a lady, towards whom Mrs. Walker gave a toss of her head. At the same moment these persons rose and walked towards the parapet. Winterbourne had asked the coachman to stop; he now descended from the carriage. His companion looked at him a moment in silence; then, while he raised his hat, she drove majestically away. Winterbourne stood there; he had turned his eyes towards Daisy and her cavalier. They evidently saw no one; they were too deeply occupied with each other. When they reached the low garden-wall they stood a moment looking off at the great flat-topped pine-clusters of the Villa Borghese; then Giovanelli seated himself familiarly upon the broad ledge of the wall. The western sun in the opposite sky sent out a brilliant shaft through a couple of cloud-bars; whereupon Daisy's companion took her parasol out of her hands and opened it. She came a little nearer and he held the parasol over her; then, still holding it, he let it rest upon her shoulder, so that both of their heads were hidden from Winterbourne. This young man lingered a moment, then he began to walk. But he walked—not towards the couple with the parasol; towards the residence of his aunt, Mrs. Costello.

IV

HE FLATTERED HIMSELF ON the following day that there was no smiling among the servants when he, at least, asked for Mrs. Miller at her hotel. This lady and her daughter, however, were not at home; and on the next day after, repeating his visit, Winterbourne again had the misfortune not to find them. Mrs. Walker's party took place on the evening of the third day, and in spite of the frigidity of his last interview with the hostess Winterbourne was among the guests. Mrs. Walker was one of those American ladies who, while residing abroad, make a point, in their own phrase, of studying European society; and she had on this occasion collected several specimens of her diversely-born fellow-mortals to serve, as it were, as text-books. When Winterbourne arrived Daisy Miller was not there; but in a few moments he saw her mother come in alone, very shyly and ruefully. Mrs. Miller's hair, above her exposed-looking temples, was more frizzled than ever. As she approached Mrs. Walker, Winterbourne also drew near.

"You see I've come all alone," said poor Mrs. Miller. "I'm so frightened; I don't know what to do; it's the first time I've ever been to a party alone—especially in this country. I wanted to bring Randolph or Eugenio, or some one, but Daisy just pushed me off by myself. I ain't used to going round alone."

"And does not your daughter intend to favour us with her society?" demanded Mrs. Walker, impressively.

"Well, Daisy's all dressed," said Mrs. Miller, with that accent of the dispassionate, if not of the philosophic, historian with which she always recorded the current incidents of her daughter's career. "She got dressed on purpose before dinner. But she's got a friend of hers there; that gentleman—the Italian—that she wanted to bring. They've got going at the piano; it seems as if they couldn't leave off. Mr. Giovanelli sings splendidly. But I guess they'll come before very long," concluded Mrs. Miller hopefully.

"I'm sorry she should come—in that way," said Mrs. Walker.

"Well, I told her that there was no use in her getting dressed before dinner if she was going to wait three hours," responded Daisy's mamma. "I didn't see the use of her putting on such a dress as that to sit round with Mr. Giovanelli."

"This is most horrible!" said Mrs. Walker, turning away and addressing herself to Winterbourne. "*Elle s'affiche.** It's her revenge for my having ventured to remonstrate with her. When she comes I shall not speak to her."

Daisy came after eleven o'clock, but she was not, on such an occasion, a young lady to wait to be spoken to. She rustled forward in radiant loveliness, smiling and chattering, carrying a large bouquet and attended by Mr. Giovanelli. Every one stopped talking, and turned and looked at her. She came straight to Mrs. Walker. "I'm afraid you thought I never was coming, so I sent mother off to tell you. I wanted to make Mr. Giovanelli practise some things before he came; you know he sings beautifully, and I want you to ask him to sing. This is Mr. Giovanelli; you know I introduced him to you; he's got the most lovely voice and he knows the most charming set of songs. I made him go over them this evening, on purpose; we had the greatest time at the hotel." Of all this Daisy delivered herself with the sweetest, brightest audibleness, looking now at her hostess and now round the room, while she gave a series of little pats, round her shoulders, to the edges of her dress. "Is there any one I know?" she asked.

"I think every one knows you!" said Mrs. Walker pregnantly, and she gave a very cursory greeting to Mr. Giovanelli. This gentleman bore himself gallantly. He smiled and bowed and showed his white teeth, he curled his moustaches and rolled his eyes, and performed all the proper functions of a handsome Italian at an evening party. He sang, very prettily, half-a-dozen songs, though Mrs. Walker afterwards declared that she had been quite unable to find out who asked him. It was apparently not Daisy who had given him his orders. Daisy sat at a distance from the piano, and though she had publicly, as it were, professed a high admiration for his singing, talked, not inaudibly, while it was going on.

"It's a pity these rooms are so small; we can't dance," she said to Winterbourne, as if she had seen him five minutes before.

*She is making a spectacle of herself (French).

"I am not sorry we can't dance," Winterbourne answered; "I don't dance."

"Of course you don't dance; you're too stiff," said Miss Daisy. "I hope you enjoyed your drive with Mrs. Walker."

"No, I didn't enjoy it; I preferred walking with you."

"We paired off, that was much better," said Daisy. "But did you ever hear anything so cool as Mrs. Walker's wanting me to get into her carriage and drop poor Mr. Giovanelli; and under the pretext that it was proper? People have different ideas! It would have been most unkind; he had been talking about that walk for ten days."

"He should not have talked about it at all," said Winterbourne; "he would never have proposed to a young lady of this country to walk about the streets with him."

"About the streets?" cried Daisy, with her pretty stare. "Where then would he have proposed to her to walk? The Pincio is not the streets, either; and I, thank goodness, am not a young lady of this country. The young ladies of this country have a dreadfully poky time of it, so far as I can learn; I don't see why I should change my habits for *them*."

"I am afraid your habits are those of a flirt," said Winterbourne gravely.

"Of course they are," she cried, giving him her little smiling stare again. "I'm a fearful, frightful flirt! Did you ever hear of a nice girl that was not? But I suppose you will tell me now that I am not a nice girl."

"You're a very nice girl, but I wish you would flirt with me, and me only," said Winterbourne.

"Ah! thank you, thank you very much; you are the last man I should think of flirting with. As I have had the pleasure of informing you, you are too stiff."

"You say that too often," said Winterbourne.

Daisy gave a delighted laugh. "If I could have the sweet hope of making you angry, I would say it again."

"Don't do that; when I am angry I'm stiffer than ever. But if you won't flirt with me, do cease at least to flirt with your friend at the piano; they don't understand that sort of thing here."

"I thought they understood nothing else!" exclaimed Daisy.

"Not in young unmarried women."

"It seems to me much more proper in young unmarried women than in old married ones," Daisy declared.

"Well," said Winterbourne, "when you deal with natives you must go by the custom of the place. Flirting is a purely American custom; it doesn't exist here. So when you show yourself in public with Mr. Giovanelli and without your mother——"

"Gracious! poor mother!" interposed Daisy.

"Though you may be flirting, Mr. Giovanelli is not; he means something else."

"He isn't preaching, at any rate," said Daisy with vivacity. "And if you want very much to know, we are neither of us flirting; we are too good friends for that; we are very intimate friends."

"Ah!" rejoined Winterbourne, "if you are in love with each other it is another affair."

She had allowed him up to this point to talk so frankly that he had no expectation of shocking her by this ejaculation; but she immediately got up, blushing visibly, and leaving him to exclaim mentally that little American flirts were the queerest creatures in the world. "Mr. Giovanelli, at least," she said, giving her interlocutor a single glance, "never says such very disagreeable things to me."

Winterbourne was bewildered; he stood staring. Mr. Giovanelli had finished singing; he left the piano and came over to Daisy. "Won't you come into the other room and have some tea?" he asked, bending before her with his decorative smile.

Daisy turned to Winterbourne, beginning to smile again. He was still perplexed, for this inconsequent smile made nothing clear, though it seemed to prove, indeed, that she had a sweetness and softness that reverted instinctively to the pardon of offences. "It has never occurred to Mr. Winterbourne to offer me any tea," she said, with her little tormenting manner.

"I have offered you advice," Winterbourne rejoined.

"I prefer weak tea!" cried Daisy, and she went off with the brilliant Giovanelli. She sat with him in the adjoining room, in the embrasure of the window, for the rest of the evening. There was an interesting performance at the piano, but neither of these young people gave heed to it. When Daisy came to take leave of Mrs. Walker, this lady conscientiously repaired the weakness of which she had been guilty at the moment of the young girl's arrival. She turned her back straight upon Miss Miller and left her to depart with what grace she might. Winterbourne was standing near the door; he saw it all. Daisy turned very pale and looked at her

mother, but Mrs. Miller was humbly unconscious of any violation
of the usual social forms. She appeared, indeed, to have felt an incongruous impulse to draw attention to her own striking obser-
vance of them. "Good night, Mrs. Walker," she said; "we've had a
beautiful evening. You see if I let Daisy come to parties without
me, I don't want her to go away without me." Daisy turned away,
looking with a pale, grave face at the circle near the door; Winterbourne saw that, for the first moment, she was too much shocked
and puzzled even for indignation. He on his side was greatly
touched.

"That was very cruel," he said to Mrs. Walker.

"She never enters my drawing-room again," replied his hostess.

Since Winterbourne was not to meet her in Mrs. Walker's
drawing-room, he went as often as possible to Mrs. Miller's hotel.
The ladies were rarely at home, but when he found them the devoted Giovanelli was always present. Very often the polished little
Roman was in the drawing-room with Daisy alone, Mrs. Miller being apparently constantly of the opinion that discretion is the better part of surveillance. Winterbourne noted, at first with surprise,
that Daisy on these occasions was never embarrassed or annoyed
by his own entrance; but he very presently began to feel that she
had no more surprises for him; the unexpected in her behaviour
was the only thing to expect. She showed no displeasure at her *tête-
à-tête* with Giovanelli being interrupted; she could chatter as
freshly and freely with two gentlemen as with one; there was always in her conversation, the same odd mixture of audacity and
puerility. Winterbourne remarked to himself that if she was seriously interested in Giovanelli it was very singular that she should
not take more trouble to preserve the sanctity of their interviews,
and he liked her the more for her innocent-looking indifference
and her apparently inexhaustible good humour. He could hardly
have said why, but she seemed to him a girl who would never be
jealous. At the risk of exciting a somewhat derisive smile on the
reader's part, I may affirm that with regard to the women who had
hitherto interested him it very often seemed to Winterbourne
among the possibilities that, given certain contingencies, he
should be afraid—literally afraid—of these ladies. He had a pleasant sense that he should never be afraid of Daisy Miller. It must be

added that this sentiment was not altogether flattering to Daisy; it was part of his conviction, or rather of his apprehension, that she would prove a very light young person.

But she was evidently very much interested in Giovanelli. She looked at him whenever he spoke; she was perpetually telling him to do this and to do that; she was constantly "chaffing" and abusing him. She appeared completely to have forgotten that Winterbourne had said anything to displease her at Mrs. Walker's little party. One Sunday afternoon, having gone to St Peter's⁹ with his aunt, Winterbourne perceived Daisy strolling about the great church in company with the inevitable Giovanelli. Presently he pointed out the young girl and her cavalier to Mrs. Costello. This lady looked at them a moment through her eyeglass, and then she said:

"That's what makes you so pensive in these days, eh?"

"I had not the least idea I was pensive," said the young man.

"You are very much pre-occupied, you are thinking of something."

"And what is it," he asked, "that you accuse me of thinking of?"

"Of that young lady's—Miss Baker's, Miss Chandler's—what's her name?—Miss Miller's intrigue with that little barber's block."

"Do you call it an intrigue," Winterbourne asked—"an affair that goes on with such peculiar publicity?"

"That's their folly," said Mrs. Costello, "it's not their merit."

"No," rejoined Winterbourne, with something of that pensiveness to which his aunt had alluded. "I don't believe that there is anything to be called an intrigue."

"I have heard a dozen people speak of it; they say she is quite carried away by him."

"They are certainly very intimate," said Winterbourne.

Mrs. Costello inspected the young couple again with her optical instrument. "He is very handsome. One easily sees how it is. She thinks him the most elegant man in the world, the finest gentleman. She has never seen anything like him; he is better even than the courier. It was the courier probably who introduced him, and if he succeeds in marrying the young lady, the courier will come in for a magnificent commission."

"I don't believe she thinks of marrying him," said Winterbourne, "and I don't believe he hopes to marry her."

"You may be very sure she thinks of nothing. She goes on from day to day, from hour to hour, as they did in the Golden Age.* I can imagine nothing more vulgar. And at the same time," added Mrs. Costello, "depend upon it that she may tell you any moment that she is 'engaged.' "

"I think that is more than Giovanelli expects," said Winterbourne.

"Who is Giovanelli?"

"The little Italian. I have asked questions about him and learned something. He is apparently a perfectly respectable little man. I believe he is in a small way a *cavaliere avvocato.*† But he doesn't move in what are called the first circles. I think it is really not absolutely impossible that the courier introduced him. He is evidently immensely charmed with Miss Miller. If she thinks him the finest gentleman in the world, he, on his side, has never found himself in personal contact with such splendour, such opulence, such expensiveness, as this young lady's. And then she must seem to him wonderfully pretty and interesting. I rather doubt whether he dreams of marrying her. That must appear to him too impossible a piece of luck. He has nothing but his handsome face to offer, and there is a substantial Mr. Miller in that mysterious land of dollars. Giovanelli knows that he hasn't a title to offer. If he were only a count or a *marchese*! He must wonder at his luck at the way they have taken him up."

"He accounts for it by his handsome face, and thinks Miss Miller a young lady *qui se passe ses fantaisies!*"‡ said Mrs. Costello.

"It is very true," Winterbourne pursued, "that Daisy and her mamma have not yet risen to that stage of—what shall I call it?—of culture, at which the idea of catching a count or a *marchese* begins. I believe that they are intellectually incapable of that conception."

"Ah! but the *cavaliere* can't believe it," said Mrs. Costello.

Of the observation excited by Daisy's "intrigue," Winterbourne gathered that day at St. Peter's sufficient evidence. A dozen of the

---

*According to the classical poets of Greece and Rome, the Golden Age was the first and best time in the world, when mankind lived in an ideal state of prosperity and happiness, free from trouble or crime.

†Gentleman lawyer (Italian).

‡Who gives into her whims, who indulges herself (French).

American colonists in Rome came to talk with Mrs. Costello, who sat on a little portable stool at the base of one of the great pilasters. The vesper-service* was going forward in splendid chants and organ-tones in the adjacent choir, and meanwhile, between Mrs. Costello and her friends, there was a great deal said about poor little Miss Miller's going really "too far." Winterbourne was not pleased with what he heard; but when, coming out upon the great steps of the church, he saw Daisy, who had emerged before him, get into an open cab with her accomplice and roll away through the cynical streets of Rome, he could not deny to himself that she was going very far indeed. He felt very sorry for her—not exactly that he believed that she had completely lost her head, but because it was painful to hear so much that was pretty and undefended and natural assigned to a vulgar place among the categories of disorder. He made an attempt after this to give a hint to Mrs. Miller. He met one day in the Corso† a friend—a tourist like himself—who had just come out of the Doria Palace,[10] where he had been walking through the beautiful gallery. His friend talked for a moment about the superb portrait of Innocent X by Velasquez,[11] which hangs in one of the cabinets of the palace, and then said, "And in the same cabinet, by-the-way, I had the pleasure of contemplating a picture of a different kind—that pretty American girl whom you pointed out to me last week." In answer to Winterbourne's inquiries, his friend narrated that the pretty American girl—prettier than ever—was seated with a companion in the secluded nook in which the great papal portrait is enshrined.

"Who was her companion?" asked Winterbourne.

"A little Italian with a bouquet in his button-hole. The girl is delightfully pretty, but I thought I understood from you the other day that she was a young lady *du meilleur monde*."‡

"So she is!" answered Winterbourne; and having assured himself that his informant had seen Daisy and her companion just five minutes before, he jumped into a cab and went to call on Mrs. Miller.

---

*Evening prayers or devotions.

†The Via del Corso, the main street in central Rome and an important thoroughfare since classical times, when it was the Via Flaminia, the road to the Adriatic.

‡Of the better social circles (French).

She was at home; but she apologised to him for receiving him in Daisy's absence.

"She's gone out somewhere with Mr. Giovanelli," said Mrs. Miller. "She's always going round with Mr. Giovanelli."

"I have noticed that they are very intimate," Winterbourne observed.

"Oh! it seems as if they couldn't live without each other!" said Mrs. Miller. "Well, he's a real gentleman, anyhow. I keep telling Daisy she's engaged!"

"And what does Daisy say?"

"Oh, she says she isn't engaged. But she might as well be!" this impartial parent resumed. "She goes on as if she was. But I've made Mr. Giovanelli promise to tell me, if *she* doesn't. I should want to write to Mr. Miller about it—shouldn't you?"

Winterbourne replied that he certainly should; and the state of mind of Daisy's mamma struck him as so unprecedented in the annals of parental vigilance that he gave up as utterly irrelevant the attempt to place her upon her guard.

After this Daisy was never at home, and Winterbourne ceased to meet her at the houses of their common acquaintance, because, as he perceived, these shrewd people had quite made up their minds that she was going too far. They ceased to invite her, and they intimated that they desired to express to observant Europeans the great truth that, though Miss Daisy Miller was a young American lady, her behaviour was not representative—was regarded by her compatriots as abnormal. Winterbourne wondered how she felt about all the cold shoulders that were turned towards her, and sometimes it annoyed him to suspect that she did not feel at all. He said to himself that she was too light and childish, too uncultivated and unreasoning, too provincial, to have reflected upon her ostracism or even to have perceived it. Then at other moments he believed that she carried about in her elegant and irresponsible little organism a defiant, passionate, perfectly observant consciousness of the impression she produced. He asked himself whether Daisy's defiance came from the consciousness of innocence or from her being, essentially, a young person of the reckless class. It must be admitted that holding oneself to a belief in Daisy's "innocence" came to seem to Winterbourne more and more a matter of fine-spun gallantry. As I have already had occasion to relate, he was angry at finding himself reduced to chopping logic about this young lady; he was vexed at his want of instinctive certitude as to how far her eccentricities were generic, national, and how far they were personal. From either view of them he had somehow missed her, and now it was too late. She was "carried away" by Mr. Giovanelli.

A few days after his brief interview with her mother, he encountered her in that beautiful abode of flowering desolation known as the Palace of the Caesars:* The early Roman spring had filled the air with bloom and perfume, and the rugged surface of the Palatine† was muffled with tender verdure. Daisy was strolling along the top of one of those great mounds of ruin that are embanked with mossy marble and paved with monumental inscriptions. It seemed to him that Rome had never been so lovely as just then. He stood looking off at the enchanting harmony of line and colour that remotely encircles the city, inhaling the softly humid odours and feeling the freshness of the year and the antiquity of the place reaffirm themselves in mysterious interfusion. It seemed to him also that Daisy had never looked so pretty; but this had been an observation of his whenever he met her. Giovanelli was at her side, and Giovanelli, too, wore an aspect of even unwonted brilliancy.

"Well," said Daisy, "I should think you would be lonesome!"

"Lonesome?" asked Winterbourne.

"You are always going round by yourself. Can't you get any one to walk with you?"

"I am not so fortunate," said Winterbourne, "as your companion."

Giovanelli, from the first, had treated Winterbourne with distinguished politeness; he listened with a deferential air to his remarks; he laughed, punctiliously, at his pleasantries; he seemed disposed to testify to his belief that Winterbourne was a superior young man. He carried himself in no degree like a jealous wooer; he had obviously a great deal of tact; he had no objection to your expecting a little humility of him. It even seemed to Winterbourne at times that Giovanelli would find a certain mental relief in being able to have a private understanding with him—to say to him, as an intelligent man, that, bless you, *he* knew how extraordinary was this young lady, and didn't flatter himself with delusive—or at least

---

*Site on the Palatine Hill where the Emperor Augustus was born and established his imperial residence.

†Four-sided plateau in Rome, south of the Forum, that rises 168 feet above sea level.

too delusive—hopes of matrimony and dollars. On this occasion he strolled away from his companion to pluck a sprig of almond blossom, which he carefully arranged in his button-hole.

"I know why you say that," said Daisy, watching Giovanelli. "Because you think I go round too much with *him*!" And she nodded at her attendant.

"Every one thinks so—if you care to know," said Winterbourne.

"Of course I care to know!" Daisy exclaimed seriously. "But I don't believe it. They are only pretending to be shocked. They don't really care a straw what I do. Besides, I don't go round so much."

"I think you will find they do care. They will show it—disagreeably."

Daisy looked at him a moment. "How—disagreeably?"

"Haven't you noticed anything?" Winterbourne asked.

"I have noticed you. But I noticed you were as stiff as an umbrella the first time I saw you."

"You will find I am not so stiff as several others," said Winterbourne, smiling.

"How shall I find it?"

"By going to see the others."

"What will they do to me?"

"They will give you the cold shoulder. Do you know what that means?"

Daisy was looking at him intently; she began to colour. "Do you mean as Mrs. Walker did the other night?"

"Exactly!" said Winterbourne.

She looked away at Giovanelli, who was decorating himself with his almond-blossom. Then looking back at Winterbourne—"I shouldn't think you would let people be so unkind!" she said.

"How can I help it?" he asked.

"I should think you would say something."

"I do say something;" and he paused a moment. "I say that your mother tells me that she believes you are engaged."

"Well, she does," said Daisy very simply.

Winterbourne began to laugh. "And does Randolph believe it?" he asked.

"I guess Randolph doesn't believe anything," said Daisy. Randolph's scepticism excited Winterbourne to farther hilarity, and he observed that Giovanelli was coming back to them. Daisy, observing it too, addressed herself again to her countryman. "Since you have mentioned it," she said, "I *am* engaged." . . . Winterbourne looked at her; he had stopped laughing. "You don't believe it!" she added.

He was silent a moment; and then, "Yes, I believe it!" he said.

"Oh, no, you don't," she answered. "Well, then—I am not!"

The young girl and her cicerone were on their way to the gate of the enclosure, so that Winterbourne, who had but lately entered, presently took leave of them. A week afterwards he went to dine at a beautiful villa on the Caelian Hill,* and, on arriving, dismissed his hired vehicle. The evening was charming, and he promised himself the satisfaction of walking home beneath the Arch of Constantine[12] and past the vaguely-lighted monuments of the Forum.[13] There was a waning moon in the sky, and her radiance was not brilliant, but she was veiled in a thin cloud-curtain which seemed to diffuse and equalise it. When, on his return from the villa (it was eleven o'clock), Winterbourne approached the dusky circle of the Colosseum,[14] it occurred to him, as a lover of the picturesque, that the interior, in the pale moonshine, would be well worth a glance. He turned aside and walked to one of the empty arches, near which, as he observed, an open carriage—one of the little Roman street-cabs— was stationed. Then he passed in among the cavernous shadows of the great structure, and emerged upon the clear and silent arena. The place had never seemed to him more impressive. One-half of the gigantic circus† was in deep shade; the other was sleeping in the luminous dusk. As he stood there he began to murmur Byron's famous lines, out of "Manfred";[15] but before he had finished his quotation he remembered that if nocturnal meditations in the Colosseum are recommended by the poets, they are deprecated by the doctors. The historic atmosphere was there, certainly; but the historic atmosphere, scientifically considered, was no better than a villainous miasma. Winterbourne walked to the middle of the arena, to take a more general glance, intending thereafter to make a hasty retreat. The great cross in the centre was covered with shadow; it was only as he drew near it that he made it out distinctly.

---

*Hill of palaces and churches that includes the public park of the Villa Celimontana and six churches that date from the fourth to the ninth centuries.

†Large building, generally oblong or oval, whose rising tiers of seats encircle a space for public spectacles, horse or chariot races, and similar events.

Then he saw that two persons were stationed upon the low steps which formed its base. One of these was a woman, seated; her companion was standing in front of her.

Presently the sound of the woman's voice came to him distinctly in the warm night-air. "Well, he looks at us as one of the old lions or tigers may have looked at the Christian martyrs!" These were the words he heard, in the familiar accent of Miss Daisy Miller.

"Let us hope he is not very hungry," responded the ingenious Giovanelli. "He will have to take me first; you will serve for dessert!"

Winterbourne stopped, with a sort of horror; and, it must be added, with a sort of relief. It was as if a sudden illumination had been flashed upon the ambiguity of Daisy's behaviour and the riddle had become easy to read. She was a young lady whom a gentleman need no longer be at pains to respect. He stood there looking at her—looking at her companion, and not reflecting that though he saw them vaguely, he himself must have been more brightly visible. He felt angry with himself that he had bothered so much about the right way of regarding Miss Daisy Miller. Then, as he was going to advance again, he checked himself; not from the fear that he was doing her injustice, but from a sense of the danger of appearing unbecomingly exhilarated by this sudden revulsion from cautious criticism. He turned away towards the entrance of the place; but as he did so he heard Daisy speak again.

"Why, it was Mr. Winterbourne! He saw me—and he cuts me!"

What a clever little reprobate she was, and how smartly she played an injured innocence! But he wouldn't cut her. Winterbourne came forward again, and went towards the great cross. Daisy had got up; Giovanelli lifted his hat. Winterbourne had now begun to think simply of the craziness, from a sanitary point of view, of a delicate young girl lounging away the evening in this nest of malaria.[16] What if she *were* a clever little reprobate? That was no reason for her dying of the *perniciosa*.* "How long have you been here?" he asked, almost brutally.

Daisy, lovely in the flattering moonlight, looked at him a moment. Then—"All the evening," she answered gently. . . . "I never saw anything so pretty."

---

*Pernicious malaria, fever (Italian).

"I am afraid," said Winterbourne, "that you will not think Roman fever[17] very pretty. This is the way people catch it. I wonder," he added, turning to Giovanelli, "that you, a native Roman, should countenance such a terrible indiscretion."

"Ah," said the handsome native, "for myself, I am not afraid."

"Neither am I—for you! I am speaking for this young lady."

Giovanelli lifted his well-shaped eyebrows and showed his brilliant teeth. But he took Winterbourne's rebuke with docility. "I told the Signorina it was a grave indiscretion; but when was the Signorina ever prudent?"

"I never was sick, and I don't mean to be!" the Signorina declared. "I don't look like much, but I'm healthy! I was bound to see the Colosseum by moonlight; I shouldn't have wanted to go home without that; and we have had the most beautiful time, haven't we, Mr. Giovanelli? If there has been any danger, Eugenio can give me some pills. He has got some splendid pills."[18]

"I should advise you," said Winterbourne, "to drive home as fast as possible and take one!"

"What you say is very wise," Giovanelli rejoined. "I will go and make sure the carriage is at hand." And he went forward rapidly.

Daisy followed with Winterbourne. He kept looking at her; she seemed not in the least embarrassed. Winterbourne said nothing; Daisy chattered about the beauty of the place. "Well, I *have* seen the Colosseum by moonlight!" she exclaimed. "That's one good thing." Then, noticing Winterbourne's silence, she asked him why he didn't speak. He made no answer; he only began to laugh. They passed under one of the dark archways; Giovanelli was in front with the carriage. Here Daisy stopped a moment, looking at the young American. "*Did* you believe I was engaged the other day?" she asked.

"It doesn't matter what I believed the other day," said Winterbourne, still laughing.

"Well, what do you believe now?"

"I believe that it makes very little difference whether you are engaged or not!"

He felt the young girl's pretty eyes fixed upon him through the thick gloom of the archway; she was apparently going to answer. But Giovanelli hurried her forward. "Quick, quick," he said; "if we get in by midnight we are quite safe."

Daisy took her seat in the carriage, and the fortunate Italian placed himself beside her. "Don't forget Eugenio's pills!" said Winterbourne, as he lifted his hat.

"I don't care," said Daisy, in a little strange tone, "whether I have Roman fever or not!" Upon this the cab-driver cracked his whip, and they rolled away over the desultory patches of the antique pavement.

Winterbourne—to do him justice, as it were—mentioned to no one that he had encountered Miss Miller, at midnight, in the Colosseum with a gentleman; but nevertheless, a couple of days later, the fact of her having been there under these circumstances was known to every member of the little American circle, and commented accordingly. Winterbourne reflected that they had of course known it at the hotel, and that, after Daisy's return, there had been an exchange of jokes between the porter and the cab-driver. But the young man was conscious at the same moment that it had ceased to be a matter of serious regret to him that the little American flirt should be "talked about" by low-minded menials. These people, a day or two later, had serious information to give: the little American flirt was alarmingly ill. Winterbourne, when the rumour came to him, immediately went to the hotel for more news. He found that two or three charitable friends had preceded him, and that they were being entertained in Mrs. Miller's salon by Randolph.

"It's going round at night," said Randolph—"that's what made her sick. She's always going round at night. I shouldn't think she'd want to—it's so plaguey dark. You can't see anything here at night, except when there's a moon. In America there's always a moon!" Mrs. Miller was invisible; she was now, at least, giving her daughter the advantage of her society. It was evident that Daisy was dangerously ill.

Winterbourne went often to ask for news of her, and once he saw Mrs. Miller, who, though deeply alarmed, was—rather to his surprise—perfectly composed, and, as it appeared, a most efficient and judicious nurse. She talked a good deal about Dr. Davis, but Winterbourne paid her the compliment of saying to himself that she was not, after all, such a monstrous goose. "Daisy spoke of you the other day," she said to him. "Half the time she doesn't know what she's saying, but that time I think she did. She gave me a message; she told me to tell you. She told me to tell you that she never was engaged to that handsome Italian. I am sure I am very glad; Mr. Giovanelli hasn't been near us since she was taken ill. I thought he was so much of a gentleman; but I don't call that very polite! A lady told me that he was afraid I was angry with him for taking Daisy round at night. Well, so I am; but I suppose he knows I'm a lady. I would scorn to scold him. Any way, she says she's not engaged. I don't know why she wanted you to know; but she said to me three times—'Mind you tell Mr. Winterbourne.' And then she told me to ask if you remembered the time you went to that castle, in Switzerland. But I said I wouldn't give any such messages as that. Only, if she is not engaged, I'm sure I'm glad to know it."

But, as Winterbourne had said, it mattered very little. A week after this the poor girl died; it had been a terrible case of the fever. Daisy's grave was in the little Protestant cemetery,[14] in an angle of the wall of imperial Rome,* beneath the cypresses and the thick spring-flowers. Winterbourne stood there beside it, with a number of other mourners; a number larger than the scandal excited by the young lady's career would have led you to expect. Near him stood Giovanelli, who came nearer still before Winterbourne turned away. Giovanelli was very pale; on this occasion he had no flower in his button-hole; he seemed to wish to say something. At last he said, "She was the most beautiful young lady I ever saw, and the most amiable." And then he added in a moment, "And she was the most innocent."

Winterbourne looked at him and presently repeated his words, "And the most innocent?"

"The most innocent!"

Winterbourne felt sore and angry. "Why the devil," he asked, "did you take her to that fatal place?"

Mr. Giovanelli's urbanity was apparently imperturbable. He looked on the ground a moment, and then he said, "For myself, I had no fear; and she wanted to go."

"That was no reason!" Winterbourne declared.

The subtle Roman again dropped his eyes. "If she had lived, I should have got nothing. She would never have married me, I am sure."

"She would never have married you?"

"For a moment I hoped so. But no. I am sure."

---

*Four square miles of the center of ancient Rome were encircled by the Aurelian Wall, erected about A.D. 270.

Winterbourne listened to him; he stood staring at the raw protuberance among the April daisies. When he turned away again Mr. Giovanelli, with his light slow step, had retired.

Winterbourne almost immediately left Rome; but the following summer he again met his aunt, Mrs. Costello, at Vevey. Mrs. Costello was fond of Vevey. In the interval Winterbourne had often thought of Daisy Miller and her mystifying manners. One day he spoke of her to his aunt—said it was on his conscience that he had done her injustice.

"I am sure I don't know," said Mrs. Costello. "How did your injustice affect her?"

"She sent me a message before her death which I didn't understand at the time. But I have understood it since. She would have appreciated one's esteem."

"Is that a modest way," asked Mrs. Costello, "of saying that she would have reciprocated one's affection?"

Winterbourne offered no answer to this question; but he presently said, "You were right in that remark that you made last summer. I was booked to make a mistake. I have lived too long in foreign parts."

Nevertheless, he went back to live at Geneva, whence there continue to come the most contradictory accounts of his motives of sojourn: a report that he is "studying" hard—an intimation that he is much interested in a very clever foreign lady.

WASHINGTON SQUARE

I

DURING A PORTION OF the first half of the present century, and more particularly during the latter part of it, there flourished and practised in the city of New York a physician who enjoyed perhaps an exceptional share of the consideration which, in the United States, has always been bestowed upon distinguished members of the medical profession. This profession in America has constantly been held in honour, and more successfully than elsewhere has put forward a claim to the epithet of "liberal." In a country in which, to play a social part, you must either earn your income or make believe that you earn it, the healing art has appeared in a high degree to combine two recognised sources of credit. It belongs to the realm of the practical, which in the United States is a great recommendation; and it is touched by the light of science — a merit appreciated in a community in which the love of knowledge has not always been accompanied by leisure and opportunity. It was an element in Dr. Sloper's reputation that his learning and his skill were very evenly balanced; he was what you might call a scholarly doctor, and yet there was nothing abstract in his remedies — he always ordered you to take something. Though he was felt to be extremely thorough, he was not uncomfortably theoretic, and if he sometimes explained matters rather more minutely than might seem of use to the patient, he never went so far (like some practitioners one has heard of) as to trust to the explanation alone, but always left behind him an inscrutable prescription. There were some doctors that left the prescription without offering any explanation at all; and he did not belong to that class either, which was after all the most vulgar. It will be seen that I am describing a clever man; and this is really the reason why Dr. Sloper had become a local celebrity. At the time at which we are chiefly concerned with him,* he was some fifty years of age, and his popularity was at its height. He was very witty, and he

---

*The novel takes place in the 1840s and 1850s.

passed in the best society of New York for a man of the world—which, indeed, he was, in a very sufficient degree. I hasten to add, to anticipate possible misconception, that he was not the least of a charlatan. He was a thoroughly honest man—honest in a degree of which he had perhaps lacked the opportunity to give the complete measure; and, putting aside the great good-nature of the circle in which he practised, which was rather fond of boasting that it possessed the "brightest" doctor in the country, he daily justified his claim to the talents attributed to him by the popular voice. He was an observer, even a philosopher, and to be bright was so natural to him, and (as the popular voice said) came so easily, that he never aimed at mere effect, and had none of the little tricks and pretensions of second-rate reputations. It must be confessed that fortune had favoured him, and that he had found the path to prosperity very soft to his tread. He had married at the age of twenty-seven, for love, a very charming girl, Miss Catherine Harrington, of New York, who, in addition to her charms, had brought him a solid dowry. Mrs. Sloper was amiable, graceful, accomplished, elegant, and in 1820 she had been one of the pretty girls of the small but promising capital which clustered about the Battery* and overlooked the Bay,† and of which the uppermost boundary was indicated by the grassy waysides of Canal Street. Even at the age of twenty-seven Austin Sloper had made his mark sufficiently to mitigate the anomaly of his having been chosen among a dozen suitors by a young woman of high fashion, who had ten thousand dollars of income and the most charming eyes in the island of Manhattan. These eyes, and some of their accompaniments, were for about five years a source of extreme satisfaction to the young physician, who was both a devoted and a very happy husband. The fact of his having married a rich woman made no difference in the line he had traced for himself, and he cultivated his profession with as definite a purpose as if he still had no other resources than his fraction of the modest patrimony

---

*Park of 21 acres, named for the battery of cannon that once lined the shore, at the southern tip of Manhattan; home to an amusement park beginning in 1823, it served as the main point of arrival for immigrants coming by ship between 1855 and 1892.

†Upper New York Bay, a sheltered, deep harbor located at the mouth of the Hudson River southeast of Manhattan; historically, one of the world's busiest ports.

which on his father's death he had shared with his brothers and sisters. This purpose had not been preponderantly to make money—it had been rather to learn something and to do something. To learn something interesting, and to do something useful—this was, roughly speaking, the programme he had sketched, and of which the accident of his wife having an income appeared to him in no degree to modify the validity. He was fond of his practise, and of exercising a skill of which he was agreeably conscious, and it was so patent a truth that if he were not a doctor there was nothing else he could be, that a doctor he persisted in being, in the best possible conditions. Of course his easy domestic situation saved him a good deal of drudgery, and his wife's affiliation to the "best people" brought him a good many of those patients whose symptoms are, if not more interesting in themselves than those of the lower orders, at least more consistently displayed. He desired experience, and in the course of twenty years he got a great deal. It must be added that it came to him in some forms which, whatever might have been their intrinsic value, made it the reverse of welcome. His first child, a little boy of extraordinary promise, as the Doctor, who was not addicted to easy enthusiasms, firmly believed, died at three years of age, in spite of everything that the mother's tenderness and the father's science could invent to save him. Two years later Mrs. Sloper gave birth to a second infant—an infant of a sex which rendered the poor child, to the Doctor's sense, an inadequate substitute for his lamented first-born, of whom he had promised himself to make an admirable man. The little girl was a disappointment; but this was not the worst. A week after her birth the young mother, who, as the phrase is, had been doing well, suddenly betrayed alarming symptoms, and before another week had elapsed Austin Sloper was a widower.

For a man whose trade was to keep people alive he had certainly done poorly in his own family; and a bright doctor who within three years loses his wife and his little boy should perhaps be prepared to see either his skill or his affection impugned. Our friend, however, escaped criticism: that is, he escaped all criticism but his own, which was much the most competent and most formidable. He walked under the weight of this very private censure for the rest of his days, and bore for ever the scars of a castigation to which the strongest hand he knew had treated him on the night that followed

II

WHEN THE CHILD WAS about ten years old, he invited his sister, Mrs. Penniman, to come and stay with him. The Miss Slopers had been but two in number, and both of them had married early in life. The younger, Mrs. Almond by name, was the wife of a prosperous merchant and the mother of a blooming family. She bloomed herself, indeed, and was a comely, comfortable, reasonable woman, and a favourite with her clever brother, who, in the matter of women, even when they were nearly related to him, was a man of distinct preferences. He preferred Mrs. Almond to his sister Lavinia, who had married a poor clergyman, of a sickly constitution and a flowery style of eloquence, and then, at the age of thirty-three, had been left a widow, without children, without fortune—with nothing but the memory of Mr. Penniman's flowers of speech, a certain vague aroma of which hovered about her own conversation. Nevertheless, he had offered her a home under his own roof, which Lavinia accepted with the alacrity of a woman who had spent ten years of her married life in the town of Poughkeepsie. The Doctor had not proposed to Mrs. Penniman to come and live with him indefinitely; he had suggested that she should make an asylum of his house while she looked about for unfurnished lodgings. It is uncertain whether Mrs. Penniman ever instituted a search for unfurnished lodgings, but it is beyond dispute that she never found them. She settled herself with her brother and never went away, and when Catherine was twenty years old her Aunt Lavinia was still one of the most striking features of her immediate *entourage*. Mrs. Penniman's own account of the matter was that she had remained to take charge of her niece's education. She had given this account, at least, to every one but the Doctor, who never asked for explanations which he could entertain himself any day with inventing. Mrs. Penniman, moreover, though she had a good deal of a certain sort of artificial assurance, shrank, for indefinable reasons, from presenting herself to her brother as a fountain of instruction. She had not a high sense of humour, but she had enough to prevent her from making this mistake; and her brother, on his side, had enough to excuse her, in her situation, for laying him under contribution during a considerable part of a lifetime. He therefore assented tacitly to the proposition which Mrs. Penniman had tacitly laid down, that it was of importance that the poor motherless girl should have a brilliant woman near her. His assent could only be tacit, for he had never been dazzled by his sister's intellectual lustre. Save when he fell in love with Catherine Harrington, he had never been dazzled, indeed, by any feminine characteristics whatever; and though he was to a certain extent what is called a ladies' doctor, his private opinion of the more complicated sex was not exalted. He regarded its complications as more curious than edifying, and he had an idea of the beauty of *reason*, which was on the whole meagrely gratified by what he observed in his female patients. His wife had been a reasonable woman, but she was a bright exception; among several things that he was sure of, this was perhaps the principal. Such a conviction, of course, did little either to mitigate or to abbreviate his widowhood; and it set a limit to his recognition, at the best, of Catherine's possibilities and of Mrs. Penniman's ministrations. He, nevertheless, at the end of six months, accepted his sister's permanent presence as an accomplished fact, and as Catherine grew older perceived that there were in effect good reasons why she should have a companion of her own imperfect sex. He was extremely polite to Lavinia, scrupulously, formally polite; and she had never seen him in anger but once in her life, when he lost his temper in a theological discussion with her late husband. With her he never discussed theology, nor, indeed, discussed anything; he contented himself with making known, very distinctly, in the form of a lucid ultimatum, his wishes with regard to Catherine.

Once, when the girl was about twelve years old, he had said to her—

"Try and make a clever woman of her, Lavinia; I should like her to be a clever woman."

Mrs. Penniman, at this, looked thoughtful a moment. "My dear Austin," she then inquired, "do you think it is better to be clever than to be good?"

"Good for what?" asked the Doctor. "You are good for nothing unless you are clever."

From this assertion Mrs. Penniman saw no reason to dissent; she possibly reflected that her own great use in the world was owing to her aptitude for many things.

"Of course I wish Catherine to be good," the Doctor said next day; "but she won't be any the less virtuous for not being a fool. I am not afraid of her being wicked; she will never have the salt of malice in her character. She is as good as good bread, as the French say; but six years hence I don't want to have to compare her to good bread and butter."

"Are you afraid she will be insipid? My dear brother, it is I who supply the butter; so you needn't fear!" said Mrs. Penniman, who had taken in hand the child's accomplishments, overlooking her at the piano, where Catherine displayed a certain talent, and going with her to the dancing-class, where it must be confessed that she made but a modest figure.

Mrs. Penniman was a tall, thin, fair, rather faded woman, with a perfectly amiable disposition, a high standard of gentility, a taste for light literature, and a certain foolish indirectness and obliquity of character. She was romantic, she was sentimental, she had a passion for little secrets and mysteries—a very innocent passion, for her secrets had hitherto always been as unpractical as addled eggs. She was not absolutely veracious; but this defect was of no great consequence, for she had never had anything to conceal. She would have liked to have a lover, and to correspond with him under an assumed name in letters left at a shop; I am bound to say that her imagination never carried the intimacy farther than this. Mrs. Penniman had never had a lover, but her brother, who was very shrewd, understood her turn of mind. "When Catherine is about seventeen," he said to himself, "Lavinia will try and persuade her that some young man with a moustache is in love with her. It will be quite untrue; no young man, with a moustache or without, will ever be in love with Catherine. But Lavinia will take it up, and talk to her about it; perhaps, even, if her taste for clandestine operations doesn't prevail with her, she will talk to me about it. Catherine won't see it, and won't believe it, fortunately for her peace of mind; poor Catherine isn't romantic."

She was a healthy well-grown child, without a trace of her mother's beauty. She was not ugly; she had simply a plain, dull, gentle countenance. The most that had ever been said for her was that she had a "nice" face, and, though she was an heiress, no one had ever thought of regarding her as a belle. Her father's opinion of her moral purity was abundantly justified; she was excellently, imperturbably good; affectionate, docile, obedient, and much addicted to speaking the truth. In her younger years she was a good deal of a romp, and, though it is an awkward confession to make about one's heroine, I must add that she was something of a glutton. She never, that I know of, stole raisins out of the pantry; but she devoted her pocket-money to the purchase of cream-cakes. As regards this, however, a critical attitude would be inconsistent with a candid reference to the early annals of any biographer. Catherine was decidedly not clever; she was not quick with her book, nor, indeed, with anything else. She was not abnormally deficient, and she mustered learning enough to acquit herself respectably in conversation with her contemporaries, among whom it must be avowed, however, that she occupied a secondary place. It is well known that in New York it is possible for a young girl to occupy a primary one. Catherine, who was extremely modest, had no desire to shine, and on most social occasions, as they are called, you would have found her lurking in the background. She was extremely fond of her father and very much afraid of him; she thought him the cleverest and handsomest and most celebrated of men. The poor girl found her account so completely in the exercise of her affections that the little tremor of fear that mixed itself with her filial passion gave the thing an extra relish rather than blunted its edge. Her deepest desire was to please him, and her conception of happiness was to know that she had succeeded in pleasing him. She had never succeeded beyond a certain point. Though on the whole he was very kind to her, she was perfectly aware of this, and to go beyond the point in question seemed to her really something to live for. What she could not know, of course, was that she disappointed him, though on three or four occasions the Doctor had been almost frank about it. She grew up peacefully and prosperously, but at the age of eighteen Mrs. Penniman had not made a clever woman of her. Dr. Sloper would have liked to be proud of his daughter; but there was nothing to be proud of in poor Catherine. There was nothing, of course, to be ashamed of; but this was not enough for the Doctor, who was a proud man and would have enjoyed being able to think of his daughter as an unusual girl. There would have been a fitness in her being pretty and graceful, intelligent and distinguished; for her mother had been the most charming woman of her little day, and as regards her father, of course he knew his own value. He had moments of irritation at having produced a commonplace child, and he even went so far at times as to take a certain satisfaction in the thought that his wife had not lived to find her out. He was naturally slow in making this discovery himself, and it was not till Catherine had become a young lady grown that he regarded the matter as settled. He gave her the benefit of a great many doubts; he was in no haste to conclude. Mrs. Penniman frequently assured him that his daughter had a delightful nature; but he knew how to interpret this assurance. It meant, to his sense, that Catherine was not wise enough to discover that her aunt was a goose—a limitation of mind that could not fail to be agreeable to Mrs. Penniman. Both she and her brother, however, exaggerated the young girl's limitations; for Catherine, though she was very fond of her aunt, and conscious of the gratitude she owed her, regarded her without a particle of that gentle dread which gave its stamp to her admiration of her father. To her mind there was nothing of the infinite about Mrs. Penniman; Catherine saw her all at once, as it were, and was not dazzled by the apparition; whereas her father's great faculties seemed, as they stretched away, to lose themselves in a sort of luminous vagueness, which indicated, not that they stopped, but that Catherine's own mind ceased to follow them.

It must not be supposed that Dr. Sloper visited his disappointment upon the poor girl, or ever let her suspect that she had played him a trick. On the contrary, for fear of being unjust to her, he did his duty with exemplary zeal, and recognised that she was a faithful and affectionate child. Besides, he was a philosopher; he smoked a good many cigars over his disappointment, and in the fulness of time he got used to it. He satisfied himself that he had expected nothing, though, indeed, with a certain oddity of reasoning. "I expect nothing," he said to himself, "so that if she gives me a surprise, it will be all clear gain. If she doesn't, it will be no loss." This was about the time Catherine had reached her eighteenth year; so that it will be seen her father had not been precipitate. At this time she seemed not only incapable of giving surprises; it was almost a question whether she could have received one—she was so quiet and irresponsive. People who expressed themselves roughly called her stolid. But she was irresponsive because she was shy, uncomfortably, painfully shy. This was not always understood, and she sometimes produced an impression of insensibility. In reality she was the softest creature in the world.

III

As a child she had promised to be tall, but when she was sixteen she ceased to grow, and her stature, like most other points in her composition, was not unusual. She was strong, however, and properly made, and, fortunately, her health was excellent. It has been noted that the Doctor was a philosopher, but I would not have answered for his philosophy if the poor girl had proved a sickly and suffering person. Her appearance of health constituted her principal claim to beauty, and her clear, fresh complexion, in which white and red were very equally distributed, was, indeed, an excellent thing to see. Her eye was small and quiet, her features were rather thick, her tresses brown and smooth. A dull, plain girl she was called by rigorous critics—a quiet, ladylike girl, by those of the more imaginative sort; but by neither class was she very elaborately discussed. When it had been duly impressed upon her that she was a young lady—it was a good while before she could believe it—she suddenly developed a lively taste for dress: a lively taste is quite the expression to use. I feel as if I ought to write it very small, her judgment in this matter was by no means infallible; it was liable to confusions and embarrassments. Her great indulgence of it was really the desire of a rather inarticulate nature to manifest itself; she sought to be eloquent in her garments, and to make up for her diffidence of speech by a fine frankness of costume. But if she expressed herself in her clothes it is certain that people were not to blame for not thinking her a witty person. It must be added that though she had the expectation of a fortune—Dr. Sloper for a long time had been making twenty thousand dollars a year by his profession and laying aside the half of it—the amount of money at her disposal was not greater than the allowance made to many poorer girls. In those days in New York there were still a few altar-fires flickering in the temple of Republican simplicity,[1] and Dr. Sloper would have been glad to see his daughter present herself, with a classic grace, as a priestess of this mild faith. It made him fairly grimace, in private, to think that a child of his should be both ugly and overdressed. For himself, he was fond of the good things of life, and he made a considerable use of them; but he had a dread of vulgarity and even a theory that it was increasing in the society that surrounded him. Moreover, the standard of luxury in the United States thirty years ago was carried by no means so high as at present, and Catherine's clever father took the old-fashioned view of the education of young persons. He had no particular theory on the subject; it had scarcely as yet become a necessity of self-defence to have a collection of theories. It simply appeared to him proper and reasonable that a well-bred young woman should not carry half her fortune on her back. Catherine's back was a broad one, and would have carried a good deal; but to the weight of the paternal displeasure she never ventured to expose it, and our heroine was twenty years old before she treated herself, for evening wear, to a red satin gown trimmed with gold fringe;[2] though this was an article which, for many years, she had coveted in secret. It made her look, when she sported it, like a woman of thirty; but oddly enough, in spite of her taste for fine clothes, she had not a grain of coquetry, and her anxiety when she put them on was as to whether they, and not she, would look well. It is a point on which history has not been explicit, but the assumption is warrantable; it was in the royal raiment just mentioned that she presented herself at a little entertainment given by her aunt, Mrs. Almond. The girl was at this time in her twenty-first year, and Mrs. Almond's party was the beginning of something very important.

Some three or four years before this, Dr. Sloper had moved his household gods up town, as they say in New York. He had been living ever since his marriage in an edifice of red brick, with granite copings and an enormous fanlight over the door, standing in a street within five minutes' walk of the City Hall,[3] which saw its best days (from the social point of view) about 1820. After this, the tide of fashion began to set steadily northward, as, indeed, in New York, thanks to the narrow channel in which it flows, it is obliged to do, and the great hum of traffic rolled farther to the right and left of Broadway. By the time the Doctor changed his residence, the murmur of trade had become a mighty uproar, which was music in the ears of all good citizens interested in the commercial development, as they delighted to call it, of their fortunate isle. Dr. Sloper's interest in this phenomenon was

only indirect—though, seeing that, as the years went on, half his patients came to be over-worked men of business, it might have been
more immediate—and when most of his neighbors' dwellings (also
ornamented with granite copings and large fanlights) had been converted into offices, warehouses, and shipping agencies, and otherwise
applied to the base uses of commerce, he determined to look out for
a quieter home. The ideal of quiet and of genteel retirement, in 1835,
was found in Washington Square, where the doctor built himself a
handsome, modern, wide-fronted house, with a big balcony before
the drawing-room windows, and a flight of white marble steps ascending to a portal which was also faced with white marble. This
structure, and many of its neighbours, which it exactly resembled,
were supposed, forty years ago, to embody the last results of architec-
tural science, and they remain to this day very solid and honourable
dwellings. In front of them was the square, containing a considerable
quantity of inexpensive vegetation, enclosed by a wooden paling,
which increased its rural and accessible appearance; and round the
corner was the more august precinct of the Fifth Avenue, taking its
origin at this point with a spacious and confident air which already
marked it for high destinies. I know not whether it is owing to the tenderness of early associations, but this portion of New York appears to
many persons the most delectable. It has a kind of established repose
which is not of frequent occurrence in other quarters of the long,
shrill city; it has a riper, richer, more honourable look than any of the
upper ramifications of the great longitudinal thoroughfare—the look
of having had something of a social history. It was here, as you might
have been informed on good authority, that you had come into a
world which appeared to offer a variety of sources of interest; it was
here that your grandmother lived, in venerable solitude, and dis-
pensed a hospitality which commended itself alike to the infant
imagination and the infant palate; it was here that you took your first
walks abroad, following the nurserymaid with unequal step and sniff-
ing up the strange odour of the ailanthus-trees* which at that time
formed the principal umbrage of the square, and diffused an aroma
that you were not yet critical enough to dislike as it deserved; it was

---

*Rapidly growing deciduous tree, also known as the "tenement palm"; has winglike
leaves and a strong, offensive odor.

here, finally, that your first school, kept by a broad-bosomed, broad-based old lady with a ferule,* who was always having tea in a blue cup, with a saucer that didn't match, enlarged the circle both of your observations and your sensations. It was here, at any rate, that my heroine spent many years of her life; which is my excuse for this topographical parenthesis.

Mrs. Almond lived much farther up town, in an embryonic street with a high number—a region where the extension of the city began to assume a theoretic air, where poplars grew beside the pavement (when there was one), and mingled their shade with the steep roofs of desultory Dutch houses, and where pigs and chickens disported themselves in the gutter. These elements of rural picturesqueness have now wholly departed from New York street scenery; but they were to be found within the memory of middle-aged persons, in quarters which now would blush to be reminded of them. Catherine had a great many cousins, and with her Aunt Almond's children, who ended by being nine in number, she lived on terms of considerable intimacy. When she was younger, they had been rather afraid of her; she was believed, as the phrase is, to be highly educated, and a person who lived in the intimacy of their Aunt Penniman had something of reflected grandeur. Mrs. Penniman, among the little Almonds, was an object of more admiration than sympathy. Her manners were strange and formidable, and her mourning robes—she dressed in black for twenty years after her husband's death, and then suddenly appeared, one morning, with pink roses in her cap—were complicated in odd, unexpected places with buckles, bugles, and pins, which discouraged familiarity. She took children too hard, both for good and for evil, and had an oppressive air of expecting subtle things of them; so that going to see her was a good deal like being taken to church and made to sit in a front pew. It was discovered after a while, however, that Aunt Penniman was but an accident in Catherine's existence, and not a part of its essence, and that when the girl came to spend a Saturday with her cousins, she was available for "follow-my-master,"† and even for leap-frog. On this basis an understanding was easily arrived at, and

---

*Stick or cane or paddle used to strike children on the hands as punishment.
†Probably a version of the childhood game "Follow My Leader," in which participants must follow and perform a chosen principal's daring or comic deeds.

for several years Catherine fraternised with her young kinsmen. I say young kinsmen, because seven of the little Almonds were boys, and Catherine had a preference for those games which are most conveniently played in trousers. By degrees, however, the little Almonds' trousers began to lengthen, and the wearers to disperse and settle themselves in life. The elder children were older than Catherine, and the boys were sent to college or placed in counting-rooms. Of the girls, one married very punctually, and the other as punctually became engaged. It was to celebrate this latter event that Mrs. Almond gave the little party I have mentioned. Her daughter was to marry a stout young stockbroker, a boy of twenty; it was thought a very good thing.

IV

Mrs. Penniman, with more buckles and bangles than ever, came of course to the entertainment, accompanied by her niece; the Doctor, too, had promised to look in later in the evening. There was to be a good deal of dancing, and before it had gone very far, Marian Almond came up to Catherine, in company with a tall young man. She introduced the young man as a person who had a great desire to make our heroine's acquaintance, and as a cousin of Arthur Townsend, her own intended.

Marian Almond was a pretty little person of seventeen, with a very small figure and a very big sash, to the elegance of whose manners matrimony had nothing to add. She already had all the airs of a hostess, receiving the company, shaking her fan, saying that with so many people to attend to she should have no time to dance. She made a long speech about Mr. Townsend's cousin, to whom she administered a tap with her fan before turning away to other cares. Catherine had not understood all that she said; her attention was given to enjoying Marian's ease of manner and flow of ideas, and to looking at the young man, who was remarkably handsome. She had succeeded, however, as she often failed to do when people were presented to her, in catching his name, which appeared to be the same as that of Marian's little stockbroker. Catherine was always agitated by an introduction; it seemed a difficult moment, and she wondered that some people—her new acquaintance at this moment, for instance—should mind it so little. She wondered what she ought to say, and what would be the consequences of her saying nothing. The consequences at present were very agreeable. Mr. Townsend, leaving her no time for embarrassment, began to talk with an easy smile, as if he had known her for a year.

"What a delightful party! What a charming house! What an interesting family! What a pretty girl your cousin is!"

These observations, in themselves of no great profundity, Mr. Townsend seemed to offer for what they were worth, and as a contribution to an acquaintance. He looked straight into Catherine's eyes. She answered nothing; she only listened, and looked at him; and he, as if he expected no particular reply, went on to say many other things in the same comfortable and natural manner. Catherine, though she felt tongue-tied, was conscious of no embarrassment; it seemed proper that he should talk, and that she should simply look at him. What made it natural was that he was so handsome, or rather, as she phrased it to herself, so beautiful. The music had been silent for a while, but it suddenly began again; and then he asked her, with a deeper, intenser, smile, if she would do him the honour of dancing with him. Even to this inquiry she gave no audible assent; she simply let him put his arm round her waist—as she did so it occurred to her more vividly than it had ever done before, that this was a singular place for a gentleman's arm to be—and in a moment he was guiding her round the room in the harmonious rotation of the polka.* When they paused, she felt that she was red; and then, for some moments, she stopped looking at him. She fanned herself, and looked at the flowers that were painted on her fan. He asked her if she would begin again, and she hesitated to answer, still looking at the flowers.

"Does it make you dizzy?" he asked, in a tone of great kindness.

Then Catherine looked up at him; he was certainly beautiful, and not at all red. "Yes," she said; she hardly knew why, for dancing had never made her dizzy.

"Ah, well, in that case," said Mr. Townsend, "we will sit still and talk. I will find a good place to sit."

He found a good place—a charming place; a little sofa that seemed meant only for two persons. The rooms by this time were very full; the dancers increased in number, and people stood close in front of them, turning their backs, so that Catherine and her companion seemed secluded and unobserved. "We will talk," the young man had said; but he still did all the talking. Catherine leaned back in her place, with her eyes fixed upon him, smiling and thinking him very clever. He had features like young men in pictures; Catherine had never seen such features—so delicate, so chiselled and finished—among the young New Yorkers whom she passed in

---

*Lively, quick-time dance of Bohemian origin.

the streets and met at parties. He was tall and slim, but he looked extremely strong. Catherine thought he looked like a statue. But a statue would not talk like that, and, above all, would not have eyes of so rare a colour. He had never been at Mrs. Almond's before, he felt very much like a stranger; and it was very kind of Catherine to take pity on him. He was Arthur Townsend's cousin—not very near; several times removed—and Arthur had brought him to present him to the family. In fact, he was a great stranger in New York. It was his native place; but he had not been there for many years. He had been knocking about the world, and living in far-away lands; he had only come back a month or two before. New York was very pleasant, only he felt lonely.

"You see, people forget you," he said, smiling at Catherine with his delightful gaze, while he leaned forward obliquely, turning towards her, with his elbows on his knees.

It seemed to Catherine that no one who had once seen him would ever forget him; but though she made this reflection she kept it to herself, almost as you would keep something precious.

They sat there for some time. He was very amusing. He asked her about the people that were near them; he tried to guess who some of them were, and he made the most laughable mistakes. He criticised them very freely, in a positive, off-hand way. Catherine had never heard any one—especially any young man—talk just like that. It was the way a young man might talk in a novel, or better still, in a play, on the stage, close before the footlights, looking at the audience, and with every one looking at him, so that you wondered at his presence of mind. And yet Mr. Townsend was not like an actor; he seemed so sincere, so natural. This was very interesting; but in the midst of it, Marian Almond came pushing through the crowd, with a little ironical cry, when she found these young people still together, which made every one turn round, and cost Catherine a conscious blush. Marian broke up their talk, and told Mr. Townsend—whom she treated as if she were already married, and he had become her cousin—to run away to her mother, who had been wishing for the last half-hour to introduce him to Mr. Almond.

"We shall meet again!" he said to Catherine as he left her, and Catherine thought it a very original speech.

Her cousin took her by the arm, and made her walk about. "I needn't ask you what you think of Morris!" the young girl exclaimed.

"Is that his name?"

"I don't ask you what you think of his name, but what you think of himself," said Marian.

"Oh, nothing particular!" Catherine answered, dissembling for the first time in her life.

"I have half a mind to tell him that!" cried Marian. "It will do him good. He's so terribly conceited."

"Conceited?" said Catherine, staring.

"So Arthur says, and Arthur knows about him."

"Oh, don't tell him!" Catherine murmured imploringly.

"Don't tell him he's conceited? I have told him so a dozen times."

At this profession of audacity, Catherine looked down at her little companion in amazement. She supposed it was because Marian was going to be married that she took so much on herself, but she wondered too, whether, when she herself should become engaged, such exploits would be expected of her.

Half an hour later she saw her Aunt Penniman sitting in the embrasure of a window, with her head a little on one side, and her gold eye-glass raised to her eyes, which were wandering about the room. In front of her was a gentleman, bending forward a little, with his back turned to Catherine. She knew his back immediately, though she had never seen it; for when he left her, at Marian's instigation, he had retreated in the best order, without turning round. Morris Townsend—the name had already become very familiar to her, as if some one had been repeating it in her ear for the last half hour— Morris Townsend was giving his impressions of the company to her aunt, as he had done to herself; he was saying clever things, and Mrs. Penniman was smiling, as if she approved of them. As soon as Catherine had perceived this she moved away; she would not have liked him to turn round and see her. But it gave her pleasure—the whole thing. That he should talk with Mrs. Penniman, with whom she lived and whom she saw and talked with every day—that seemed to keep him near her, and to make him even easier to contemplate than if she herself had been the object of his civilities; and that Aunt Lavinia should like him, should not be shocked or startled by what he said, this also appeared to the girl a personal gain; for Aunt Lavinia's standard was extremely high, planted as it was over the grave of her late husband, in which, as she had convinced every one, the very genius of conversation was buried. One of the Almond boys, as Catherine called him, invited our heroine to dance a quadrille,* and for a quarter of an hour her feet at least were occupied. This time she was not dizzy; her head was very clear. Just when the dance was over, she found herself in the crowd face to face with her father. Dr. Sloper had usually a little smile, never a very big one, and with his little smile playing in his clear eyes and on his neatly-shaved lips, he looked at his daughter's crimson gown.

"Is it possible that this magnificent person is my child?" he said.

You would have surprised him if you had told him so; but it is a literal fact that he almost never addressed his daughter save in the ironical form. Whenever he addressed her he gave her pleasure; but she had to cut her pleasure out of the piece, as it were. There were portions left over, light remnants and snippets of irony, which she never knew what to do with, which seemed too delicate for her own use; and yet Catherine, lamenting the limitations of her understanding, felt that they were too valuable to waste, and had a belief that if they passed over her head they yet contributed to the general sum of human wisdom.

"I am not magnificent," she said, mildly, wishing that she had put on another dress.

"You are sumptuous, opulent, expensive," her father rejoined. "You look as if you had eighty thousand a year."

"Well, so long as I haven't——" said Catherine illogically. Her conception of her prospective wealth was as yet very indefinite.

"So long as you haven't you shouldn't look as if you had. Have you enjoyed your party?"

Catherine hesitated a moment; and then, looking away, "I am rather tired," she murmured. I have said that this entertainment was the beginning of something important for Catherine. For the second time in her life she made an indirect answer; and the beginning of a period of dissimulation is certainly a significant date. Catherine was not so easily tired as that.

Nevertheless, in the carriage, as they drove home, she was as quiet as if fatigue had been her portion. Dr. Sloper's manner of addressing his sister Lavinia had a good deal of resemblance to the tone he had adopted towards Catherine.

---

*Square dance, of French derivation, made up of five sections and usually performed by four couples.

"Who was the young man that was making love to you?" he presently asked.

"Oh, my good brother!" murmured Mrs. Penniman, in deprecation.

"He seemed uncommonly tender. Whenever I looked at you, for half an hour, he had the most devoted air."

"The devotion was not to me," said Mrs. Penniman. "It was to Catherine; he talked to me of her."

Catherine had been listening with all her ears. "Oh, Aunt Penniman!" she exclaimed faintly.

"He is very handsome; he is very clever; he expressed himself with a great deal—a great deal of felicity," her aunt went on.

"He is in love with this regal creature, then?" the Doctor inquired humorously.

"Oh, father," cried the girl, still more faintly, devoutly thankful the carriage was dark.

"I don't know that; but he admired her dress."

Catherine did not say to herself in the dark, "My dress only?" Mrs. Penniman's announcement struck her by its richness, not by its meagreness.

"You see," said her father, "he thinks you have eighty thousand a year."

"I don't believe he thinks of that," said Mrs. Penniman; "he is too refined."

"He must be tremendously refined not to think of that!"

"Well, he is!" Catherine exclaimed, before she knew it.

"I thought you had gone to sleep," her father answered. "The hour has come!" he added to himself. "Lavinia is going to get up a romance for Catherine. It's a shame to play such tricks on the girl. What is the gentleman's name?" he went on, aloud.

"I didn't catch it, and I didn't like to ask him. He asked to be introduced to me," said Mrs. Penniman, with a certain grandeur; "but you know how indistinctly Jefferson speaks." Jefferson was Mr. Almond. "Catherine, dear, what was the gentleman's name?"

For a minute, if it had not been for the rumbling of the carriage, you might have heard a pin drop.

"I don't know, Aunt Lavinia," said Catherine, very softly. And, with all his irony, her father believed her.

V

He learned what he had asked some three or four days later, after Morris Townsend, with his cousin, had called in Washington Square. Mrs. Penniman did not tell her brother, on the drive home, that she had intimated to this agreeable young man, whose name she did not know, that, with her niece, she should be very glad to see him; but she was greatly pleased, and even a little flattered, when late on a Sunday afternoon, the two gentlemen made their appearance. His coming with Arthur Townsend made it more natural and easy; the latter young man was on the point of becoming connected with the family, and Mrs. Penniman had remarked to Catherine that, as he was going to marry Marian, it would be polite in him to call. These events came to pass late in the autumn, and Catherine and her aunt had been sitting together in the closing dusk, by the firelight, in the high back-parlour.

Arthur Townsend fell to Catherine's portion, while his companion placed himself on the sofa, beside Mrs. Penniman. Catherine had hitherto not been a harsh critic; she was easy to please—she liked to talk with young men. But Marian's betrothed, this evening, made her feel vaguely fastidious; he sat looking at the fire and rubbing his knees with his hands. As for Catherine, she scarcely even pretended to keep up the conversation; her attention had fixed itself on the other side of the room; she was listening to what went on between the other Mr. Townsend and her aunt. Every now and then he looked over at Catherine herself and smiled, as if to show that what he said was for her benefit too. Catherine would have liked to change her place, to go and sit near them, where she might see and hear him better. But she was afraid of seeming bold—of looking eager; and, besides, it would not have been polite to Marian's little suitor. She wondered why the other gentleman had picked out her aunt—how he came to have so much to say to Mrs. Penniman, to whom, usually, young men were not especially devoted. She was not at all jealous of Aunt Lavinia, but she was a little envious, and above all she wondered; for Morris Townsend was an object on which she found that her imagination could exercise itself indefinitely. His cousin had been describing a house that he had taken in view of his union with Marian, and the domestic conveniences he meant to introduce into it; how Marian wanted a larger one, and Mrs. Almond recommended a smaller one, and how he himself was convinced that he had got the neatest house in New York.

"It doesn't matter," he said; "it's only for three or four years. At the end of three or four years we'll move. That's the way to live in New York—to move every three or four years. Then you always get the last thing. It's because the city's growing so quick—you've got to keep up with it. It's going straight up town—that's where New York's going. If I wasn't afraid Marian would be lonely, I'd go up there—right up to the top—and wait for it. Only have to wait ten years—they'd all come up after you. But Marian says she wants some neighbours—she doesn't want to be a pioneer. She says that if she's got to be the first settler she had better go out to Minnesota. I guess we'll move up little by little; when we get tired of one street we'll go higher. So you see we'll always have a new house; it's a great advantage to have a new house; you get all the latest improvements. They invent everything all over again about every five years, and it's a great thing to keep up with the new things. I always try and keep up with the new things of every kind. Don't you think that's a good motto for a young couple—to keep 'going higher'? That's the name of that piece of poetry—what do they call it?— *Excelsior!*"[4]

Catherine bestowed on her junior visitor only just enough attention to feel that this was not the way Mr. Morris Townsend had talked the other night, or that he was talking now to her fortunate aunt. But suddenly his aspiring kinsman became more interesting. He seemed to have become conscious that she was affected by his companion's presence, and he thought it proper to explain it.

"My cousin asked me to bring him, or I shouldn't have taken the liberty. He seemed to want very much to come; you know he's awfully sociable. I told him I wanted to ask you first, but he said Mrs. Penniman had invited him. He isn't particular what he says when he wants to come somewhere! But Mrs. Penniman seems to think it's all right."

"We are very glad to see him," said Catherine. And she wished to talk more about him; but she hardly knew what to say. "I never saw him before," she went on presently.

Arthur Townsend stared.

"Why, he told me he talked with you for over half an hour the other night."

"I mean before the other night. That was the first time."

"Oh, he has been away from New York—he has been all round the world. He doesn't know many people here, but he's very sociable, and he wants to know every one."

"Every one?" said Catherine.

"Well, I mean all the good ones. All the pretty young ladies—like Mrs. Penniman!" And Arthur Townsend gave a private laugh.

"My aunt likes him very much," said Catherine.

"Most people like him—he's so brilliant."

"He's more like a foreigner," Catherine suggested.

"Well, I never knew a foreigner!" said young Townsend, in a tone which seemed to indicate that his ignorance had been optional.

"Neither have I," Catherine confessed, with more humility. "They say they are generally brilliant," she added, vaguely.

"Well, the people of this city are clever enough for me. I know some of them that think they are too clever for me; but they ain't!"

"I suppose you can't be too clever," said Catherine, still with humility.

"I don't know. I know some people that call my cousin too clever."

Catherine listened to this statement with extreme interest, and a feeling that if Morris Townsend had a fault it would naturally be that one. But she did not commit herself, and in a moment she asked:—"Now that he has come back, will he stay here always?"

"Ah," said Arthur, "if he can get something to do."

"Something to do?"

"Some place or other; some business."

"Hasn't he got any?" said Catherine, who had never heard of a young man—of the upper class—in this situation.

"No; he's looking round. But he can't find anything."

"I am very sorry," Catherine permitted herself to observe.

"Oh, he doesn't mind," said young Townsend. "He takes it easy—he isn't in a hurry. He is very particular."

Catherine thought he naturally would be, and gave herself up for some moments to the contemplation of this idea, in several of its bearings.

"Won't his father take him into his business—his office?" she at last inquired.

"He hasn't got any father—he has only got a sister. Your sister can't help you much."

It seemed to Catherine that if she were his sister she would disprove this axiom. "Is she—is she pleasant?" she asked in a moment.

"I don't know—I believe she's very respectable," said young Townsend. And then he looked across to his cousin and began to laugh. "Look here, we are talking about you," he added.

Morris Townsend paused in his conversation with Mrs. Penniman, and stared, with a little smile. Then he got up, as if he were going.

"As far as you are concerned, I can't return the compliment," he said to Catherine's companion. "But as regards Miss Sloper, it's another affair."

Catherine thought this little speech wonderfully well turned; but she was embarrassed by it, and she also got up. Morris Townsend stood looking at her and smiling; he put out his hand for farewell. He was going, without having said anything to her; but even on these terms she was glad to have seen him.

"I will tell her what you have said—when you go!" said Mrs. Penniman, with an insinuating laugh.

Catherine blushed, for she felt almost as if they were making sport of her. What in the world could this beautiful young man have said? He looked at her still, in spite of her blush; but very kindly and respectfully.

"I have had no talk with you," he said, "and that was what I came for. But it will be a good reason for coming another time; a little pretext—if I am obliged to give one. I am not afraid of what your aunt will say when I go."

With this the two young men took their departure; after which Catherine, with her blush still lingering, directed a serious and interrogative eye to Mrs. Penniman. She was incapable of elaborate artifice, and she resorted to no jocular device—to no affectation of the belief that she had been maligned—to learn what she desired.

"What did you say you would tell me?" she asked.

Mrs. Penniman came up to her, smiling and nodding a little, looked her all over, and gave a twist to the knot of ribbon in her neck. "It's a great secret, my dear child; but he is coming a-courting!"

Catherine was serious still. "Is that what he told you!"

"He didn't say so exactly. But he left me to guess it. I'm a good guesser."

"Do you mean a-courting me?"

"Not me, certainly, miss; though I must say he is a hundred times more polite to a person who has no longer extreme youth to recommend her than most of the young men. He is thinking of some one else." And Mrs. Penniman gave her niece a delicate little kiss. "You must be very gracious to him."

Catherine stared—she was bewildered. "I don't understand you," she said; "he doesn't know me."

"Oh yes, he does; more than you think. I have told him all about you."

"Oh, Aunt Penniman!" murmured Catherine, as if this had been a breach of trust. "He is a perfect stranger—we don't know him." There was infinite modesty in the poor girl's "we."

Aunt Penniman, however, took no account of it; she spoke even with a touch of acrimony. "My dear Catherine, you know very well that you admire him!"

"Oh, Aunt Penniman!" Catherine could only murmur again. It might very well be that she admired him—though this did not seem to her a thing to talk about. But that this brilliant stranger—this sudden apparition, who had barely heard the sound of her voice—took that sort of interest in her that was expressed by the romantic phrase of which Mrs. Penniman had just made use: this could only be a figment of the restless brain of Aunt Lavinia, whom every one knew to be a woman of powerful imagination.

VI

Mrs. Penniman even took for granted at times that other people had as much imagination as herself; so that when, half an hour later, her brother came in, she addressed him quite on this principle.

"He has just been here, Austin; it's such a pity you missed him."

"Whom in the world have I missed?" asked the Doctor.

"Mr. Morris Townsend; he has made us such a delightful visit."

"And who in the world is Mr. Morris Townsend?"

"Aunt Penniman means the gentleman—the gentleman whose name I couldn't remember," said Catherine.

"The gentleman at Elizabeth's party who was so struck with Catherine," Mrs. Penniman added.

"Oh, his name is Morris Townsend, is it? And did he come here to propose to you?"

"Oh, father," murmured the girl for all answer, turning away to the window, where the dusk had deepened to darkness.

"I hope he won't do that without your permission," said Mrs. Penniman, very graciously.

"After all, my dear, he seems to have yours," her brother answered.

Lavinia simpered, as if this might not be quite enough, and Catherine, with her forehead touching the window-panes, listened to this exchange of epigrams as reservedly as if they had not each been a pin-prick in her own destiny.

"The next time he comes," the Doctor added, "you had better call me. He might like to see me."

Morris Townsend came again, some five days afterwards; but Dr. Sloper was not called as he was absent from home at the time. Catherine was with her aunt when the young man's name was brought in, and Mrs. Penniman, effacing herself and protesting, made a great point of her niece's going into the drawing-room alone.

"This time it's for you—for you only," she said. "Before, when he talked to me, it was only preliminary—it was to gain my confidence.

Literally, my dear, I should not have the *courage* to show myself to-day."

And this was perfectly true. Mrs. Penniman was not a brave woman, and Morris Townsend had struck her as a young man of great force of character, and of remarkable powers of satire; a keen, resolute, brilliant nature, with which one must exercise a great deal of tact. She said to herself that he was "imperious," and she liked the word and the idea. She was not the least jealous of her niece, and she had been perfectly happy with Mr. Penniman, but in the bottom of her heart she permitted herself the observation: "That's the sort of husband I should have had!" He was certainly much more imperious—she ended by calling it imperial—than Mr. Penniman.

So Catherine saw Mr. Townsend alone, and her aunt did not come in even at the end of the visit. The visit was a long one; he sat there—in the front parlour, in the biggest arm-chair—for more than an hour. He seemed more at home this time—more familiar; lounging a little in the chair, slapping a cushion that was near him with his stick, and looking round the room a good deal, and at the objects it contained, as well as at Catherine; whom, however, he also contemplated freely. There was a smile of respectful devotion in his handsome eyes which seemed to Catherine almost solemnly beautiful; it made her think of a young knight in a poem. His talk, however, was not particularly knightly; it was light and easy and friendly; it took a practical turn, and he asked a number of questions about herself—what were her tastes—if she liked this and that—what were her habits. He said to her, with his charming smile, "Tell me about yourself; give me a little sketch." Catherine had very little to tell, and she had no talent for sketching; but before he went she had confided to him that she had a secret passion for the theatre, which had been but scantily gratified, and a taste for operatic music—that of Bellini and Donizetti,[5] in especial (it must be remembered in extenuation of this primitive young woman that she held these opinions in an age of general darkness)—which she rarely had an occasion to hear, except on the hand-organ. She confessed that she was not particularly fond of literature. Morris Townsend agreed with her that books were tiresome things; only, as he said, you had to read a good many before you found it out. He had been to places that people had written books about, and they were not a bit like the descriptions. To see for yourself—that was the great thing; he always tried to see for himself.

He had seen all the principal actors—he had been to all the best theatres in London and Paris. But the actors were always like the authors—they always exaggerated. He liked everything to be natural. Suddenly he stopped, looking at Catherine with his smile.

"That's what I like you for; you are so natural! Excuse me," he added; "you see I am natural myself!"

And before she had time to think whether she excused him or not—which afterwards, at leisure, she became conscious that she did—he began to talk about music, and to say that it was his greatest pleasure in life. He had heard all the great singers in Paris and London—Pasta and Rubini and Lablache[6]—and when you had done that, you could say that you knew what singing was.

"I sing a little myself," he said; "some day I will show you. Not today, but some other time."

And then he got up to go; he had omitted, by accident, to say that he would sing to her if she would play to him. He thought of this after he got into the street; but he might have spared his compunction, for Catherine had not noticed the lapse. She was thinking only that "some other time" had a delightful sound; it seemed to spread itself over the future.

This was all the more reason, however, though she was ashamed and uncomfortable, why she should tell her father that Mr. Morris Townsend had called again. She announced the fact abruptly, almost violently, as soon as the Doctor came into the house; and having done so—it was her duty—she took measures to leave the room. But she could not leave it fast enough; her father stopped her just as she reached the door.

"Well, my dear, did he propose to you to-day?" the Doctor asked.

This was just what she had been afraid he would say; and yet she had no answer ready. Of course she would have liked to take it as a joke—as her father must have meant it; and yet she would have liked, also, in denying it, to be a little positive, a little sharp; so that he would perhaps not ask the question again. She didn't like it—it made her unhappy. But Catherine could never be sharp; and for a moment she only stood, with her hand on the door-knob, looking at her satiric parent, and giving a little laugh.

"Decidedly," said the Doctor to himself, "my daughter is not brilliant!"

But he had no sooner made this reflection than Catherine found something; she had decided on the whole to take the thing as a joke.

"Perhaps he will do it the next time!" she exclaimed, with a repetition of her laugh. And she quickly got out of the room.

The Doctor stood staring; he wondered whether his daughter were serious. Catherine went straight to her own room, and by the time she reached it she bethought herself that there was something else—something better—she might have said. She almost wished, now, that her father would ask his question again, so that she might reply:— "Oh yes, Mr. Morris Townsend proposed to me, and I refused him!"

The Doctor, however, began to put his questions elsewhere; it naturally having occurred to him that he ought to inform himself properly about this handsome young man who had formed the habit of running in and out of his house. He addressed himself to the elder of his sisters, Mrs. Almond—not going to her for the purpose; there was no such hurry as that—but having made a note of the matter for the first opportunity. The Doctor was never eager, never impatient nor nervous; but he made notes of everything, and he regularly consulted his notes. Among them the information he obtained from Mrs. Almond about Morris Townsend took its place.

"Lavinia has already been to ask me," she said. "Lavinia is most excited; I don't understand it. It's not, after all, Lavinia that the young man is supposed to have designs upon. She is very peculiar."

"Ah, my dear," the Doctor replied, "she has not lived with me these twelve years without my finding it out!"

"She has got such an artificial mind," said Mrs. Almond, who always enjoyed an opportunity to discuss Lavinia's peculiarities with her brother. "She didn't want me to tell you that she had asked me about Mr. Townsend; but I told her I would. She always wants to conceal everything."

"And yet at moments no one blurts things out with such crudity. She is like a revolving lighthouse; pitch darkness alternating with a dazzling brilliancy! But what did you tell her?" the Doctor asked.

"What I tell you; that I know very little of him."

"Lavinia must have been disappointed at that," said the Doctor; "she would prefer him to have been guilty of some romantic crime. However, we must make the best of people. They tell me our gentleman is the cousin of the little boy to whom you are about to entrust the future of your little girl."

"Arthur is not a little boy; he is a very old man; you and I will never be so old. He is a distant relation of Lavinia's *protégé*. The name is the same, but I am given to understand that there are Townsends and Townsends. So Arthur's mother tells me; she talked about 'branches'—younger branches, elder branches, inferior branches—as if it were a royal house. Arthur, it appears, is of the reigning line, but poor Lavinia's young man is not. Beyond this, Arthur's mother knows very little about him; she has only a vague story that he has been 'wild.' But I know his sister a little, and she is a very nice woman. Her name is Mrs. Montgomery; she is a widow, with a little property and five children. She lives in the Second Avenue."

"What does Mrs. Montgomery say about him?"

"That he has talents by which he might distinguish himself."

"Only he is lazy, eh?"

"She doesn't say so."

"That's family pride," said the Doctor. "What is his profession?"

"He hasn't got any; he is looking for something. I believe he was once in the Navy."

"Once? What is his age?"

"I suppose he is upwards of thirty. He must have gone into the Navy very young. I think Arthur told me that he inherited a small property—which was perhaps the cause of his leaving the Navy— and that he spent it all in a few years. He travelled all over the world, lived abroad, amused himself. I believe it was a kind of system, a theory he had. He has lately come back to America, with the intention, as he tells Arthur, of beginning life in earnest."

"Is he in earnest about Catherine, then?"

"I don't see why you should be incredulous," said Mrs. Almond. "It seems to me that you have never done Catherine justice. You must remember that she has the prospect of thirty thousand a year."

The Doctor looked at his sister a moment, and then, with the slightest touch of bitterness:—"You at least appreciate her," he said.

Mrs. Almond blushed.

"I don't mean that is her only merit; I simply mean that it is a great one. A great many young men think so; and you appear to me never to have been properly aware of that. You have always had a little way of alluding to her as an unmarriageable girl."

"My allusions are as kind as yours, Elizabeth," said the Doctor, frankly. "How many suitors has Catherine had, with all her expectations—how much attention has she ever received? Catherine is not unmarriageable, but she is absolutely unattractive. What other reason is there for Lavinia being so charmed with the idea that there is a lover in the house? There has never been one before, and Lavinia, with her sensitive, sympathetic nature, is not used to the idea. It affects her imagination. I must do the young men of New York the justice to say that they strike me as very disinterested. They prefer pretty girls— lively girls—girls like your own. Catherine is neither pretty nor lively."

"Catherine does very well; she has a style of her own—which is more than my poor Marian has, who has no style at all," said Mrs. Almond. "The reason Catherine has received so little attention is that she seems to all the young men to be older than themselves. She is so large, and she dresses—so richly. They are rather afraid of her, I think; she looks as if she had been married already, and you know they don't like married women. And if our young men appear disinterested," the Doctor's wiser sister went on, "it is because they marry, as a general thing, so young, before twenty-five, at the age of innocence and sincerity, before the age of calculation. If they only waited a little, Catherine would fare better."

"As a calculation? Thank you very much," said the Doctor.

"Wait till some intelligent man of forty comes along, and he will be delighted with Catherine," Mrs. Almond continued.

"Mr. Townsend is not old enough, then; his motives may be pure."

"It is very possible that his motives are pure; I should be very sorry to take the contrary for granted. Lavinia is sure of it, and, as he is a very prepossessing youth, you might give him the benefit of the doubt."

Dr. Sloper reflected a moment.

"What are his present means of subsistence?"

"I have no idea. He lives, as I say, with his sister."

"A widow, with five children? Do you mean he lives *upon* her?"

Mrs. Almond got up, and with a certain impatience: "Had you not better ask Mrs. Montgomery herself?" she inquired.

"Perhaps I may come to that," said the Doctor. "Did you say the Second Avenue?" He made a note of the Second Avenue.

VII

HE WAS, HOWEVER, BY no means so much in earnest as this might seem to indicate; and, indeed, he was more than anything else amused with the whole situation. He was not in the least in a state of tension or of vigilance, with regard to Catherine's prospects; he was even on his guard against the ridicule that might attach itself to the spectacle of a house thrown into agitation by its daughter and heiress receiving attentions unprecedented in its annals. More than this, he went so far as to promise himself some entertainment from the little drama—if drama it was—of which Mrs. Penniman desired to represent the ingenious Mr. Townsend as the hero. He had no intention, as yet, of regulating the *dénouement*. He was perfectly willing, as Elizabeth had suggested, to give the young man the benefit of every doubt. There was no great danger in it; for Catherine, at the age of twenty-two, was after all a rather mature blossom, such as could be plucked from the stem only by a vigorous jerk. The fact that Morris Townsend was poor—was not of necessity against him; the Doctor had never made up his mind that his daughter should marry a rich man. The fortune she would inherit struck him as a very sufficient provision for two reasonable persons, and if a penniless swain who could give a good account of himself should enter the lists, he should be judged quite upon his personal merits. There were other things besides. The Doctor thought it very vulgar to be precipitate in accusing people of mercenary motives, inasmuch as his door had as yet not been in the least besieged by fortune-hunters; and, lastly, he was very curious to see whether Catherine might really be loved for her moral worth. He smiled as he reflected that poor Mr. Townsend had been only twice to the house, and he said to Mrs. Penniman that the next time he should come she must ask him to dinner.

He came very soon again, and Mrs. Penniman had of course great pleasure in executing this mission. Morris Townsend accepted her invitation with equal good grace, and the dinner took place a few days later. The Doctor had said to himself, justly enough, that they must not have the young man alone; this would partake too much of the nature of encouragement. So two or three other persons were invited; but Morris Townsend, though he was by no means the ostensible, was the real, occasion of the feast. There is every reason to suppose that he desired to make a good impression; and if he fell short of this result, it was not for want of a good deal of intelligent effort. The Doctor talked to him very little during dinner; but he observed him attentively, and after the ladies had gone out he pushed him the wine and asked him several questions. Morris was not a young man who needed to be pressed, and he found quite enough encouragement in the superior quality of the claret. The Doctor's wine was admirable, and it may be communicated to the reader that while he sipped it Morris reflected that a cellar-full of good liquor—there was evidently a cellar-full here—would be a most attractive idiosyncrasy in a father-in-law. The Doctor was struck with his appreciative guest; he saw that he was not a commonplace young man. "He has ability," said Catherine's father, "decided ability; he has a very good head if he chooses to use it. And he is uncommonly well turned out; quite the sort of figure that pleases the ladies. But I don't think I like him." The Doctor, however, kept his reflections to himself, and talked to his visitors about foreign lands, concerning which Morris offered him more information than he was ready, as he mentally phrased it, to swallow. Dr. Sloper had travelled but little, and he took the liberty of not believing everything this anecdotical idler narrated. He prided himself on being something of a physiognomist,* and while the young man, chatting with easy assurance, puffed his cigar and filled his glass again, the Doctor sat with his eyes quietly fixed on his bright, expressive face. "He has the assurance of the devil himself," said Morris's host; "I don't think I ever saw such assurance. And his powers of invention are most remarkable. He is very knowing; they were not so knowing as that in my time. And a good head, did I say? I should think so—after a bottle of Madeira, and a bottle and a half of claret?"

After dinner Morris Townsend went and stood before Catherine, who was standing before the fire in her red satin gown.

---

*Practitioner of a now-discredited science in which character and disposition were thought to be legible in a body's lineaments and facial features.

"He doesn't like me—he doesn't like me at all!" said the young man.

"Who doesn't like you?" asked Catherine.

"Your father; extraordinary man!"

"I don't see how you know," said Catherine, blushing.

"I feel; I am very quick to feel."

"Perhaps you are mistaken."

"Ah, well; you ask him and you will see."

"I would rather not ask him, if there is any danger of his saying what you think."

Morris looked at her with an air of mock melancholy.

"It wouldn't give you any pleasure to contradict him?"

"I never contradict him," said Catherine.

"Will you hear me abused without opening your lips in my defence?"

"My father won't abuse you. He doesn't know you enough."

Morris Townsend gave a loud laugh, and Catherine began to blush again.

"I shall never mention you," she said, to take refuge from her confusion.

"That is very well; but it is not quite what I should have liked you to say. I should have liked you to say: 'If my father doesn't think well of you, what does it matter?' "

"Ah, but it would matter; I couldn't say that!" the girl exclaimed.

He looked at her for a moment, smiling a little; and the Doctor, if he had been watching him just then, would have seen a gleam of fine impatience in the sociable softness of his eye. But there was no impatience in his rejoinder—none, at least, save what was expressed in a little appealing sigh. "Ah, well, then, I must not give up the hope of bringing him round!"

He expressed it more frankly to Mrs. Penniman, later in the evening. But before that he sang two or three songs at Catherine's timid request; not that he flattered himself that this would help to bring her father round. He had a sweet, light tenor voice, and when he had finished, every one made some exclamation—every one, that is, save Catherine, who remained intensely silent. Mrs. Penniman declared that his manner of singing was "most artistic," and Dr. Sloper said it was "very taking—very taking indeed;" speaking loudly and distinctly, but with a certain dryness.

"He doesn't like me—he doesn't like me at all," said Morris Townsend, addressing the aunt in the same manner as he had done the niece. "He thinks I'm all wrong."

Unlike her niece, Mrs. Penniman asked for no explanation. She only smiled very sweetly, as if she understood everything; and, unlike Catherine too, she made no attempt to contradict him. "Pray, what does it matter?" she murmured softly.

"Ah, you say the right thing!" said Morris, greatly to the gratification of Mrs. Penniman, who prided herself on always saying the right thing.

The Doctor, the next time he saw his sister Elizabeth, let her know that he had made the acquaintance of Lavinia's *protégé*.

"Physically," he said, "he's uncommonly well set up. As an anatomist, it is really a pleasure to me to see such a beautiful structure; although, if people were all like him, I suppose there would be very little need for doctors."

"Don't you see anything in people but their bones?" Mrs. Almond rejoined. "What do you think of him as a father?"

"As a father? Thank Heaven I am not his father!"

"No; but you are Catherine's. Lavinia tells me she is in love."

"She must get over it. He is not a gentleman."

"Ah, take care! Remember that he is a branch of the Townsends."

"He is not what I call a gentleman. He has not the soul of one. He is extremely insinuating; but it's a vulgar nature. I saw through it in a minute. He is altogether too familiar—I hate familiarity. He is a plausible coxcomb."

"Ah, well," said Mrs. Almond; "if you make up your mind so easily, it's a great advantage."

"I don't make up my mind easily. What I tell you is the result of thirty years of observation; and in order to be able to form that judgment in a single evening, I have had to spend a lifetime in study."

"Very possibly you are right. But the thing is for Catherine to see it."

"I will present her with a pair of spectacles!" said the Doctor.

VIII

IF IT WERE TRUE that she was in love, she was certainly very quiet about it; but the Doctor was of course prepared to admit that her quietness might mean volumes. She had told Morris Townsend that she would not mention him to her father, and she saw no reason to retract this vow of discretion. It was no more than decently civil, of course, that after having dined in Washington Square, Morris should call there again; and it was no more than natural that, having been kindly received on this occasion, he should continue to present himself. He had had plenty of leisure on his hands; and thirty years ago, in New York, a young man of leisure had reason to be thankful for aids to self-oblivion. Catherine said nothing to her father about these visits, though they had rapidly become the most important, the most absorbing thing in her life. The girl was very happy. She knew not as yet what would come of it; but the present had suddenly grown rich and solemn. If she had been told she was in love, she would have been a good deal surprised; for she had an idea that love was an eager and exacting passion, and her own heart was filled in these days with the impulses of self-effacement and sacrifice. Whenever Morris Townsend had left the house, her imagination projected itself, with all its strength, into the idea of his soon coming back; but if she had been told at such a moment that he would not return for a year, or even that he would never return, she would not have complained nor rebelled, but would have humbly accepted the decree, and sought for consolation in thinking over the times she had already seen him, the words he had spoken, the sound of his voice, of his tread, the expression of his face. Love demands certain things as a right; but Catherine had no sense of her rights; she had only a consciousness of immense and unexpected favours. Her very gratitude for these things had hushed itself; for it seemed to her that there would be something of impudence in making a festival of her secret. Her father suspected Morris Townsend's visits, and noted her reserve. She seemed to beg pardon for it; she looked at him constantly in silence, as if she meant to say that she said nothing because she was afraid of irritating him. But the poor girl's dumb eloquence irritated him more than anything else would have done, and he caught himself murmuring more than once that it was a grievous pity his only child was a simpleton. His murmurs, however, were inaudible; and for a while he said nothing to any one. He would have liked to know exactly how often young Townsend came; but he had determined to ask no questions of the girl herself—to say nothing more to her that would show that he watched her. The Doctor had a great idea of being largely just: he wished to leave his daughter her liberty, and interfere only when the danger should be proved. It was not in his manner to obtain information by indirect methods, and it never even occurred to him to question the servants. As for Lavinia, he hated to talk to her about the matter; she annoyed him with her mock romanticism. But he had to come to this. Mrs. Penniman's convictions as regards the relations of her niece and the clever young visitor who saved appearances by coming ostensibly for both the ladies—Mrs. Penniman's convictions had passed into a riper and richer phase. There was to be no crudity in Mrs. Penniman's treatment of the situation; she had become as un-communicative as Catherine herself. She was tasting of the sweets of concealment; she had taken up the line of mystery. "She would be enchanted to be able to prove to herself that she is persecuted," said the Doctor; and when at last he questioned her, he was sure she would contrive to extract from his words a pretext for this belief.

"Be so good as to let me know what is going on in the house," he said to her, in a tone which, under the circumstances, he himself deemed genial.

"Going on, Austin?" Mrs. Penniman exclaimed. "Why, I am sure I don't know! I believe that last night the old gray cat had kittens?"

"At her age?" said the Doctor. "The idea is startling—almost shocking. Be so good as to see that they are all drowned. But what else has happened?"

"Ah, the dear little kittens!" cried Mrs. Penniman. "I wouldn't have them drowned for the world!"

Her brother puffed his cigar a few moments in silence. "Your sympathy with kittens, Lavinia," he presently resumed, "arises from a feline element in your own character."

"Cats are very graceful, and very clean," said Mrs. Penniman, smiling.

"And very stealthy. You are the embodiment both of grace and of neatness; but you are wanting in frankness."

"You certainly are not, dear brother."

"I don't pretend to be graceful, though I try to be neat. Why haven't you let me know that Mr. Morris Townsend is coming to the house four times a week?"

Mrs. Penniman lifted her eyebrows. "Four times a week?"

"Five times, if you prefer it. I am away all day, and I see nothing. But when such things happen, you should let me know."

Mrs. Penniman, with her eyebrows still raised, reflected intently. "Dear Austin," she said at last, "I am incapable of betraying a confidence. I would rather suffer anything."

"Never fear; you shall not suffer. To whose confidence is it you allude? Has Catherine made you take a vow of eternal secrecy?"

"By no means. Catherine has not told me as much as she might. She has not been very trustful."

"It is the young man, then, who has made you his confidant? Allow me to say that it is extremely indiscreet of you to form secret alliances with young men. You don't know where they may lead you."

"I don't know what you mean by an alliance," said Mrs. Penniman. "I take a great interest in Mr. Townsend; I won't conceal that. But that's all."

"Under the circumstances, that is quite enough. What is the source of your interest in Mr. Townsend?"

"Why," said Mrs. Penniman, musing, and then breaking into her smile, "that he is so interesting!"

The Doctor felt that he had need of his patience. "And what makes him interesting?—his good looks?"

"His misfortunes, Austin."

"Ah, he has had misfortunes? That, of course, is always interesting. Are you at liberty to mention a few of Mr. Townsend's?"

"I don't know that he would like it," said Mrs. Penniman. "He has told me a great deal about himself—he has told me, in fact, his whole history. But I don't think I ought to repeat those things. He would tell them to you, I am sure, if he thought you would listen to him kindly. With kindness you may do anything with him."

The Doctor gave a laugh. "I shall request him very kindly, then, to leave Catherine alone."

"Ah!" said Mrs. Penniman, shaking her forefinger at her brother, with her little finger turned out, "Catherine has probably said something to him kinder than that!"

"Said that she loved him? Do you mean that?"

Mrs. Penniman fixed her eyes on the floor. "As I tell you, Austin, she doesn't confide in me."

"You have an opinion, I suppose, all the same. It is that I ask you for; though I don't conceal from you that I shall not regard it as conclusive."

Mrs. Penniman's gaze continued to rest on the carpet; but at last she lifted it, and then her brother thought it very expressive. "I think Catherine is very happy; that is all I can say."

"Townsend is trying to marry her—is that what you mean?"

"He is greatly interested in her."

"He finds her such an attractive girl?"

"Catherine has a lovely nature, Austin," said Mrs. Penniman, "and Mr. Townsend has had the intelligence to discover that."

"With a little help from you, I suppose. My dear Lavinia," cried the Doctor, "you are an admirable aunt!"

"So Mr. Townsend says, "observed Lavinia, smiling.

"Do you think he is sincere?" asked her brother.

"In saying that?"

"No; that's of course. But in his admiration for Catherine?"

"Deeply sincere. He has said to me the most appreciative, the most charming things about her. He would say them to you, if he were sure you would listen to him—gently."

"I doubt whether I can undertake it. He appears to acquire a great deal of gentleness."

"He is a sympathetic, sensitive nature," said Mrs. Penniman.

Her brother puffed his cigar again in silence. "These delicate qualities have survived his vicissitudes, eh? All this while you haven't told me about his misfortunes."

"It is a long story," said Mrs. Penniman, "and I regard it as a sacred trust. But I suppose there is no objection to my saying that he has been wild—he frankly confesses that. But he has paid for it."

"That's what has impoverished him, eh?"

"I don't mean simply in money. He is very much alone in the world."

"Do you mean that he has behaved so badly that his friends have given him up?"

"He has had false friends, who have deceived and betrayed him."

"He seems to have some good ones too. He has a devoted sister, and half a dozen nephews and nieces."

Mrs. Penniman was silent a minute. "The nephews and nieces are children, and the sister is not a very attractive person."

"I hope he doesn't abuse her to you," said the Doctor; "for I am told he lives upon her."

"Lives upon her?"

"Lives with her, and does nothing for himself; it is about the same thing."

"He is looking for a position—most earnestly," said Mrs. Penniman. "He hopes every day to find one."

"Precisely. He is looking for it here—over there in the front parlour. The position of husband of a weak-minded woman with a large fortune would suit him to perfection!"

Mrs. Penniman was truly amiable, but she now gave signs of temper. She rose with much animation, and stood for a moment looking at her brother. "My dear Austin," she remarked, "if you regard Catherine as a weak-minded woman, you are particularly mistaken!" And with this she moved majestically away.

IX

It was a regular custom with the family in Washington Square to go and spend Sunday evening at Mrs. Almond's. On the Sunday after the conversation I have just narrated, this custom was not intermitted; and on this occasion, towards the middle of the evening, Dr. Sloper found reason to withdraw to the library, with his brother-in-law, to talk over a matter of business. He was absent some twenty minutes, and when he came back into the circle, which was enlivened by the presence of several friends of the family, he saw that Morris Townsend had come in and had lost as little time as possible in seating himself on a small sofa, beside Catherine. In the large room, where several different groups had been formed, and the hum of voices and of laughter was loud, these two young persons might confabulate, as the Doctor phrased it to himself, without attracting attention. He saw in a moment, however, that his daughter was painfully conscious of his own observation. She sat motionless, with her eyes bent down, staring at her open fan, deeply flushed, shrinking together as if to minimise the indiscretion of which she confessed herself guilty.

The Doctor almost pitied her. Poor Catherine was not defiant; she had no genius for bravado; and as she felt that her father viewed her companion's attentions with an unsympathising eye, there was nothing but discomfort for her in the accident of seeming to challenge him. The Doctor felt, indeed, so sorry for her that he turned away, to spare her the sense of being watched; and he was so intelligent a man that, in his thoughts, he rendered a sort of poetic justice to her situation.

"It must be deucedly pleasant for a plain, inanimate girl like that to have a beautiful young fellow come and sit down beside her and whisper to her that he is her slave — if that is what this one whispers. No wonder she likes it, and that she thinks me a cruel tyrant; which of course she does, though she is afraid — she hasn't the animation necessary — to admit it to herself. Poor old Catherine!" mused the

Doctor; "I verily believe she is capable of defending me when Townsend abuses me!"

And the force of this reflection, for the moment, was such in making him feel the natural opposition between his point of view and that of an infatuated child, that he said to himself that he was perhaps after all taking things too hard and crying out before he was hurt. He must not condemn Morris Townsend unheard. He had a great aversion to taking things too hard; he thought that half the discomfort and many of the disappointments of life come from it; and for an instant he asked himself whether, possibly, he did not appear ridiculous to this intelligent young man, whose private perception of incongruities he suspected of being keen. At the end of a quarter of an hour Catherine had got rid of him, and Townsend was now standing before the fireplace in conversation with Mrs. Almond.

"We will try him again," said the Doctor. And he crossed the room and joined his sister and her companion, making her a sign that she should leave the young man to him. She presently did so, while Morris looked at him, smiling, without a sign of evasiveness in his affable eye.

"He's amazingly conceited!" thought the Doctor; and then he said aloud: "I am told you are looking out for a position."

"Oh, a position is more than I should presume to call it," Morris Townsend answered. "That sounds so fine. I should like some quiet work—something to turn an honest penny."

"What sort of thing should you prefer?"

"Do you mean what am I fit for? Very little, I am afraid. I have nothing but my good right arm, as they say in the melodramas."

"You are too modest," said the Doctor. "In addition to your good right arm, you have your subtle brain. I know nothing of you but what I see; but I see by your physiognomy that you are extremely intelligent."

"Ah," Townsend murmured, "I don't know what to answer when you say that! You advise me, then, not to despair?"

And he looked at his interlocutor as if the question might have a double meaning. The Doctor caught the look and weighed it a moment before he replied. "I should be very sorry to admit that a robust and well-disposed young man need ever despair. If he doesn't succeed in one thing, he can try another. Only, I should add, he should choose his line with discretion."

"Ah, yes, with discretion," Morris Townsend repeated, sympathetically. "Well, I have been indiscreet, formerly; but I think I have got over it. I am very steady now." And he stood a moment, looking down at his remarkably neat shoes. Then at last, "Were you kindly intending to propose something for my advantage?" he inquired, looking up and smiling.

"Damn his impudence!" the Doctor exclaimed, privately. But in a moment he reflected that he himself had, after all, touched first upon this delicate point, and that his words might have been construed as an offer of assistance. "I have no particular proposal to make," he presently said; "but it occurred to me to let you know that I have you in my mind. Sometimes one hears of opportunities. For instance — should you object to leaving New York—to going to a distance?"

"I am afraid I shouldn't be able to manage that. I must seek my fortune here or nowhere. You see," added Morris Townsend, "I have ties—I have responsibilities here. I have a sister, a widow, from whom I have been separated for a long time, and to whom I am almost everything. I shouldn't like to say to her that I must leave her. She rather depends upon me, you see."

"Ah, that's very proper; family feeling is very proper," said Dr. Sloper. "I often think there is not enough of it in our city. I think I have heard of your sister."

"It is possible, but I rather doubt it; she lives so very quietly."

"As quietly, you mean," the Doctor went on, with a short laugh, "as a lady may do who has several young children."

"Ah, my little nephews and nieces—that's the very point! I am helping to bring them up," said Morris Townsend. "I am a kind of amateur tutor. I give them lessons."

"That's very proper, as I say; but it is hardly a career."

"It won't make my fortune!" the young man confessed.

"You must not be too much bent on a fortune," said the Doctor. "But I assure you I will keep you in mind; I won't lose sight of you!"

"If my situation becomes desperate I shall perhaps take the liberty of reminding you!" Morris rejoined, raising his voice a little, with a brighter smile, as his interlocutor turned away.

Before he left the house the Doctor had a few words with Mrs. Almond.

"I should like to see his sister," he said. "What do you call her? Mrs. Montgomery. I should like to have a little talk with her."

"I will try and manage it," Mrs. Almond responded. "I will take the first opportunity of inviting her, and you shall come and meet her. Unless, indeed," Mrs. Almond added, "she first takes it into her head to be sick and to send for you."

"Ah no, not that; she must have trouble enough without that. But it would have its advantages, for then I should see the children. I should like very much to see the children."

"You are very thorough. Do you want to catechise them about their uncle?"

"Precisely. Their uncle tells me he has charge of their education, that he saves their mother the expense of school-bills. I should like to ask them a few questions in the commoner branches."

"He certainly has not the cut of a schoolmaster!" Mrs. Almond said to herself a short time afterwards, as she saw Morris Townsend in a corner bending over her niece, who was seated.

And there was, indeed, nothing in the young man's discourse at this moment that savoured of the pedagogue.

"Will you meet me somewhere to-morrow or next day?" he said, in a low tone, to Catherine.

"Meet you?" she asked, lifting her frightened eyes.

"I have something particular to say to you—very particular."

"Can't you come to the house? Can't you say it there?"

Townsend shook his head gloomily. "I can't enter your doors again!"

"Oh, Mr. Townsend!" murmured Catherine. She trembled as she wondered what had happened, whether her father had forbidden it.

"I can't in self-respect," said the young man. "Your father has insulted me."

"Insulted you?"

"He has taunted me with my poverty."

"Oh, you are mistaken—you misunderstood him!" Catherine spoke with energy, getting up from her chair.

"Perhaps I am too proud—too sensitive. But would you have me otherwise?" he asked, tenderly.

"Where my father is concerned, you must not be sure. He is full of goodness," said Catherine.

"He laughed at me for having no position! I took it quietly; but only because he belongs to you."

"I don't know," said Catherine; "I don't know what he thinks. I am sure he means to be kind. You must not be too proud."

"I will be proud only of you," Morris answered. "Will you meet me in the Square in the afternoon?"

A great blush on Catherine's part had been the answer to the declaration I have just quoted. She turned away, heedless of his question.

"Will you meet me?" he repeated. "It is very quiet there; no one need see us—toward dusk?"

"It is you who are unkind, it is you who laugh, when you say such things as that."

"My dear girl!" the young man murmured.

"You know how little there is in me to be proud of. I am ugly and stupid."

Morris greeted this remark with an ardent murmur, in which she recognised nothing articulate but an assurance that she was his own dearest.

But she went on. "I am not even—I am not even——" And she paused a moment.

"You are not what?"

"I am not even brave."

"Ah, then, if you are afraid, what shall we do?"

She hesitated awhile; then at last—"You must come to the house," she said; "I am not afraid of that."

"I would rather it were in the Square," the young man urged. "You know how empty it is, often. No one will see us."

"I don't care who sees us! But leave me now."

He left her resignedly; he had got what he wanted. Fortunately he was ignorant that half an hour later, going home with her father and feeling him near, the poor girl, in spite of her sudden declaration of courage, began to tremble again. Her father said nothing; but she had an idea his eyes were fixed upon her in the darkness. Mrs. Penniman also was silent; Morris Townsend had told her that her niece preferred, unromantically, an interview in a chintz-covered parlour to a sentimental tryst beside a fountain sheeted with dead leaves, and she was lost in wonderment at the oddity—almost the perversity—of the choice.

X

CATHERINE RECEIVED THE YOUNG man the next day on the ground she had chosen—amid the chaste upholstery of a New York drawing-room furnished in the fashion of fifty years ago. Morris had swallowed his pride and made the effort necessary to cross the threshold of her too derisive parent—an act of magnanimity which could not fail to render him doubly interesting.

"We must settle something—we must take a line," he declared, passing his hand through his hair and giving a glance at the long narrow mirror which adorned the space between the two windows, and which had as its base a little gilded bracket covered by a thin slab of white marble, supporting in its turn a backgammon board folded together in the shape of two volumes, two shining folios inscribed in letters of greenish gilt, *History of England*. If Morris had been pleased to describe the master of the house as a heartless scoffer, it is because he thought him too much on his guard, and this was the easiest way to express his own dissatisfaction—a dissatisfaction which he had made a point of concealing from the Doctor. It will probably seem to the reader, however, that the Doctor's vigilance was by no means excessive, and that these two young people had an open field. Their intimacy was now considerable, and it may appear that for a shrinking and retiring person our heroine had been liberal of her favours. The young man, within a few days, had made her listen to things for which she had not supposed that she was prepared; having a lively foreboding of difficulties, he proceeded to gain as much ground as possible in the present. He remembered that fortune favours the brave, and even if he had forgotten it, Mrs. Penniman would have remembered it for him. Mrs. Penniman delighted of all things in a drama, and she flattered herself that a drama would now be enacted. Combining as she did the zeal of the prompter with the impatience of the spectator, she had long since done her utmost to pull up the curtain. She, too, expected to figure in the performance—to be the confidant, the

Chorus, to speak the epilogue. It may even be said that there were times when she lost sight altogether of the modest heroine of the play, in the contemplation of certain great passages which would naturally occur between the hero and herself.

What Morris had told Catherine at last was simply that he loved her, or rather adored her. Virtually, he had made known as much already—his visits had been a series of eloquent intimations of it. But now he had affirmed it in lover's vows, and, as a memorable sign of it, he had passed his arm round the girl's waist and taken a kiss. This happy certitude had come sooner than Catherine expected, and she had regarded it, very naturally, as a priceless treasure. It may even be doubted whether she had ever definitely expected to possess it; she had not been waiting for it, and she had never said to herself that at a given moment it must come. As I have tried to explain, she was not eager and exacting; she took what was given her from day to day; and if the delightful custom of her lover's visits, which yielded her a happiness in which confidence and timidity were strangely blended, had suddenly come to an end, she would not only not have spoken of herself as one of the forsaken, but she would not have thought of herself as one of the disappointed. After Morris had kissed her, the last time he was with her, as a ripe assurance of his devotion, she begged him to go away, to leave her alone, to let her think. Morris went away, taking another kiss first. But Catherine's meditations had lacked a certain coherence. She felt his kisses on her lips and on her cheeks for a long time afterwards; the sensation was rather an obstacle than an aid to reflection. She would have liked to see her situation all clearly before her, to make up her mind what she should do if, as she feared, her father should tell her that he disapproved of Morris Townsend. But all that she could see with any vividness was that it was terribly strange that any one should disapprove of him; that there must in that case be some mistake, some mystery, which in a little while would be set at rest. She put off deciding and choosing; before the vision of a conflict with her father she dropped her eyes and sat motionless, holding her breath and waiting. It made her heart beat, it was intensely painful. When Morris kissed her and said these things—that also made her heart beat; but this was worse, and it frightened her. Nevertheless, today, when the young man spoke of settling something, taking a line, she felt that it was the truth, and she answered very simply and without hesitating.

"We must do our duty," she said; "we must speak to my father. I will do it to-night; you must do it to-morrow."

"It is very good of you to do it first," Morris answered. "The young man—the happy lover—generally does that. But just as you please!"

It pleased Catherine to think that she should be brave for his sake, and in her satisfaction she even gave a little smile. "Women have more tact," she said; "they ought to do it first. They are more conciliating; they can persuade better."

"You will need all your powers of persuasion. But after all," Morris added, "you are irresistible."

"Please don't speak that way—and promise me this. To-morrow, when you talk with father, you will be very gentle and respectful."

"As much so as possible," Morris promised. "It won't be much use, but I shall try. I certainly would rather have you easily than have to fight for you."

"Don't talk about fighting; we shall not fight."

"Ah, we must be prepared," Morris rejoined; "you especially, because for you it must come hardest. Do you know the first thing your father will say to you?"

"No, Morris; please tell me."

"He will tell you I am mercenary."

"Mercenary?"

"It's a big word; but it means a low thing. It means that I am after your money."

"Oh!" murmured Catherine, softly.

The exclamation was so deprecating and touching that Morris indulged in another little demonstration of affection. "But he will be sure to say it," he added.

"It will be easy to be prepared for that," Catherine said. "I shall simply say that he is mistaken—that other men may be that way, but that you are not."

"You must make a great point of that, for it will be his own great point."

Catherine looked at her lover a minute, and then she said, "I shall persuade him. But I am glad we shall be rich," she added.

Morris turned away, looking into the crown of his hat. "No, it's a misfortune," he said at last. "It is from that our difficulty will come."

"Well, if it is the worst misfortune, we are not so unhappy. Many people would not think it so bad. I will persuade him, and after that we shall be very glad we have money."

Morris Townsend listened to this robust logic in silence. "I will leave my defence to you; it's a charge that a man has to stoop to defend himself from."

Catherine on her side was silent for a while; she was looking at him while he looked, with a good deal of fixedness, out of the window. "Morris," she said, abruptly, "are you very sure you love me?"

He turned round, and in a moment he was bending over her. "My own dearest, can you doubt it?"

"I have only known it five days," she said; "but now it seems to me as if I could never do without it."

"You will never be called upon to try!" And he gave a little tender, reassuring laugh. Then, in a moment, he added, "There is something you must tell me, too." She had closed her eyes after the last word she uttered, and kept them closed; and at this she nodded her head, without opening them. "You must tell me," he went on, "that if your father is dead against me, if he absolutely forbids our marriage, you will still be faithful."

Catherine opened her eyes, gazing at him, and she could give no better promise than what he read there.

"You will cleave to me?" said Morris. "You know you are your own mistress—you are of age."

"Ah, Morris!" she murmured, for all answer. Or rather not for all; for she put her hand into his own. He kept it awhile, and presently he kissed her again. This is all that need be recorded of their conversation; but Mrs. Penniman, if she had been present, would probably have admitted that it was as well it had not taken place beside the fountain in Washington Square.

XI

CATHERINE LISTENED FOR HER father when he came in that evening, and she heard him go to his study. She sat quiet, though her heart was beating fast, for nearly half an hour; then she went and knocked at his door—a ceremony without which she never crossed the threshold of this apartment. On entering it now she found him in his chair beside the fire, entertaining himself with a cigar and the evening paper.

"I have something to say to you," she began very gently; and she sat down in the first place that offered.

"I shall be very happy to hear it, my dear," said her father. He waited—waited, looking at her, while she stared, in a long silence, at the fire. He was curious and impatient, for he was sure she was going to speak of Morris Townsend; but he let her take her own time, for he was determined to be very mild.

"I am engaged to be married!" Catherine announced at last, still staring at the fire.

The Doctor was startled; the accomplished fact was more than he had expected. But he betrayed no surprise. "You do right to tell me," he simply said. "And who is the happy mortal whom you have honoured with your choice?"

"Mr. Morris Townsend." And as she pronounced her lover's name, Catherine looked at him. What she saw was her father's still gray eye and his clear-cut, definite smile. She contemplated these objects for a moment, and then she looked back at the fire; it was much warmer.

"When was this arrangement made?" the Doctor asked.

"This afternoon—two hours ago."

"Was Mr. Townsend here?"

"Yes, father; in the front parlour." She was very glad that she was not obliged to tell him that the ceremony of their betrothal had taken place out under the bare ailantus-trees.

"Is it serious?" said the Doctor.

"Very serious, father."

Her father was silent a moment. "Mr. Townsend ought to have told me."

"He means to tell you to-morrow."

"After I know all about it from you? He ought to have told me before. Does he think I didn't care—because I left you so much liberty?"

"Oh, no," said Catherine; "he knew you would care. And we have been so much obliged to you for—for the liberty."

The Doctor gave a short laugh. "You might have made a better use of it, Catherine."

"Please don't say that, father," the girl urged, softly, fixing her dull and gentle eyes upon him.

He puffed his cigar awhile, meditatively. "You have gone very fast," he said at last.

"Yes," Catherine answered simply; "I think we have."

Her father glanced at her an instant, removing his eyes from the fire. "I don't wonder Mr. Townsend likes you. You are so simple and so good. "

"I don't know why it is—but he *does* like me. I am sure of that."

"And are you very fond of Mr. Townsend?"

"I like him very much, of course—or I shouldn't consent to marry him."

"But you have known him a very short time, my dear."

"Oh," said Catherine, with some eagerness, "it doesn't take long to like a person—when once you begin."

"You must have begun very quickly. Was it the first time you saw him—that night at your aunt's party?"

"I don't know, father," the girl answered. "I can't tell you about that."

"Of course; that's your own affair. You will have observed that I have acted on that principle. I have not interfered, I have left you your liberty, I have remembered that you are no longer a little girl—that you have arrived at years of discretion."

"I feel very old—and very wise," said Catherine, smiling faintly.

"I am afraid that before long you will feel older and wiser yet. I don't like your engagement."

"Ah!" Catherine exclaimed, softly, getting up from her chair.

"No, my dear. I am sorry to give you pain; but I don't like it. You should have consulted me before you settled it. I have been too easy with you, and I feel as if you had taken advantage of my indulgence. Most decidedly, you should have spoken to me first."

Catherine hesitated a moment, and then—"It was because I was afraid you wouldn't like it!" she confessed.

"Ah, there it is! You had a bad conscience."

"No, I have not a bad conscience, father!" the girl cried out, with considerable energy. "Please don't accuse me of anything so dreadful." These words, in fact, represented to her imagination something very terrible indeed, something base and cruel, which she associated with malefactors and prisoners. "It was because I was afraid—afraid——" she went on.

"If you were afraid, it was because you had been foolish!"

"I was afraid you didn't like Mr. Townsend."

"You are quite right. I don't like him."

"Dear father, you don't know him," said Catherine, in a voice so timidly argumentative that it might have touched him.

"Very true; I don't know him intimately. But I know him enough. I have my impression of him. You don't know him either."

She stood before the fire, with her hands lightly clasped in front of her; and her father, leaning back in his chair and looking up at her, made this remark with a placidity that might have been irritating.

I doubt, however, whether Catherine was irritated, though she broke into a vehement protest. "I don't know him?" she cried. "Why, I know him—better than I have ever known any one!"

"You know a part of him—what he has chosen to show you. But you don't know the rest."

"The rest? What is the rest?"

"Whatever it may be. There is sure to be plenty of it."

"I know what you mean," said Catherine, remembering how Morris had forewarned her. "You mean that he is mercenary."

Her father looked up at her still, with his cold, quiet, reasonable eye. "If I meant it, my dear, I should say it! But there is an error I wish particularly to avoid—that of rendering Mr. Townsend more interesting to you by saying hard things about him."

"I won't think them hard, if they are true," said Catherine.

"If you don't, you will be a remarkably sensible young woman!"

"They will be your reasons, at any rate; and you will want me to hear your reasons."

The Doctor smiled a little. "Very true. You have a perfect right to ask for them." And he puffed his cigar a few moments. "Very well, then, without accusing Mr. Townsend of being in love only with your fortune—and with the fortune that you justly expect—I will say that there is every reason to suppose that these good things have entered into his calculation more largely than a tender solicitude for your happiness strictly requires. There is, of course, nothing impossible in an intelligent young man entertaining a disinterested affection for you. You are an honest, amiable girl, and an intelligent young man might easily find it out. But the principal thing that we know about this young man—who is, indeed, very intelligent— leads us to suppose that, however much he may value your personal merits, he values your money more. The principal thing we know about him is that he has led a life of dissipation, and has spent a fortune of his own in doing so. That is enough for me, my dear. I wish you to marry a young man with other antecedents—a young man who could give positive guarantees. If Morris Townsend has spent his own fortune in amusing himself, there is every reason to believe that he would spend yours."

The Doctor delivered himself of these remarks slowly, deliberately, with occasional pauses and prolongations of accent, which made no great allowance for poor Catherine's suspense as to his conclusion. She sat down at last, with her head bent and her eyes still fixed upon him; and strangely enough—I hardly know how to tell it—even while she felt that what he said went so terribly against her, she admired his neatness and nobleness of expression. There was something hopeless and oppressive in having to argue with her father; but she too, on her side, must try to be clear. He was so quiet; he was not at all angry; and she, too, must be quiet. But her very effort to be quiet made her tremble.

"That is not the principal thing we know about him," she said; and there was a touch of her tremor in her voice. "There are other things—many other things. He has very high abilities—he wants so much to do something. He is kind, and generous, and true," said poor Catherine, who had not suspected hitherto the resources of her eloquence. "And his fortune—his fortune that he spent—was very small!"

"All the more reason he shouldn't have spent it," cried the Doctor, getting up with a laugh. Then as Catherine, who had also risen to her feet again, stood there in her rather angular earnestness, wishing so much and expressing so little, he drew her towards him and kissed her. "You won't think me cruel?" he said, holding her a moment.

This question was not reassuring; it seemed to Catherine, on the contrary, to suggest possibilities which made her feel sick. But she answered coherently enough—"No, dear father; because if you knew how I feel—and you must know, you know everything—you would be so kind, so gentle."

"Yes, I think I know how you feel," the Doctor said. "I will be very kind—be sure of that. And I will see Mr. Townsend to-morrow. Meanwhile, and for the present, be so good as to mention to no one that you are engaged."

XII

ON THE MORROW, IN the afternoon, he stayed at home, awaiting Mr. Townsend's call—a proceeding by which it appeared to him (justly perhaps, for he was a very busy man) that he paid Catherine's suitor great honour, and gave both these young people so much the less to complain of. Morris presented himself with a countenance sufficiently serene—he appeared to have forgotten the "insult" for which he had solicited Catherine's sympathy two evenings before, and Dr. Sloper lost no time in letting him know that he had been prepared for his visit.

"Catherine told me yesterday what has been going on between you," he said. "You must allow me to say that it would have been becoming of you to give me notice of your intentions before they had gone so far."

"I should have done so," Morris answered, "if you had not had so much the appearance of leaving your daughter at liberty. She seems to me quite her own mistress."

"Literally, she is. But she has not emancipated herself morally quite so far, I trust, as to choose a husband without consulting me. I have left her at liberty, but I have not been in the least indifferent. The truth is that your little affair has come to a head with a rapidity that surprises me. It was only the other day that Catherine made your acquaintance."

"It was not long ago, certainly," said Morris, with great gravity. "I admit that we have not been slow to—to arrive at an understanding. But that was very natural, from the moment we were sure of ourselves—and of each other. My interest in Miss Sloper began the first time I saw her."

"Did it not by chance precede your first meeting?" the Doctor asked.

Morris looked at him an instant. "I certainly had already heard that she was a charming girl."

"A charming girl—that's what you think her?"

"Assuredly. Otherwise I should not be sitting here."

The Doctor meditated a moment. "My dear young man," he said at last, "you must be very susceptible. As Catherine's father, I have, I trust, a just and tender appreciation of her many good qualities; but I don't mind telling you that I have never thought of her as a charming girl, and never expected any one else to do so."

Morris Townsend received this statement with a smile that was not wholly devoid of deference. "I don't know what I might think of her if I were her father. I can't put myself in that place. I speak from my own point of view."

"You speak very well," said the Doctor; "but that is not all that is necessary. I told Catherine yesterday that I disapproved of her engagement."

"She let me know as much, and I was very sorry to hear it. I am greatly disappointed." And Morris sat in silence awhile, looking at the floor.

"Did you really expect I would say I was delighted, and throw my daughter into your arms?"

"Oh, no; I had an idea you didn't like me."

"What gave you the idea?"

"The fact that I am poor."

"That has a harsh sound," said the Doctor, "but it is about the truth—speaking of you strictly as a son-in-law. Your absence of means, of a profession, of visible resources or prospects, places you in a category from which it would be imprudent for me to select a husband for my daughter, who is a weak young woman with a large fortune. In any other capacity I am perfectly prepared to like you. As a son-in-law, I abominate you!"

Morris Townsend listened respectfully. "I don't think Miss Sloper is a weak woman," he presently said.

"Of course you must defend her—it's the least you can do. But I have known my child twenty years, and you have known her six weeks. Even if she were not weak, however, you would still be a penniless man."

"Ah, yes; that is *my* weakness! And therefore, you mean, I am mercenary—I only want your daughter's money."

"I don't say that. I am not obliged to say it; and to say it, save under stress of compulsion, would be very bad taste. I say simply that you belong to the wrong category."

"But your daughter doesn't marry a category," Townsend urged, with his handsome smile. "She marries an individual—an individual whom she is so good as to say she loves."

"An individual who offers so little in return!"

"Is it possible to offer more than the most tender affection and a lifelong devotion?" the young man demanded.

"It depends how we take it. It is possible to offer a few other things besides, and not only is it possible, but it's usual. A lifelong devotion is measured after the fact; and meanwhile it is customary in these cases to give a few material securities. What are yours? A very handsome face and figure, and a very good manner. They are excellent as far as they go, but they don't go far enough."

"There is one thing you should add to them," said Morris; "the word of a gentleman!"

"The word of a gentleman that you will always love Catherine? You must be a very fine gentleman to be sure of that."

"The word of a gentleman that I am not mercenary; that my affection for Miss Sloper is as pure and disinterested a sentiment as was ever lodged in a human breast! I care no more for her fortune than for the ashes in that grate."

"I take note—I take note," said the Doctor. "But having done so, I turn to our category again. Even with that solemn vow on your lips, you take your place in it. There is nothing against you but an accident, if you will; but with my thirty years' medical practice, I have seen that accidents may have far-reaching consequences."

Morris smoothed his hat—it was already remarkably glossy—and continued to display a self-control which, as the Doctor was obliged to admit, was extremely creditable to him. But his disappointment was evidently keen.

"Is there nothing I can do to make you believe in me?"

"If there were I should be sorry to suggest it, for—don't you see?—I don't want to believe in you!" said the Doctor, smiling.

"I would go and dig in the fields."

"That would be foolish."

"I will take the first work that offers, to-morrow."

"Do so by all means—but for your own sake, not for mine."

"I see; you think I am an idler!" Morris exclaimed, a little too much in the tone of a man who has made a discovery. But he saw his error immediately and blushed.

"It doesn't matter what I think, when once I have told you I don't think of you as a son-in-law."

But Morris persisted. "You think I would squander her money."

The Doctor smiled. "It doesn't matter, as I say; but I plead guilty to that."

"That's because I spent my own, I suppose," said Morris. "I frankly confess that. I have been wild. I have been foolish. I will tell you every crazy thing I ever did, if you like. There were some great follies among the number—I have never concealed that. But I have sown my wild oats. Isn't there some proverb about a reformed rake?[7] I was not a rake, but I assure you I have reformed. It is better to have amused oneself for a while and have done with it. Your daughter would never care for a milksop; and I will take the liberty of saying that you would like one quite as little. Besides, between my money and hers there is a great difference. I spent my own; it was because it was my own that I spent it. And I made no debts; when it was gone I stopped. I don't owe a penny in the world."

"Allow me to inquire what you are living on now—though I admit," the Doctor added, "that the question, on my part, is inconsistent."

"I am living on the remnants of my property," said Morris Townsend.

"Thank you!" the Doctor gravely replied.

Yes, certainly, Morris's self-control was laudable. "Even admitting I attach an undue importance to Miss Sloper's fortune," he went on, "would not that be in itself an assurance that I should take good care of it?"

"That you should take too much care would be quite as bad as that you should take too little. Catherine might suffer as much by your economy as by your extravagance."

"I think you are very unjust!" The young man made this declaration decently, civilly, without violence.

"It is your privilege to think so, and I surrender my reputation to you! I certainly don't flatter myself I gratify you."

"Don't you care a little to gratify your daughter? Do you enjoy the idea of making her miserable?"

"I am perfectly resigned to her thinking me a tyrant for a twelvemonth."

"For a twelvemonth!" exclaimed Morris, with a laugh.

"For a lifetime, then! She may as well be miserable in that way as in the other."

Here at last Morris lost his temper. "Ah, you are not polite, sir!" he cried.

"You push me to it—you argue too much."

"I have a great deal at stake."

"Well, whatever it is," said the Doctor, "you have lost it!"

"Are you sure of that?" asked Morris; "are you sure your daughter will give me up?"

"I mean, of course, you have lost it as far as I am concerned. As for Catherine's giving you up—no, I am not sure of it. But as I shall strongly recommend it, as I have a great fund of respect and affection in my daughter's mind to draw upon, and as she has the sentiment of duty developed in a very high degree, I think it extremely possible."

Morris Townsend began to smooth his hat again. "I, too, have a fund of affection to draw upon!" he observed at last.

The Doctor at this point showed his own first symptoms of irritation. "Do you mean to defy me?"

"Call it what you please, sir! I mean not to give your daughter up!"

The Doctor shook his head. "I haven't the least fear of your pining away your life. You are made to enjoy it."

Morris gave a laugh. "Your opposition to my marriage is all the more cruel, then! Do you intend to forbid your daughter to see me again?"

"She is past the age at which people are forbidden, and I am not a father in an old-fashioned novel. But I shall strongly urge her to break with you."

"I don't think she will," said Morris Townsend.

"Perhaps not. But I shall have done what I could."

"She has gone too far," Morris went on.

"To retreat? Then let her stop where she is."

"Too far to stop, I mean."

The Doctor looked at him a moment; Morris had his hand on the door. "There is a great deal of impertinence in your saying it."

"I will say no more, sir!" Morris answered; and, making his bow, he left the room.

XIII

IT MAY BE THOUGHT the Doctor was too positive, and Mrs. Almond intimated as much. But as he said, he had his impression; it seemed to him sufficient, and he had no wish to modify it. He had passed his life in estimating people (it was part of the medical trade), and in nineteen cases out of twenty he was right.

"Perhaps Mr. Townsend is the twentieth case," Mrs. Almond suggested.

"Perhaps he is, though he doesn't look to me at all like a twentieth case. But I will give him the benefit of the doubt, and, to make sure, I will go and talk to Mrs. Montgomery. She will almost certainly tell me I have done right; but it is just possible that she will prove to me that I have made the greatest mistake of my life. If she does, I will beg Mr. Townsend's pardon. You needn't invite her to meet me, as you kindly proposed; I will write her a frank letter, telling her how matters stand, and asking leave to come and see her."

"I am afraid the frankness will be chiefly on your side. The poor little woman will stand up for her brother, whatever he may be."

"Whatever he may be? I doubt that. People are not always so fond of their brothers."

"Ah," said Mrs. Almond, "when it's a question of thirty thousand a year coming into a family——"

"If she stands up for him on account of the money, she will be a humbug. If she is a humbug I shall see it. If I see it, I won't waste time with her."

"She is not a humbug—she is an exemplary woman. She will not wish to play her brother a trick simply because he is selfish."

"If she is worth talking to, she will sooner play him a trick than that he should play Catherine one. Has she seen Catherine, by the way—does she know her?"

"Not to my knowledge. Mr. Townsend can have had no particular interest in bringing them together."

"If she is an exemplary woman, no. But we shall see to what extent she answers your description."

"I shall be curious to hear her description of you!" said Mrs. Almond, with a laugh. "And, meanwhile, how is Catherine taking it?"

"As she takes everything—as a matter of course."

"Doesn't she make a noise? Hasn't she made a scene?"

"She is not scenic."

"I thought a love-lorn maiden was always scenic."

"A fantastic widow is more so. Lavinia has made me a speech; she thinks me very arbitrary."

"She has a talent for being in the wrong," said Mrs. Almond. "But I am very sorry for Catherine, all the same."

"So am I. But she will get over it."

"You believe she will give him up?"

"I count upon it. She has such an admiration for her father."

"Oh, we know all about that! But it only makes me pity her the more. It makes her dilemma the more painful, and the effort of choosing between you and her lover almost impossible."

"If she can't choose, all the better."

"Yes, but he will stand there entreating her to choose, and Lavinia will pull on that side."

"I am glad she is not on my side; she is capable of ruining an excellent cause. The day Lavinia gets into your boat it capsizes. But she had better be careful," said the Doctor. "I will have no treason in my house!"

"I suspect she will be careful; for she is at bottom very much afraid of you."

"They are both afraid of me—harmless as I am!" the Doctor answered. "And it is on that that I build—on the salutary terror I inspire!"

XIV

HE WROTE HIS FRANK letter to Mrs. Montgomery, who punctually
answered it, mentioning an hour at which he might present himself
in the Second Avenue. She lived in a neat little house of red brick,
which had been freshly painted, with the edges of the bricks very
sharply marked out in white. It has now disappeared, with its companions, to make room for a row of structures more majestic. There
were green shutters upon the windows, without slats, but pierced
with little holes, arranged in groups; and before the house was a
diminutive yard, ornamented with a bush of mysterious character,
and surrounded by a low wooden paling, painted in the same green
as the shutters. The place looked like a magnified baby-house, and
might have been taken down from a shelf in a toy-shop. Dr. Sloper,
when he went to call, said to himself, as he glanced at the objects
I have enumerated, that Mrs. Montgomery was evidently a thrifty
and self-respecting little person—the modest proportions of her
dwelling seemed to indicate that she was of small stature—who took
a virtuous satisfaction in keeping herself tidy, and had resolved that,
since she might not be splendid, she would at least be immaculate.
She received him in a little parlour, which was precisely the parlour
he had expected: a small unspeckled bower, ornamented with a
desultory foliage of tissue-paper, and with clusters of glass drops, amid
which—to carry out the analogy—the temperature of the leafy season was maintained by means of a cast-iron stove, emitting a dry blue
flame, and smelling strongly of varnish. The walls were embellished
with engravings swathed in pink gauze, and the tables ornamented
with volumes of extracts from the poets, usually bound in black cloth
stamped with florid designs in jaundiced gilt. The Doctor had time
to take cognisance of these details; for Mrs. Montgomery, whose con-
duct he pronounced under the circumstances inexcusable, kept him
waiting some ten minutes before she appeared. At last, however, she
rustled in, smoothing down a stiff poplin dress, with a little frightened
flush in a gracefully rounded cheek.

She was a small, plump, fair woman, with a bright, clear eye, and an extraordinary air of neatness and briskness. But these qualities were evidently combined with an unaffected humility, and the Doctor gave her his esteem as soon as he had looked at her. A brave little person, with lively perceptions, and yet a disbelief in her own talent for social, as distinguished from practical, affairs—this was his rapid mental *résumé* of Mrs. Montgomery, who, as he saw, was flattered by what she regarded as the honour of his visit. Mrs. Montgomery, in her little red house in the Second Avenue, was a person for whom Dr. Sloper was one of the great men, one of the fine gentlemen of New York; and while she fixed her agitated eyes upon him, while she clasped her mittened hands together in her glossy poplin lap, she had the appearance of saying to herself that he quite answered her idea of what a distinguished guest would naturally be. She apologised for being late; but he interrupted her.

"It doesn't matter," he said; "for while I sat here I had time to think over what I wish to say to you, and to make up my mind how to begin."

"Oh, do begin!" murmured Mrs. Montgomery.

"It is not so easy," said the Doctor, smiling. "You will have gathered from my letter that I wish to ask you a few questions, and you may not find it very comfortable to answer them."

"Yes; I have thought what I should say. It is not very easy."

"But you must understand my situation—my state of mind. Your brother wishes to marry my daughter, and I wish to find out what sort of a young man he is. A good way to do so seemed to be to come and ask you; which I have proceeded to do."

Mrs. Montgomery evidently took the situation very seriously; she was in a state of extreme moral concentration. She kept her pretty eyes, which were illumined by a sort of brilliant modesty, attached to his own countenance, and evidently paid the most earnest attention to each of his words. Her expression indicated that she thought his idea of coming to see her a very superior conception, but that she was really afraid to have opinions on strange subjects.

"I am extremely glad to see you," she said, in a tone which seemed to admit, at the same time, that this had nothing to do with the question.

The Doctor took advantage of this admission. "I didn't come to see you for your pleasure; I came to make you say disagreeable things — and you can't like that. What sort of a gentleman is your brother?"

Mrs. Montgomery's illuminated gaze grew vague, and began to wander. She smiled a little, and for some time made no answer, so that the Doctor at last became impatient. And her answer, when it came, was not satisfactory. "It is difficult to talk about one's brother."

"Not when one is fond of him, and when one has plenty of good to say."

"Yes, even then, when a good deal depends on it," said Mrs. Montgomery.

"Nothing depends on it, for you."

"I mean for — for —— " and she hesitated.

"For your brother himself. I see!"

"I mean for Miss Sloper," said Mrs. Montgomery.

The Doctor liked this; it had the accent of sincerity. "Exactly; that's the point. If my poor girl should marry your brother, everything — as regards her happiness — would depend on his being a good fellow. She is the best creature in the world, and she could never do him a grain of injury. He, on the other hand, if he should not be all that we desire, might make her very miserable. That is why I want you to throw some light upon his character, you know. Of course, you are not bound to do it. My daughter, whom you have never seen, is nothing to you; and I, possibly, am only an indiscreet and impertinent old man. It is perfectly open to you to tell me that my visit is in very bad taste and that I had better go about my business. But I don't think you will do this; because I think we shall interest you, my poor girl and I. I am sure that if you were to see Catherine, she would interest you very much. I don't mean because she is interesting in the usual sense of the word, but because you would feel sorry for her. She is so soft, so simple-minded, she would be such an easy victim! A bad husband would have remarkable facilities for making her miserable; for she would have neither the intelligence nor the resolution to get the better of him, and yet she would have an exaggerated power of suffering. I see," added the Doctor, with his most insinuating, his most professional laugh, "you are already interested!"

"I have been interested from the moment he told me he was engaged," said Mrs. Montgomery.

"Ah! he says that — he calls it an engagement?"

"Oh, he has told me you didn't like it."

"Did he tell you that I don't like *him*?"

"Yes, he told me that too. I said I couldn't help it!" added Mrs. Montgomery.

"Of course you can't. But what you can do is to tell me I am right—to give me an attestation, as it were." And the Doctor accompanied this remark with another professional smile.

Mrs. Montgomery, however, smiled not at all; it was obvious that she could not take the humorous view of his appeal. "That is a good deal to ask," she said at last.

"There can be no doubt of that; and I must, in conscience, remind you of the advantages a young man marrying my daughter would enjoy. She has an income of ten thousand dollars in her own right, left her by her mother; if she marries a husband I approve, she will come into almost twice as much more at my death."

Mrs. Montgomery listened in great earnestness to this splendid financial statement; she had never heard thousands of dollars so familiarly talked about. She flushed a little with excitement. "Your daughter will be immensely rich," she said softly.

"Precisely—that's the bother of it."

"And if Morris should marry her, he—he——" And she hesitated timidly.

"He would be master of all that money? By no means. He would be master of the ten thousand a year that she has from her mother; but I should leave every penny of my fortune, earned in the laborious exercise of my profession, to public institutions."

Mrs. Montgomery dropped her eyes at this, and sat for some time gazing at the straw matting which covered her floor.

"I suppose it seems to you," said the Doctor, laughing, "that in so doing I should play your brother a very shabby trick."

"Not at all. That is too much money to get possession of so easily, by marrying. I don't think it would be right."

"It's right to get all one can. But in this case your brother wouldn't be able. If Catherine marries without my consent, she doesn't get a penny from my own pocket."

"Is that certain?" asked Mrs. Montgomery, looking up.

"As certain as that I sit here!"

"Even if she should pine away?"

"Even if she should pine to a shadow, which isn't probable."

"Does Morris know this?"

"I shall be most happy to inform him!" the Doctor exclaimed.

Mrs. Montgomery resumed her meditations, and her visitor, who was prepared to give time to the affair, asked himself whether, in spite of her little conscientious air, she was not playing into her brother's hands. At the same time he was half ashamed of the ordeal to which he had subjected her, and was touched by the gentleness with which she bore it. "If she were a humbug," he said, "she would get angry; unless she be very deep indeed. It is not probable that she is as deep as that."

"What makes you dislike Morris so much?" she presently asked, emerging from her reflections.

"I don't dislike him in the least as a friend, as a companion. He seems to me a charming fellow, and I should think he would be excellent company. I dislike him, exclusively, as a son-in-law. If the only office of a son-in-law were to dine at the paternal table, I should set a high value upon your brother. He dines capitally. But that is a small part of his function, which, in general, is to be a protector, and care-taker of my child, who is singularly ill-adapted to take care of herself. It is there that he doesn't satisfy me. I confess I have nothing but my impression to go by; but I am in the habit of trusting my impression. Of course you are at liberty to contradict it flat. He strikes me as selfish and shallow."

Mrs. Montgomery's eyes expanded a little, and the Doctor fancied he saw the light of admiration in them. "I wonder you have discovered he is selfish!" she exclaimed.

"Do you think he hides it so well?"

"Very well indeed," said Mrs. Montgomery. "And I think we are all rather selfish," she added quickly.

"I think so too; but I have seen people hide it better than he. You see I am helped by a habit I have of dividing people into classes, into types. I may easily be mistaken about your brother as an individual, but his type is written on his whole person."

"He is very good-looking," said Mrs. Montgomery.

The Doctor eyed her a moment. "You women are all the same! But the type to which your brother belongs was made to be the ruin of you, and you were made to be its handmaids and victims. The sign of the type in question is the determination—sometimes terrible in its quiet intensity—to accept nothing of life but its pleasures, and to secure these pleasures chiefly by the aid of your complaisant sex. Young men of this class never do anything for themselves that they can get other people to do for them, and it is the infatuation, the devotion, the superstition of others, that keeps them going. These others in ninety-nine cases out of a hundred are women. What our young friends chiefly insist upon is that some one else shall suffer for them; and women do that sort of thing, as you must know, wonderfully well." The Doctor paused a moment, and then he added abruptly, "You have suffered immensely for your brother!"

This exclamation was abrupt, as I say, but it was also perfectly calculated. The Doctor had been rather disappointed at not finding his compact and comfortable little hostess surrounded in a more visible degree by the ravages of Morris Townsend's immorality; but he had said to himself that this was not because the young man had spared her, but because she had contrived to plaster up her wounds. They were aching there, behind the varnished stove, the festooned engravings, beneath her own neat little poplin bosom; and if he could only touch the tender spot, she would make a movement that would betray her. The words I have just quoted were an attempt to put his finger suddenly upon the place; and they had some of the success that he looked for. The tears sprang for a moment to Mrs. Montgomery's eyes, and she indulged in a proud little jerk of the head.

"I don't know how you have found that out!" she exclaimed.

"By a philosophic trick—by what they call induction. You know you have always your option of contradicting me. But kindly answer me a question. Don't you give your brother money? I think you ought to answer that."

"Yes, I have given him money," said Mrs. Montgomery.

"And you have not had much to give him?"

She was silent for a moment. "If you ask me for a confession of poverty, that is easily made. I am very poor."

"One would never suppose it from your—your charming house," said the Doctor. "I learned from my sister that your income was moderate, and your family numerous."

"I have five children," Mrs. Montgomery observed; "but I am happy to say I can bring them up decently."

"Of course you can—accomplished and devoted as you are! But your brother has counted them over, I suppose?"

"Counted them over?"

"He knows there are five, I mean. He tells me it is he that brings them up."

Mrs. Montgomery stared a moment, and then quickly—"Oh, yes; he teaches them—Spanish."

The Doctor laughed out. "That must take a great deal off your hands! Your brother also knows, of course, that you have very little money."

"I have often told him so!" Mrs. Montgomery exclaimed, more unreservedly than she had yet spoken. She was apparently taking some comfort in the Doctor's clairvoyance.

"Which means that you have often occasion to, and that he often sponges on you. Excuse the crudity of my language; I simply express a fact. I don't ask you how much of your money he has had, it is none of my business. I have ascertained what I suspected—what I wished." And the Doctor got up, gently smoothing his hat. "Your brother lives on you," he said as he stood there.

Mrs. Montgomery quickly rose from her chair, following her visitor's movements with a look of fascination. But then, with a certain inconsequence—"I have never complained of him!" she said.

"You needn't protest—you have not betrayed him. But I advise you not to give him any more money."

"Don't you see it is in my interest that he should marry a rich person?" she asked. "If, as you say, he lives on me, I can only wish to get rid of him, and to put obstacles in the way of his marrying is to increase my own difficulties."

"I wish very much you would come to me with your difficulties," said the Doctor. "Certainly, if I throw him back on your hands, the least I can do is to help you to bear the burden. If you will allow me to say so, then, I shall take the liberty of placing in your hands, for the present, a certain fund for your brother's support."

Mrs. Montgomery stared; she evidently thought he was jesting; but she presently saw that he was not, and the complication of her feelings became painful. "It seems to me that I ought to be very much offended with you," she murmured.

"Because I have offered you money? That's a superstition," said the Doctor. "You must let me come and see you again, and we will talk about these things. I suppose that some of your children are girls."

"I have two little girls," said Mrs. Montgomery.

"Well, when they grow up, and begin to think of taking husbands, you will see how anxious you will be about the moral character of these gentlemen. Then you will understand this visit of mine!"

"Ah, you are not to believe that Morris's moral character is bad!"

The Doctor looked at her a little, with folded arms. "There is something I should greatly like—as a moral satisfaction. I should like to hear you say—'He is abominably selfish!' "

The words came out with the grave distinctness of his voice, and they seemed for an instant to create, to poor Mrs. Montgomery's troubled vision, a material image. She gazed at it an instant, and then she turned away. "You distress me, sir!" she exclaimed. "He is, after all, my brother, and his talents, his talents——" On these last words her voice quavered, and before he knew it she had burst into tears.

"His talents are first-rate!" said the Doctor. "We must find the proper field for them!" And he assured her most respectfully of his regret at having so greatly discomposed her. "It's all for my poor Catherine," he went on. "You must know her, and you will see."

Mrs. Montgomery brushed away her tears and blushed at having shed them. "I should like to know your daughter," she answered; and then, in an instant—"Don't let her marry him!"

Dr. Sloper went away with the words gently humming in his ears—"Don't let her marry him!" They gave him the moral satisfaction of which he had just spoken, and their value was the greater that they had evidently cost a pang to poor little Mrs. Montgomery's family pride.

XV

HE HAD BEEN PUZZLED by the way that Catherine carried herself;
her attitude at this sentimental crisis seemed to him unnaturally
passive. She had not spoken to him again after that scene in the library, the day before his interview with Morris; and a week had
elapsed without making any change in her manner. There was
nothing in it that appealed for pity, and he was even a little disappointed at her not giving him an opportunity to make up for his
harshness by some manifestation of liberality which should operate
as a compensation. He thought a little of offering to take her for a
tour in Europe; but he was determined to do this only in case she
should seem mutely to reproach him. He had an idea that she would
display a talent for mute reproaches, and he was surprised at not
finding himself exposed to these silent batteries. She said nothing,
either tacitly, or explicitly, and as she was never very talkative, there
was no especial eloquence in her reserve. And poor Catherine was
not sulky—a style of behaviour for which she had too little histrionic
talent; she was simply very patient. Of course she was thinking over
her situation, and she was apparently doing so in a deliberate and
unimpassioned manner, with a view of making the best of it.

"She will do as I have bidden her," said the Doctor, and he made
the further reflection that his daughter was not a woman of a great
spirit. I know not whether he had hoped for a little more resistance
for the sake of a little more entertainment; but he said to himself, as
he had said before, that though it might have its momentary alarms,
paternity was, after all, not an exciting vocation.

Catherine meanwhile had made a discovery of a very different
sort; it had become vivid to her that there was a great excitement in
trying to be a good daughter. She had an entirely new feeling, which
may be described as a state of expectant suspense about her own actions. She watched herself as she would have watched another person, and wondered what she would do. It was as if this other person,
who was both herself and not herself, had suddenly sprung into

being, inspiring her with a natural curiosity as to the performance of untested functions.

"I am glad I have such a good daughter," said her father, kissing her, after the lapse of several days.

"I am trying to be good," she answered, turning away, with a conscience not altogether clear.

"If there is anything you would like to say to me, you know you must not hesitate. You needn't feel obliged to be so quiet. I shouldn't care that Mr. Townsend should be a frequent topic of conversation, but whenever you have anything particular to say about him I shall be very glad to hear it."

"Thank you," said Catherine; "I have nothing particular at present."

He never asked her whether she had seen Morris again, because he was sure that if this had been the case she would tell him. She had in fact not seen him, she had only written him a long letter. The letter at least was long for her; and, it may be added, that it was long for Morris; it consisted of five pages, in a remarkably neat and handsome hand. Catherine's handwriting was beautiful, and she was even a little proud of it; she was extremely fond of copying, and possessed volumes of extracts which testified to this accomplishment; volumes which she had exhibited one day to her lover, when the bliss of feeling that she was important in his eyes was exceptionally keen. She told Morris in writing that her father had expressed the wish that she should not see him again, and that she begged he would not come to the house until she should have "made up her mind." Morris replied with a passionate epistle, in which he asked to what, in Heaven's name, she wished to make up her mind. Had not her mind been made up two weeks before, and could it be possible that she entertained the idea of throwing him off? Did she mean to break down at the very beginning of their ordeal, after all the promises of fidelity she had both given and extracted? And he gave an account of his own interview with her father—an account not identical at all points with that offered in these pages. "He was terribly violent," Morris wrote; "but you know my self-control. I have need of it all when I remember that I have it in my power to break in upon your cruel captivity." Catherine sent him in answer to this, a note of three lines. "I am in great trouble; do not doubt of my affection, but let me wait a little and think." The idea of a struggle with her father, of setting up her will against his own, was heavy on her soul, and it kept her formally submissive, as a great physical weight keeps us motionless. It never entered into her mind to throw her lover off; but from the first she tried to assure herself that there would be a peaceful way out of their difficulty. The assurance was vague, for it contained no element of positive conviction that her father would change his mind. She only had an idea that if she should be very good, the situation would in some mysterious manner improve. To be good, she must be patient, respectful, abstain from judging her father too harshly, and from committing any act of open defiance. He was perhaps right, after all, to think as he did; by which Catherine meant not in the least that his judgment of Morris's motives in seeking to marry her was perhaps a just one, but that it was probably natural and proper that conscientious parents should be suspicious and even unjust. There were probably people in the world as bad as her father supposed Morris to be, and if there were the slightest chance of Morris being one of these sinister persons, the Doctor was right in taking it into account. Of course he could not know what she knew, how the purest love and truth were seated in the young man's eyes; but Heaven, in its time, might appoint a way of bringing him to such knowledge. Catherine expected a good deal of Heaven, and referred to the skies the initiative, as the French say,* in dealing with her dilemma. She could not imagine herself imparting any kind of knowledge to her father, there was something superior even in his injustice and absolute in his mistakes. But she could at least be good, and if she were only good enough, Heaven would invent some way of reconciling all things—the dignity of her father's errors and the sweetness of her own confidence, the strict performance of her filial duties and the enjoyment of Morris Townsend's affection. Poor Catherine would have been glad to regard Mrs. Penniman as an illuminating agent, a part which this lady herself indeed was but imperfectly prepared to play. Mrs. Penniman took too much satisfaction in the sentimental shadows of this little drama to have, for the moment, any great interest in dissipating them. She wished the plot to thicken, and the advice

---

*The French expression *s'en remettre au ciel l'initiative* means, roughly, "to leave the enterprise to Heaven."

that she gave her niece tended, in her own imagination, to produce
this result. It was rather incoherent counsel, and from one day to
another it contradicted itself; but it was pervaded by an earnest desire that Catherine should do something striking. "You must *act*,
my dear; in your situation the great thing is to act," said Mrs. Penniman, who found her niece altogether beneath her opportunities.
Mrs. Penniman's real hope was that the girl would make a secret
marriage, at which she should officiate as brideswoman or duenna.
She had a vision of this ceremony being performed in some subterranean chapel—subterranean chapels in New York were not frequent,
but Mrs. Penniman's imagination was not chilled by trifles—and of
the guilty couple—she liked to think of poor Catherine and her
suitor as the guilty couple—being shuffled away in a fast-whirling
vehicle to some obscure lodging in the suburbs, where she would
pay them (in a thick veil) clandestine visits, where they would en-
dure a period of romantic privation, and where ultimately, after she
should have been their earthly providence, their intercessor, their
advocate, and their medium of communication with the world,
they should be reconciled to her brother in an artistic tableau, in
which she herself should be somehow the central figure. She hesitated as yet to recommend this course to Catherine, but she attempted to draw an attractive picture of it to Morris Townsend. She
was in daily communication with the young man, whom she kept
informed by letters of the state of affairs in Washington Square. As
he had been banished, as she said, from the house, she no longer
saw him; but she ended by writing to him that she longed for an interview. This interview could take place only on neutral ground,
and she bethought herself greatly before selecting a place of meeting. She had an inclination for Greenwood Cemetery,[8] but she gave
it up as too distant; she could not absent herself for so long, as she
said, without exciting suspicion. Then she thought of the Battery,
but that was rather cold and windy, besides one's being exposed to
intrusion from the Irish emigrants who at this point alight, with large
appetites, in the New World; and at last she fixed upon an oyster sa-
loon in the Seventh Avenue, kept by a negro—an establishment of
which she knew nothing save that she had noticed it in passing. She
made an appointment with Morris Townsend to meet him there,
and she went to the tryst at dusk, enveloped in an impenetrable veil.
He kept her waiting for half-an-hour—he had almost the whole

XVI

THEY HAD OF COURSE immediately spoken of Catherine.

"Did she send me a message, or—or anything?" Morris asked. He appeared to think that she might have sent him a trinket or a lock of her hair.

Mrs. Penniman was slightly embarrassed, for she had not told her niece of her intended expedition. "Not exactly a message," she said; "I didn't ask her for one, because I was afraid to—to excite her."

"I am afraid she is not very excitable!" And Morris gave a smile of some bitterness.

"She is better than that. She is steadfast—she is true!"

"Do you think she will hold fast then?"

"To the death!"

"Oh, I hope it won't come to that," said Morris.

"We must be prepared for the worst, and that is what I wish to speak to you about."

"What do you call the worst?"

"Well," said Mrs. Penniman, "my brother's hard, intellectual nature."

"Oh, the devil!"

"He is impervious to pity," Mrs. Penniman added, by way of explanation.

"Do you mean that he won't come round?"

"He will never be vanquished by argument. I have studied him. He will be vanquished only by the accomplished fact."

"The accomplished fact?"

"He will come round afterwards," said Mrs. Penniman, with extreme significance. "He cares for nothing but facts; he must be met by facts!"

"Well," rejoined Morris, "it is a fact that I wish to marry his daughter. I met him with that the other day, but he was not at all vanquished."

Mrs. Penniman was silent a little, and her smile beneath the shadow of her capacious bonnet, on the edge of which her black veil was arranged curtain-wise, fixed itself upon Morris's face with a still more tender brilliancy. "Marry Catherine first, and meet him afterwards!" she exclaimed.

"Do you recommend that?" asked the young man, frowning heavily.

She was a little frightened, but she went on with considerable boldness. "That is the way I see it: a private marriage—a private marriage." She repeated the phrase because she liked it.

"Do you mean that I should carry Catherine off? What do they call it—elope with her?"

"It is not a crime when you are driven to it," said Mrs. Penniman. "My husband, as I have told you, was a distinguished clergyman; one of the most eloquent men of his day. He once married a young couple that had fled from the house of the young lady's father. He was so interested in their story. He had no hesitation, and everything came out beautifully. The father was afterwards reconciled, and thought everything of the young man. Mr. Penniman married them in the evening, about seven o'clock. The church was so dark, you could scarcely see; and Mr. Penniman was intensely agitated; he was so sympathetic. I don't believe he could have done it again."

"Unfortunately Catherine and I have not Mr. Penniman to marry us," said Morris.

"No, but you have me!" rejoined Mrs. Penniman, expressively. "I can't perform the ceremony, but I can help you. I can watch."

"The woman's an idiot," thought Morris; but he was obliged to say something different. It was not, however, materially more civil. "Was it in order to tell me this that you requested I would meet you here?"

Mrs. Penniman had been conscious of a certain vagueness in her errand, and of not being able to offer him any very tangible reward for his long walk. "I thought perhaps you would like to see one who is so near to Catherine," she observed with considerable majesty. "And also," she added, "that you would value an opportunity of sending her something."

Morris extended his empty hands with a melancholy smile. "I am greatly obliged to you, but I have nothing to send."

"Haven't you a *word?*" asked his companion, with her suggestive smile coming back.

Morris frowned again. "Tell her to hold fast," he said, rather curtly.

"That is a good word—a noble word. It will make her happy for many days. She is very touching, very brave," Mrs. Penniman went on, arranging her mantle and preparing to depart. While she was so engaged she had an inspiration. She found the phrase that she could boldly offer as a vindication of the step she had taken. "If you marry Catherine at all risks," she said, "you will give my brother a proof of your being what he pretends to doubt."

"What he pretends to doubt?"

"Don't you know what that is?" Mrs. Penniman asked, almost playfully.

"It does not concern me to know," said Morris, grandly.

"Of course it makes you angry."

"I despise it," Morris declared.

"Ah, you know what it is, then?" asked Mrs. Penniman, shaking her finger at him. "He pretends that you like—you like the money."

Morris hesitated a moment; and then, as if he spoke advisedly—"I *do* like the money!"

"Ah, but not—but not as he means it. You don't like it more than Catherine?"

He leaned his elbows on the table and buried his head in his hands, "You torture me!" he murmured. And, indeed, this was almost the effect of the poor lady's too importunate interest in his situation.

But she insisted on making her point. "If you marry her in spite of him, he will take for granted that you expect nothing of him, and are prepared to do without it. And so he will see that you are disinterested."

Morris raised his head a little, following this argument. "And what shall I gain by that?"

"Why, that he will see that he has been wrong in thinking that you wished to get his money."

"And seeing that I wish he would go to the deuce with it, he will leave it to a hospital. Is that what you mean?" asked Morris.

"No, I don't mean that; though that would be very grand!" Mrs. Penniman quickly added. "I mean that having done you such an injustice, he will think it his duty, at the end, to make some amends."

Morris shook his head, though it must be confessed he was a little struck with this idea. "Do you think he is so sentimental?"

"He is not sentimental," said Mrs. Penniman; "but, to be perfectly fair to him, I think he has, in his own narrow way, a certain sense of duty."

There passed through Morris Townsend's mind a rapid wonder as to what he might, even under a remote contingency, be indebted to from the action of this principle in Dr. Sloper's breast, and the inquiry exhausted itself in his sense of the ludicrous. "Your brother has no duties to me," he said presently, "and I none to him."

"Ah, but he has duties to Catherine."

"Yes, but you see that on that principle Catherine has duties to him as well."

Mrs. Penniman got up, with a melancholy sigh, as if she thought him very unimaginative. "She has always performed them faithfully; and now do you think she has no duties to *you?*" Mrs. Penniman always, ever, in conversation, italicised her personal pronouns.

"It would sound harsh to say so! I am so grateful for her love," Morris added.

"I will tell her you said that! And now, remember that if you need me, I am there." And Mrs. Penniman, who could think of nothing more to say, nodded vaguely in the direction of Washington Square.

Morris looked some moments at the sanded floor of the shop; he seemed to be disposed to linger a moment. At last, looking up with a certain abruptness, "It is your belief that if she marries me he will cut her off?" he asked.

Mrs. Penniman stared a little, and smiled. "Why, I have explained to you what I think would happen—that in the end it would be the best thing to do."

"You mean that, whatever she does, in the long run she will get the money?"

"It doesn't depend upon her, but upon you. Venture to appear as disinterested as you are!" said Mrs. Penniman ingeniously. Morris dropped his eyes on the sanded floor again, pondering this; and she pursued. "Mr. Penniman and I had nothing, and we were very happy. Catherine, moreover, has her mother's fortune, which, at the time my sister-in-law married, was considered a very handsome one."

"Oh, don't speak of that!" said Morris; and, indeed, it was quite superfluous, for he had contemplated the fact in all its lights.

"Austin married a wife with money—why shouldn't you?"

"Ah! but your brother was a doctor," Morris objected.

"Well, all young men can't be doctors!"

"I should think it an extremely loathsome profession," said Morris, with an air of intellectual independence. Then, in a moment, he went on rather inconsequently, "Do you suppose there is a will already made in Catherine's favour?"

"I suppose so—even doctors must die; and perhaps a little in mine," Mrs. Penniman frankly added.

"And you believe he would certainly change it—as regards Catherine?"

"Yes; and then change it back again."

"Ah, but one can't depend on that!" said Morris.

"Do you want to *depend* on it?" Mrs. Penniman asked.

Morris blushed a little. "Well, I am certainly afraid of being the cause of an injury to Catherine."

"Ah! you must not be afraid. Be afraid of nothing, and everything will go well!"

And then Mrs. Penniman paid for her cup of tea, and Morris paid for his oyster stew, and they went out together into the dimly-lighted wilderness of the Seventh Avenue. The dusk had closed in completely and the street lamps were separated by wide intervals of a pavement in which cavities and fissures played a disproportionate part. An omnibus,* emblazoned with strange pictures, went tumbling over the dislocated cobblestones.

"How will you go home?" Morris asked, following this vehicle with an interested eye. Mrs. Penniman had taken his arm.

She hesitated a moment. "I think this manner would be pleasant," she said; and she continued to let him feel the value of his support.

So he walked with her through the devious ways of the west side of the town, and through the bustle of gathering nightfall in populous streets, to the quiet precinct of Washington Square. They lingered a moment at the foot of Dr. Sloper's white marble steps, above which a spotless white door, adorned with a glittering silver plate, seemed to figure, for Morris, the closed portal of happiness;

---

*Four-wheeled public vehicle that usually travels along a fixed route and carries a number of passengers; modern usage has shortened this term to "bus."

and then Mrs. Penniman's companion rested a melancholy eye upon a lighted window in the upper part of the house.

"That is my room—my dear little room!" Mrs. Penniman remarked.

Morris started. "Then I needn't come walking round the square to gaze at it."

"That's as you please. But Catherine's is behind; two noble windows on the second floor. I think you can see them from the other street."

"I don't want to see them, ma'am!" And Morris turned his back to the house.

"I will tell her you have been *here*, at any rate," said Mrs. Penniman, pointing to the spot where they stood; "and I will give her your message—that she is to hold fast!"

"Oh, yes! of course. You know I write her all that."

"It seems to say more when it is spoken! And remember, if you need me, that I am *there*"; and Mrs. Penniman glanced at the third floor.

On this they separated, and Morris, left to himself, stood looking at the house a moment; after which he turned away, and took a gloomy walk round the Square, on the opposite side, close to the wooden fence. Then he came back, and paused for a minute in front of Dr. Sloper's dwelling. His eyes travelled over it; they even rested on the ruddy windows of Mrs. Penniman's apartment. He thought it a devilish comfortable house.

XVII

Mrs. Penniman told Catherine that evening—the two ladies were sitting in the back parlour—that she had had an interview with Morris Townsend; and on receiving this news the girl started with a sense of pain. She felt angry for the moment; it was almost the first time she had ever felt angry. It seemed to her that her aunt was meddlesome; and from this came a vague apprehension that she would spoil something.

"I don't see why you should have seen him. I don't think it was right," Catherine said.

"I was so sorry for him—it seemed to me some one ought to see him."

"No one but I," said Catherine, who felt as if she were making the most presumptuous speech of her life, and yet at the same time had an instinct that she was right in doing so.

"But you wouldn't, my dear," Aunt Lavinia rejoined; "and I didn't know what might have become of him."

"I have not seen him, because my father has forbidden it," Catherine said, very simply.

There was a simplicity in this, indeed, which fairly vexed Mrs. Penniman. "If your father forbade you to go to sleep, I suppose you would keep awake!" she commented.

Catherine looked at her. "I don't understand you. You seem to be very strange."

"Well, my dear, you will understand me some day!" And Mrs. Penniman, who was reading the evening paper, which she perused daily from the first line to the last, resumed her occupation. She wrapped herself in silence; she was determined Catherine should ask her for an account of her interview with Morris. But Catherine was silent for so long, that she almost lost patience; and she was on the point of remarking to her that she was very heartless, when the girl at last spoke.

"What did he say?" she asked.

"He said he is ready to marry you any day, in spite of everything."

Catherine made no answer to this, and Mrs. Penniman almost lost patience again; owing to which she at last volunteered the information that Morris looked very handsome, but terribly haggard.

"Did he seem sad?" asked her niece.

"He was dark under the eyes," said Mrs. Penniman. "So different from when I first saw him; though I am not sure that if I had seen him in this condition the first time, I should not have been even more struck with him. There is something brilliant in his very misery."

This was, to Catherine's sense, a vivid picture, and though she disapproved, she felt herself gazing at it. "Where did you see him?" she asked presently.

"In—in the Bowery; at a confectioner's," said Mrs. Penniman, who had a general idea that she ought to dissemble a little.

"Whereabouts is the place?" Catherine inquired, after another pause.

"Do you wish to go there, my dear?" said her aunt.

"Oh, no!" And Catherine got up from her seat and went to the fire, where she stood looking awhile at the glowing coals.

"Why are you so dry, Catherine?" Mrs. Penniman said at last.

"So dry?"

"So cold—so irresponsive."

The girl turned, very quickly. "Did *he* say that?"

Mrs. Penniman hesitated a moment. "I will tell you what he said. He said he feared only one thing—that you would be afraid."

"Afraid of what?"

"Afraid of your father."

Catherine turned back to the fire again, and then, after a pause, she said—"I *am* afraid of my father."

Mrs. Penniman got quickly up from her chair and approached her niece. "Do you mean to give him up, then?"

Catherine for some time never moved; she kept her eyes on the coals. At last she raised her head and looked at her aunt. "Why do you push me so?" she asked.

"I don't push you. When have I spoken to you before?"

"It seems to me that you have spoken to me several times."

"I am afraid it is necessary, then, Catherine," said Mrs. Penniman, with a good deal of solemnity. "I am afraid you don't feel the importance——" She paused a little; Catherine was looking at her. "The importance of not disappointing that gallant young heart!"

And Mrs. Penniman went back to her chair, by the lamp, and, with a little jerk, picked up the evening paper again.

Catherine stood there before the fire, with her hands behind her, looking at her aunt, to whom it seemed that the girl had never had just this dark fixedness in her gaze. "I don't think you understand— or that you know me," she said.

"If I don't, it is not wonderful; you trust me so little."

Catherine made no attempt to deny this charge, and for some- time more nothing was said. But Mrs. Penniman's imagination was restless, and the evening paper failed on this occasion to enchain it.

"If you succumb to the dread of your father's wrath," she said, "I don't know what will become of us."

"Did *he* tell you to say these things to me?"

"He told me to use my influence."

"You must be mistaken," said Catherine. "He trusts me."

"I hope he may never repent of it!" And Mrs. Penniman gave a little sharp slap to her newspaper. She knew not what to make of her niece, who had suddenly become stern and contradictious.

This tendency on Catherine's part was presently even more ap- parent. "You had much better not make any more appointments with Mr. Townsend," she said. "I don't think it is right."

Mrs. Penniman rose with considerable majesty. "My poor child, are you jealous of me?" she inquired.

"Oh, Aunt Lavinia!" murmured Catherine, blushing.

"I don't think it is your place to teach me what is right."

On this point Catherine made no concession.

"It can't be right to deceive."

"I certainly have not deceived *you*!"

"Yes; but I promised my father——"

"I have no doubt you promised your father. But I have promised him nothing!"

Catherine had to admit this, and she did so in silence. "I don't believe Mr. Townsend himself likes it," she said at last.

"Doesn't like meeting me?"

"Not in secret."

"It was not in secret; the place was full of people."

"But it was a secret place—away off in the Bowery."

Mrs. Penniman flinched a little. "Gentlemen enjoy such things," she remarked, presently. "I know what gentlemen like."

"My father wouldn't like it, if he knew."

"Pray, do you propose to inform him?" Mrs. Penniman inquired.

"No, Aunt Lavinia. But please don't do it again."

"If I do it again, you will inform him: is that what you mean? I do not share your dread of my brother; I have always known how to defend my own position. But I shall certainly never again take any step on your behalf; you are much too thankless. I knew you were not a spontaneous nature, but I believed you were firm, and I told your father that he would find you so. I am disappointed—but your father will not be!" And with this, Mrs. Penniman offered her niece a brief good-night, and withdrew to her own apartment.

XVIII

CATHERINE SAT ALONE BY the parlour fire—sat there for more than an hour, lost in her meditations. Her aunt seemed to her aggressive and foolish, and to see it so clearly—to judge Mrs. Penniman so positively—made her feel old and grave. She did not resent the imputation of weakness; it made no impression on her, for she had not the sense of weakness, and she was not hurt at not being appreciated. She had an immense respect for her father and she felt that to displease him would be a misdemeanour analogous to an act of profanity in a great temple: but her purpose had slowly ripened, and she believed that her prayers had purified it of its violence. The evening advanced, and the lamp burned dim without her noticing it; her eyes were fixed upon her terrible plan. She knew her father was in his study—that he had been there all the evening; from time to time she expected to hear him move. She thought he would perhaps come, as he sometimes came, into the parlour. At last the clock struck eleven, and the house was wrapped in silence; the servants had gone to bed. Catherine got up and went slowly to the door of the library, where she waited a moment, motionless. Then she knocked, and then she waited again. Her father had answered her, but she had not the courage to turn the latch. What she had said to her aunt was true enough—she was afraid of him; and in saying that she had no sense of weakness she meant that she was not afraid of herself. She heard him move within, and he came and opened the door for her.

"What is the matter?" asked the Doctor. "You are standing there like a ghost."

She went into the room, but it was some time before she contrived to say what she had come to say. Her father, who was in his dressing-gown and slippers, had been busy at his writing-table, and after looking at her for some moments, and waiting for her to speak, he went and seated himself at his papers again. His back was turned to her—she began to hear the scratching of his pen. She remained near the door, with her heart thumping beneath her bodice; and she was very glad that his back was turned, for it seemed to her that she could more easily address herself to this portion of his person than to his face. At last she began, watching it while she spoke.

"You told me that if I should have anything more to say about Mr. Townsend you would be glad to listen to it."

"Exactly, my dear," said the Doctor, not turning round, but stopping his pen.

Catherine wished it would go on, but she herself continued. "I thought I would tell you that I have not seen him again, but that I should like to do so."

"To bid him good-bye?" asked the Doctor.

The girl hesitated a moment. "He is not going away."

The Doctor wheeled slowly round in his chair, with a smile that seemed to accuse her of an epigram; but extremes meet, and Catherine had not intended one. "It is not to bid him good-bye, then?" her father said.

"No, father, not that; at least, not for ever. I have not seen him again, but I should like to see him," Catherine repeated.

The Doctor slowly rubbed his under lip with the feather of his quill.

"Have you written to him?"

"Yes, four times."

"You have not dismissed him, then. Once would have done that."

"No," said Catherine; "I have asked him—asked him to wait."

Her father sat looking at her, and she was afraid he was going to break out into wrath; his eyes were so fine and cold.

"You are a dear, faithful child," he said at last. "Come here to your father." And he got up, holding out his hands toward her.

The words were a surprise, and they gave her an exquisite joy. She went to him, and he put his arm round her tenderly, soothingly; and then he kissed her. After this he said—

"Do you wish to make me very happy?"

"I should like to—but I am afraid I can't," Catherine answered.

"You can if you will. It all depends on your will."

"Is it to give him up?" said Catherine.

"Yes, it is to give him up."

And he held her still, with the same tenderness, looking into her face and resting his eyes on her averted eyes. There was a long silence; she wished he would release her.

"You are happier than I, father," she said, at last.

"I have no doubt you are unhappy just now. But it is better to be unhappy for three months and get over it, than for many years and never get over it."

"Yes, if that were so," said Catherine.

"It would be so; I am sure of that." She answered nothing, and he went on. "Have you no faith in my wisdom, in my tenderness, in my solicitude for your future?"

"Oh, father!" murmured the girl.

"Don't you suppose that I know something of men: their vices, their follies, their falsities?"

She detached herself, and turned upon him. "He is not vicious — he is not false!"

Her father kept looking at her with his sharp, pure eye. "You make nothing of my judgment, then?"

"I can't believe that!"

"I don't ask you to believe it, but to take it on trust."

Catherine was far from saying to herself that this was an ingenious sophism; but she met the appeal none the less squarely. "What has he done — what do you know?"

"He has never done anything — he is a selfish idler."

"Oh, father, don't abuse him!" she exclaimed, pleadingly.

"I don't mean to abuse him; it would be a great mistake. You may do as you choose," he added, turning away.

"I may see him again?"

"Just as you choose."

"Will you forgive me?"

"By no means."

"It will only be for once."

"I don't know what you mean by once. You must either give him up or continue the acquaintance."

"I wish to explain — to tell him to wait."

"To wait for what?"

"Till you know him better — till you consent."

"Don't tell him any such nonsense as that. I know him well enough, and I shall never consent."

"But we can wait a long time," said poor Catherine, in a tone which was meant to express the humblest conciliation, but which had upon her father's nerves the effect of an iteration not characterised by tact.

The Doctor answered, however, quietly enough: "Of course you can wait till I die, if you like."

Catherine gave a cry of natural horror.

"Your engagement will have one delightful effect upon you; it will make you extremely impatient for that event."

Catherine stood staring, and the Doctor enjoyed the point he made. It came to Catherine with the force—or rather with the vague impressiveness—of a logical axiom which it was not in her province to controvert; and yet, though it was a scientific truth, she felt wholly unable to accept it.

"I would rather not marry, if that were true," she said.

"Give me a proof of it, then; for it is beyond a question that by engaging yourself to Morris Townsend you simply wait for my death."

She turned away, feeling sick and faint; and the Doctor went on. "And if you wait for it with impatience, judge, if you please, what *his* eagerness will be!"

Catherine turned it over—her father's words had such an authority for her that her very thoughts were capable of obeying him. There was a dreadful ugliness in it, which seemed to glare at her through the interposing medium of her own feebler reason. Suddenly, however, she had an inspiration—she almost knew it to be an inspiration.

"If I don't marry before your death, I will not after," she said.

To her father, it must be admitted, this seemed only another epigram; and as obstinacy, in unaccomplished minds, does not usually select such a mode of expression, he was the more surprised at this wanton play of a fixed idea.*

"Do you mean that for an impertinence?" he inquired; an inquiry of which, as he made it, he quite perceived the grossness.

"An impertinence? Oh, father, what terrible things you say!"

"If you don't wait for my death, you might as well marry immediately; there is nothing else to wait for."

---

*Obsession; from *idée fixe* (French).

For some time Catherine made no answer; but finally she said—

"I think Morris—little by little—might persuade you."

"I shall never let him speak to me again. I dislike him too much."

Catherine gave a long, low sigh; she tried to stifle it, for she had made up her mind that it was wrong to make a parade of her trouble, and to endeavour to act upon her father by the meretricious aid of emotion. Indeed, she even thought it wrong—in the sense of being inconsiderate—to attempt to act upon his feelings at all; her part was to effect some gentle, gradual change in his intellectual perception of poor Morris's character. But the means of effecting such a change were at present shrouded in mystery, and she felt miserably helpless and hopeless. She had exhausted all arguments, all replies. Her father might have pitied her, and in fact he did so; but he was sure he was right.

"There is one thing you can tell Mr. Townsend, when you see him again," he said: "that if you marry without my consent, I don't leave you a farthing of money. That will interest him more than anything else you can tell him."

"That would be very right," Catherine answered. "I ought not in that case have a farthing of your money."

"My dear child," the Doctor observed, laughing, "your simplicity is touching. Make that remark, in that tone, and with that expression of countenance, to Mr. Townsend and take a note of his answer. It won't be polite—it will express irritation; and I shall be glad of that, as it will put me in the right; unless, indeed—which is perfectly possible—you should like him the better for being rude to you."

"He will never be rude to me," said Catherine, gently.

"Tell him what I say, all the same."

She looked at her father, and her quiet eyes filled with tears.

"I think I will see him, then," she murmured, in her timid voice.

"Exactly as you choose!" And he went to the door and opened it for her to go out. The movement gave her a terrible sense of his turning her off.

"It will be only once, for the present," she added, lingering a moment.

"Exactly as you choose," he repeated, standing there with his hand on the door. "I have told you what I think. If you see him, you will be an ungrateful, cruel child; you will have given your old father the greatest pain of his life."

This was more than the poor girl could bear; her tears overflowed, and she moved towards her grimly consistent parent with a pitiful cry. Her hands were raised in supplication, but he sternly evaded this appeal. Instead of letting her sob out her misery on his shoulder, he simply took her by the arm and directed her course across the threshold, closing the door gently but firmly behind her. After he had done so, he remained listening. For a long time there was no sound; he knew that she was standing outside. He was sorry for her, as I have said; but he was so sure he was right. At last he heard her move away, and then her footstep creaked faintly upon the stairs.

The Doctor took several turns round his study, with his hands in his pockets, and a thin sparkle, possibly of irritation, but partly also of something like humour, in his eye. "By Jove," he said to himself, "I believe she will stick—I believe she will stick!" And this idea of Catherine "sticking" appeared to have a comical side, and to offer a prospect of entertainment. He determined, as he said to himself, to see it out.

XIX

IT WAS FOR REASONS connected with this determination that on the morrow he sought a few words of private conversation with Mrs. Penniman. He sent for her to the library, and he there informed her that he hoped very much that, as regarded this affair of Catherine's, she would mind her *p*'s and *q*'s.

"I don't know what you mean by such an expression," said his sister. "You speak as if I were learning the alphabet."

"The alphabet of common sense is something you will never learn," the Doctor permitted himself to respond.

"Have you called me here to insult me?" Mrs. Penniman inquired.

"Not at all. Simply to advise you. You have taken up young Townsend; that's your own affair. I have nothing to do with your sentiments, your fancies, your affections, your delusions; but what I request of you is that you will keep these things to yourself. I have explained my views to Catherine; she understands them perfectly, and anything that she does further in the way of encouraging Mr. Townsend's attentions will be in deliberate opposition to my wishes. Anything that you should do in the way of giving her aid and comfort will be — permit me the expression — distinctly treasonable. You know high treason is a capital offence; take care how you incur the penalty."

Mrs. Penniman threw back her head, with a certain expansion of the eye which she occasionally practised. "It seems to me that you talk like a great autocrat."

"I talk like my daughter's father."

"Not like your sister's brother!" cried Lavinia.

"My dear Lavinia," said the Doctor, "I sometimes wonder whether I am your brother. We are so extremely different. In spite of differences, however, we can, at a pinch, understand each other; and that is the essential thing just now. Walk straight with regard to Mr. Townsend; that's all I ask. It is highly probable you have been corresponding with him for the last three weeks—perhaps even seeing him. I don't ask you—you needn't tell me." He had a moral conviction that she would contrive to tell a fib about the matter, which it would disgust him to listen to. "Whatever you have done, stop doing it. That's all I wish."

"Don't you wish also by chance to murder your child?" Mrs. Penniman inquired.

"On the contrary, I wish to make her live and be happy."

"You will kill her; she passed a dreadful night."

"She won't die of one dreadful night, nor of a dozen. Remember that I am a distinguished physician."

Mrs. Penniman hesitated a moment. Then she risked her retort. "Your being a distinguished physician has not prevented you from already losing *two members* of your family!"

She had risked it, but her brother gave her such a terribly incisive look—a look so like a surgeon's lancet* —that she was frightened at her courage. And he answered her in words that corresponded to the look: "It may not prevent me, either, from losing the society of still another."

Mrs. Penniman took herself off, with whatever air of depreciated merit was at her command, and repaired to Catherine's room, where the poor girl was closeted. She knew all about her dreadful night, for the two had met again, the evening before, after Catherine left her father. Mrs. Penniman was on the landing of the second floor when her niece came upstairs. It was not remarkable that a person of so much subtlety should have discovered that Catherine had been shut up with the Doctor. It was still less remarkable that she should have felt an extreme curiosity to learn the result of this interview, and that this sentiment, combined with her great amiability and generosity, should have prompted her to regret the sharp words lately exchanged between her niece and herself. As the unhappy girl came into sight, in the dusky corridor, she made a lively demonstration of sympathy. Catherine's bursting heart was equally oblivious. She only knew that her aunt was taking her into her arms. Mrs. Penniman drew her into Catherine's own room, and the two women sat there together, far into the small hours; the younger one

---

*Pointed and often double-edged surgical instrument used for making small incisions.

with her head on the other's lap, sobbing and sobbing at first in a soundless, stifled manner, and then at last perfectly still. It gratified Mrs. Penniman to be able to feel conscientiously that this scene virtually removed the interdict which Catherine had placed upon her further communion with Morris Townsend. She was not gratified, however, when, in coming back to her niece's room before breakfast, she found that Catherine had risen and was preparing herself for this meal.

"You should not go to breakfast," she said; "you are not well enough, after your fearful night."

"Yes, I am very well, and I am only afraid of being late."

"I can't understand you!" Mrs. Penniman cried. "You should stay in bed for three days."

"Oh, I could never do that!" said Catherine, to whom this idea presented no attractions.

Mrs. Penniman was in despair, and she noted, with extreme annoyance, that the trace of the night's tears had completely vanished from Catherine's eyes. She had a most impracticable *physique*. "What effect do you expect to have upon your father," her aunt demanded, "if you come plumping down, without a vestige of any sort of feeling, as if nothing in the world had happened?"

"He would not like me to lie in bed," said Catherine, simply.

"All the more reason for your doing it. How else do you expect to move him?"

Catherine thought a little. "I don't know how; but not in that way. I wish to be just as usual." And she finished dressing, and according to her aunt's expression, went plumping down into the paternal presence. She was really too modest for consistent pathos.

And yet it was perfectly true that she had had a dreadful night. Even after Mrs. Penniman left her she had had no sleep. She lay staring at the uncomforting gloom, with her eyes and ears filled with the movement with which her father had turned her out of his room, and of the words in which he had told her that she was a heartless daughter. Her heart was breaking. She had heart enough for that. At moments it seemed to her that she believed him, and that to do what she was doing, a girl must indeed be bad. She *was* bad; but she couldn't help it. She would try to appear good, even if her heart were perverted; and from time to time she had a fancy that she might accomplish something by ingenious concessions to form,

Henry James

though she should persist in caring for Morris. Catherine's ingenuities were indefinite, and we are not called upon to expose their hollowness. The best of them perhaps showed itself in that freshness of aspect which was so discouraging to Mrs. Penniman, who was amazed at the absence of haggardness in a young woman who for a whole night had lain quivering beneath a father's curse. Poor Catherine was conscious of her freshness; it gave her a feeling about the future which rather added to the weight upon her mind. It seemed a proof that she was strong and solid and dense, and would live to a great age—longer than might be generally convenient; and this idea was depressing, for it appeared to saddle her with a pretension the more, just when the cultivation of any pretension was inconsistent with her doing right. She wrote that day to Morris Townsend, requesting him to come and see her on the morrow; using very few words, and explaining nothing. She would explain everything face to face.

XX

ON THE MORROW, IN the afternoon, she heard his voice at the door, and his step in the hall. She received him in the big, bright front-parlour, and she instructed the servant that if any one should call she was particularly engaged. She was not afraid of her father's coming in, for at that hour he was always driving about town. When Morris stood there before her, the first thing that she was conscious of was that he was even more beautiful to look at than fond recollection had painted him; the next was that he had pressed her in his arms. When she was free again it appeared to her that she had now indeed thrown herself into the gulf of defiance, and even, for an instant, that she had been married to him.

He told her that she had been very cruel, and had made him very unhappy; and Catherine felt acutely the difficulty of her destiny, which forced her to give pain in such opposite quarters. But she wished that, instead of reproaches, however tender, he would give her help; he was certainly wise enough, and clever enough, to invent some issue from their troubles. She expressed this belief, and Morris received the assurance as if he thought it natural; but he interrogated, at first—as was natural too—rather than committed himself to marking out a course.

"You should not have made me wait so long," he said. "I don't know how I have been living; every hour seemed like years. You should have decided sooner."

"Decided?" Catherine asked.

"Decided whether you would keep me or give me up."

"Oh, Morris," she cried, with a long tender murmur, "I never thought of giving you up!"

"What, then, were you waiting for?" The young man was ardently logical.

"I thought my father might—might——" and she hesitated.

"Might see how unhappy you were?"

"Oh, no! But that he might look at it differently."

"And now you have sent for me to tell me that at last he does so. Is that it?"

This hypothetical optimism gave the poor girl a pang. "No, Morris," she said solemnly, "he looks at it still the same way."

"Then why have you sent for me?"

"Because I wanted to see you!" cried Catherine piteously.

"That's an excellent reason, surely. But did you want to look at me only? Have you nothing to tell me?"

His beautiful persuasive eyes were fixed upon her face, and she wondered what answer would be noble enough to make to such a gaze as that. For a moment her own eyes took it in, and then—"I *did* want to look at you!" she said, gently. But after this speech, most inconsistently, she hid her face.

Morris watched her for a moment, attentively. "Will you marry me to-morrow?" he asked suddenly.

"To-morrow?"

"Next week, then. Any time within a month."

"Isn't it better to wait?" said Catherine.

"To wait for what?"

She hardly knew for what; but this tremendous leap alarmed her. "Till we have thought about it a little more."

He shook his head, sadly and reproachfully. "I thought you had been thinking about it these three weeks. Do you want to turn it over in your mind for five years? You have given me more than time enough. My poor girl," he added in a moment, "you are not sincere!"

Catherine coloured from brow to chin, and her eyes filled with tears. "Oh, how can you say that?" she murmured.

"Why, you must take me or leave me," said Morris, very reasonably. "You can't please your father and me both; you must choose between us."

"I have chosen you!" she said, passionately.

"Then marry me next week."

She stood gazing at him. "Isn't there any other way?"

"None that I know of for arriving at the same result. If there is, I should be happy to hear of it."

Catherine could think of nothing of the kind, and Morris's luminosity seemed almost pitiless. The only thing she could think of was that her father might after all come round, and she articulated, with an awkward sense of her helplessness in doing so, a wish that this miracle might happen.

"Do you think it is in the least degree likely?" Morris asked.

"It would be, if he could only know you!"

"He can know me if he will. What is to prevent it?"

"His ideas, his reasons," said Catherine. "They are so—so terribly strong." She trembled with the recollection of them yet.

"Strong?" cried Morris. "I would rather you should think them weak."

"Oh, nothing about my father is weak!" said the girl.

Morris turned away, walking to the window, where he stood looking out. "You are terribly afraid of him!" he remarked at last.

She felt no impulse to deny it, because she had no shame in it; for if it was no honour to herself, at least it was an honour to him. "I suppose I must be," she said, simply.

"Then you don't love me—not as I love you. If you fear your father more than you love me, then your love is not what I hoped it was."

"Ah, my friend!" she said, going to him.

"Do *I* fear anything?" he demanded, turning round on her. "For your sake what am I not ready to face?"

"You are noble—you are brave!" she answered, stopping short at a distance that was almost respectful.

"Small good it does me, if you are so timid."

"I don't think that I am—*really*," said Catherine.

"I don't know what you mean by 'really.' It is really enough to make us miserable."

"I should be strong enough to wait—to wait a long time."

"And suppose after a long time your father should hate me worse than ever?"

"He wouldn't—he couldn't!"

"He would be touched by my fidelity? Is that what you mean? If he is so easily touched, then why should you be afraid of him?"

This was much to the point, and Catherine was struck by it.

"I will try not to be," she said. And she stood there, submissively, the image, in advance, of a dutiful and responsible wife. This image could not fail to recommend itself to Morris Townsend, and he continued to give proof of the high estimation in which he held her. It could only have been at the prompting of such a sentiment that he presently mentioned to her that the course recommended by Mrs. Penniman was an immediate union, regardless of consequences.

"Yes, Aunt Penniman would like that," Catherine said, simply—and yet with a certain shrewdness. It must, however, have been in pure simplicity, and from motives quite untouched by sarcasm, that, a few moments after, she went on to say to Morris that her father had given her a message for him. It was quite on her conscience to deliver this message, and had the mission been ten times more painful she would have as scrupulously performed it. "He told me to tell you—to tell you very distinctly, and directly from himself, that if I marry without his consent, I shall not inherit a penny of his fortune. He made a great point of this. He seemed to think—he seemed to think——"

Morris flushed, as any young man of spirit might have flushed at an imputation of baseness.

"What did he seem to think?"

"That it would make a difference."

"It *will* make a difference—in many things. We shall be by many thousands of dollars the poorer; and that is a great difference. But it will make none in my affection."

"We shall not want the money," said Catherine; "for you know I have a good deal myself."

"Yes, my dear girl, I know you have something. And he can't touch that!"

"He would never," said Catherine. "My mother left it to me."

Morris was silent awhile. "He was very positive about this, was he?" he asked at last. "He thought such a message would annoy me terribly, and make me throw off the mask, eh?"

"I don't know what he thought," said Catherine, wearily.

"Please tell him that I care for his message as much as for that!" And Morris snapped his fingers sonorously.

"I don't think I could tell him that."

"Do you know you sometimes disappoint me?" said Morris.

"I should think I might. I disappoint every one—father and Aunt Penniman."

"Well, it doesn't matter with me, because I am fonder of you than they are."

"Yes, Morris," said the girl, with her imagination—what there was of it—swimming in this happy truth, which seemed, after all, invidious to no one.

"Is it your belief that he will stick to it—stick to it for ever, to this idea of disinheriting you?—that your goodness and patience will never wear out his cruelty?"

"The trouble is that if I marry you, he will think I am not good. He will think that a proof."

"Ah, then, he will never forgive you!"

This idea, sharply expressed by Morris's handsome lips, renewed for a moment, to the poor girl's temporarily pacified conscience, all its dreadful vividness. "Oh, you must love me very much!" she cried.

"There is no doubt of that, my dear!" her lover rejoined. "You don't like that word 'disinherited,'" he added in a moment.

"It isn't the money; it is that he should—that he should feel so."

"I suppose it seems to you a kind of curse," said Morris. "It must be very dismal. But don't you think," he went on presently, "that if you were to try to be very clever, and to set rightly about it, you might in the end conjure it away? Don't you think," he continued further, in a tone of sympathetic speculation, "that a really clever woman, in your place, might bring him round at last? Don't you think——"

Here, suddenly, Morris was interrupted; these ingenious inquiries had not reached Catherine's ears. The terrible word "disinheritance," with all its impressive moral reprobation, was still ringing there; seemed indeed to gather force as it lingered. The mortal chill of her situation struck more deeply into her childlike heart, and she was overwhelmed by a feeling of loneliness and danger. But her refuge was there, close to her, and she put out her hands to grasp it. "Ah, Morris," she said, with a shudder, "I will marry you as soon as you please!" And she surrendered herself, leaning her head on his shoulder.

"My dear good girl!" he exclaimed, looking down at his prize. And then he looked up again rather vaguely, with parted lips and lifted eyebrows.

XXI

Dr. Sloper very soon imparted his conviction to Mrs. Almond, in the same terms in which he had announced it to himself. "She's going to stick, by Jove! she's going to stick."

"Do you mean that she is going to marry him?" Mrs. Almond inquired.

"I don't know that; but she is not going to break down. She is going to drag out the engagement, in the hope of making me relent."

"And shall you not relent?"

"Shall a geometrical proposition relent? I am not so superficial."

"Doesn't geometry treat of surfaces?" asked Mrs. Almond, who, as we know, was clever, smiling.

"Yes; but it treats of them profoundly. Catherine and her young man are my surfaces; I have taken their measure."

"You speak as if it surprised you."

"It is immense; there will be a great deal to observe."

"You are shockingly cold-blooded!" said Mrs. Almond.

"I need to be, with all this hot blood about me. Young Townsend indeed is cool; I must allow him that merit."

"I can't judge him," Mrs. Almond answered; "but I am not at all surprised at Catherine."

"I confess I am a little; she must have been so deucedly divided and bothered."

"Say it amuses you outright! I don't see why it should be such a joke that your daughter adores you."

"It is the point where the adoration stops that I find it interesting to fix."

"It stops where the other sentiment begins."

"Not at all—that would be simple enough. The two things are extremely mixed up, and the mixture is extremely odd. It will produce some third element, and that's what I am waiting to see. I wait with suspense—with positive excitement; and that is a sort of emotion that

I didn't suppose Catherine would ever provide for me. I am really very much obliged to her."

"She will cling," said Mrs. Almond; "she will certainly cling."

"Yes; as I say, she will stick."

"Cling is prettier. That's what those very simple natures always do, and nothing could be simpler than Catherine. She doesn't take many impressions; but when she takes one she keeps it. She is like a copper kettle that receives a dent; you may polish up the kettle, but you can't efface the mark."

"We must try and polish up Catherine," said the Doctor. "I will take her to Europe."

"She won't forget him in Europe."

"He will forget her, then."

Mrs. Almond looked grave. "Should you really like that?"

"Extremely!" said the Doctor.

Mrs. Penniman, meanwhile, lost little time in putting herself again in communication with Morris Townsend. She requested him to favour her with another interview, but she did not on this occasion select an oyster-saloon as the scene of their meeting. She proposed that he should join her at the door of a certain church, after service on Sunday afternoon, and she was careful not to appoint the place of worship which she usually visited, and where, as she said, the congregation would have spied upon her. She picked out a less elegant resort, and on issuing from its portal at the hour she had fixed she saw the young man standing apart. She offered him no recognition till she had crossed the street and he had followed her to some distance. Here, with a smile — "Excuse my apparent want of cordiality," she said. "You know what to believe about that. Prudence before everything." And on his asking her in what direction they should walk, "Where we shall be least observed," she murmured.

Morris was not in high good-humour, and his response to this speech was not particularly gallant. "I don't flatter myself we shall be much observed anywhere." Then he turned recklessly toward the centre of the town. "I hope you have come to tell me that he has knocked under," he went on.

"I am afraid I am not altogether a harbinger of good; and yet, too, I am to a certain extent a messenger of peace. I have been thinking a great deal, Mr. Townsend," said Mrs. Penniman.

"You think too much."

"I suppose I do; but I can't help it; my mind is so terribly active. When I give myself, I give myself. I pay the penalty in my headaches, my famous headaches—a perfect circlet of pain! But I carry it as a queen carries her crown. Would you believe that I have one now? I wouldn't, however, have missed our rendezvous for anything. I have something very important to tell you."

"Well let's have it," said Morris.

"I was perhaps a little headlong the other day in advising you to marry immediately. I have been thinking it over, and now I see it just a little differently."

"You seem to have a great many different ways of seeing the same object."

"Their number is infinite!" said Mrs. Penniman, in a tone which seemed to suggest that this convenient faculty was one of her brightest attributes.

"I recommend you to take one way and stick to it," Morris replied.

"Ah! but it isn't easy to choose. My imagination is never quiet, never satisfied. It makes me a bad adviser, perhaps; but it makes me a capital friend!"

"A capital friend who gives bad advice!" said Morris.

"Not intentionally—and who hurries off, at every risk, to make the most humble excuses!"

"Well, what do you advise me now?"

"To be very patient; to watch and wait."

"And is that bad advice or good?"

"That is not for me to say," Mrs. Penniman rejoined, with some dignity. "I only pretend it's sincere."

"And will you come to me next week and recommend something different and equally sincere?"

"I may come to you next week and tell you that I am in the streets!"

"In the streets?"

"I have had a terrible scene with my brother, and he threatens, if anything happens, to turn me out of the house. You know I am a poor woman."

Morris had a speculative idea that she had a little property; but he naturally did not press this.

'I should be very sorry to see you suffer martyrdom for me," he said. "But you make your brother out a regular Turk."*

Mrs. Penniman hesitated a little.

"I certainly do not regard Austin as a satisfactory Christian."

" And am I to wait till he is converted?"

"Wait at any rate till he is less violent. Bide your time, Mr. Townsend; remember the prize is great!"

Morris walked along some time in silence, tapping the railings and gateposts very sharply with his stick.

"You certainly are devilish inconsistent!" he broke out at last. "I have already got Catherine to consent to a private marriage."

Mrs. Penniman was indeed inconsistent, for at this news she gave a little jump of gratification.

"Oh! when and where?" she cried. And then she stopped short.

Morris was a little vague about this.

"That isn't fixed; but she consents. It's deuced awkward, now, to back out."

Mrs. Penniman, as I say, had stopped short; and she stood there with her eyes fixed, brilliantly, on her companion.

"Mr. Townsend," she proceeded, "shall I tell you something? Catherine loves you so much that you may do anything."

This declaration was slightly ambiguous, and Morris opened his eyes.

"I am happy to hear it! But what do you mean by 'anything'?"

"You may postpone—you may change about; she won't think the worse of you."

Morris stood there still, with his raised eyebrows; then he said simply and rather dryly—"Ah!" After this he remarked to Mrs. Penniman that if she walked so slowly she would attract notice, and he succeeded, after a fashion, in hurrying her back to the domicile of which her tenure had become so insecure.

---

*Brutal or tyrannical person.

XXII

He had slightly misrepresented the matter in saying that Catherine had consented to take the great step. We left her just now declaring that she would burn her ships behind her; but Morris, after having elicited this declaration, had become conscious of good reasons for not taking it up. He avoided, gracefully enough, fixing a day, though he left her under the impression that he had his eye on one. Catherine may have had her difficulties; but those of her circumspect suitor are also worthy of consideration. The prize was certainly great; but it was only to be won by striking the happy mean between precipitancy and caution. It would be all very well to take one's jump and trust to Providence; Providence was more especially on the side of clever people, and clever people were known by an indisposition to risk their bones. The ultimate reward of a union with a young woman who was both unattractive and impoverished ought to be connected with immediate disadvantages by some very palpable chain. Between the fear of losing Catherine and her possible fortune altogether, and the fear of taking her too soon and finding this possible fortune as void of actuality as a collection of emptied bottles, it was not comfortable for Morris Townsend to choose; a fact that should be remembered by readers disposed to judge harshly of a young man who may have struck them as making but an indifferently successful use of fine natural parts. He had not forgotten that in any event Catherine had her own ten thousand a year; he had devoted an abundance of meditation to this circumstance. But with his fine parts he rated himself high, and he had a perfectly definite appreciation of his value, which seemed to him inadequately represented by the sum I have mentioned. At the same time he reminded himself that this sum was considerable, that everything is relative, and that if a modest income is less desirable than a large one, the complete absence of revenue is nowhere accounted an advantage. These reflections gave him plenty of occupation, and made it necessary that he should trim his sail. Dr. Sloper's opposition was the unknown quantity in the problem he had to work out. The natural way to work it out was by marrying Catherine; but in mathematics there are many short cuts, and Morris was not without a hope that he should yet discover one. When Catherine took him at his word and consented to renounce the attempt to mollify her father, he drew back skilfully enough, as I have said, and kept the wedding-day still an open question. Her faith in his sincerity was so complete that she was incapable of suspecting that he was playing with her; her trouble just now was of another kind. The poor girl had an admirable sense of honour; and from the moment she had brought herself to the point of violating her father's wish, it seemed to her that she had no right to enjoy his protection. It was on her conscience that she ought to live under his roof only so long as she conformed to his wisdom. There was a great deal of glory in such a position, but poor Catherine felt that she had forfeited her claim to it. She had cast her lot with a young man against whom he had solemnly warned her, and broken the contract under which he provided her with a happy home. She could not give up the young man, so she must leave the home; and the sooner the object of her preference offered her another, the sooner her situation would lose its awkward twist. This was close reasoning; but it was commingled with an infinite amount of merely instinctive penitence. Catherine's days, at this time, were dismal, and the weight of some of her hours was almost more than she could bear. Her father never looked at her, never spoke to her. He knew perfectly what he was about, and this was part of a plan. She looked at him as much as she dared (for she was afraid of seeming to offer herself to his observation), and she pitied him for the sorrow she had brought upon him. She held up her head and busied her hands, and went about her daily occupations; and when the state of things in Washington Square seemed intolerable, she closed her eyes and indulged herself with an intellectual vision of the man for whose sake she had broken a sacred law. Mrs. Penniman, of the three persons in Washington Square, had much the most of the manner that belongs to a great crisis. If Catherine was quiet, she was quietly quiet, as I may say, and her pathetic effects, which there was no one to notice, were entirely unstudied and unintended. If the Doctor was stiff and dry and absolutely indifferent to the presence of his companions, it was so lightly, neatly, easily done, that you would have had to know him well to discover that on the whole he rather enjoyed having to be so disagreeable. But Mrs. Penniman was elaborately reserved and significantly silent; there was a richer rustle in the very deliberate movements to which she confined herself, and when she occasionally spoke, in connection with some very trivial event, she had the air of meaning something deeper than what she said. Between Catherine and her father nothing had passed since the evening she went to speak to him in his study. She had something to say to him—it seemed to her she ought to say it; but she kept it back, for fear of irritating him. He also had something to say to her; but he was determined not to speak first. He was interested, as we know, in seeing how, if she were left to herself, she would "stick." At last she told him she had seen Morris Townsend again, and that their relations remained quite the same.

"I think we shall marry—before very long. And probably, meanwhile, I shall see him rather often; about once a week, not more."

The Doctor looked at her coldly from head to foot, as if she had been a stranger. It was the first time his eyes had rested on her for a week, which was fortunate, if that was to be their expression. "Why not three times a day?" he asked. "What prevents your meeting as often as you choose?"

She turned away a moment; there were tears in her eyes. Then she said, "It is better once a week."

"I don't see how it is better. It is as bad as it can be. If you flatter yourself that I care for little modifications of that sort, you are very much mistaken. It is as wrong of you to see him once a week as it would be to see him all day long. Not that it matters to me, however."

Catherine tried to follow these words, but they seemed to lead towards a vague horror from which she recoiled. "I think we shall marry pretty soon," she repeated at last.

Her father gave her his dreadful look again, as if she were some one else. "Why do you tell me that? It's no concern of mine."

"Oh, father!" she broke out, "don't you care, even if you do feel so?"

"Not a button. Once you marry, it's quite the same to me when or where or why you do it; and if you think to compound for your folly by hoisting your flag in this way, you may spare yourself the trouble."

With this he turned away. But the next day he spoke to her of his own accord, and his manner was somewhat changed. "Shall you be married within the next four or five months?" he asked.

"I don't know, father," said Catherine. "It is not very easy for us to make up our minds."

"Put it off, then, for six months, and in the meantime I will take you to Europe. I should like you very much to go."

It gave her such delight, after his words of the day before, to hear that he should "like" her to do something, and that he still had in his heart any of the tenderness of preference, that she gave a little exclamation of joy. But then she became conscious that Morris was not included in this proposal, and that—as regards really going— she would greatly prefer to remain at home with him. But she blushed, none the less, more comfortably than she had done of late. "It would be delightful to go to Europe," she remarked, with a sense that the idea was not original, and that her tone was not all it might be.

"Very well, then, we will go. Pack up your clothes."

"I had better tell Mr. Townsend," said Catherine.

Her father fixed his cold eyes upon her. "If you mean that you had better ask his leave, all that remains to me is to hope he will give it."

The girl was sharply touched by the pathetic ring of the words; it was the most calculated, the most dramatic little speech the Doctor had ever uttered. She felt that it was a great thing for her, under the circumstances, to have this fine opportunity of showing him her respect; and yet there was something else that she felt as well, and that she presently expressed. "I sometimes think that if I do what you dislike so much, I ought not to stay with you."

"To stay with me?"

"If I live with you, I ought to obey you."

"If that's your theory, it's certainly mine," said the Doctor, with a dry laugh.

"But if I don't obey you, I ought not to live with you—to enjoy your kindness and protection."

This striking argument gave the Doctor a sudden sense of having underestimated his daughter; it seemed even more than worthy of a young woman who had revealed the quality of unaggressive obstinacy. But it displeased him—displeased him deeply, and he signified as much. "That idea is in very bad taste," he said. "Did you get it from Mr. Townsend?"

"Oh no; it's my own!" said Catherine eagerly.

"Keep it to yourself, then," her father answered, more than ever determined she should go to Europe.

XXIII

I_F M_{ORRIS} T_{OWNSEND} _{WAS} not to be included in this journey, no more was Mrs. Penniman, who would have been thankful for an invitation, but who (to do her justice) bore her disappointment in a perfectly lady-like manner. "I should enjoy seeing the works of Raphael[9] and the ruins—the ruins of the Pantheon,"* she said to Mrs. Almond; "but on the other hand, I shall not be sorry to be alone and at peace for the next few months in Washington Square. I want rest; I have been through so much in the last four months." Mrs. Almond thought it rather cruel that her brother should not take poor Lavinia abroad; but she easily understood that, if the purpose of his expedition was to make Catherine forget her lover, it was not in his interest to give his daughter this young man's best friend as a companion. "If Lavinia had not been so foolish, she might visit the ruins of the Pantheon," she said to herself; and she continued to regret her sister's folly, even though the latter assured her that she had often heard the relics in question most satisfactorily described by Mr. Penniman. Mrs. Penniman was perfectly aware that her brother's motive in undertaking a foreign tour was to lay a trap for Catherine's constancy; and she imparted this conviction very frankly to her niece.

"He thinks it will make you forget Morris," she said (she always called the young man "Morris" now); "out of sight, out of mind, you know. He thinks that all the things you will see over there will drive him out of your thoughts."

Catherine looked greatly alarmed. "If he thinks that, I ought to tell him beforehand."

Mrs. Penniman shook her head. "Tell him afterwards, my dear! After he has had all the trouble and the expense! That's the way to

---

*Circular temple in Rome dedicated to the gods, built by Emperor Hadrian between A.D. 118 and 125; its design influenced numerous architects from the Renaissance onward.

serve him." And she added, in a softer key, that it must be delightful to think of those who love us among the ruins of the Pantheon.

Her father's displeasure had cost the girl, as we know, a great deal of deep-welling sorrow—sorrow of the purest and most generous kind, without a touch of resentment or rancour; but for the first time, after he had dismissed with such contemptuous brevity her apology for being a charge upon him, there was a spark of anger in her grief. She had felt his contempt; it had scorched her; that speech about her bad taste made her ears burn for three days. During this period she was less considerate; she had an idea—a rather vague one, but it was agreeable to her sense of injury—that now she was absolved from penance, and might do what she chose. She chose to write to Morris Townsend to meet her in the Square and take her to walk about the town. If she were going to Europe out of respect to her father, she might at least give herself this satisfaction. She felt in every way at present more free and more resolute; there was a force that urged her. Now at last, completely and unreservedly, her passion possessed her.

Morris met her at last, and they took a long walk. She told him immediately what had happened—that her father wished to take her away. It would be for six months, to Europe; she would do absolutely what Morris should think best. She hoped inexpressibly that he would think it best she should stay at home. It was some time before he said what he thought: he asked, as they walked along, a great many questions. There was one that especially struck her; it seemed so incongruous.

"Should you like to see all those celebrated things over there?"

"Oh, no, Morris!" said Catherine quite deprecatingly.

"Gracious Heaven, what a dull woman!" Morris exclaimed to himself.

"He thinks I will forget you," said Catherine; "that all these things will drive you out of my mind."

"Well, my dear, perhaps they will!"

"Please don't say that," Catherine answered gently, as they walked along. "Poor father will be disappointed."

Morris gave a little laugh. "Yes, I verily believe that your poor father will be disappointed! But you will have seen Europe," he added humorously. "What a take-in!"

"I don't care for seeing Europe," Catherine said.

"You ought to care, my dear. And it may mollify your father."

Catherine, conscious of her obstinacy, expected little of this, and could not rid herself of the idea that in going abroad and yet remaining firm, she should play her father a trick. "Don't you think it would be a kind of deception?" she asked.

"Doesn't he want to deceive you?" cried Morris. "It will serve him right! I really think you had better go."

"And not be married for so long?"

"Be married when you come back. You can buy your wedding-clothes in Paris." And then Morris, with great kindness of tone, explained his view of the matter. It would be a good thing that she should go; it would put them completely in the right. It would show they were reasonable and willing to wait. Once they were so sure of each other, they could afford to wait—what had they to fear? If there was a particle of chance that her father would be favourably affected by her going, that ought to settle it; for, after all, Morris was very unwilling to be the cause of her being disinherited. It was not for himself, it was for her and for her children. He was willing to wait for her; it would be hard, but he could do it. And over there, among beautiful scenes and noble monuments, perhaps the old gentleman would be softened; such things were supposed to exert a humanising influence. He might be touched by her gentleness, her patience, her willingness to make any sacrifice but *that* one; and if she should appeal to him some day, in some celebrated spot—in Italy, say, in the evening; in Venice, in a gondola, by moonlight—if she should be a little clever about it and touch the right chord, perhaps he would fold her in his arms and tell her that he forgave her. Catherine was immensely struck with this conception of the affair, which seemed eminently worthy of her lover's brilliant intellect; though she viewed it askance in so far as it depended upon her own powers of execution. The idea of being "clever" in a gondola by moonlight appeared to her to involve elements of which her grasp was not active. But it was settled between them that she should tell her father that she was ready to follow him obediently anywhere, making the mental reservation that she loved Morris Townsend more than ever.

She informed the Doctor she was ready to embark, and he made rapid arrangements for this event. Catherine had many farewells to make, but with only two of them are we actively concerned. Mrs. Penniman took a discriminating view of her niece's journey; it seemed to her very proper that Mr. Townsend's destined bride should wish to embellish her mind by a foreign tour.

"You leave him in good hands," she said, pressing her lips to Catherine's forehead. (She was very fond of kissing people's foreheads; it was an involuntary expression of sympathy with the intellectual part.) "I shall see him often; I shall feel like one of the vestals of old, tending the sacred flame."*

"You behave beautifully about not going with us," Catherine answered, not presuming to examine this analogy.

"It is my pride that keeps me up," said Mrs. Penniman, tapping the body of her dress, which always gave forth a sort of metallic ring.

Catherine's parting with her lover was short, and few words were exchanged.

"Shall I find you just the same when I come back?" she asked; though the question was not the fruit of scepticism.

"The same—only more so!" said Morris, smiling.

It does not enter into our scheme to narrate in detail Dr. Sloper's proceedings in the Eastern hemisphere. He made the grand tour of Europe, travelled in considerable splendour, and (as was to have been expected in a man of his high cultivation) found so much in art and antiquity to interest him, that he remained abroad, not for six months, but for twelve. Mrs. Penniman, in Washington Square, accommodated herself to his absence. She enjoyed her uncontested dominion in the empty house, and flattered herself that she made it more attractive to their friends than when her brother was at home. To Morris Townsend, at least, it would have appeared that she made it singularly attractive. He was altogether her most frequent visitor, and Mrs. Penniman was very fond of asking him to tea. He had his chair—a very easy one—at the fireside in the back-parlour (when the great mahogany sliding-doors, with silver knobs and hinges, which divided this apartment from its more formal neighbour, were closed), and he used to smoke cigars in the Doctor's study, where he often spent an hour in turning over the curious collections of its absent proprietor. He thought Mrs. Penniman a goose, as we know; but he was no goose himself, and, as a young

---

*In Roman religion, the six Vestal Virgins watched over the fire of Vesta, the goddess of the state hearth.

man of luxurious tastes and scanty resources, he found the house a perfect castle of indolence. It became for him a club with a single member. Mrs. Penniman saw much less of her sister than while the Doctor was at home; for Mrs. Almond had felt moved to tell her that she disapproved of her relations with Mr. Townsend. She had no business to be so friendly to a young man of whom their brother thought so meanly, and Mrs. Almond was surprised at her levity in foisting a most deplorable engagement upon Catherine.

"Deplorable?" cried Lavinia. "He will make her a lovely husband!"

"I don't believe in lovely husbands," said Mrs. Almond; "I only believe in good ones. If he marries her, and she comes into Austin's money, they may get on. He will be an idle, amiable, selfish, and doubtless tolerably good-natured fellow. But if she doesn't get the money and he finds himself tied to her, Heaven have mercy on her! He will have none. He will hate her for his disappointment, and take his revenge; he will be pitiless and cruel. Woe betide poor Catherine! I recommend you to talk a little with his sister; it's a pity Catherine can't marry *her!*"

Mrs. Penniman had no appetite whatever for conversation with Mrs. Montgomery, whose acquaintance she made no trouble to cultivate; and the effect of this alarming forecast of her niece's destiny was to make her think it indeed a thousand pities that Mr. Townsend's generous nature should be embittered. Bright enjoyment was his natural element, and how could he be comfortable if there should prove to be nothing to enjoy? It became a fixed idea with Mrs. Penniman that he should yet enjoy her brother's fortune, on which she had acuteness enough to perceive that her own claim was small.

"If he doesn't leave it to Catherine, it certainly won't be to leave it to me," she said.

XXIV

THE DOCTOR, DURING THE first six months he was abroad, never spoke to his daughter of their little difference; partly on system, and partly because he had a great many other things to think about. It was idle to attempt to ascertain the state of her affections without direct inquiry, because, if she had not had an expressive manner among the familiar influences of home, she failed to gather animation from the mountains of Switzerland or the monuments of Italy. She was always her father's docile and reasonable associate—going through their sight-seeing in deferential silence, never complaining of fatigue, always ready to start at the hour he had appointed overnight, making no foolish criticisms and indulging in no refinements of appreciation. "She is about as intelligent as the bundle of shawls," the Doctor said; her main superiority being that while the bundle of shawls sometimes got lost, or tumbled out of the carriage, Catherine was always at her post, and had a firm and ample seat. But her father had expected this, and he was not constrained to set down her intellectual limitations as a tourist to sentimental depression; she had completely divested herself of the characteristics of a victim, and during the whole time that they were abroad she never uttered an audible sigh. He supposed she was in correspondence with Morris Townsend; but he held his peace about it, for he never saw the young man's letters, and Catherine's own missives were always given to the courier to post. She heard from her lover with considerable regularity, but his letters came enclosed in Mrs. Penniman's; so that whenever the Doctor handed her a packet addressed in his sister's hand, he was an involuntary instrument of the passion he condemned. Catherine made this reflection, and six months earlier she would have felt bound to give him warning; but now she deemed herself absolved. There was a sore spot in her heart that his own words had made when once she spoke to him as she thought honour prompted; she would try and please him as far as she could, but she would never speak that way again. She read her lover's letters in secret.

178

One day, at the end of the summer, the two travellers found themselves in a lonely valley of the Alps. They were crossing one of the passes, and on the long ascent they had got out of the carriage and had wandered much in advance. After a while the Doctor descried a footpath which, leading through a transverse valley, would bring them out, as he justly supposed, at a much higher point of the ascent. They followed this devious way and finally lost the path; the valley proved very wild and rough, and their walk became rather a scramble. They were good walkers, however, and they took their adventure easily; from time to time they stopped, that Catherine might rest; and then she sat upon a stone and looked about her at the hard-featured rocks and the glowing sky. It was late in the afternoon, in the last of August; night was coming on, and, as they had reached a great elevation, the air was cold and sharp. In the west there was a great suffusion of cold, red light, which made the sides of the little valley look only the more rugged and dusky. During one of their pauses, her father left her and wandered away to some high place, at a distance, to get a view. He was out of sight; she sat there alone, in the stillness, which was just touched by the vague murmur, somewhere, of a mountain brook. She thought of Morris Townsend, and the place was so desolate and lonely that he seemed very far away. Her father remained absent a long time; she began to wonder what had become of him. But at last he reappeared, coming towards her in the clear twilight, and she got up, to go on. He made no motion to proceed, however, but came close to her, as if he had something to say. He stopped in front of her and stood looking at her with eyes that had kept the light of the flushing snow-summits on which they had just been fixed. Then, abruptly, in a low tone, he asked her an unexpected question—

"Have you given him up?"

The question was unexpected, but Catherine was only superficially unprepared.

"No, father!" she answered.

He looked at her again, for some moments, without speaking.

"Does he write to you?" he asked.

"Yes—about twice a month."

The Doctor looked up and down the valley, swinging his stick; then he said to her, in the same low tone—

"I am very angry."

She wondered what he meant—whether he wished to frighten her. If he did, the place was well chosen; this hard, melancholy dell, abandoned by the summer light, made her feel her loneliness. She looked around her, and her heart grew cold; for a moment her fear was great. But she could think of nothing to say, save to murmur gently, "I am sorry."

"You try my patience," her father went on, "and you ought to know what I am, I am not a very good man. Though I am very smooth externally, at bottom I am very passionate; and I assure you I can be very hard."

She could not think why he told her these things. Had he brought her there on purpose, and was it part of a plan? What was the plan? Catherine asked herself. Was it to startle her suddenly into a retraction—to take an advantage of her by dread? Dread of what? The place was ugly and lonely, but the place could do her no harm. There was a kind of still intensity about her father which made him dangerous, but Catherine hardly went so far as to say to herself that it might be part of his plan to fasten his hand—the neat, fine, supple hand of a distinguished physician—in her throat. Nevertheless, she receded a step. "I am sure you can be anything you please," she said. And it was her simple belief.

"I am very angry," he replied, more sharply.

"Why has it taken you so suddenly?"

"It has not taken me suddenly. I have been raging inwardly for the last six months. But just now this seemed a good place to flare out. It's so quiet, and we are alone."

"Yes, it's very quiet," said Catherine vaguely, looking about her. "Won't you come back to the carriage?"

"In a moment. Do you mean that in all this time you have not yielded an inch?"

"I would if I could, father; but I can't."

The Doctor looked round him too. "Should you like to be left in such a place as this, to starve?"

"What do you mean?" cried the girl.

"That will be your fate—that's how he will leave you."

He would not touch her, but he had touched Morris. The warmth came back to her heart. "That is not true, father," she broke out, "and you ought not to say it! It is not right, and it's not true!"

He shook his head slowly. "No, it's not right, because you won't believe it. But it *is* true. Come back to the carriage."

He turned away, and she followed him; he went faster, and was presently much in advance. But from time to time he stopped, without turning round, to let her keep up with him, and she made her way forward with difficulty, her heart beating with the excitement of having for the first time spoken to him in violence. By this time it had grown almost dark, and she ended by losing sight of him. But she kept her course, and after a little, the valley making a sudden turn, she gained the road, where the carriage stood waiting. In it sat her father, rigid and silent; in silence, too, she took her place beside him.

It seemed to her, later, in looking back upon all this, that for days afterwards not a word had been exchanged between them. The scene had been a strange one, but it had not permanently affected her feeling towards her father, for it was natural, after all, that he should occasionally make a scene of some kind, and he had let her alone for six months. The strangest part of it was that he had said he was not a good man; Catherine wondered a great deal what he had meant by that. The statement failed to appeal to her credence, and it was not grateful to any resentment that she entertained. Even in the utmost bitterness that she might feel, it would give her no satisfaction to think him less complete. Such a saying as that was a part of his great subtlety—men so clever as he might say anything and mean anything. And as to his being hard, that surely, in a man, was a virtue.

He let her alone for six months more—six months during which she accommodated herself without a protest to the extension of their tour. But he spoke again at the end of this time; it was at the very last, the night before they embarked for New York, in the hotel at Liverpool. They had been dining together in a great dim, musty sitting-room; and then this cloth had been removed, and the Doctor walked slowly up and down. Catherine at last took her candle to go to bed, but her father motioned her to stay.

"What do you mean to do when you get home?" he asked, while she stood there with her candle in her hand.

"Do you mean about Mr. Townsend?"

"About Mr. Townsend."

"We shall probably marry."

The Doctor took several turns again while she waited. "Do you hear from him as much as ever?"

"Yes; twice a month," said Catherine, promptly.

"And does he always talk about marriage?"

"Oh, yes! That is, he talks about other things too, but he always says something about that."

"I am glad to hear he varies his subjects; his letters might otherwise be monotonous."

"He writes beautifully," said Catherine, who was very glad of a chance to say it.

"They always write beautifully. However, in a given case that doesn't diminish the merit. So, as soon as you arrive, you are going off with him?"

This seemed a rather gross way of putting it, and something that there was of dignity in Catherine resented it. "I cannot tell you till we arrive," she said.

"That's reasonable enough," her father answered. "That's all I ask of you—that you *do* tell me, that you give me definite notice. When a poor man is to lose his only child, he likes to have an inkling of it beforehand."

"Oh, father, you will not lose me!" Catherine said, spilling her candle-wax.

"Three days before will do," he went on, "if you are in a position to be positive then. He ought to be very thankful to me, do you know. I have done a mighty good thing for him in taking you abroad; your value is twice as great, with all the knowledge and taste that you have acquired. A year ago, you were perhaps a little limited—a little rustic; but now you have seen everything, and appreciated everything, and you will be a most entertaining companion. We have fattened the sheep for him before he kills it!" Catherine turned away, and stood staring at the blank door. "Go to bed," said her father; "and, as we don't go aboard till noon, you may sleep late. We shall probably have a most uncomfortable voyage."

XXV

THE VOYAGE WAS INDEED uncomfortable, and Catherine, on arriving in New York, had not the compensation of "going off," in her father's phrase, with Morris Townsend. She saw him, however, the day after she landed; and, in the meantime, he formed a natural subject of conversation between our heroine and her Aunt Lavinia, with whom, the night she disembarked, the girl was closeted for a long time before either lady retired to rest.

"I have seen a great deal of him," said Mrs. Penniman. "He is not very easy to know. I suppose you think you know him; but you don't, my dear. You will some day; but it will only be after you have lived with him. I may almost say *I* have lived with him," Mrs. Penniman proceeded, while Catherine stared. "I think I know him now; I have had such remarkable opportunities. You will have the same—or rather, you will have better!" and Aunt Lavinia smiled. "Then you will see what I mean. It's a wonderful character, full of passion and energy, and just as true!"

Catherine listened with a mixture of interest and apprehension. Aunt Lavinia was intensely sympathetic, and Catherine, for the past year, while she wandered through foreign galleries and churches, and rolled over the smoothness of posting roads, nursing the thoughts that never passed her lips, had often longed for the company of some intelligent person of her own sex. To tell her story to some kind woman—at moments it seemed to her that this would give her comfort, and she had more than once been on the point of taking the landlady, or the nice young person from the dressmaker's into her confidence. If a woman had been near her she would on certain occasions have treated such a companion to a fit of weeping; and she had an apprehension that, on her return, this would form her response to Aunt Lavinia's first embrace. In fact, however, the two ladies had met, in Washington Square, without tears, and when they found themselves alone together a certain dryness fell upon the girl's emotion. It came over her with a greater force that Mrs. Penniman had enjoyed a whole year of her lover's society, and it was not a pleasure to hear her aunt explain and interpret the young man, speaking of him as if her own knowledge of him were supreme. It was not that Catherine was jealous; but her sense of Mrs. Penniman's innocent falsity, which had lain dormant, began to haunt her again, and she was glad that she was safely at home. With this, however, it was a blessing to be able to talk of Morris, to sound his name, to be with a person who was not unjust to him.

"You have been very kind to him," said Catherine. "He has written me that, often. I shall never forget that, Aunt Lavinia."

"I have done what I could; it has been very little. To let him come and talk to me, and give him his cup of tea—that was all. Your Aunt Almond thought it was too much, and used to scold me terribly; but she promised me, at least, not to betray me."

"To betray you?"

"Not to tell your father. He used to sit in your father's study!" said Mrs. Penniman, with a little laugh.

Catherine was silent a moment. This idea was disagreeable to her, and she was reminded again, with pain, of her aunt's secretive habits. Morris, the reader may be informed, had had the tact not to tell her that he sat in her father's study. He had known her but for a few months, and her aunt had known her for fifteen years; and yet he would not have made the mistake of thinking that Catherine would see the joke of the thing. "I am sorry you made him go into father's room," she said, after a while.

"I didn't make him go; he went himself. He liked to look at the books, and at all those things in the glass cases. He knows all about them; he knows all about everything."

Catherine was silent again; then, "I wish he had found some employment," she said.

"He has found some employment! It's beautiful news, and he told me to tell you as soon as you arrived. He has gone into partnership with a commission-merchant. It was all settled, quite suddenly, a week ago."

This seemed to Catherine indeed beautiful news; it had a fine prosperous air. "Oh, I'm so glad!" she said; and now, for a moment, she was disposed to throw herself on Aunt Lavinia's neck.

"It's much better than being under some one; and he has never been used to that," Mrs. Penniman went on. "He is just as good as his partner—they are perfectly equal! You see how right he was to wait. I should like to know what your father can say now! They have got an office in Duane Street, and little printed cards; he brought me one to show me. I have got it in my room, and you shall see it to-morrow. That's what he said to me the last time he was here—'You see how right I was to wait!' He has got other people under him, instead of being subordinate. He could never be a subordinate; I have often told him I could never think of him in that way."

Catherine assented to this proposition, and was very happy to know that Morris was his own master; but she was deprived of the satisfaction of thinking that she might communicate this news in triumph to her father. Her father would care equally little whether Morris were established in business or transported for life. Her trunks had been brought into her room, and further reference to her lover was for a short time suspended, while she opened them and displayed to her aunt some of the spoils of foreign travel. These were rich and abundant; and Catherine had brought home a present to every one—to every one save Morris, to whom she had brought simply her undiverted heart. To Mrs. Penniman she had been lavishly generous, and Aunt Lavinia spent half-an-hour in unfolding and folding again, with little ejaculations of gratitude and taste. She marched about for some time in a splendid cashmere shawl, which Catherine had begged her to accept, settling it on her shoulders, and twisting down her head to see how low the point descended behind.

"I shall regard it only as a loan," she said. "I will leave it to you again when I die; or rather," she added, kissing her niece again, "I will leave it to your first-born little girl!" And draped in her shawl, she stood there smiling.

"You had better wait till she comes," said Catherine.

"I don't like the way you say that," Mrs. Penniman rejoined, in a moment. "Catherine, are you changed?"

"No; I am the same."

"You have not swerved a line?"

"I am exactly the same," Catherine repeated, wishing her aunt were a little less sympathetic.

"Well, I am glad!" and Mrs. Penniman surveyed her cashmere in the glass. Then, "How is your father?" she asked in a moment, with her eyes on her niece. "Your letters were so meagre—I could never tell!"

"Father is very well."

"Ah, you know what I mean," said Mrs. Penniman, with a dignity to which the cashmere gave a richer effect. "Is he still implacable!"

"Oh, yes!"

"Quite unchanged?"

"He is, if possible, more firm."

Mrs. Penniman took off her great shawl, and slowly folded it up. "That is very bad. You had no success with your little project?"

"What little project?"

"Morris told me all about it. The idea of turning the tables on him, in Europe; of watching him, when he was agreeably impressed by some celebrated sight—he pretends to be so artistic, you know—and then just pleading with him and bringing him round."

"I never tried it. It was Morris's idea; but if he had been with us, in Europe, he would have seen that father was never impressed in that way. He *is* artistic—tremendously artistic; but the more celebrated places we visited, and the more he admired them, the less use it would have been to plead with him. They seemed only to make him more determined—more terrible," said poor Catherine. "I shall never bring him round, and I expect nothing now."

"Well, I must say," Mrs. Penniman answered, "I never supposed you were going to give it up."

"I have given it up. I don't care now."

"You have grown very brave," said Mrs. Penniman, with a short laugh. "I didn't advise you to sacrifice your property."

"Yes, I am braver than I was. You asked me if I had changed; I have changed in that way. Oh," the girl went on, "I have changed very much. And it isn't my property. If *he* doesn't care for it, why should I?"

Mrs. Penniman hesitated. "Perhaps he does care for it."

"He cares for it for my sake, because he doesn't want to injure me. But he will know—he knows already—how little he need be afraid about that. Besides," said Catherine, "I have got plenty of money of my own. We shall be very well off; and now hasn't he got his business? I am delighted about that business." She went on talking, showing a good deal of excitement as she proceeded. Her aunt had never seen her with just this manner and Mrs. Penniman, observing her, set it down to foreign travel, which had made her more positive, more mature. She thought also that Catherine had improved in appearance; she looked rather handsome. Mrs. Penniman wondered whether Morris Townsend would be struck with that. While she was engaged in this speculation, Catherine broke out, with a certain sharpness, "Why are you so contradictory, Aunt Penniman? You seem to think one thing at one time, and another at another. A year ago, before I went away, you wished me not to mind about displeasing father; and now you seem to recommend me to take another line. You change about so."

This attack was unexpected, for Mrs. Penniman was not used, in any discussion, to seeing the war carried into her own country—possibly because the enemy generally had doubts of finding subsistence there. To her own consciousness, the flowery fields of her reason had rarely been ravaged by a hostile force. It was perhaps on this account that in defending them she was majestic rather than agile.

"I don't know what you accuse me of, save of being too deeply interested in your happiness. It is the first time I have been told I am capricious. That fault is not what I am usually reproached with."

"You were angry last year that I wouldn't marry immediately, and now you talk about my winning my father over. You told me it would serve him right if he should take me to Europe for nothing. Well, he has taken me for nothing, and you ought to be satisfied. Nothing is changed—nothing but my feeling about father. I don't mind nearly so much now. I have been as good as I could, but he doesn't care. Now I don't care either. I don't know whether I have grown bad; perhaps I have. But I don't care for that. I have come home to be married—that's all I know. That ought to please you, unless you have taken up some new idea; you are so strange. You may do as you please; but you must never speak to me again about pleading with father. I shall never plead with him for anything; that is all over. He has put me off. I am come home to be married."

This was a more authoritative speech than she had ever heard on her niece's lips, and Mrs. Penniman was proportionately startled. She was indeed a little awe-struck, and the force of the girl's emotion and resolution left her nothing to reply. She was easily frightened, and she always carried off her discomfiture by a concession; a concession which was often accompanied, as in the present case, by a little nervous laugh.

XXVI

IF SHE HAD DISTURBED her niece's temper—she began from this moment forward to talk a good deal about Catherine's temper, an article which up to that time had never been mentioned in connection with our heroine—Catherine had opportunity, on the morrow, to recover her serenity. Mrs. Penniman had given her a message from Morris Townsend, to the effect that he would come and welcome her home on the day after her arrival. He came in the afternoon; but, as may be imagined, he was not on this occasion made free of Dr. Sloper's study. He had been coming and going, for the past year, so comfortably and irresponsibly, that he had a certain sense of being wronged by finding himself reminded that he must now limit his horizon to the front-parlour, which was Catherine's particular province.

"I am very glad you have come back," he said; "it makes me very happy to see you again." And he looked at her, smiling, from head to foot; though it did not appear, afterwards, that he agreed with Mrs. Penniman (who, womanlike, went more into details) in thinking her embellished.

To Catherine he appeared resplendent; it was some time before she could believe again that this beautiful young man was her own exclusive property. They had a great deal of characteristic lovers' talk—a soft exchange of inquiries and assurances. In these matters Morris had an excellent grace, which flung a picturesque interest even over the account of his début in the commission-business—a subject as to which his companion earnestly questioned him. From time to time he got up from the sofa where they sat together, and walked about the room; after which he came back, smiling and passing his hand through his hair. He was unquiet, as was natural in a young man who has just been re-united to a long-absent mistress, and Catherine made the reflection that she had never seen him so excited. It gave her pleasure, somehow, to note this fact. He asked her questions about her travels, to some of which she was unable to reply, for she had forgotten the names of places and the order of her father's journey. But for the moment she was so happy, so lifted up by the belief that her troubles at last were over, that she forgot to be ashamed of her meagre answers. It seemed to her now that she could marry him without the remnant of a scruple or a single tremor save those that belonged to joy. Without waiting for him to ask, she told him that her father had come back in exactly the same state of mind—that he had not yielded an inch.

"We must not expect it now," she said, "and we must do without it."

Morris sat looking and smiling. "My poor dear girl!" he exclaimed.

"You mustn't pity me," said Catherine; "I don't mind it now—I am used to it."

Morris continued to smile, and then he got up and walked about again. "You had better let me try him!"

"Try to bring him over? You would only make him worse," Catherine answered, resolutely.

"You say that because I managed it so badly before. But I should manage it differently now. I am much wiser; I have had a year to think of it. I have more tact."

"Is that what you have been thinking of for a year?"

"Much of the time. You see, the idea sticks in my crop. I don't like to be beaten."

"How are you beaten if we marry."

"Of course, I am not beaten on the main issue; but I am, don't you see, on all the rest of it—on the question of my reputation, of my relations with my own children, if we should have any."

"We shall have enough for our children—we shall have enough for everything. Don't you expect to succeed in business?"

"Brilliantly, and we shall certainly be very comfortable. But it isn't of the mere material comfort I speak; it is of the moral comfort," said Morris—"of the intellectual satisfaction!"

"I have great moral comfort now," Catherine declared, very simply.

"Of course you have. But with me it is different. I have staked my pride on proving to your father that he is wrong; and now that I am at the head of a flourishing business, I can deal with him as an equal. I have a capital plan—do let me go at him!"

He stood before her with his bright face, his jaunty air, his hands in his pockets; and she got up, with her eyes resting on his own. "Please don't, Morris; please don't," she said; and there was a certain mild, sad firmness in her tone which he heard for the first time. "We must ask no favours of him—we must ask nothing more. He won't relent, and nothing good will come of it. I know it now—I have a very good reason."

"And pray what is your reason?"

She hesitated to bring it out, but at last it came. "He is not very fond of me!"

"Oh, bother!" cried Morris, angrily.

"I wouldn't say such a thing without being sure. I saw it, I felt it, in England, just before he came away. He talked to me one night—the last night; and then it came over me. You can tell when a person feels that way. I wouldn't accuse him if he hadn't made me feel that way. I don't accuse him; I just tell you that that's how it is. He can't help it; we can't govern our affections. Do I govern mine? mightn't he say that to me? It's because he is so fond of my mother, whom we lost so long ago. She was beautiful, and very, very brilliant; he is always thinking of her. I am not at all like her; Aunt Penniman has told me that. Of course it isn't my fault; but neither is it his fault. All I mean is, it's true; and it's a stronger reason for his never being reconciled than simply his dislike for you."

"Simply?" cried Morris, with a laugh, "I am much obliged for that!"

"I don't mind about his disliking you now; I mind everything less. I feel differently; I feel separated from my father."

"Upon my word," said Morris, "you are a queer family!"

"Don't say that—don't say anything unkind," the girl entreated. "You must be very kind to me now, because, Morris—because," and she hesitated a moment—"because I have done a great deal for you."

"Oh, I know that, my dear!"

She had spoken up to this moment without vehemence or outward sign of emotion, gently, reasoningly, only trying to explain. But her emotion had been ineffectually smothered, and it betrayed itself at last in the trembling of her voice. "It is a great thing to be separated like that from your father, when you have worshipped him before. It has made me very unhappy; or it would have made me so if I didn't love you. You can tell when a person speaks to you as if—as if——"

"As if what?"

"As if they despised you!" said Catherine, passionately. "He spoke that way the night before we sailed. It wasn't much, but it was enough, and I thought of it on the voyage, all the time. Then I made up my mind. I will never ask him for anything again, or expect anything from him. It would not be natural now. We must be very happy together, and we must not seem to depend upon his forgiveness. And Morris, Morris, you must never despise me!"

This was an easy promise to make, and Morris made it with fine effect. But for the moment he undertook nothing more onerous.

XXVII

THE DOCTOR, OF COURSE, on his return, had a good deal of talk with his sisters. He was at no great pains to narrate his travels or to communicate his impressions of distant lands to Mrs. Penniman, upon whom he contented himself with bestowing a memento of his enviable experience, in the shape of a velvet gown. But he conversed with her at some length about matters nearer home, and lost no time in assuring her that he was still an inflexible father.

"I have no doubt you have seen a great deal of Mr. Townsend, and done your best to console him for Catherine's absence," he said. "I don't ask you, and you needn't deny it. I wouldn't put the question to you for the world, and expose you to the inconvenience of having to—a—excogitate an answer. No one has betrayed you, and there has been no spy upon your proceedings. Elizabeth has told no tales, and has never mentioned you except to praise your good looks and good spirits. The thing is simply an inference of my own—an induction, as the philosophers say. It seems to me likely that you would have offered an asylum to an interesting sufferer. Mr. Townsend has been a good deal in the house; there is something in the house that tells me so. We doctors, you know, end by acquiring fine perceptions, and it is impressed upon my sensorium that he has sat in these chairs, in a very easy attitude, and warmed himself at that fire. I don't grudge him the comfort of it; it is the only one he will ever enjoy at my expense. It seems likely, indeed, that I shall be able to economise at his own. I don't know what you may have said to him, or what you may say hereafter; but I should like you to know that if you have encouraged him to believe that he will gain anything by hanging on, or that I have budged a hair's breadth from the position I took up a year ago, you have played him a trick for which he may exact reparation. I'm not sure that he may not bring a suit against you. Of course you have done it conscientiously; you have made yourself believe that I can be tired out. This is the most base-less hallucination that ever visited the brain of a genial optimist. I am not in the least tired; I am as fresh as when I started; I am good for fifty years yet. Catherine appears not to have budged an inch either; she is equally fresh; so we are about where we were before. This, however, you know as well as I. What I wish is simply to give you notice of my own state of mind! Take it to heart, dear Lavinia. Beware of the just resentment of a deluded fortune-hunter!"

"I can't say I expected it," said Mrs. Penniman. "And I had a sort of foolish hope that you would come home without that odious ironical tone with which you treat the most sacred subjects."

"Don't undervalue irony, it is often of great use. It is not, however, always necessary, and I will show you how gracefully I can lay it aside. I should like to know whether you think Morris Townsend will hang on."

"I will answer you with your own weapons," said Mrs. Penniman. "You had better wait and see!"

"Do you call such a speech as that one of my own weapons? I never said anything so rough."

"He will hang on long enough to make you very uncomfortable, then."

"My dear Lavinia," exclaimed the Doctor, "do you call that irony? I call it pugilism."

Mrs. Penniman, however, in spite of her pugilism, was a good deal frightened, and she took counsel of her fears. Her brother meanwhile took counsel, with many reservations, of Mrs. Almond, to whom he was no less generous than to Lavinia, and a good deal more communicative.

"I suppose she has had him there all the while," he said. "I must look into the state of my wine! You needn't mind telling me now; I have already said all I mean to say to her on the subject."

"I believe he was in the house a good deal," Mrs. Almond answered. "But you must admit that your leaving Lavinia quite alone was a great change for her, and that it was natural she should want some society."

"I do admit that, and that is why I shall make no row about the wine; I shall set it down as compensation to Lavinia. She is capable of telling me that she drank it all herself. Think of the inconceivable bad taste, in the circumstances, of that fellow making free with the house—or coming there at all! If that doesn't describe him, he is indescribable."

"His plan is to get what he can. Lavinia will have supported him for a year," said Mrs. Almond. "It's so much gained."

"She will have to support him for the rest of his life, then!" cried the Doctor. "But without wine, as they say at the *table d'hôte*."*

"Catherine tells me he has set up a business, and is making a great deal of money."

The Doctor stared. "She has not told me that—and Lavinia didn't deign. Ah!" he cried, "Catherine has given me up. Not that it matters, for all that the business amounts to."

"She has not given up Mr. Townsend," said Mrs. Almond. "I saw that in the first half-minute. She has come home exactly the same."

"Exactly the same; not a grain more intelligent. She didn't notice a stick or a stone all the while we were away—not a picture nor a view, not a statue nor a cathedral."

"How could she notice? She had other things to think of; they are never for an instant out of her mind. She touches me very much."

"She would touch me if she didn't irritate me. That's the effect she has upon me now. I have tried everything upon her; I really have been quite merciless. But it is of no use whatever; she is absolutely *glued*. I have passed, in consequence, into the exasperated stage. At first I had a good deal of a certain genial curiosity about it; I wanted to see if she really would stick. But, good Lord, one's curiosity is satisfied! I see she is capable of it, and now she can let go."

"She will never let go," said Mrs. Almond.

"Take care, or you will exasperate me too. If she doesn't let go, she will be shaken off—sent tumbling into the dust! That's a nice position for my daughter. She can't see that if you are going to be pushed you had better jump. And then she will complain of her bruises."

"She will never complain," said Mrs. Almond.

"That I shall object to even more. But the deuce will be that I can't prevent anything."

"If she is to have a fall," said Mrs. Almond, with a gentle laugh, "we must spread as many carpets as we can." And she carried out this idea by showing a great deal of motherly kindness to the girl.

---

*At a hotel or inn, communal dining offered to guests as part of the cost of the stay (French).

Mrs. Penniman immediately wrote to Morris Townsend. The intimacy between these two was by this time consummate, but I must content myself with noting but a few of its features. Mrs. Penniman's own share in it was a singular sentiment, which might have been misinterpreted, but which in itself was not discreditable to the poor lady. It was a romantic interest in this attractive and unfortunate young man, and yet it was not such an interest as Catherine might have been jealous of. Mrs. Penniman had not a particle of jealousy of her niece. For herself, she felt as if she were Morris's mother or sister—a mother or sister of an emotional temperament—and she had an absorbing desire to make him comfortable and happy. She had striven to do so during the year that her brother left her an open field, and her efforts had been attended with the success that has been pointed out. She had never had a child of her own, and Catherine, whom she had done her best to invest with the importance that would naturally belong to a youthful Penniman, had only partly rewarded her zeal. Catherine, as an object of affection and solicitude, had never had that picturesque charm which (as it seemed to her) would have been a natural attribute of her own progeny. Even the maternal passion in Mrs. Penniman would have been romantic and factitious, and Catherine was not constituted to inspire a romantic passion. Mrs. Penniman was as fond of her as ever, but she had grown to feel that with Catherine she lacked opportunity. Sentimentally speaking, therefore, she had (though she had not disinherited her niece) adopted Morris Townsend, who gave her opportunity in abundance. She would have been very happy to have a handsome and tyrannical son, and would have taken an extreme interest in his love affairs. This was the light in which she had come to regard Morris, who had conciliated her at first, and made his impression by his delicate and calculated deference—a sort of exhibition to which Mrs. Penniman was particularly sensitive. He had largely abated his deference afterwards, for he economised his resources, but the impression was made, and the young man's very brutality came to have a sort of filial value. If Mrs. Penniman had had a son, she would probably have been afraid of him, and at this stage of our narrative she was certainly afraid of Morris Townsend. This was one of the results of his domestication in Washington Square. He took his ease with her—as, for that matter, he would certainly have done with his own mother.

XXVIII

THE LETTER WAS A word of warning; it informed him that the Doctor had come home more impracticable than ever. She might have reflected that Catherine would supply him with all the information he needed on this point; but we know that Mrs. Penniman's reflections were rarely just; and, moreover, she felt that it was not for her to depend on what Catherine might do. She was to do her duty, quite irrespective of Catherine. I have said that her young friend took his ease with her, and it is an illustration of the fact that he made no answer to her letter. He took note of it, amply; but he lighted his cigar with it, and he waited, in tranquil confidence that he should receive another. "His state of mind really freezes my blood," Mrs. Penniman had written, alluding to her brother; and it would have seemed that upon this statement she could hardly improve. Nevertheless, she wrote again, expressing herself with the aid of a different figure. "His hatred of you burns with a lurid flame—the flame that never dies," she wrote. "But it doesn't light up the darkness of your future. If my affection could do so, all the years of your life would be an eternal sunshine. I can extract nothing from C.; she is so terribly secretive, like her father. She seems to expect to be married very soon, and has evidently made preparations in Europe—quantities of clothing, ten pairs of shoes, etc. My dear friend, you cannot set up in married life simply with a few pairs of shoes, can you? Tell me what you think of this. I am intensely anxious to see you; I have so much to say. I miss you dreadfully; the house seems so empty without you. What is the news down town? Is the business extending? That dear little business—I think it's so brave of you! Couldn't I come to your office?—just for three minutes? I might pass for a customer—is that what you call them. I might come in to buy something—some shares or some railroad things. *Tell me what you think of this plan.* I would carry a little reticule,* like a woman of the people."

---

*Small pocketbook or workbag, carried by women on the arm or in the hand.

In spite of the suggestion about the reticule, Morris appeared to think poorly of the plan, for he gave Mrs. Penniman no encouragement whatever to visit his office, which he had already represented to her as a place peculiarly and unnaturally difficult to find. But as she persisted in desiring an interview—up to the last, after months of intimate colloquy, she called these meetings "interviews"—he agreed that they should take a walk together, and was even kind enough to leave his office for this purpose, during the hours at which business might have been supposed to be liveliest. It was no surprise to him, when they met at a street-corner, in a region of empty lots and undeveloped pavements (Mrs. Penniman being attired as much as possible like a "woman of the people"), to find that, in spite of her urgency, what she chiefly had to convey to him was the assurance of her sympathy. Of such assurances, however, he had already a voluminous collection, and it would not have been worth his while to forsake a fruitful avocation merely to hear Mrs. Penniman say, for the thousandth time, that she had made his cause her own. Morris had something of his own to say. It was an easy thing to bring out, and while he turned it over the difficulty made him acrimonious.

"Oh yes, I know perfectly that he combines the properties of a lump of ice and a red-hot coal," he observed. "Catherine has made it thoroughly clear, and you have told me so till I am sick of it. You needn't tell me again; I am perfectly satisfied. He will never give us a penny; I regard that as mathematically proved."

Mrs. Penniman at this point had an inspiration.

"Couldn't you bring a lawsuit against him?" She wondered that this simple expedient had never occurred to her before.

"I will bring a lawsuit against *you*," said Morris, "if you ask me any more such aggravating questions. A man should know when he is beaten," he added, in a moment. "I must give her up!"

Mrs. Penniman received this declaration in silence, though it made her heart beat a little. It found her by no means unprepared, for she had accustomed herself to the thought that, if Morris should decidedly not be able to get her brother's money, it would not do for him to marry Catherine without it. "It would not do" was a vague way of putting the thing; but Mrs. Penniman's natural affection completed the idea, which, though it had not as yet been so crudely expressed between them as in the form that Morris had just given it, had nevertheless been implied so often, in certain easy intervals of talk, as he sat stretching his legs in the Doctor's well-stuffed arm-chairs, that she had grown first to regard it with an emotion which she flattered herself was philosophic, and then to have a secret tenderness for it. The fact that she kept her tenderness secret proves, of course, that she was ashamed of it; but she managed to blink her shame by reminding herself that she was, after all, the official protector of her niece's marriage. Her logic would scarcely have passed muster with the Doctor. In the first place, Morris *must* get the money, and she would help him to it. In the second, it was plain it would never come to him, and it would be a grievous pity he should marry without it—a young man who might so easily find something better. After her brother had delivered himself, on his return from Europe, of that incisive little address that has been quoted, Morris's cause seemed so hopeless that Mrs. Penniman fixed her attention exclusively upon the latter branch of her argument. If Morris had been her son, she would certainly have sacrificed Catherine to a superior conception of his future; and to be ready to do so as the case stood was therefore even a finer degree of devotion. Nevertheless, it checked her breath a little to have the sacrificial knife, as it were, suddenly thrust into her hand.

Morris walked along a moment, and then he repeated, harshly—

"I must give her up!"

"I think I understand you," said Mrs. Penniman, gently.

"I certainly say it distinctly enough—brutally and vulgarly enough."

He was ashamed of himself, and his shame was uncomfortable; and as he was extremely intolerant of discomfort, he felt vicious and cruel. He wanted to abuse somebody, and he began, cautiously—for he was always cautious—with himself.

"Couldn't you take her down a little?" he asked.

"Take her down?"

"Prepare her—try and ease me off."

Mrs. Penniman stopped, looking at him very solemnly.

"My poor Morris, do you know how much she loves you?"

"No, I don't. I don't want to know. I have always tried to keep from knowing. It would be too painful."

"She will suffer much," said Mrs. Penniman.

"You must console her. If you are as good a friend to me as you pretend to be, you will manage it."

Mrs. Penniman shook her head, sadly.

"You talk of my 'pretending' to like you; but I can't pretend to hate you. I can only tell her I think very highly of you; and how will that console her for losing you?"

"The Doctor will help you. He will be delighted at the thing being broken off, and, as he is a knowing fellow, he will invent something to comfort her."

"He will invent a new torture!" cried Mrs. Penniman. "Heaven deliver her from her father's comfort. It will consist of his crowing over her and saying, 'I told you so!' "

Morris coloured a most uncomfortable red.

"If you don't console her any better than you console me, you certainly won't be of much use! It's a damned disagreeable necessity; I feel it extremely, and you ought to make it easy for me."

"I will be your friend for life!" Mrs. Penniman declared.

"Be my friend *now*!" And Morris walked on.

She went with him; she was almost trembling.

"Should you like me to tell her?" she asked.

"You mustn't tell her, but you can—you can——." And he hesitated, trying to think what Mrs. Penniman could do. "You can explain to her why it is. It's because I can't bring myself to step in between her and her father—to give him the pretext he grasps at so eagerly (it's a hideous sight) for depriving her of her rights."

Mrs. Penniman felt with remarkable promptitude the charm of this formula.

"That's so like you," she said; "it's so finely felt."

Morris gave his stick an angry swing.

"Oh botheration!" he exclaimed perversely.

Mrs. Penniman, however, was not discouraged.

"It may turn out better than you think. Catherine is, after all, so very peculiar." And she thought she might take it upon herself to assure him that, whatever happened, the girl would be very quiet—she wouldn't make a noise. They extended their walk, and, while they proceeded, Mrs. Penniman took upon herself other things besides, and ended by having assumed a considerable burden; Morris being ready enough, as may be imagined, to put everything off upon her. But he was not for a single instant the dupe of her blundering alacrity; he knew that of what she promised she was competent to perform but an insignificant fraction, and the more she professed her willingness to serve him, the greater fool he thought her.

"What will you do if you don't marry her?" she ventured to inquire in the course of this conversation.

"Something brilliant," said Morris. "Shouldn't you like me to do something brilliant?"

The idea gave Mrs. Penniman exceeding pleasure.

"I shall feel sadly taken in if you don't."

"I shall have to, to make up for this. This isn't at all brilliant, you know."

Mrs. Penniman mused a little, as if there might be some way of making out that it was; but she had to give up the attempt, and, to carry off the awkwardness of failure, she risked a new inquiry.

"Do you mean—do you mean another marriage?"

Morris greeted this question with a reflection which was hardly the less impudent from being inaudible. "Surely, women are more crude than men!" And then he answered audibly—

"Never in the world!"

Mrs. Penniman felt disappointed and snubbed, and she relieved herself in a little vaguely sarcastic cry. He was certainly perverse.

"I give her up not for another woman, but for a wider career!" Morris announced.

This was very grand; but still Mrs. Penniman, who felt that she had exposed herself, was faintly rancorous.

"Do you mean never to come to see her again?" she asked, with some sharpness.

"Oh no, I shall come again; but what is the use of dragging it out? I have been four times since she came back, and it's terribly awkward work. I can't keep it up indefinitely; she oughtn't to expect that, you know. A woman should never keep a man dangling!" he added, finely.

"Ah, but you must have your last parting!" urged his companion, in whose imagination the idea of last partings occupied a place inferior in dignity only to that of first meetings.

XXIX

HE CAME AGAIN, WITHOUT managing the last parting; and again and again, without finding that Mrs. Penniman had as yet done much to pave the path of retreat with flowers. It was devilish awkward, as he said, and he felt a lively animosity for Catherine's aunt, who, as he had now quite formed the habit of saying to himself, had dragged him into the mess and was bound in common charity to get him out of it. Mrs. Penniman, to tell the truth, had, in the seclusion of her own apartment—and, I may add, amid the suggestiveness of Catherine's, which wore in those days the appearance of that of a young lady laying out her *trousseau** — Mrs. Penniman had measured her responsibilities, and taken fright at their magnitude. The task of preparing Catherine and easing off Morris presented difficulties which increased in the execution, and even led the impulsive Lavinia to ask herself whether the modification of the young man's original project had been conceived in a happy spirit. A brilliant future, a wider career, a conscience exempt from the reproach of interference between a young lady and her natural rights—these excellent things might be too troublesomely purchased. From Catherine herself Mrs. Penniman received no assistance whatever; the poor girl was apparently without suspicion of her danger. She looked at her lover with eyes of undiminished trust, and though she had less confidence in her aunt than in a young man with whom she had exchanged so many tender vows, she gave her no handle for explaining or confessing. Mrs. Penniman, faltering and wavering, declared Catherine was very stupid, put off the great scene, as she would have called it, from day to day, and wandered about very uncomfortably, primed, to repletion, with her apology, but unable to bring it to the light. Morris's own scenes were very small ones just now; but even these were beyond his strength. He made his visits as

---

*Bride's collection of clothing, jewelry, house linens, and the like, assembled in anticipation of her marriage.

brief as possible, and, while he sat with his mistress, found terribly little to talk about. She was waiting for him, in vulgar parlance, to name the day; and so long as he was unprepared to be explicit on this point, it seemed a mockery to pretend to talk about matters more abstract. She had no airs and no arts; she never attempted to disguise her expectancy. She was waiting on his good pleasure, and would wait modestly and patiently; his hanging back at this supreme time might appear strange, but of course he must have a good reason for it. Catherine would have made a wife of the gentle old-fashioned pattern—regarding reasons as favours and windfalls, but no more expecting one every day than she would have expected a bouquet of camellias. During the period of her engagement, how-ever, a young lady even of the most slender pretensions counts upon more bouquets than at other times; and there was a want of perfume in the air at this moment which at last excited the girl's alarm.

"Are you sick?" she asked of Morris. "You seem so restless, and you look pale."

"I am not at all well," said Morris; and it occurred to him that, if he could only make her pity him enough, he might get off.

"I am afraid you are overworked; you oughtn't to work so much."

"I must do that." And then he added, with a sort of calculated brutality, "I don't want to owe you everything!"

"Ah, how can you say that?"

"I am too proud," said Morris.

"Yes—you are too proud!"

"Well, you must take me as I am," he went on, "you can never change me."

"I don't want to change you," she said, gently. "I will take you as you are!" And she stood looking at him.

"You know people talk tremendously about a man's marrying a rich girl," Morris remarked. "It's excessively disagreeable."

"But I am not rich!" said Catherine.

"You are rich enough to make me talked about!"

"Of course you are talked about. It's an honour!"

"It's an honour I could easily dispense with."

She was on the point of asking him whether it were not a compen-sation for this annoyance that the poor girl who had the misfortune to bring it upon him, loved him so dearly and believed in him so truly; but she hesitated, thinking that this would perhaps seem an exacting speech, and while she hesitated, he suddenly left her.

The next time he came, however, he brought it out, and she told him again that he was too proud. He repeated that he couldn't change, and this time she felt the impulse to say that with a little effort he might change.

Sometimes he thought that if he could only make a quarrel with her it might help him; but the question was how to quarrel with a young woman who had such treasures of concession. "I suppose you think the effort is all on your side!" he was reduced to exclaiming. "Don't you believe that I have my own effort to make?"

"It's all yours now," she said. "My effort is finished and done with!"

"Well, mine is not."

"We must bear things together," said Catherine. "That's what we ought to do."

Morris attempted a natural smile. "There are some things which we can't very well bear together—for instance, separation."

"Why do you speak of separation?"

"Ah! you don't like it; I knew you wouldn't!"

"Where are you going, Morris?" she suddenly asked.

He fixed his eye on her a moment, and for a part of that moment she was afraid of it. "Will you promise not to make a scene?"

"A scene!—do I make scenes?"

"All women do!" said Morris, with the tone of large experience.

"I don't. Where are you going?"

"If I should say I was going away on business, should you think it very strange?"

She wondered a moment, gazing at him. "Yes—no. Not if you will take me with you."

"Take you with me—on business?"

"What is your business? Your business is to be with me."

"I don't earn my living with you," said Morris. "Or rather," he cried with a sudden inspiration, "that's just what I do—or what the world says I do!"

This ought perhaps to have been a great stroke, but it miscarried. "Where are you going?" Catherine simply repeated.

"To New Orleans. About buying some cotton."

"I am perfectly willing to go to New Orleans," Catherine said.

"Do you suppose I would take you to a nest of yellow fever?"* cried Morris. "Do you suppose I would expose you at such a time as this?"

"If there is yellow fever, why should you go? Morris, you must not go!"

"It is to make six thousand dollars," said Morris. "Do you grudge me that satisfaction?"

"We have no need of six thousand dollars. You think too much about money!"

"You can afford to say that? This is a great chance; we heard of it last night." And he explained to her in what the chance consisted; and told her a long story, going over more than once several of the details, about the remarkable stroke of business which he and his partner had planned between them.

But Catherine's imagination, for reasons best known to herself, absolutely refused to be fired. "If you can go to New Orleans, I can go," she said. "Why shouldn't you catch yellow fever quite as easily as I? I am every bit as strong as you, and not in the least afraid of any fever. When we were in Europe, we were in very unhealthy places; my father used to make me take some pills. I never caught anything, and I never was nervous. What will be the use of six thousand dollars if you die of a fever? When persons are going to be married, they oughtn't to think so much about business. You shouldn't think about cotton, you should think about me. You can go to New Orleans some other time—there will always be plenty of cotton. It isn't the moment to choose—we have waited too long already." She spoke more forcibly and volubly than he had ever heard her, and she held his arm in her two hands.

"You said you wouldn't make a scene!" cried Morris. "I call this a scene."

"It's you that are making it! I have never asked you anything before. We have waited too long already." And it was a comfort to her to think that she had hitherto asked so little; it seemed to make her right to insist the greater now.

Morris bethought himself a little. "Very well, then; we won't talk

---

*Dangerous, mosquito-borne infectious disease found in hot climates and characterized by vomiting, high fever, liver degeneration, and jaundice (hence its name).

about it any more. I will transact my business by letter." And he began to smooth his hat, as if to take leave.

"You won't go?" And she stood looking up at him.

He could not give up his idea of provoking a quarrel; it was so much the simplest way! He bent his eyes on her upturned face, with the darkest frown he could achieve. "You are not discreet. You mustn't bully me!"

But, as usual, she conceded everything. "No, I am not discreet; I know I am too pressing. But isn't it natural? It is only for a moment."

"In a moment you may do a great deal of harm. Try and be calmer the next time I come."

"When will you come?"

"Do you want to make conditions?" Morris asked. "I will come next Saturday."

"Come to-morrow," Catherine begged; "I want you to come to-morrow. I will be very quiet," she added; and her agitation had by this time become so great that the assurance was not unbecoming. A sudden fear had come over her; it was like the solid conjunction of a dozen disembodied doubts, and her imagination, at a single bound, had traversed an enormous distance. All her being, for the moment, centred in the wish to keep him in the room.

Morris bent his head and kissed her forehead. "When you are quiet, you are perfection," he said; "but when you are violent you are not in character."

It was Catherine's wish that there should be no violence about her save the beating of her heart, which she could not help; and she went on, as gently as possible, "Will you promise to come to-morrow?"

"I said Saturday!" Morris answered, smiling. He tried a frown at one moment, a smile at another; he was at his wit's end.

"Yes, Saturday too," she answered, trying to smile. "But to-morrow first." He was going to the door, and she went with him, quickly. She leaned her shoulder against it; it seemed to her that she would do anything to keep him.

"If I am prevented from coming to-morrow, you will say I have deceived you!" he said.

"How can you be prevented? You can come if you will."

"I am a busy man—I am not a dangler!" cried Morris, sternly.

His voice was so hard and unnatural that, with a helpless look at him, she turned away; and then he quickly laid his hand on the door-knob. He felt as if he were absolutely running away from her. But in an instant she was close to him again, and murmuring in a tone none the less penetrating for being low, "Morris, you are going to leave me."

"Yes, for a little while."

"For how long?"

"Till you are reasonable again."

"I shall never be reasonable in that way!" And she tried to keep him longer; it was almost a struggle. "Think of what I have done!" she broke out. "Morris, I have given up everything!"

"You shall have everything back!"

"You wouldn't say that if you didn't mean something. What is it?—what has happehed?—what have I done?—what has changed you?"

"I will write to you—that is better," Morris stammered.

"Ah, you won't come back!" she cried, bursting into tears.

"Dear Catherine," he said, "don't believe that! I promise you that you shall see me again!" And he managed to get away and to close the door behind him.

XXX

It was almost her last outbreak of passive grief; at least, she never indulged in another that the world knew anything about. But this one was long and terrible; she flung herself on the sofa and gave herself up to her misery. She hardly knew what had happened; ostensibly she had only had a difference with her lover, as other girls had had before, and the thing was not only not a rupture, but she was under no obligation to regard it even as a menace. Nevertheless, she felt a wound, even if he had not dealt it; it seemed to her that a mask had suddenly fallen from his face. He had wished to get away from her; he had been angry and cruel, and said strange things, with strange looks. She was smothered and stunned; she buried her head in the cushions, sobbing and talking to herself. But at last she raised herself, with the fear that either her father or Mrs. Penniman would come in; and then she sat there, staring before her, while the room grew darker. She said to herself that perhaps he would come back to tell her he had not meant what he said; and she listened for his ring at the door, trying to believe that this was probable. A long time passed, but Morris remained absent; the shadows gathered; the evening settled down on the meagre elegance of the light, clear-coloured room; the fire went out. When it had grown dark, Catherine went to the window and looked out; she stood there for half an hour, on the mere chance that he would come up the steps. At last she turned away, for she saw her father come in. He had seen her at the window looking out, and he stopped a moment at the bottom of the white steps, and gravely, with an air of exaggerated courtesy, lifted his hat to her. The gesture was so incongruous to the condition she was in, this stately tribute of respect to a poor girl despised and forsaken was so out of place, that the thing gave her a kind of horror, and she hurried away to her room. It seemed to her that she had given Morris up.

She had to show herself half an hour later, and she was sustained at table by the immensity of her desire that her father should not perceive that anything had happened. This was a great help to her afterwards, and it served her (though never as much as she supposed) from the first. On this occasion Dr. Sloper was rather talkative. He told a great many stories about a wonderful poodle that he had seen at the house of an old lady whom he visited professionally. Catherine not only tried to appear to listen to the anecdotes of the poodle, but she endeavoured to interest herself in them, so as not to think of her scene with Morris. That perhaps was an hallucination; he was mistaken, she was jealous; people didn't change like that from one day to another. Then she knew that she had had doubts before—strange suspicions, that were at once vague and acute— and that he had been different ever since her return from Europe: whereupon she tried again to listen to her father, who told a story so remarkably well. Afterwards she went straight to her own room; it was beyond her strength to undertake to spend the evening with her aunt. All the evening, alone, she questioned herself. Her trouble was terrible; but was it a thing of her imagination, engendered by an extravagant sensibility, or did it represent a clear-cut reality, and had the worst that was possible actually come to pass? Mrs. Penniman, with a degree of tact that was as unusual as it was commendable, took the line of leaving her alone. The truth is, that her suspicions having been aroused, she indulged a desire, natural to a timid person, that the explosion should be localised. So long as the air still vibrated she kept out of the way.

She passed and repassed Catherine's door several times in the course of the evening, as if she expected to hear a plaintive moan behind it. But the room remained perfectly still; and accordingly, the last thing before retiring to her own couch, she applied for admittance. Catherine was sitting up, and had a book that she pretended to be reading. She had no wish to go to bed, for she had no expectation of sleeping. After Mrs. Penniman had left her she sat up half the night, and she offered her visitor no inducement to remain. Her aunt came stealing in very gently, and approached her with great solemnity.

"I am afraid you are in trouble, my dear. Can I do anything to help you?"

"I am not in any trouble whatever, and do not need any help," said Catherine, fibbing roundly, and proving thereby that not only our faults, but our most involuntary misfortunes, tend to corrupt our morals.

"Has nothing happened to you?"

"Nothing whatever."

"Are you very sure, dear?"

"Perfectly sure."

"And can I really do nothing for you?"

"Nothing, aunt, but kindly leave me alone," said Catherine.

Mrs. Penniman, though she had been afraid of too warm a welcome before, was now disappointed at so cold a one; and in relating afterwards, as she did to many persons, and with considerable variations of detail, the history of the termination of her niece's engagement, she was usually careful to mention that the young lady, on a certain occasion, had "hustled" her out of the room. It was characteristic of Mrs. Penniman that she related this fact, not in the least out of malignity to Catherine, whom she very sufficiently pitied, but simply from a natural disposition to embellish any subject that she touched.

Catherine, as I have said, sat up half the night, as if she still expected to hear Morris Townsend ring at the door. On the morrow this expectation was less unreasonable; but it was not gratified by the reappearance of the young man. Neither had he written; there was not a word of explanation or reassurance. Fortunately for Catherine she could take refuge from her excitement, which had now become intense, in her determination that her father should see nothing of it. How well she deceived her father we shall have occasion to learn; but her innocent arts were of little avail before a person of the rare perspicacity of Mrs. Penniman. This lady easily saw that she was agitated, and if there was any agitation going forward, Mrs. Penniman was not a person to forfeit her natural share in it. She returned to the charge the next evening, and requested her niece to lean upon her—to unburden her heart. Perhaps she should be able to explain certain things that now seemed dark, and that she knew more about than Catherine supposed. If Catherine had been frigid the night before, to-day she was haughty.

"You are completely mistaken, and I have not the least idea what you mean. I don't know what you are trying to fasten on me, and I have never had less need of any one's explanations in my life."

In this way the girl delivered herself, and from hour to hour kept her aunt at bay. From hour to hour Mrs. Penniman's curiosity grew. She would have given her little finger to know what Morris had said and done, what tone he had taken, what pretext he had found. She wrote to him, naturally, to request an interview; but she received, as naturally, no answer to her petition. Morris was not in a writing mood; for Catherine had addressed him two short notes which met with no acknowledgment. These notes were so brief that I may give them entire. "Won't you give me some sign that you didn't mean to be so cruel as you seemed on Tuesday?"—that was the first; the other was a little longer. "If I was unreasonable or suspicious, on Tuesday—if I annoyed you or troubled you in any way—I beg your forgiveness, and I promise never again to be so foolish. I am punished enough, and I don't understand. Dear Morris, you are killing me!" These notes were despatched on the Friday and Saturday; but Saturday and Sunday passed without bringing the poor girl the satisfaction she desired. Her punishment accumulated; she continued to bear it, however, with a good deal of superficial fortitude. On Saturday morning, the Doctor, who had been watching in silence, spoke to his sister Lavinia.

"The thing has happened—the scoundrel has backed out!"

"Never!" cried Mrs. Penniman, who had bethought herself what she should say to Catherine, but was not provided with a line of defence against her brother, so that indignant negation was the only weapon in her hands.

"He has begged for a reprieve, then, if you like that better!"

"It seems to make you very happy that your daughter's affections have been trifled with."

"It does," said the Doctor; "for I had foretold it! It's a great pleasure to be in the right."

"Your pleasures make one shudder!" his sister exclaimed.

Catherine went rigidly through her usual occupations; that is, up to the point of going with her aunt to church on Sunday morning. She generally went to afternoon service as well; but on this occasion her courage faltered, and she begged of Mrs. Penniman to go without her.

"I am sure you have a secret," said Mrs. Penniman, with great significance, looking at her rather grimly.

"If I have, I shall keep it!" Catherine answered, turning away.

Mrs. Penniman started for church; but before she had arrived, she stopped and turned back, and before twenty minutes had elapsed she re-entered the house, looked into the empty parlours, and then went upstairs and knocked at Catherine's door. She got no answer;

Catherine was not in her room, and Mrs. Penniman presently ascertained that she was not in the house. "She has gone to him, she has fled!" Lavinia cried, clasping her hands with admiration and envy. But she soon perceived that Catherine had taken nothing with her—all her personal property in her room was intact—and then she jumped at the hypothesis that the girl had gone forth, not in tenderness, but in resentment. "She has followed him to his own door—she has burst upon him in his own apartment!" It was in these terms that Mrs. Penniman depicted to herself her niece's errand, which, viewed in this light, gratified her sense of the picturesque only a shade less strongly than the idea of a clandestine marriage. To visit one's lover, with tears and reproaches, at his own residence, was an image so agreeable to Mrs. Penniman's mind that she felt a sort of aesthetic disappointment at its lacking, in this case, the harmonious accompaniments of darkness and storm. A quiet Sunday afternoon appeared an inadequate setting for it; and, indeed, Mrs. Penniman was quite out of humour with the conditions of the time, which passed very slowly as she sat in the front-parlour, in her bonnet and her cashmere shawl, awaiting Catherine's return.

This event at last took place. She saw her—at the window—mount the steps, and she went to await her in the hall, where she pounced upon her as soon as she had entered the house, and drew her into the parlour, closing the door with solemnity. Catherine was flushed, and her eye was bright. Mrs. Penniman hardly knew what to think.

"May I venture to ask where you have been?" she demanded.

"I have been to take a walk," said Catherine. "I thought you had gone to church."

"I did go to church; but the service was shorter than usual. And pray where did you walk?"

"I don't know!" said Catherine.

"Your ignorance is most extraordinary! Dear Catherine, you can trust me."

"What am I to trust you with?"

"With your secret—your sorrow."

"I have no sorrow!" said Catherine fiercely.

"My poor child," Mrs. Penniman insisted, "you can't deceive me. I know everything. I have been requested to—a—to converse with you."

"I don't want to converse!"

"It will relieve you. Don't you know Shakespeare's lines?—'the grief that does not speak!'[10] My dear girl, it is better as it is."

"What is better?" Catherine asked.

She was really too perverse. A certain amount of perversity was to be allowed for in a young lady whose lover had thrown her over; but not such an amount as would prove inconvenient to his apologists. "That you should be reasonable," said Mrs. Penniman, with some sternness. "That you should take counsel of worldly prudence, and submit to practical considerations. That you should agree to—a—separate."

Catherine had been ice up to this moment, but at this word she flamed up. "Separate? What do you know about our separating?"

Mrs. Penniman shook her head with a sadness in which there was almost a sense of injury. "Your pride is my pride and your susceptibilities are mine. I see your side perfectly, but I also"—and she smiled with melancholy suggestiveness—"I also see the situation as a whole!"

This suggestiveness was lost upon Catherine, who repeated her violent inquiry. "Why do you talk about separation; what do you know about it?"

"We must study resignation," said Mrs. Penniman, hesitating, but sententious at a venture.

"Resignation to what?"

"To a change of—of our plans."

"My plans have not changed!" said Catherine, with a little laugh.

"Ah, but Mr. Townsend's have," her aunt answered very gently.

"What do you mean?"

There was an imperious brevity in the tone of this inquiry, against which Mrs. Penniman felt bound to protest; the information with which she had undertaken to supply her niece was after all a favour. She had tried sharpness, and she had tried sternness; but neither would do; she was shocked at the girl's obstinacy. "Ah, well," she said, "if he hasn't told you! . . ." and she turned away.

Catherine watched her a moment in silence; then she hurried after her, stopping her before she reached the door. "Told me what? What do you mean? What are you hinting at and threatening me with?"

"Isn't it broken off?" asked Mrs. Penniman.

"My engagement? Not in the least!"

"I beg your pardon in that case. I have spoken too soon!"

"Too soon! Soon or late," Catherine broke out, "you speak foolishly and cruelly!"

"What has happened between you then?" asked her aunt, struck by the sincerity of this cry. "For something certainly has happened."

"Nothing has happened but that I love him more and more!"

Mrs. Penniman was silent an instant. "I suppose that's the reason you went to see him this afternoon."

Catherine flushed as if she had been struck. "Yes, I did go to see him! But that's my own business."

"Very well, then; we won't talk about it." And Mrs. Penniman moved towards the door again. But she was stopped by a sudden imploring cry from the girl.

"Aunt Lavinia, *where* has he gone?"

"Ah, you admit then that he has gone away? Didn't they know at his house?"

"They said he had left town. I asked no more questions; I was ashamed," said Catherine simply enough.

"You needn't have taken so compromising a step if you had had a little more confidence in me," Mrs. Penniman observed, with a good deal of grandeur.

"Is it to New Orleans?" Catherine went on, irrelevantly.

It was the first time Mrs. Penniman had heard of New Orleans in this connection; but she was averse to letting Catherine know that she was in the dark. She attempted to strike an illumination from the instructions she had received from Morris. "My dear Catherine," she said, "when a separation has been agreed upon, the farther he goes away the better."

"Agreed upon? Has he agreed upon it with you?" A consummate sense of her aunt's meddlesome folly had come over her during the last five minutes, and she was sickened at the thought that Mrs. Penniman had been let loose, as it were, upon her happiness.

"He certainly has sometimes advised with me," said Mrs. Penniman.

"Is it you then that have changed him and made him so unnatural?" Catherine cried. "Is it you that have worked on him and taken him from me! He doesn't belong to you, and I don't see how you have anything to do with what is between us! Is it you that have made this plot and told him to leave me? How could you be so wicked, so cruel? What have I ever done to you; why can't you leave me alone? I was afraid you would spoil everything; for you *do* spoil everything you touch! I was afraid of you all the time we were abroad; I had no rest when I thought that you were always talking to him." Catherine went on with growing vehemence, pouring out in her bitterness and in the clairvoyance of her passion (which suddenly, jumping all processes, made her judge her aunt finally and without appeal), the uneasiness which had lain for so many months upon her heart.

Mrs. Penniman was scared and bewildered; she saw no prospect of introducing her little account of the purity of Morris's motives. "You are a most ungrateful girl!" she cried. "Do you scold me for talking with him! I am sure we never talked of anything but you!"

"Yes; and that was the way you worried him; you made him tired of my very name! I wish you had never spoken of me to him; I never asked your help!"

"I am sure if it hadn't been for me he would never have come to the house, and you would never have known what he thought of you," Mrs. Penniman rejoined with a good deal of justice.

"I wish he never had come to the house, and that I never had known it! That's better than this," said poor Catherine.

"You are a very ungrateful girl," Aunt Lavinia repeated.

Catherine's outbreak of anger and the sense of wrong gave her, while they lasted, the satisfaction that comes from all assertion of force; they hurried her along, and there is always a sort of pleasure in cleaving the air. But at the bottom she hated to be violent, and she was conscious of no aptitude for organised resentment. She calmed herself with a great effort, but with great rapidity, and walked about the room a few moments, trying to say to herself that her aunt had meant everything for the best. She did not succeed in saying it with much conviction, but after a little she was able to speak quietly enough.

"I am not ungrateful, but I am very unhappy. It's hard to be grateful for that," she said. "Will you please tell me where he is?"

"I haven't the least idea; I am not in secret correspondence with him!" And Mrs. Penniman wished indeed that she were, so that she might let him know how Catherine abused her, after all she had done.

"Was it a plan of his, then, to break off——?" By this time Catherine had become completely quiet.

Mrs. Penniman began again to have a glimpse of her chance for explaining. "He shrank—he shrank," she said. "He lacked courage, but it was the courage to injure you! He couldn't bear to bring down on you your father's curse."

Catherine listened to this with her eyes fixed upon her aunt, and continued to gaze at her for some time afterwards. "Did he tell you to say that?"

"He told me to say many things—all so delicate, so discriminating. And he told me to tell you he hoped you wouldn't despise him."

"I don't," said Catherine. And then she added: "And will he stay away for ever?"

"Oh, for ever is a long time. Your father, perhaps, won't live for ever."

"Perhaps not."

"I am sure you appreciate—you understand—even though your heart bleeds," said Mrs. Penniman. "You doubtless think him too scrupulous. So do I, but I respect his scruples. What he asks of you is that you should do the same."

Catherine was still gazing at her aunt, but she spoke, at last, as if she had not heard or not understood her. "It has been a regular plan, then. He has broken it off deliberately; he has given me up."

"For the present, dear Catherine. He has put it off, only."

"He has left me alone," Catherine went on.

"Haven't you *me*?" asked Mrs. Penniman, with much expression.

Catherine shook her head slowly. "I don't believe it!" and she left the room.

XXXI

THOUGH SHE HAD FORCED herself to be calm, she preferred practising this virtue in private, and she forbore to show herself at tea—a repast which, on Sundays, at six o'clock, took the place of dinner. Dr. Sloper and his sister sat face to face, but Mrs. Penniman never met her brother's eye.

Late in the evening she went with him, but without Catherine, to their sister Almond's, where, between the two ladies, Catherine's unhappy situation was discussed with a frankness that was conditioned by a good deal of mysterious reticence on Mrs. Penniman's part.

"I am delighted he is not to marry her," said Mrs. Almond, "but he ought to be horsewhipped all the same."

Mrs. Penniman, who was shocked at her sister's coarseness, replied that he had been actuated by the noblest of motives—the desire not to impoverish Catherine.

"I am very happy that Catherine is not to be impoverished—but I hope he may never have a penny too much! And what does the poor girl say to *you*?" Mrs. Almond asked.

"She says I have a genius for consolation," said Mrs. Penniman.

This was the account of the matter that she gave to her sister, and it was perhaps with the consciousness of genius that, on her return that evening to Washington Square, she again presented herself for admittance at Catherine's door. Catherine came and opened it; she was apparently very quiet.

"I only want to give you a little word of advice," she said. "If your father asks you, say that everything is going on."

Catherine stood there, with her hand on the knob, looking at her aunt, but not asking her to come in. "Do you think he will ask me?"

"I am sure he will. He asked me just now, on our way home from your Aunt Elizabeth's. I explained the whole thing to your Aunt Elizabeth. I said to your father I know nothing about it."

"Do you think he will ask me, when he sees—when he sees——?" But here Catherine stopped.

"The more he sees, the more disagreeable he will be," said her aunt.

"He shall see as little as possible!" Catherine declared.

"Tell him you are to be married."

"So I am," said Catherine, softly; and she closed the door upon her aunt.

She could not have said this two days later—for instance, on Tuesday, when she at last received a letter from Morris Townsend. It was an epistle of considerable length, measuring five large square pages, and written at Philadelphia. It was an explanatory document, and it explained a great many things, chief among which were the considerations that had led the writer to take advantage of an urgent "professional" absence to try and banish from his mind the image of one whose path he had crossed only to scatter it with ruins. He ventured to expect but partial success in this attempt, but he could promise her that, whatever his failure, he would never again interpose between her generous heart and her brilliant prospects and filial duties. He closed with an intimation that his professional pursuits might compel him to travel for some months, and with the hope that when they should each have accommodated themselves to what was sternly involved in their respective positions—even should this result not be reached for years—they should meet as friends, as fellow-sufferers, as innocent but philosophic victims of a great social law. That her life should be peaceful and happy was the dearest wish of him who ventured still to subscribe himself her most obedient servant. The letter was beautifully written, and Catherine, who kept it for many years after this, was able, when her sense of the bitterness of its meaning and the hollowness of its tone had grown less acute, to admire its grace of expression. At present, for a long time after she received it, all she had to help her was the determination, daily more rigid, to make no appeal to the compassion of her father.

He suffered a week to elapse, and then one day, in the morning, at an hour at which she rarely saw him, he strolled into the back-parlour. He had watched his time, and he found her alone. She was sitting with some work, and he came and stood in front of her. He was going out, he had on his hat and was drawing on his gloves.

"It doesn't seem to me that you are treating me just now with all the consideration I deserve," he said in a moment.

"I don't know what I have done," Catherine answered, with her eyes on her work.

"You have apparently quite banished from your mind the request I made you at Liverpool, before we sailed; the request that you would notify me in advance before leaving my house."

"I have not left your house!" said Catherine.

"But you intend to leave it, and by what you gave me to understand, your departure must be impending. In fact, though you are still here in body, you are already absent in spirit. Your mind has taken up its residence with your prospective husband, and you might quite as well be lodged under the conjugal roof, for all the benefit we get from your society."

"I will try and be more cheerful!" said Catherine.

"You certainly ought to be cheerful; you ask a great deal if you are not. To the pleasure of marrying a brilliant young man, you add that of having your own way; you strike me as a very lucky young lady!"

Catherine got up; she was suffocating. But she folded her work, deliberately and correctly, bending her burning face upon it. Her father stood where he had planted himself; she hoped he would go, but he smoothed and buttoned his gloves, and then he rested his hands upon his hips.

"It would be a convenience to me to know when I may expect to have an empty house," he went on. "When you go, your aunt marches."

She looked at him at last, with a long silent gaze, which, in spite of her pride and her resolution, uttered part of the appeal she had tried not to make. Her father's cold gray eye sounded her own, and he insisted on his point.

"Is it to-morrow? Is it next week, or the week after?"

"I shall not go away!" said Catherine.

The Doctor raised his eyebrows. "Has he backed out?"

"I have broken off my engagement."

"Broken it off?"

"I have asked him to leave New York, and he has gone away for a long time."

The Doctor was both puzzled and disappointed, but he solved his perplexity by saying to himself that his daughter simply misrepresented—justifiably, if one would, but nevertheless, misrepresented—the facts; and he eased off his disappointment, which was that of a man losing a chance for a little triumph that he had rather counted on, by a few words that he uttered aloud.

"How does he take his dismissal?"

"I don't know!" said Catherine, less ingeniously than she had hitherto spoken.

"You mean you don't care? You are rather cruel, after encouraging him and playing with him for so long!"

The Doctor had his revenge after all.

XXXII

OUR STORY HAS HITHERTO moved with very short steps, but as it approaches its termination it must take a long stride. As time went on, it might have appeared to the Doctor that his daughter's account of her rupture with Morris Townsend, mere bravado as he had deemed it, was in some degree justified by the sequel. Morris remained as rigidly and unremittingly absent as if he had died of a broken heart, and Catherine had apparently buried the memory of this fruitless episode as deep as if it had terminated by her own choice. We know that she had been deeply and incurably wounded, but the Doctor had no means of knowing it. He was certainly curious about it, and would have given a good deal to discover the exact truth; but it was his punishment that he never knew—his punishment, I mean, for the abuse of sarcasm in his relations with his daughter. There was a good deal of effective sarcasm in her keeping him in the dark, and the rest of the world conspired with her, in this sense, to be sarcastic. Mrs. Penniman told him nothing, partly because he never questioned her—he made too light of Mrs. Penniman for that—and partly because she flattered herself that a tormenting reserve, and a serene profession of ignorance, would avenge her for his theory that she had meddled in the matter. He went two or three times to see Mrs. Montgomery, but Mrs. Montgomery had nothing to impart. She simply knew that her brother's engagement was broken off, and now that Miss Sloper was out of danger, she preferred not to bear witness in any way against Morris. She had done so before—however unwillingly—because she was sorry for Miss Sloper; but she was not sorry for Miss Sloper now—not at all sorry. Morris had told her nothing about his relations with Miss Sloper at the time, and he had told her nothing since. He was always away, and he very seldom wrote to her; she believed he had gone to California. Mrs. Almond had, in her sister's phrase, "taken up" Catherine violently since the recent catastrophe; but though the girl was very grateful to her for her kindness, she revealed no secrets, and the good lady could give the Doctor no satisfaction. Even, however, had she been able to narrate to him the private history of his daughter's unhappy love-affair, it would have given her a certain comfort to leave him in ignorance; for Mrs. Almond was at this time not altogether in sympathy with her brother. She had guessed for herself that Catherine had been cruelly jilted—she knew nothing from Mrs. Penniman, for Mrs. Penniman had not ventured to lay the famous explanation of Morris's motives before Mrs. Almond, though she had thought it good enough for Catherine—and she pronounced her brother too consistently indifferent to what the poor creature must have suffered and must still be suffering. Dr. Sloper had his theory, and he rarely altered his theories. The marriage would have been an abominable one, and the girl had had a blessed escape. She was not to be pitied for that, and to pretend to condole with her would have been to make concessions to the idea that she had ever had a right to think of Morris.

"I put my foot on this idea from the first, and I keep it there now," said the Doctor. "I don't see anything cruel in that; one can't keep it there too long." To this Mrs. Almond more than once replied that if Catherine had got rid of her incongruous lover, she deserved the credit of it, and that to bring herself to her father's enlightened view of the matter must have cost her an effort that he was bound to appreciate.

"I am by no means sure she has got rid of him," the Doctor said. "There is not the smallest probability that, after having been as obstinate as a mule for two years, she suddenly became amenable to reason. It is infinitely more probable that he got rid of her."

"All the more reason you should be gentle with her."

"I *am* gentle with her. But I can't do the pathetic; I can't pump up tears, to look graceful, over the most fortunate thing that ever happened to her."

"You have no sympathy," said Mrs. Almond; "that was never your strong point. You have only to look at her to see that, right or wrong, and whether the rupture came from herself or from him, her poor little heart is grievously bruised."

"Handling bruises—and even dropping tears on them—doesn't make them any better! My business is to see she gets no more knocks, and that I shall carefully attend to. But I don't at all recognise your description of Catherine. She doesn't strike me in the least as a young woman going about in search of a moral poultice. In fact, she seems to me much better than while the fellow was hanging about. She is perfectly comfortable and blooming; she eats and sleeps, takes her usual exercise, and overloads herself, as usual, with finery. She is always knitting some purse or embroidering some handkerchief, and it seems to me she turns these articles out about as fast as ever. She hasn't much to say; but when had she anything to say? She had her little dance, and now she is sitting down to rest. I suspect that, on the whole, she enjoys it."

"She enjoys it as people enjoy getting rid of a leg that has been crushed. The state of mind after amputation is doubtless one of comparative repose."

"If your leg is a metaphor for young Townsend, I can assure you he has never been crushed. Crushed? Not he! He is alive and perfectly intact, and that's why I am not satisfied."

"Should you have liked to kill him?" asked Mrs. Almond.

"Yes, very much. I think it is quite possible that it is all a blind."

"A blind?"*

"An arrangement between them. *Il fait le mort,*† as they say in France; but he is looking out of the corner of his eye. You can depend upon it he has not burned his ships; he has kept one to come back in. When I am dead, he will set sail again, and then she will marry him."

"It is interesting to know that you accuse your only daughter of being the vilest of hypocrites," said Mrs. Almond.

"I don't see what difference her being my only daughter makes. It is better to accuse one than a dozen. But I don't accuse any one. There is not the smallest hypocrisy about Catherine, and I deny that she even pretends to be miserable."

The Doctor's idea that the thing was a "blind" had its intermissions and revivals; but it may be said on the whole to have increased as he grew older; together with his impression of Catherine's blooming and comfortable condition. Naturally, if he had not found grounds for viewing her as a lovelorn maiden during the year or two that followed her great trouble, he found none at a time when she had

---

*Thing or action intended to conceal one's real design; pretence or pretext.
†That is, he is lying low; literally, "he's playing dead" (French).

completely recovered her self-possession. He was obliged to recognise the fact that if the two young people were waiting for him to get out of the way, they were at least waiting very patiently. He had heard from time to time that Morris was in New York; but he never remained there long, and, to the best of the Doctor's belief, had no communication with Catherine. He was sure they never met, and he had reason to suspect that Morris never wrote to her. After the letter that has been mentioned, she heard from him twice again, at considerable intervals; but on none of these occasions did she write herself. On the other hand, as the Doctor observed, she averted herself rigidly from the idea of marrying other people. Her opportunities for doing so were not numerous, but they occurred often enough to test her disposition. She refused a widower, a man with a genial temperament, a handsome fortune, and three little girls (he had heard that she was very fond of children, and he pointed to his own with some confidence); and she turned a deaf ear to the solicitations of a clever young lawyer, who, with the prospect of a great practice, and the reputation of a most agreeable man, had had the shrewdness, when he came to look about him for a wife, to believe that she would suit him better than several younger and prettier girls. Mr. Macalister, the widower, had desired to make a marriage of reason, and had chosen Catherine for what he supposed to be her latent matronly qualities; but John Ludlow, who was a year the girl's junior, and spoken of always as a young man who might have his "pick," was seriously in love with her. Catherine, however, would never look at him; she made it plain to him that she thought he came to see her too often. He afterwards consoled himself, and married a very different person, little Miss Sturtevant, whose attractions were obvious to the dullest comprehension. Catherine, at the time of these events, had left her thirtieth year well behind her, and had quite taken her place as an old maid. Her father would have preferred she should marry, and he once told her that he hoped she would not be too fastidious. "I should like to see you an honest man's wife before I die," he said. This was after John Ludlow had been compelled to give it up, though the Doctor had advised him to persevere. The Doctor exercised no further pressure, and had the credit of not "worrying" at all over his daughter's singleness. In fact he worried rather more than appeared, and there were considerable periods during which he felt sure that Morris Townsend was hidden behind some door. "If he is not, why doesn't she marry?" he asked himself. "Limited as her intelligence may be, she must understand perfectly well that she is made to do the usual thing." Catherine, however, became an admirable old maid. She formed habits, regulated her days upon a system of her own, interested herself in charitable institutions, asylums, hospitals, and aid-societies; and went generally, with an even and noiseless step, about the rigid business of her life. This life had, however, a secret history as well as a public one—if I may talk of the public history of a mature and diffident spinster for whom publicity had always a combination of terrors. From her own point of view the great facts of her career were that Morris Townsend had trifled with her affection, and that her father had broken its spring. Nothing could ever alter these facts; they were always there, like her name, her age, her plain face. Nothing could ever undo the wrong or cure the pain that Morris had inflicted on her, and nothing could ever make her feel towards her father as she felt in her younger years. There was something dead in her life, and her duty was to try and fill the void. Catherine recognised this duty to the utmost; she had a great disapproval of brooding and moping. She had of course no faculty for quenching memory in dissipation; but she mingled freely in the usual gaieties of the town, and she became at last an inevitable figure at all respectable entertainments. She was greatly liked, and as time went on she grew to be a sort of kindly maiden-aunt to the younger portion of society. Young girls were apt to confide to her their love-affairs (which they never did to Mrs. Penniman), and young men to be fond of her without knowing why. She developed a few harmless eccentricities; her habits, once formed, were rather stiffly maintained; her opinions, on all moral and social matters, were extremely conservative; and before she was forty she was regarded as an old-fashioned person, and an authority on customs that had passed away. Mrs. Penniman, in comparison, was quite a girlish figure; she grew younger as she advanced in life. She lost none of her relish for beauty and mystery, but she had little opportunity to exercise it. With Catherine's later wooers she failed to establish relations as intimate as those which had given her so many interesting hours in the society of Morris Townsend. These gentlemen had an indefinable mistrust of her good offices, and they never talked to her about Catherine's charms. Her ringlets, her buckles and bangles glistened more brightly with each succeeding year, and she remained quite the same officious and imaginative Mrs. Penniman, and the odd mixture of impetuosity and circumspection, that we have hitherto known. As regards one point, however, her circumspection prevailed, and she must be given due credit for it. For upwards of seventeen years she never mentioned Morris Townsend's name to her niece. Catherine was grateful to her, but this consistent silence, so little in accord with her aunt's character, gave her a certain alarm, and she could never wholly rid herself of a suspicion that Mrs. Penniman sometimes had news of him.

XXXIII

LITTLE BY LITTLE DR. SLOPER had retired from his profession; he visited only those patients in whose symptoms he recognized a certain originality. He went again to Europe, and remained two years; Catherine went with him, and on this occasion Mrs. Penniman was of the party. Europe apparently had few surprises for Mrs. Penniman, who frequently remarked, in the most romantic sites—"You know I am very familiar with all this." It should be added that such remarks were usually not addressed to her brother, or yet to her niece, but to fellow-tourists who happened to be at hand, or even to the cicerone* or the goat-herd in the foreground.

One day, after his return from Europe, the Doctor said something to his daughter that made her start—it seemed to come from so far out of the past.

"I should like you to promise me something before I die."

"Why do you talk about your dying?" she asked.

"Because I am sixty-eight years old."

"I hope you will live a long time," said Catherine.

"I hope I shall! But some day I shall take a bad cold, and then it will not matter much what any one hopes. That will be the manner of my exit, and when it takes place, remember I told you so. Promise me not to marry Morris Townsend after I am gone."

This was what made Catherine start, as I have said; but her start was a silent one, and for some moments she said nothing. "Why do you speak of him?" she asked at last.

"You challenge everything I say. I speak of him because he's a topic, like any other. He's to be seen, like any one else, and he is still looking for a wife—having had one and got rid of her, I don't

---

*Tour guide who explains the antiquities or curiosities of a place; termed such for the great Roman orator Cicero, who was known for his knowledge and eloquence.

know by what means. He has lately been in New York, and at your cousin Marian's house; your Aunt Elizabeth saw him there."

"They neither of them told me," said Catherine.

"That's their merit; it's not yours. He has grown fat and bald, and he has not made his fortune. But I can't trust those facts alone to steel your heart against him, and that's why I ask you to promise."

"Fat and bald": these words presented a strange image to Catherine's mind, out of which the memory of the most beautiful young man in the world had never faded. "I don't think you understand," she said. "I very seldom think of Mr. Townsend."

"It will be very easy for you to go on, then. Promise me, after my death, to do the same."

Again, for some moments, Catherine was silent; her father's request deeply amazed her; it opened an old wound and made it ache afresh. "I don't think I can promise that," she answered.

"It would be a great satisfaction," said her father.

"You don't understand. I can't promise that."

The Doctor was silent a minute. "I ask you for a particular reason. I am altering my will."

This reason failed to strike Catherine; and indeed she scarcely understood it. All her feelings were merged in the sense that he was trying to treat her as he had treated her years before. She had suffered from it then; and now all her experience, all her acquired tranquillity and rigidity, protested. She had been so humble in her youth that she could now afford to have a little pride, and there was something in this request, and in her father's thinking himself so free to make it, that seemed an injury to her dignity. Poor Catherine's dignity was not aggressive; it never sat in state; but if you pushed far enough you could find it. Her father had pushed very far.

"I can't promise," she simply repeated.

"You are very obstinate," said the Doctor.

"I don't think you understand."

"Please explain, then."

"I can't explain," said Catherine. "And I can't promise."

"Upon my word," her father exclaimed, "I had no idea how obstinate you are!"

She knew herself that she was obstinate, and it gave her a certain joy. She was now a middle-aged woman.

About a year after this, the accident that the Doctor had spoken of occurred; he took a violent cold. Driving out to Bloomingdale* one April day to see a patient of unsound mind, who was confined in a private asylum for the insane, and whose family greatly desired a medical opinion from an eminent source, he was caught in a spring shower, and being in a buggy, without a hood, he found himself soaked to the skin. He came home with an ominous chill, and on the morrow he was seriously ill. "It is congestion of the lung,"† he said to Catherine; "I shall need very good nursing. It will make no difference, for I shall not recover; but I wish everything to be done, to the smallest detail, as if I should. I hate an ill-conducted sick-room; and you will be so good as to nurse me on the hypothesis that I shall get well." He told her which of his fellow-physicians to send for, and gave her a multitude of minute directions; it was quite on the optimistic hypothesis that she nursed him. But he had never been wrong in his life, and he was not wrong now. He was touching his seventieth year, and though he had a very well-tempered constitution, his hold upon life had lost its firmness. He died after three weeks' illness, during which Mrs. Penniman, as well as his daughter, had been assiduous at his bedside.

On his will being opened after a decent interval, it was found to consist of two portions. The first of these dated from ten years back, and consisted of a series of dispositions by which he left the great mass of property to his daughter, with becoming legacies to his two sisters. The second was a codicil, of recent origin, maintaining the annuities to Mrs. Penniman and Mrs. Almond, but reducing Catherine's share to a fifth of what he had first bequeathed her. "She is amply provided for from her mother's side," the document ran, "never having spent more than a fraction of her income from this source; so that her fortune is already more than sufficient to attract those unscrupulous adventurers whom she has given me reason to believe that she persists in regarding as an interesting class." The

---

*The Bloomingdale Insane Asylum, built in 1821 on land in northern Manhattan now occupied by Columbia University.

†Probably pneumonia, an inflammation caused by bacteria; a leading cause of death before the discovery of antibiotics.

large remainder of his property, therefore, Dr. Sloper had divided into seven unequal parts, which he left, as endowments, to as many different hospitals and schools of medicine, in various cities of the Union.

To Mrs. Penniman it seemed monstrous that a man should play such tricks with other people's money; for after his death, of course, as she said, it was other people's. "Of course you will dispute the will," she remarked, fatuously, to Catherine.

"Oh no," Catherine answered, "I like it very much. Only I wish it had been expressed a little differently!"

XXXIV

IT WAS HER HABIT to remain in town very late in the summer; she preferred the house in Washington Square to any other habitation whatever and it was under protest that she used to go to the seaside for the month of August. At the sea she spent her month at an hotel. The year that her father died she intermitted this custom altogether, not thinking it consistent with deep mourning; and the year after that she put off her departure till so late that the middle of August found her still in the heated solitude of Washington Square. Mrs. Penniman, who was fond of a change, was usually eager for a visit to the country; but this year she appeared quite content with such rural impressions as she could gather, at the parlour window, from the ailantus-trees behind the wooden paling. The peculiar fragrance of this vegetation used to diffuse itself in the evening air, and Mrs. Penniman, on the warm nights of July, often sat at the open window and inhaled it. This was a happy moment for Mrs. Penniman; after the death of her brother she felt more free to obey her impulses. A vague oppression had disappeared from her life, and she enjoyed a sense of freedom of which she had not been conscious since the memorable time, so long ago, when the Doctor went abroad with Catherine and left her at home to entertain Morris Townsend. The year that had elapsed since her brother's death reminded her of that happy time, because, although Catherine, in growing older, had become a person to be reckoned with, yet her society was not a very different thing, as Mrs. Penniman said, from that of a tank of cold water. The elder lady hardly knew what use to make of this larger margin of her life; she sat and looked at it very much as she had often sat, with her poised needle in her hand, before her tapestry-frame. She had a confident hope, however, that her rich impulses, her talent for embroidery, would still find their application, and this confidence was justified before many months had elapsed.

Catherine continued to live in her father's house in spite of its being represented to her that a maiden-lady of quiet habits might find a more convenient abode in one of the smaller dwellings, with brown stone fronts, which had at this time begun to adorn the transverse thoroughfares in the upper part of the town. She liked the earlier structure—it had begun by this time to be called an "old" house—and proposed to herself to end her days in it. If it was too large for a pair of unpretending gentlewomen, this was better than the opposite fault; for Catherine had no desire to find herself in closer quarters with her aunt. She expected to spend the rest of her life in Washington Square, and to enjoy Mrs. Penniman's society for the whole of this period; as she had a conviction that, long as she might live, her aunt would live at least as long, and always retain her brilliancy and activity. Mrs. Penniman suggested to her the idea of a rich vitality.

On one of those warm evenings in July of which mention has been made, the two ladies sat together at an open window, looking out on the quiet Square. It was too hot for lighted lamps, for reading, or for work; it might have appeared too hot even for conversation, Mrs. Penniman having long been speechless. She sat forward in the window, half on the balcony, humming a little song. Catherine was within the room, in a low rocking-chair, dressed in white, and slowly using a large palmetto fan.* It was in this way, at this season, that the aunt and niece, after they had had tea, habitually spent their evenings.

"Catherine," said Mrs. Penniman at last, "I am going to say something that will surprise you."

"Pray do," Catherine answered; "I like surprises. And it is so quiet now."

"Well, then, I have seen Morris Townsend."

If Catherine was surprised, she checked the expression of it; she gave neither a start nor an exclamation. She remained, indeed, for some moments intensely still, and this may very well have been a symptom of emotion. "I hope he was well," she said at last.

"I don't know; he is a great deal changed. He would like very much to see you."

"I would rather not see him," said Catherine, quickly.

---

*Fan made from one of several smaller species of palms, such as the dwarf fan-palm or the cabbage palmetto.

"I was afraid you would say that. But you don't seem surprised!"

"I am—very much."

"I met him at Marian's," said Mrs. Pennimam. "He goes to Marian's, and they are so afraid you will meet him there. It's my belief that that's why he goes. He wants so much to see you." Catherine made no response to this, and Mrs. Penniman went on. "I didn't know him at first; he is so remarkably changed. But he knew me in a minute. He says I am not in the least changed. You know how polite he always was. He was coming away when I came, and we walked a little distance together. He is still very handsome, only, of course, he looks older, and he is not so—so animated as he used to be. There was a touch of sadness about him; but there was a touch of sadness about him before—especially when he went away. I am afraid he has not been very successful—that he has never got thoroughly established. I don't suppose he is sufficiently plodding, and that, after all, is what succeeds in this world." Mrs. Penniman had not mentioned Morris Townsend's name to her niece for upwards of the fifth of a century; but now that she had broken the spell, she seemed to wish to make up for lost time, as if there had been a sort of exhilaration in hearing herself talk of him. She proceeded, however, with considerable caution, pausing occasionally to let Catherine give some sign. Catherine gave no other sign than to stop the rocking of her chair and the swaying of her fan; she sat motionless and silent. "It was on Tuesday last," said Mrs. Penniman, "and I have been hesitating ever since about telling you. I didn't know how you might like it. At last I thought that it was so long ago that you would probably not have any particular feeling. I saw him again, after meeting him at Marian's. I met him in the street, and he went a few steps with me. The first thing he said was about you; he asked ever so many questions. Marian didn't want me to speak to you; she didn't want you to know that they receive him. I told him I was sure that after all these years you couldn't have any feeling about that; you couldn't grudge him the hospitality of his own cousin's house. I said you would be bitter indeed if you did that. Marian has the most extraordinary ideas about what happened between you; she seems to think he behaved in some very unusual manner. I took the liberty of reminding her of the real facts, and placing the story in its true light. *He* has no bitterness, Catherine, I can assure you; and he might be excused for it, for things have not gone well with him.

He has been all over the world, and tried to establish himself everywhere; but his evil star was against him. It is most interesting to hear him talk of his evil star. Everything failed; everything but his—you know, you remember—his proud, high spirit. I believe he married some lady somewhere in Europe. You know they marry in such a peculiar matter-of-course way in Europe; a marriage of reason* they call it. She died soon afterwards; as he said to me, she only flitted across his life. He has not been in New York for ten years; he came back a few days ago. The first thing he did was to ask me about you. He had heard you had never married; he seemed very much interested about that. He said you had been the real romance of his life."

Catherine had suffered her companion to proceed from point to point, and pause to pause, without interrupting her; she fixed her eyes on the ground and listened. But the last phrase I have quoted was followed by a pause of peculiar significance, and then, at last, Catherine spoke. It will be observed that before doing so she had received a good deal of information about Morris Townsend. "Please say no more; please don't follow up that subject."

"Doesn't it interest you?" asked Mrs. Penniman, with a certain timorous archness.

"It pains me," said Catherine.

"I was afraid you would say that. But don't you think you could get used to it? He wants so much to see you."

"Please don't, Aunt Lavinia," said Catherine, getting up from her seat. She moved quickly away, and went to the other window, which stood open to the balcony; and here, in the embrasure, concealed from her aunt by the white curtains, she remained a long time, looking out into the warm darkness. She had had a great shock; it was as if the gulf of the past had suddenly opened, and a spectral figure had risen out of it. There were some things she believed she had got over, some feelings that she had thought of as dead; but apparently there was a certain vitality in them still. Mrs. Penniman had made them stir themselves. It was but a momentary agitation, Catherine said to herself; it would presently pass away. She was trembling, and her heart was beating so that she could feel it;

---

*Marriage of convenience; from *mariage de raison* (French).

XXXV

HER REFRESHED ATTENTION TO this gentleman had not those limits of which Catherine desired, for herself, to be conscious; it lasted long enough to enable her to wait another week before speaking of him again. It was under the same circumstances that she once more attacked the subject. She had been sitting with her niece in the evening; only on this occasion, as the night was not so warm, the lamp had been lighted, and Catherine had placed herself near it with a morsel of fancy-work. Mrs. Penniman went and sat alone for half an hour on the balcony; then she came in, moving vaguely about the room. At last she sank into a seat near Catherine, with clasped hands, and a little look of excitement.

"Shall you be angry if I speak to you again about *him?*" she asked.

Catherine looked up at her quietly. "Who is *he?*"

"He whom you once loved."

"I shall not be angry, but I shall not like it."

"He sent you a message," said Mrs. Penniman. "I promised him to deliver it, and I must keep my promise."

In all these years Catherine had had time to forget how little she had to thank her aunt for in the season of her misery; she had long ago forgiven Mrs. Penniman for taking too much upon herself. But for a moment this attitude of interposition and disinterestedness, this carrying of messages and redeeming of promises, brought back the sense that her companion was a dangerous woman. She had said she would not be angry; but for an instant she felt sore. "I don't care what you do with your promise!" she answered.

Mrs. Penniman, however, with her high conception of the sanctity of pledges, carried her point. "I have gone too far to retreat," she said, though precisely what this meant she was not at pains to explain. "Mr. Townsend wishes most particularly to see you, Catherine; he believes that if you knew how much, and why, he wishes it, you would consent to do so."

"There can be no reason," said Catherine; "no good reason."

"His happiness depends upon it. Is not that a good reason?" asked Mrs. Penniman, impressively.

"Not for me. My happiness does not."

"I think you will be happier after you have seen him. He is going away again—going to resume his wanderings. It is a very lonely, restless, joyless life. Before he goes, he wishes to speak to you; it is a fixed idea with him—he is always thinking of it. He has something very important to say to you. He believes that you never understood him—that you never judged him rightly, and the belief has always weighed upon him terribly. He wishes to justify himself; he believes that in a very few words he could do so. He wishes to meet you as a friend."

Catherine listened to this wonderful speech, without pausing in her work; she had now had several days to accustom herself to think of Morris Townsend again as an actuality. When it was over she said simply, "Please say to Mr. Townsend that I wish he would leave me alone."

She had hardly spoken when a sharp, firm ring at the door vibrated through the summer night. Catherine looked up at the clock; it marked a quarter-past nine—a very late hour for visitors especially in the empty condition of the town. Mrs. Penniman at the same moment gave a little start, and then Catherine's eyes turned quickly to her aunt. They met Mrs. Penniman's and sounded them for a moment, sharply. Mrs. Penniman was blushing; her look was a conscious one; it seemed to confess something. Catherine guessed its meaning, and rose quickly from her chair.

"Aunt Penniman," she said, in a tone that scared her companion, "have you taken *the liberty* . . . ?"

"My dearest Catherine," stammered Mrs. Penniman, "just wait till you see him!"

Catherine had frightened her aunt, but she was also frightened herself; she was on the point of rushing to give orders to the servant, who was passing to the door, to admit no one; but the fear of meeting her visitor checked her.

"Mr. Morris Townsend."

This was what she heard, vaguely but recognisably articulated by the domestic, while she hesitated. She had her back turned to the door of the parlour, and for some moments she kept it turned, feeling that he had come in. He had not spoken, however, and at last she faced about. Then she saw a gentleman standing in the middle of the room, from which her aunt had discreetly retired.

She would never have known him. He was forty-five years old, and his figure was not that of the straight, slim young man she remembered. But it was a very fine person, and a fair and lustrous beard, spreading itself upon a well-presented chest, contributed to its effect. After a moment Catherine recognised the upper half of the face, which, though her visitor's clustering locks had grown thin, was still remarkably handsome. He stood in a deeply deferential attitude, with his eyes on her face. "I have ventured—I have ventured," he said; and then he paused, looking about him, as if he expected her to ask him to sit down. It was the old voice; but it had not the old charm. Catherine, for a minute, was conscious of a distinct determination not to invite him to take a seat. Why had he come? It was wrong for him to come. Morris was embarrassed, but Catherine gave him no help. It was not that she was glad of his embarrassment; on the contrary, it excited all her own liabilities of this kind, and gave her great pain. But how could she welcome him when she felt so vividly that he ought not to have come? "I wanted so much—I was determined," Morris went on. But he stopped again; it was not easy. Catherine still said nothing, and he may well have recalled with apprehension her ancient faculty of silence. She continued to look at him, however, and as she did so she made the strangest observation. It seemed to be he, and yet not he; it was the man who had been everything, and yet this person was nothing. How long ago it was—how old she had grown—how much she had lived! She had lived on something that was connected with *him*, and she had consumed it in doing so. This person did not look unhappy. He was fair and well-preserved, perfectly dressed, mature and complete. As Catherine looked at him, the story of his life defined itself in his eyes; he had made himself comfortable, and he had never been caught. But even while her perception opened itself to this, she had no desire to catch him; his presence was painful to her, and she only wished he would go.

"Will you not sit down?" he asked.

"I think we had better not," said Catherine.

"I offend you by coming?" He was very grave; he spoke in a tone of the richest respect.

"I don't think you ought to have come."

"Did not Mrs. Penniman tell you—did she not give you my message?"

"She told me something, but I did not understand."

"I wish you would let *me* tell you—let me speak for myself."

"I don't think it is necessary," said Catherine.

"Not for you, perhaps, but for me. It would be a great satisfaction—and I have not many." He seemed to be coming nearer; Catherine turned away. "Can we not be friends again?" he asked.

"We are not enemies," said Catherine. "I have none but friendly feelings to you."

"Ah, I wonder whether you know the happiness it gives me to hear you say that!" Catherine uttered no intimation that she measured the influence of her words; and he presently went on, "You have not changed—the years have passed happily for you."

"They have passed very quietly," said Catherine.

"They have left no marks; you are admirably young." This time he succeeded in coming nearer—he was close to her; she saw his glossy perfumed beard, and his eyes above it looking strange and hard. It was very different from his old—from his young—face. If she had first seen him this way she would not have liked him. It seemed to her that he was smiling, or trying to smile. "Catherine," he said, lowering his voice, "I have never ceased to think of you."

"Please don't say those things," she answered.

"Do you hate me?"

"Oh no," said Catherine.

Something in her tone discouraged him, but in a moment he recovered himself. "Have you still some kindness for me, then?"

"I don't know why you have come here to ask me such things!" Catherine exclaimed.

"Because for many years it has been the desire of my life that we should be friends again."

"That is impossible."

"Why so? Not if you will allow it."

"I will not allow it!" said Catherine.

He looked at her again in silence. "I see, my presence troubles you and pains you. I will go away; but you must give me leave to come again."

"Please don't come again," she said.

"Never?—never?"

She made a great effort; she wished to say something that would make it impossible he should ever again cross her threshold. "It is wrong of you. There is no propriety in it—no reason for it."

"Ah, dearest lady, you do me injustice!" cried Morris Townsend. "We have only waited, and now we are free."

"You treated me badly," said Catherine.

"Not if you think of it rightly. You had your quiet life with your father—which was just what I could not make up my mind to rob you of."

"Yes; I had that."

Morris felt it to be a considerable damage to his cause that he could not add that she had had something more besides; for it is needless to say that he had learnt the contents of Doctor Sloper's will. He was nevertheless not at a loss. "There are worse fates than that!" he exclaimed with expression; and he might have been supposed to refer to his own unprotected situation. Then he added, with a deeper tenderness, "Catherine, have you never forgiven me?"

"I forgave you years ago, but it is useless for us to attempt to be friends."

"Not if we forget the past. We have still a future, thank God!"

"I can't forget—I don't forget," said Catherine. "You treated me too badly. I felt it very much; I felt it for years." And then she went on, with her wish to show him that he must not come to her this way, "I can't begin again—I can't take it up. Everything is dead and buried. It was too serious; it made a great change in my life. I never expected to see you here."

"Ah, you are angry!" cried Morris, who wished immensely that he could extort some flash of passion from her mildness. In that case he might hope.

"No, I am not angry. Anger does not last, that way, for years. But there are other things. Impressions last, when they have been strong.—But I can't talk."

Morris stood stroking his beard, with a clouded eye. "Why have you never married?" he asked abruptly. "You have had opportunities."

"I didn't wish to marry."

"Yes, you are rich, you are free; you had nothing to gain."

"I had nothing to gain," said Catherine.

Morris looked vaguely round him, and gave a deep sigh.

"Well, I was in hopes that we might still have been friends."

"I meant to tell you, by my aunt, in answer to your message—if you had waited for an answer—that it was unnecessary for you to come in that hope."

"Good-bye, then," said Morris. "Excuse my indiscretion."

He bowed, and she turned away—standing there, averted, with her eyes on the ground, for some moments after she had heard him close the door of the room.

In the hall he found Mrs. Penniman, fluttered and eager; she appeared to have been hovering there under the irreconcilable promptings of her curiosity and her dignity.

"That was a precious plan of yours!" said Morris, clapping on his hat.

"Is she so hard!" asked Mrs. Penniman.

"She doesn't care a button for me—with her confounded little dry manner."

"Was it very dry?" pursued Mrs. Penniman, with solicitude.

Morris took no notice of her question; he stood musing an instant, with his hat on. "But why the deuce, then, would she never marry?"

"Yes—why indeed?" sighed Mrs. Penniman. And then, as if from a sense of the inadequacy of this explanation, "But you will not despair—you will come back?"

"Come back? Damnation!" And Morris Townsend strode out of the house, leaving Mrs. Penniman staring.

Catherine, meanwhile, in the parlour, picking up her morsel of fancy-work, had seated herself with it again—for life, as it were.

ENDNOTES

Daisy Miller

1. (p. 5) *Newport and Saratoga:* Newport, Rhode Island, and Saratoga Springs, New York, were fashionable resort destinations in the nineteenth century. Newport contained a number of palatial mansions, including The Breakers, Cornelius Vanderbilt's former summerhouse. Similarly, Saratoga Springs served as a chief social and sporting center, attracting thoroughbred horse racing aficionados, beginning in 1863, and elite gamblers, who frequented a casino built in 1867.

2. (p. 5) *to the Ocean House or to Congress Hall:* The Ocean House, built in 1840, was a well-known summer hotel in Newport, Rhode Island. Congress Hall, a fashionable resort in Saratoga Springs, New York, was destroyed in a fire in 1868 and rebuilt in 1870.

3. (p. 6) *the little metropolis of Calvinism:* Geneva became an important center of the Protestant Reformation with the arrival of John Calvin, a French theologian and religious reformer, in 1536. Calvinism emphasized the essential sinfulness of man, the salvation of the elect by God's grace, and the supremacy of Scriptures in the revelation of truth.

4. (p. 6) *he had been put to school there as a boy, and he had afterwards gone to college there:* In 1860 the James family lived in Geneva, where seventeen-year-old Henry was enrolled in the Academy as a special student. In *Transatlantic Sketches* (1875), he confesses an "old-time kindness for Geneva, to which I was introduced years ago, in my schooldays, when I was as good an idler as the best."

5. (p. 20) *sylph:* A sylph is an imaginary or elemental spirit who inhabits the air and is mortal but soulless. The existence of such beings was first stipulated by the medieval physician Paracelsus, who found a different being to correspond with each of the four elements: air, fire, water, and earth.

6. (p. 29) *the unhappy Bonivard:* The Genevan patriot François Bonivard (1493–1570) took up arms against the reigning dukes of Savoy and was subsequently imprisoned in 1530 in the castle of Chillon, where he was incarcerated in an underground jail cell from 1532 until 1536.

7. (p. 32) *that pretty novel of Cherbuliez's—'Paule Méré':* This novel was published in 1864 by French novelist, critic, and historian Victor Cherbuliez (1829–1899). The narrative follows a carefree heroine who is hurt by slander and disappointed by a weak hero. In *Transatlantic Sketches* (1875) James described *Paule Méré* as "a tale [written] expressly to prove that frank nature is out of favor (in Geneva)." Cherbuliez's heroine, James wrote, "dies of a broken heart because her spontaneity passes for impropriety." James eventually met Cherbuliez in Paris, where they were both guests at Gustave Flaubert's apartment in 1875 and 1876. In a letter to Thomas Sergeant Perry, James recalled that the members of Flaubert's Parisian circle held Cherbuliez in some contempt.

8. (p. 45) *Villa Borghese:* This famous villa, surrounded by beautiful gardens, statues, and fountains, was designed by architects Flaminio Ponzio and Giovanni Vasanzio and built at the beginning of the seventeenth century for Cardinal Scipione Caffarelli Borghese, the favorite nephew of Pope Paul V.

9. (p. 51) *St Peter's:* St. Peter's Basilica is the church of the popes in Rome. A major pilgrimage site, it was begun by Pope Julius II in 1506 and completed in 1615 under Paul V. Its dome rises directly above the high altar, which contains the shrine of Saint Peter the Apostle.

10. (p. 53) *Doria Palace:* The Palazzo Doria Pamphili, in the Via del Corso, dates back to the 1440s, when it was built by the Doria-Pamphili, a prominent Roman noble clan who distinguished themselves by serving the Roman Curia, a group of Vatican bureaus that assist the pope in his jurisdiction over the Roman Catholic church. The palace galleries contain works by Raphael, Caravaggio, and Bernini.

11. (p. 53) *the superb portrait of Innocent X by Velasquez:* This portrait of Pope Innocent X, who served as pontiff from 1644 to 1655, was completed by the Spanish artist Diego Velásquez between 1650 and 1651. The painting, considered "too truthful" by its papal subject, depicts a stern, indeed suspicious pope.

12. (p. 57) *the Arch of Constantine:* One of three surviving ancient Roman triumphal arches in Rome, it was hastily erected in A.D. 312 by Constantine, the first Christian emperor of Rome, to celebrate his victory over Maxentius.

13. (p. 57) *the Forum:* Situated between the Palatine and Capitoline Hills, the Roman Forum was the scene of public meetings, legal courts, and gladiatorial combats in republican times. Under the Roman Empire, it was a center for religious and secular spectacles and ceremonies.

14. (p. 57) *the Colosseum:* A 50,000-seat oval stadium measuring one-third of a mile around and inaugurated in A.D. 80, the Colosseum was

the site of gladiatorial contests, wild animal spectacles, sham battles, and, when flooded, naval displays.

15. (p. 57) *Byron's famous lines, out of "Manfred"*: In act 3, scene 4 of Lord Byron's dramatic poem *Manfred*, the eponymous hero, recalling a youthful visit to the Colosseum, meditates on the "ruinous perfection" of the "noble wreck":

> And thou didst shine, thou rolling moon, upon
> All this, and cast a wide and tender light,
> Which soften'd down the hoar austerity
> Of rugged desolation, and fill'd up,
> As 'twere anew, the gaps of centuries;
> Leaving that beautiful which still was so,
> And making that which was not, till the place
> Became religion, and the heart ran o'er
> With silent worship of the great of old, —
> The dead but sceptred sovereigns, who still rule
> Our spirits from their urns.

As Susan Koprince notes (*Arizona Quarterly* 42 [1986], pp. 293–304), both Byron and James regard the Colosseum as a site of ambivalence — a place of both beauty and death. Unlike Manfred, however, Winterbourne is derivative to the bone: Rather than express the immediacy of his own heart, he quotes someone else.

16. (p. 58) *this nest of malaria*: Originally thought to be the result of the unwholesome atmosphere — foul and poisonous emanations from rotting flesh and vegetation (hence the Italian name *mal'aria*, meaning "bad air") — that permeated Italy's marshy districts, malaria was recognized in the early twentieth century to be a group of febrile diseases transmitted by mosquitoes of the genus *Anopheles*.

17. (p. 58) *Roman fever*: Beginning in the third century, malaria was associated with the marshes of the Roman Campagna (the area immediately surrounding Rome). Familiarly termed "Roman fever," it frequently protected Rome from foreign invaders felled by the deadly illness.

18. (p. 59) *splendid pills*: The pills were probably quinine, from the seventeenth to the early twentieth centuries the best and only remedy for malaria. Made from the bark of the cinchona tree, quinine suppresses the action of malaria parasites and also acts as a preventative.

19. (p. 61) *the little Protestant cemetery*: In 1873 James described this burial ground as "one of the solemn places of Rome": "Here is a mixture

of tears and smiles, of stones and flowers, of mourning cypresses and radiant sky, which gives us the impression of our looking back at death from the brighter side of the grave." He focused in particular on the gravestone of a young woman named Miss Bathurst, who drowned in the Tiber River in 1824. Her inscription read: "If thou art young and lovely, build not thereon, for she who lies beneath thy feet in death was the loveliest flower ever cropt in its bloom." According to James, this epitaph "affects us irresistibly as a case for tears on the spot. The whole elaborate inscription indeed says something over and beyond all it does say."

Washington Square

1. (p. 74) *the temple of Republican simplicity:* In the late eighteenth century, during the years of the early American Republic, citizens showed their independence from British manufacturing concerns by wearing simple, homespun fabrics. In her 1897 biography of Martha Washington, Anne Hollingsworth Wharton reports that visitors to the First Lady frequently "felt rebuked by the plainness of her apparel and her example of persistent industry, while we were extravagantly dressed idlers, a name not very creditable in these perilous times."

2. (p. 75) *a red satin gown trimmed with gold fringe:* This is a reference to the embellished letter "A" worn by Hester Prynne in Nathaniel Hawthorne's novel, *The Scarlet Letter* (1850). The letter is woven from "fine red cloth" and "surrounded with an elaborate embroidery and fantastic flourishes of gold thread."

3. (p. 75) *within five minutes' walk of the City Hall:* The narrator refers to the affluent New York neighborhood around Lower Broadway, where City Hall was built in 1803. A visiting Englishman, John Lambert, remarked in 1807 that the district's "lofty and well built" town houses opened onto "large commodious shops of every description."

4. (p. 86) *Excelsior!:* In this 1841 poem by Henry Wadsworth Longfellow (1807–1882), a handsome young traveler ignores a village's offers of help and hospitality, and instead goes forth into a snowstorm, where he dies bearing the banner "Excelsior!"—meaning "Higher!" or "Upward!"

5. (p. 91) *Bellini and Donizetti:* Vincenzo Bellini (1801–1835) was a popular Romantic operatic composer known for his expressive melodies and interpretive sensitivity; among his works are *La sonnambula* (1831; *The Sleepwalker)* and *Norma* (1831). His longer-lived Italian peer, Gaetano Donizetti (1797–1848), achieved fame with such Romantic operas as *Anna Bolena*, which debuted in Milan in 1830, and *Lucia di Lammermoor*, which opened in Naples in 1835.

6. (p. 92) *Pasta and Rubini and Lablache:* Three mid-nineteenth-century opera singers: Giuditta Pasta (1798–1865), an Italian soprano; Adelaide Cornelli-Rubini (c.1796–1874), a French, later Italian, mezzo-soprano; and Luigi Lablache (1794–1858), an Italian bass.

7. (p. 122) *"Isn't there some proverb about a reformed rake?"*: The proverb appears in Samuel Richardson's novel *Clarissa* (1747–1748): "To what a bad choice is many a worthy woman betrayed, by that false and inconsiderate notion, That a reformed rake makes the best husband!"

8. (p. 137) *Greenwood Cemetery:* Green-Wood Cemetery was founded in rural Brooklyn in 1838. By the 1850s, it was the final resting place of such well-known Americans as Horace Greeley, Louis Comfort Tiffany, and Henry Ward Beecher. A major tourist attraction in the nineteenth-century, the cemetery drew some 500,000 visitors annually.

9. (p. 173) *the works of Raphael:* Italian painter, draughtsman, and architect Raphael Sanzio (1483–1529), one of the most important painters of the High Renaissance, is well known for his decorative painting of the Stanza della Segnatura and other papal apartments in the Vatican.

10. (p. 212) *"the grief that does not speak!"*: A reference to Shakespeare's *Macbeth* (act 4, scene 4) in which Malcolm, hearing the news that Macduff's wife and children have been mercilessly slaughtered, cries out, "Merciful heaven! / What, man! Ne'er pull your hat upon your brows; / Give sorrow words: the grief that does not speak / Whispers the o'er-fraught heart and bids it break."

INSPIRED BY *DAISY MILLER* AND *WASHINGTON SQUARE*

More than fifty film adaptations of Henry James's novels appeared during the twentieth century, and the urge to depict the Jamesian world in cinema shows no signs of dampening. In the late 1990s alone, four books were made into films: Jane Campion's *The Portrait of a Lady* (1996), Agnieszka Holland's *Washington Square* (1997), Ian Softely's *The Wings of the Dove* (1997), and James Ivory's *The Golden Bowl* (2000). For a time James was heralded as the "next Jane Austen"—that is, the next classic novelist to become the darling of moviegoers.

Washington Square was adapted for the cinema in 1949 as *The Heiress*, produced and directed by film legend William Wyler, who worked with a screenplay adapted from the hit 1948 Broadway play of the same name, written by Augustus and Ruth Goetz. The Goetzes and Wyler focused James's narrative into a sharp drama that is intense and sophisticated. Olivia de Havilland stars as Catherine, in the finest performance of her career; when the beautiful and imperious de Havilland walks through the gilded drawing rooms of her Washington Square manor (the sets are opulent), she seems almost to be slumming. The charming Montgomery Clift is her suitor, Morris Townsend, and Sir Ralph Richardson portrays Dr. Austin Sloper with intelligence and nuance. Wyler's picture was nominated for eight Academy Awards, and de Havilland earned an Oscar. (The play *The Heiress* was revived on Broadway in 1976 and again in 1995; the 1995 production, starring Cherry Jones, won four Tony awards, including Best Revival of a Play.)

Washington Square was again filmed in 1997, in a production directed by Agnieszka Holland and with a screenplay by Carol Doyle. The dynamic among the small, excellent cast moves the drama swiftly with an arousing tension. Jennifer Jason Leigh portrays Catherine Sloper with a fine pathos. Albert Finney plays a stern Dr. Sloper, and Maggie Smith steals the movie as Aunt Lavinia Penniman, whose gregariousness lends the film most of its humor.

Ben Chaplin plays an earnest, charismatic Morris Townsend, who seems almost as naive as Catherine; his revelatory argument with her forms a marvelous climax. Light, skillful camera shots trace the characters throughout this adept and emotional adaptation.

Peter Bogdanovich's *Daisy Miller* (1974) was the first in a string of disastrous movies that nearly ended the once-great director's career. Cybill Shepherd, in her first starring role, played the title character and was lambasted for being one-dimensional and without charm; audiences found Daisy, with her careless umbrella turns and coquettish hair flips, obnoxious, irritating, and self-involved. If for nothing else, the film was praised for its faithfulness to the original text in both its plot and its settings. The success Bogdanovich had won with his previous movies—*The Last Picture Show* (1971), *What's Up, Doc?* (1972), and *Paper Moon* (1973)—allowed him to gain access to the exact locations James names in his book. Scenes were shot at the Coliseum in Rome and at the stunning Château de Chillon and Hôtel des Trois Couronnes in Vevey, Switzerland.

COMMENTS & QUESTIONS

In this section, we aim to provide the reader with an array of perspectives on the text, as well as questions that challenge those perspectives. The commentary has been culled from sources as diverse as reviews contemporaneous with the works, letters written by the author, literary criticism of later generations, and appreciations written throughout the works' history. Following the commentary, a series of questions seeks to filter Henry James's Daisy Miller and Washington Square *through a variety of voices and bring about a richer understanding of these enduring works.*

Comments

HENRY JAMES

I must thank you very tenderly for your generous little despatch on the subject of "Daisy Miller." I am charmed to think that she struck a sympathetic chord in your imagination, and that having been, in fact, so harshly treated by fate and public opinion, she has had it made up to her in posthumous honors.

—from a letter to Mrs. William Dean Howells (August 14, 1878)

THE SPECTATOR

No doubt there is a wonderful skill in the writer who, avowedly refusing to tell you what can properly be called a story,—loving above all things to depict excursions of the heart and mind which fade away and end in nothing,—can yet interest you so deeply as he does in his delineation of these unfulfilled intentions of men, these *manqué* and tentative deviations into regions not adapted for embodiment into the substance of life. One might perhaps say that Mr. Henry James has discerned in relation to literature what has long been known in relation to art,—that with artists of any genius, "sketches" are apt to be more satisfying than finished pictures. But then the sketches we like so much in artists' studios are, though unfinished pictures, still pictures of what the painter has been most struck with, pictures in which he has given all that struck him most, and left only what did not strike him to be filled in by the fancy of the public. Now Mr. Henry James does not give us sketches of the striking features in what he sees of human life and passion, so much as finished pictures of the little nooks and bays into which human caprice occasionally drifts, when the main current of life's deeper interests has left us for a moment on one side, and rushed past us. He does not half-paint what is striking; he prefers rather to paint with wonderful care and precision what is not striking, or only striking by its contrast with what is usually thought so. As in his "study" of Daisy Miller, he loves to paint that aspect of life which is commonly mistaken for its main aspect; or if it is so, is so only because, in the particular case of the character he thus studies, the preparatory antecedents of action or passion as they show themselves in other beings, have taken up an accidental preponderance, and superseded the interest of the action or passion to which they are usually only preparatory. Mr. Henry James is not so much a novelist as an episodist, if such a term be allowable. But he is a wonderful episodist.

—March 1, 1879

THE SPECTATOR

In [Mr. Henry James's] pictures, most passions fade away; most influences fail of their characteristic effect; most comedies are spoiled; most tragedies break down before the tragic crisis; most catastrophes, as the Irishman would say, never come off; while that which fulfils its function most completely in the world is the power, inherent in most of us, to spoil or hamper the life of other people, an agency the conspicuous success of which almost all Mr. James's writings commemorate.

There has never been a more adequate illustration of this tendency of Mr. Henry James's than the dismal tale entitled *Washington Square*, in which there is no agreeable character, only one likeable character,—we mean the plain, mute, tenacious heroine, of whom we are told that "she knew she was obstinate, and it gave her a certain joy,"—no very detestable character, nothing but common-place affectionateness, common-place and even vulgar selfishness, somewhat more than common-place cruelty and cynicism, very common-place insincerity, and very common-place misery. Mr. Henry James seems to take quite a pleasure in making us study this leaden-coloured group of emotions, and take home to our hearts that life, even among well-to-do New Yorkers who have something like culture, and care to study Europe, is like that,—a scene where a girl may make a romance to herself out of the selfish love-making of a thoroughly indifferent and underbred man, where her only near relations will be likely to injure her by false sentimentality or cruel scorn, where each phase of her disappointment is more miserable than the last, where she loses her love for her father in fighting for a worthless lover, and loses her love for her lover in the exposure caused by her father's refusal to give her his money, and where, finally, her aunt makes everything meaner by her *fade* sentimental falsehood, and yet is never sufficiently found out to be got rid of and sent away. In short, *Washington Square* might be described as the story of how a dull girl's nature was lit up by passion for a mock-hero, how the father tried to cut it out of her as he would have performed a surgical operation, and only succeeded in cutting out of her all love for himself; how the aunt fanned the flame with her fancy falsehoods, and made it burn brighter and brighter, till the object of the passion showed himself in his true colours; and how after that it smouldered away and went out, leaving the life in which it had been lit a little blunter, a little duller, and a little more tolerant of bare surroundings than it found it. The story is marvellously clever.

—February 5, 1881

H. G. WELLS

James begins by taking it for granted that a novel is a work of art that must be judged by its oneness. Some one gave him that idea in the beginning of things and he has never found it out. He doesn't find things out. He doesn't even seem to want to find things out. He accepts very readily and then—elaborates. . . . The thing his novel is *about* is always there. It is like a church lit but without a congregation to distract you, with every light and line focused on the high altar. And on the altar, very reverently placed, intensely there, is a dead kitten, an egg-shell, a bit of string.

—from *Boon* (1915)

JAMES RUSSELL LOWELL

Whoever takes an interest, whether of mere curiosity or of critical foreboding, in the product and tendency of our younger literature, must have had his attention awakened and detained by the writings of Mr. James. Whatever else they may be, they are not common, and have that air of good breeding which is the token of whatever is properly called literature. They are not the overflow of a shallow talent for improvisation too full of self to be contained, but show everywhere the marks of intelligent purpose and of the graceful ease that comes only of conscientious training. Undoubtedly there was a large capital of native endowment to start from—a mind of singular subtlety and refinement; a faculty of rapid observation, yet patient of rectifying afterthought; senses daintily alive to every aesthetic suggestion; and a frank enthusiasm, kept within due bounds by the double-consciousness of humor. But it is plain that Mr. James is fortunate enough to possess, or to be possessed by, that finer sixth sense which we call the artistic, and which controls, corrects, and discontents. His felicities, therefore, are not due to a lucky turn of the dice, but to forethought and afterthought.

—from *The Function of the Poet and Other Essays* (1920)

EDMUND WILSON

Henry James stands out today as unique among our fiction writers of the nineteenth century in having devoted wholeheartedly to literature the full span of a long life and brought to it first-rate abilities. Beside James's half century of achievement, with its energy, continuity and variety, the production of Hawthorne looks furtive and meager and the work of Poe's brief years fragmentary. Alone among our novelists of the past, Henry James managed to master his art and to practice it on an impressive scale, to stand up to popular pressures so as not to break down or peter out, and to build up what the French call an *oeuvre*.

—from *The Triple Thinkers* (1938)

Questions

1. Early critics spoke of these short novels as "dismal," as requiring us to "study this leaden-colored group of emotions." The characters are paltry, the issues private, the actions utterly without grandeur; there are no tremendous sins or heroic virtues—these are the criticisms. Are they just? Even if true, do they miss James's point?

2. Does Henry James, in his depiction of Catherine and Daisy, get the psychology of women right? Or does he leave out or get wrong things that any woman writer would not?

3. Can Henry James be described as a realist?

4. Is it the social milieu in these short novels that determines not only the action, but also what the characters feel and what they do? Are the characters independent of their environment? Or are they controlled by it?

5. These novels have been widely read for a long time; there are numerous movie versions of both. What is the source of their popularity? From reading *The Spectator*'s criticism from 1881, one would think there is no pleasure to be found in reading these novels. But certainly reading them is more than just study, more than just an academic exercise. In the end, what is it about them that gives us pleasure?

FOR FURTHER READING

Selected Works by Henry James

Watch and Ward (1871)
A Passionate Pilgrim and Other Stories (1875)
Transatlantic Sketches (1875)
Roderick Hudson (1876)
The American (1877)
The Europeans (1878)
An International Episode (1879)
Hawthorne (1879)
The Portrait of a Lady (1881)
The Bostonians (1886)
The Princess Casamassima (1886)
The Aspern Papers (1888)
The Spoils of Poynton (1897)
What Maisie Knew (1897)
The Turn of the Screw (1898)
The Awkward Age (1899)
The Sacred Fount (1901)
The Wings of the Dove (1902)
The Ambassadors (1903)
The Golden Bowl (1904)
The Outcry (1911)
The Complete Notebooks of Henry James. Edited by Leon Edel and
    Lyall H. Powers. New York: Oxford University Press, 1987.
Henry James: Letters. Edited by Leon Edel. Vol. 2: 1875–1883.
    Cambridge, MA: Belknap Press, 1975.

Biography

Edel, Leon. *The Life of Henry James, Vol. 1: 1843–1889.* 2 vols. New York: Penguin, 1977.

Lewis, R. W. B. *The Jameses: A Family Narrative.* New York: Farrar, Straus, and Giroux, 1991.

Criticism

Bell, Ian F. A. "'This Exchange of Epigrams': Commodity and Style in *Washington Square.*" *Journal of American Studies* 19:1 (1985), pp. 49–68.

———. "Money, History and Writing in Henry James: Assaying *Washington Square.*" In *Henry James: Fiction as History*, edited by Ian F. A. Bell. Totowa, NJ: Barnes and Noble, 1984, pp. 11–48.

Bell, Millicent. *Meaning in Henry James.* Cambridge, MA: Harvard University Press, 1991.

Berlant, Lauren. "Fancy-Work and Fancy Foot-Work: Motives for Silence in *Washington Square.*" *Criticism* 29:4 (1987), pp. 439–458.

Davidson, Cathy N. "'Circumsexualocution' in Henry James's *Daisy Miller.*" *Arizona Quarterly* 32 (1977), pp. 353–366.

Fielder, Leslie A. *Love and Death in the American Novel.* Revised edition. 1966. New York: Stein and Day, 1982.

Gard, Roger, ed. *Henry James: The Critical Heritage.* London and New York: Routledge and Kegan Paul, 1968.

Howland, Bette. "Washington Square, the Family Plot." *Raritan* 15:4 (1996), pp. 88–110.

James's "Daisy Miller": The Story, the Play, the Critics. Edited by William T. Stafford. New York: Scribner, 1963.

Johnson, Lisa. "Daisy Miller: Cowboy Feminist." *Henry James Review* 22 (2001), pp. 41–58.

Klein, Marcus. "*Washington Square*, or Downtown with Henry James." *Arizona Quarterly* 53 (1997), pp. 7–21.

Long, Robert Emmet. "James's *Washington Square*: The Hawthorne Relation." *New England Quarterly* 46:4 (1973), pp. 573–590.

Lukacs, Paul. "Unambiguous Ambiguity: The International Theme of *Daisy Miller.*" *Studies in American Fiction* 16:2 (1988), pp. 209–216.

Scheiber, Andrew J. "The Doctor's Order: Eugenic Anxiety in Henry James's *Washington Square.*" *Literature and Medicine* 15 (1996), pp. 244–262.

Swaab, Peter. "The End of Embroidery: From *Washington Square* to *The Heiress.*" In *Henry James on Stage and Screen*, edited by John R. Bradley. New York: Palgrave, 2000, pp. 56–71.

Wadsworth, Sarah A. "Innocence Abroad: Henry James and the Re-Invention of the American Woman Abroad." *Henry James Review* 22:2 (2001), pp. 107–127.

Wardley, Lynn. "Reassembling Daisy Miller." *American Literary History* 3:2 (1991), pp. 232–254.

Weisbuch, Robert. "James and the American Sacred." *Henry James Review* 22:3 (2001), pp. 217–228.

Wilkinson, Myler. "Henry James and the Ethical Moment." *Henry James Review* 11 (1990), pp. 153–175.

Historical Context

Bender, Thomas. *The Unfinished City: New York and the Metropolitan Idea.* New York: New Press, 2002.

Cohen, Patricia Cline. *A Calculating People: The Spread of Numeracy in Early America.* Chicago: University of Chicago Press, 1982.

Kline, Morris. "Geometry." In *Encyclopedia Americana.* Grolier Online, 2002, http://80-go.grolier.com.osiyou.cc.columbia.edu:2048/gol (Oct. 22, 2003).

Mlodinow, Leonard. *Euclid's Window: The Story of Geometry from Parallel Lines to Hyperspace.* New York: Free Press, 2001.

Poovey, Mary. "Figures of Arithmetic, Figures of Speech: The Discourse of Statistics in the 1830s." In *Questions of Evidence: Proof, Practice, and Persuasion across the Disciplines*, edited by James Chandler, Arnold I. Davidson, and Harry Harootunian. Chicago: University of Chicago Press, 1994, pp. 401–421.

Richards, Joan L. *Mathematical Visions: The Pursuit of Geometry in Victorian England.* Boston: Academic Press, 1988.

Democracy

Berlant, Lauren. "Uncle Sam Needs a Wife: Citizenship and Denegation." In *Materializing Democracy: Toward a Revitalized Cultural Politics*, edited by Russ Castronovo and Dana D. Nelson. Durham, NC: Duke University Press, 2002, pp. 144–174.

Castiglia, Chris. "The Genealogy of a Democratic Crush." In *Materializing Democracy: Toward a Revitalized Cultural Politics*, edited by Russ Castronovo and Dana D. Nelson. Durham, NC: Duke University Press, 2002.

Castronovo, Russ. *Necro Citizenship: Death, Eroticism, and the Public Sphere in the Nineteenth-Century United States.* Durham, NC: Duke University Press, 2001.

——. "Souls That Matter: Social Death and the Pedagogy of Democratic Citizenship." In *Materializing Democracy: Toward a Revitalized Cultural Politics*, edited by Russ Castronovo and Dana D. Nelson. Durham, NC: Duke University Press, 2002, pp. 116–143.

Dimock, Wai Chee. "Rethinking Space, Rethinking Rights: Literature, Law, and Science." In *Materializing Democracy: Toward a Revitalized Cultural Politics*, edited by Russ Castonovo and Dana D. Nelson. Durham, NC: Duke University Press, 2002, pp. 248–266.

Nelson, Dana D. "Representative/Democracy: The Political Work of Countersymbolic Representation." In *Materializing Democracy: Toward a Revitalized Cultural Politics*, edited by Russ Castonovo and Dana D. Nelson. Durham, NC: Duke University Press, 2002, pp. 218–247.

Other Works Cited in the Introduction

Giles, Paul. "Transnationalism and Classic American Literature." *PMLA* 118 (2003), pp. 62–77.

James, Henry. *Daisy Miller; Pandora; The Patagonia; and Other Tales.* New York: Charles Scribner's Sons, 1909.

——. *The Portrait of a Lady.* New York: Penguin, 1986.